Nina Milne has loved Mills & Boon, since as a child she discovered stacks of M&B books 'hidden' in the airing cupboard so is thrilled to now write for them. Nina spent her childhood in England, US and France. Since then she has acquired an English degree, one hero-husband, three gorgeous children and a house in Brighton where she plans to stay. After all she can now transport herself via her characters to anywhere in the world whilst sitting in pyjamas in her study. Bliss!

Traci Douglass is a *USA TODAY* bestselling romance author with Mills & Boon, Entangled Publishing and Tule Publishing, and has an MFA in Writing Popular Fiction from Seton Hill University. She writes sometimes funny, usually awkward, always emotional stories about strong, quirky, wounded characters overcoming past adversity to find their forever person. Heartfelt Healing Happily Ever Afters. Connect with her through her website: tracidouglassbooks.com

Maisey Yates is a *New York Times* bestselling author of over one hundred romance novels. Whether she's writing strong, hard working cowboys, dissolute princes or multigenerational family stories, she loves getting lost in fictional worlds. An avid knitter with a dangerous yarn addiction and an aversion to housework, Maisey lives with her husband and three kids in rural Oregon. Check out her website, maiseyyates.com or find her on Facebook.

Passion in Paradise

Passion in Paradise:
Stolen Moments

NINA MILNE

TRACI DOUGLASS

MAISEY YATES

MILLS & BOON

First Published in Great Britain 2022
By Mills & Boon, an imprint of HarperCollins*Publishers,* Ltd
1 London Bridge Street, London, SE1 9GF

www.harpercollins.co.uk

HarperCollins*Publishers*
1st Floor, Watermarque Building,
Ringsend Road, Dublin 4, Ireland

PASSION IN PARADISE: STOLEN MOMENTS
© 2022 Harlequin Enterprises ULC.

Claiming His Secret Royal Heir © 2017 Nina Milne
Their Hot Hawaiian Fling © 2020 Traci Douglass
The Spaniard's Stolen Bride © 2019 Maisey Yates

ISBN: 978-0-263-30491-6

CLAIMING HIS
SECRET ROYAL HEIR

NINA MILNE

To the memory of my very lovely
'Nanni'—I still miss you.

CHAPTER ONE

August 15th—Online Celebrity News with April Fotherington

Who will be the new Lycander Princess?

All bets are off!

It's official! Lady Kaitlin Derwent is no longer a contender for the position of Lycander Bride—the people's favourite aristo announced that her new squeeze for the foreseeable future is Daniel Harrington, CEO of Harrington's Legal Services.

Who'd have thought it?

Exit Lady Kaitlin!

So Prince Frederick, ruler of Lycander, is on the lookout for a new bride.

Who will it be?

Will it be the type of woman who graced his arm and his bed back in his playboy days, before the tragic death of his older brother and the scandalous death of Prince Alphonse, his flamboyant father, in a house of ill repute propelled him to the throne?

FREDERICK II OF the House of Petrelli, Prince and Ruler of Lycander, stopped reading and pushed his screen across the ornate carved desk, resplendent with gilt—a royal gift from an English monarch of yore.

The phrase pounded his brain—*tragic death of his older brother*—but he forced his features to remain calm, and made himself focus on the man standing in front of him: Marcus Alrikson, his chief advisor. After all, he needed all the advice he could get.

'I don't understand what the problem is—this article is nothing more than a gossip fest. And it's old news.'

Marcus shook his head. '*That* is the problem. The article serves to remind the people of your past.'

'Don't you mean my sordid, scandalous and immoral past?' Might as well tell it like it is, he thought.

'If you like,' Marcus returned evenly. 'The bigger problem is that we both know you are holding on to the crown by your fingertips. The people did not want you on the throne because of your past—so any reminder causes damage.'

'I understand that.'

The all too familiar guilt twisted his insides—the people had wanted his brother on the throne. Axel had been born to this. He would have been the ideal ruler to bring prosperity and calm to the land after their father's turbulent rule.

But Axel was dead and buried—victim of a car crash that should have been Frederick's destiny. Frederick should have been in that car on his way to a State dinner; instead he'd asked Axel to step in and take his place and his big brother had—no questions asked. So Frederick had attended a party on board a glitzy yacht to celebrate a business deal...and Axel had died.

The dark secret tarnished Frederick's soul, weighted his conscience.

And now Lycander was stuck with the black sheep of the royal line and the people were threatening to revolt. Bleak determination hardened inside him. He would keep the crown safe, whatever the cost—he owed that at least to Axel's memory.

'So what do you suggest?'

'I suggest you find a new bride—someone like Lady Kaitlin. Your proposed alliance with Kaitlin was a popular one. It showed the people that you had decided to settle down with a suitable bride, that you'd changed—proof there would be no repeat of your father's disastrous marriages.'

'I *have* decided to settle down.' To bind himself to a lifestyle he'd once sworn to avoid and the formulation of a cold-blooded alliance undertaken for the sake of the throne. 'But Kaitlin is no longer an option—she has fallen in love with another man.'

Irritation sparked inside him. He wished Kaitlin well, but it was hard to believe that the cool, poised Lady Kaitlin had succumbed to so foolish an emotion.

'Which is not good news for Lycander.'

Marcus resumed pacing, each stride swallowing up a metre of the marble floor, taking him past yet another portrait of one of Frederick's ancestors.

'Kaitlin was the perfect bride—her background is impeccable and she reminded the people of Lycander brides of the past.'

Unlike the succession of actresses, models and gold diggers Frederick's father had married.

'The people loved her.'

Unlike you.

The unspoken words hovered in the air between them.

'I understand all this. But Kaitlin is history.'

'Yes. And right now the press is *focused* on your history. That article zones in on your former flames—the actresses, the socialites, the models. Giselle, Mariana, Sunita… Hell, this reporter, April, even tried to track them down.'

Frederick froze.

Sunita.

Images flashed across his mind; memory reached across the chasm of tragedy.

Sunita.

Shared laughter, sheer beauty, almond-shaped eyes of a brown that veered from tawny to light, dependent on her mood. The raven sheen of her silken hair, the glow of her skin, the lissom length of her legs.

Sunita.

The woman who had left him—the woman he'd allowed to go...

Without preamble, he pulled his netbook back towards him, eyes scanning the article.

But where is Sunita now?

This is where it becomes a little mysterious.

Mere weeks after the end of her relationship with the Prince of Lycander—which, according to several sources, she ended abruptly—Sunita decided to 'take a break' from her highly lucrative modelling career to 'rediscover her roots'.

This involved a move to Mumbai, where her mother reportedly hailed from. But the trail ends there, and to all intents and purposes Sunita seems to have vanished.

'Frederick?' Marcus's voice pulled him from the article and he looked up to see his chief advisor's forehead crease into a frown. 'What is it?'

'Nothing.' Under the sceptical gaze Frederick shrugged. 'It just sounds unlike Sunita to give up her career.'

Sunita had been one of the most ambitious people he knew—had been defined by that ambition, had had her career aspirations and goals mapped out with well-lit beacons. The idea of her jacking it all in seemed far-fetched at best.

Marcus drummed his fingers on his thigh. 'Could her disappearance have anything to do with you?'

'No.'

'What happened?'

'We spent a few weeks together—she moved on.'

'*She* moved on?'

Damn. 'We moved on.'

'Why?'

Keep it together. This is history. 'She decided to call it a day as she'd garnered sufficient publicity from our connection.'

Marcus raised his eyebrows. 'So she used you for publicity?'

'Yes. To be fair, she was upfront about that from the start.'

More fool him for thinking she'd changed her mind as time had gone on. He'd believed their time together, the long conversations, the laughter, had meant something. Well, he'd been wrong. Sunita had been after publicity and then she'd cut and run. Yet there had been something in her expression that morning…a transitory shadow in her tawny eyes, an errant twist of her hands that had belied the glib words dropping from her lips. But he hadn't called her on it.

Enough! The past was over and did not bear dwelling on because—as he knew with soul-wrenching certainty—it could not be changed.

Marcus's dark blue eyes met his as he resumed pacing. 'So weeks after this publicity stunt she disappeared off the modelling scene? That doesn't make sense.'

It didn't. But it had nothing to do with him. Two years

ago Sunita had affected him in ways he didn't want to remember. He'd missed her once she'd gone—an unheard-of weakness he'd knocked on the head and buried. Easy come, easy go. That was the Playboy Prince's motto. Sunita had gone—he'd accepted it. And then, mere months after her departure, Axel had died and his life had changed for ever.

'I'll look into it,' Marcus said. 'But right now you need to focus on this list. Potential brides. A princess, a lady and a *marquesa*. Take your pick.'

Frederick accepted the piece of paper but didn't so much as glance down. 'What do you mean, "look into it"?'

'If there is any chance of potential scandal we need to shut it down now. So I plan to find Sunita before April Fotherington or any other reporter does.'

'Then what?'

'Then I'll send someone to talk to her. Or go myself.'

'No!' The refusal came with a vehemence that surprised him. However it had ended, his time with Sunita had marked something—his last moments of joy before catastrophe occurred, perhaps. He didn't want her life tainted…didn't want Marcus or his minions to find her if she didn't want to be found.

'It needs to be done.' Marcus leant forward, his hands on the edge of the desk. 'I understand you don't like it, but you can't take even the smallest risk that there is a scandal floating around out there. The crown is at stake. The throne is rocking, Frederick, and if it topples it will be a Humpty Dumpty scenario.'

Great! A Humpty Dumpty scenario—exactly what he needed. Of course he could choose to ignore the warning, but that would be foolish. Marcus knew his stuff. The sensible option would be to allow Marcus to go ahead, investigate and deal with any problem. But for some reason every fibre of his being cavilled—dammit, stupid though it sounded, it wasn't the *honourable* thing to do.

A small mocking smile tilted his lips as he faced his chief advisor..Frederick of Lycander—man of honour. Axel would be proud of him. 'Fine. *I'll* check out Sunita.'

Marcus's blue eyes narrowed. 'With all due respect, that's nuts and you know it. The press will jump on it.'

'Then let them jump. I'm the boss and this is what's going to happen.'

'Why?'

'Because it's the right thing to do.' And for once he'd like to stand on a tiny wedge of the moral high ground. 'What would Axel have done? Sent you in to spy on a woman he'd dated?'

'Axel would never have got himself into a position where it was necessary.'

'Touché. But I have and I will deal with it.' His brain whirred as he thought it through. 'I can schedule a trip to Mumbai—I'd like to follow up on how the Schools for All project is rolling out anyway.'

It was a project set up by Axel, but Frederick had taken it over and had every intention of making it into a success.

'I'll locate Sunita, confirm there is no scandal, and then I'll come back and find a wife from your shortlist. No argument.' A mirthless smile touched his lips. 'Don't worry. I'll be discreet.'

August 17th, Mumbai

Sunita stared down at the screen and reread the article for approximately the millionth time in three days as a mini-tornado of panic whirled and soared around her tummy.

She told herself that she was climbing the heights of irrationality. April Fotherington *hadn't* found her—she was safe here in this spacious, anonymous Mumbai apartment, surrounded by cool white walls and the hustle and bustle of a city she'd come to love. Soon enough the flicker of interest the article might ignite would die out. No one had discovered her secret thus far—there was no reason to believe they would now. She was safe. *They* were safe.

But she couldn't help the sudden lurch of fear as she gazed round the living room and the evidence of the life she'd created. Signs of her baby son were everywhere—a wooden toy box in the corner, the cheerful play mat by the sofa, board books, beakers... She knew all too well how quickly life could change, be upended and destroyed.

Stop. No one would take Amil away. Alphonse of Lycander was dead, and he had been the greatest threat—a man who had fought virulent custody battles for four of his children and used his position and wealth to win them all. She had no doubt he would have done the same for his grandchild—would have used the might and power of his sovereignty to win Amil.

Just as Frederick still might.

The peal of the doorbell jolted her from her thoughts and a scud of panic skittered through her. It couldn't be her grandmother and Amil—they had only left a little while before. *Chill*. They could have forgotten something, it could be a neighbour, or a delivery or—

Only one way to find out.

Holding her breath, she peered through the peephole.

Shock dizzied her—she blinked and prayed the man at her door was a figment of her overheated imagination, brought on by reading the article so many times. The alternative was too ghastly to contemplate. But, however many times she blinked, Prince Frederick of Lycander was still right there.

What to do? What to do? Ignore him?

But what if he waited outside? What if he was still there when Amil came back? Or what if he went away and returned when Amil was here? What if he was here to take Amil?

Enough. She had not got this far to give up now. She was no longer that ten-year-old girl, reeling from her mother's death, powerless to stop the father she had never known from taking her. No longer that eleven, twelve, thirteen-year-old girl at the mercy of her stepmother and sisters who had graduated with honours from *Cinderella* school.

She'd escaped them without the help of a handsome prince and left that feeling of powerlessness far behind. No way was she going back there—especially now, when her son was at stake.

Adrenalin surged through her body as she did what life had taught her—moved forward to face up to whatever was about to be thrown at her. She might dodge it, catch it, or punch it, but she would confront it on her own terms.

True to her motto, she pulled the door open and raised her eyebrows in aloof surprise. 'Your Highness,' she said. 'What are you doing here?'

Stepping out into the communal hall, she closed the door behind her, searching his gaze for a sign that he knew about Amil.

'I came to see *you*. April Fotherington wrote an article saying you'd vanished.'

Sunita forced herself not to lean back against the wall in relief. Instead, she maintained her façade of reserve as they stood and studied each other. Against her will, her stomach nosedived and her hormones cartwheeled. Memories of the totally wrong sort streamed through her mind and fizzed through her veins as she drank him in. The same corn-blond hair, the same hazel eyes...

No, not the same. His eyes were now haunted by shadows and his lips no longer turned upward in insouciance. Prince Frederick looked like a man who hadn't smiled in a while. Little wonder after the loss of his brother and his father, followed by a troubled ascent to the throne.

Instinctively she stepped closer, wanting to offer comfort. 'I saw the article. But before we discuss that, I'm sorry for your losses. I wanted to send condolences but...'

It had been too risky, and it had seemed wrong somehow—to send condolences whilst pregnant with his baby, whom she intended to keep secret from him.

'Why didn't you?'

The seemingly casual question held an edge and she tensed.

'If all your girlfriends had done that you'd still be reading them now. I didn't feel our brief relationship gave me the right.'

Disingenuous, but there was some truth there. For a second she could almost taste the bitter disappointment with herself for succumbing to the Playboy Prince's charms and falling into bed with him. Hell—she might as well have carved the notch on his four-poster bed herself.

She'd woken the morning after and known what she had to do—the only way forward to salvage some pride and dignity. End it on *her* terms, before he did. It had been the only option, but even as she had done it there had been a tiny part of her that had hoped he'd stop her, ask her to stay. But of course he hadn't. The Playboy Prince wouldn't change. People didn't change—Sunita knew that.

Anyway this was history. *Over and done with.*

'I am offering condolences now.'

'Thank you. But, as I said, that's not why I am here.'

'The article?'

'Yes. I'd like to talk—perhaps we could go inside.'

'No!' *Tone it down, Sunita.* 'This is my home, Frederick, my private sanctuary. I want to keep it that way.'

He eyed her for a moment and she forced herself to hold his gaze.

'Then where would you suggest? Preferably somewhere discreet.'

'In case the press spot us and tips me as the next candidate for Lycander Bride?'

The words were out before she could stop them; obscure hurt touched her with the knowledge he didn't want to be seen with her.

'Something like that. You're my unofficial business.'

For a moment there was a hint of the Frederick she'd known in the warmth of his voice, and more memories threatened to surface. Of warmth and laughter, touch and taste.

'My official reason for this trip is charity business— I'm patron of an educational charity that is rolling out some new schools.'

The tang of warmth had disappeared; instead impatience vibrated from him as he shifted from foot to foot.

'Are you sure we can't talk inside? It shouldn't take long. All I want is the solution to April's mystery.'

Sunita checked the hollow laughter before it could fall from her lips. Was that *all* he wanted? Easy-peasy, lemon-squeezy.

'I'm sure we can't talk here.'

Think. But coherent thought was nigh on impossible. Raw panic combined with her body's reaction to his proximity had unsettled her, sheer awareness wrong-footed her. *Think.* Yet her mind drew a blank as to any possible location, any café where she and Amil weren't regulars.

Fear displaced all other emotion—Frederick must not find out about Amil. Not now, not like this. One day, yes, but at a time of her choice—when it was right and safe for Amil.

'I'll just grab a coat and we can go.'

'A coat?'

'It's monsoon season.'

Sunita turned, opened the door, and slipped inside, her mind racing to formulate a plan. She'd always been able to think on her feet, after all. If Frederick wanted a solution to the mystery of her disappearance from the modelling scene, then that was what she would provide.

Grabbing her phone, she pressed speed dial and waited.

'Sunita?'

'Hey, Sam. I need a favour. A *big* favour.'

CHAPTER TWO

FREDERICK WATCHED AS she opened the door and sidled out. Coatless, he couldn't help but notice. What was going on? Anyone would think she had the Lycander Crown Jewels tucked away in there. Hell, maybe she did. Or maybe something was wrong.

Disquiet flickered and he closed it down. He'd vowed emotion would not come into play here. He and Sunita were history—the sole reason for his presence was to ensure no scandal would touch Lycander and topple him, Humpty Dumpty-style.

They exited the building and emerged onto the heat-soaked pavement, thronged with an almost impossible mass of people, alive with the shouts of the hawkers who peddled their wares and the thrum of the seemingly end-less cars that streamed along the road. Horns blared, and the smell of cumin, coriander and myriad spices mingled with the delicate scents of the garlands of flowers on offer and the harsher fumes of pollution.

Sunita walked slightly ahead, and he took the oppor-tunity to study her. The past two years had done nothing to detract from her beauty—her hair shone with a lustre that should have the manufacturer of whatever brand of shampoo she used banging at her door, and her impossibly long legs and slender waist were unchanged.

Yet there was a difference. The Sunita he'd known had dressed to be noticed, but today her outfit was simple and anonymous—cut-off jeans, a loose dark blue T-shirt and blue sandals. It was an ensemble that made her blend in with the crowd. Even the way she walked seemed altered—somehow different from the way she had once sashayed down the catwalk.

Once.

And therein lay the crux of the matter. The more he thought about it, the more he recalled the vibrant, publicity-loving, career-orientated Sunita he'd known, the less possible it seemed that she had traded the life path she'd planned for an anonymous existence. His research of the past two days had confirmed that mere weeks after Sunita had ended their association she'd thrown it all away and melted into obscurity.

'How did you find me?'

'It wasn't easy.'

Or so Marcus had informed him. Sunita's agent had refused point-blank to respond to his discreet enquiries, but Marcus had ways and means, and had eventually procured the address through 'contacts'—whatever that meant.

'Was it my agent? Was it Harvey?'

'No. But whoever it was I promise you they did you a favour.'

'Some favour.'

'You mean you aren't happy to see me?' he deadpanned.

A shadow of a smile threatened to touch her lips and he fought the urge to focus on those lips in more detail.

'Pass.'

Raising an arm, she hailed a taxi and they waited until the yellow and black vehicle had screeched through the traffic to stop by the kerb.

Once inside she leant forward to speak to the driver.

'Sunshine Café, please,' she said, and then sat back. 'I'm taking you to meet the solution to your mystery. The reason I stayed in India.'

Her eyes slid away from him for a fraction of a second and then back again as she inhaled an audible breath.

'His name is Sam Matthews. He used to be a photographer, but he's moved here and set up a beach café.'

'A boyfriend?'

Such a simple answer—Sunita had given it all up for love. A small stab of jealousy pierced his ribcage, caught him unawares. *Get real, Frederick.* So what if she walked straight into someone else's arms, into the real thing? That had never been his destiny. *Know your limitations. Easy come, easy go.* Two stellar life mottos.

'Yes.'

'Must be some boyfriend to have persuaded you to throw away your career. You told me once that nothing was more important to you than success.'

'I meant it at the time.'

'So you gave up stardom and lucre for love.'

A small smile touched her lips. 'Yes, I did.'

'And you're happy? Sam makes you happy?'

Her hands twisted on her lap in a small convulsive movement. She looked down as if in surprise, then back up as she nodded. 'Yes.'

A spectrum of emotion showed in her brown eyes—regret, guilt, defiance,—he couldn't settle on what it was, and then it was gone.

'I'm happy.'

Job done. Sunita had a boyfriend and she'd moved on with her life. There was no dangerous scandal to uncover. A simple case of over-vigilance from his chief advisor. He could stop the taxi now and return to his hotel.

Yet…something felt off. He could swear Sunita was

watching him, assessing his reactions. Just like two years ago when she'd called it a day. Or maybe it was his own ego seeing spectres—perhaps he didn't *want* to believe another woman had ricocheted from him to perfect love. Sunita to Sam, Kaitlin to Daniel—there was a definite pattern emerging.

He glanced out of the window at the busy beach, scattered with parasols and bodies, as the taxi slowed to a halt.

'We're here,' she announced.

What the hell? He might as well meet this paragon who had upended Sunita's plans, her career, her life, in a way he had not.

Damn it. There was that hint of chagrin again. Not classy, Frederick. Not royal behaviour.

Minutes later they approached a glass-fronted restaurant nestled at the corner of a less populated section of sand, under the shade of two fronded palms. Once inside, Frederick absorbed the warm yet uncluttered feel achieved by the wooden floor, high exposed beam ceiling and polished wooden tables and slatted chairs. A long sweeping bar added to the ambience, as did the hum of conversation.

Sunita moved forward. 'Hey, Sam.'

Frederick studied the man who stood before them. There was more than a hint of wariness in his eyes and stance. Chestnut wavy hair, average height, average build, light brown eyes that returned his gaze with an answering assessment.

Sunita completed the introduction. 'Sam, Frederick— Frederick, Sam. Right, now that's done...'

'Perhaps you and I could have a drink and a catch-up? For old times' sake.'

The suggestion brought on by an instinctive unease, augmented by the look of reluctance on her face. Something wasn't right. She hadn't wanted him to so much as peek into her apartment, and she could have simply *told* him about Sam. Instead she'd brought him here to see him, as if to provide tangible proof of his existence.

'Sure.' Sunita glanced at her watch. 'But I can't be too long.'

Sam indicated a staircase. 'There's a private room you can use upstairs, if you want to chat without attracting attention.'

'Great. Thank you,' Frederick said, and stepped back to allow the couple to walk together.

Their body language indicated that they were...*comfortable* with each other. They walked side by side, but there was no accidental brush of a hand, no quick glance of appreciation or anticipation, no chemistry or any sign of the awareness that had shimmered in the air since he himself had set eyes on Sunita.

They entered a small room with a wooden table and chairs by a large glass window that overlooked the beach. Sam moved over to the window, closed the shutters and turned to face them. 'If you tell me what you'd like to drink, I'll have it sent up.'

'You're welcome to join us,' Frederick said smoothly, and saw the look of caution in Sam's brown eyes intensify as he shook his head.

'I'd love to, but we're extremely busy and one of my staff members didn't turn up today, so I'm afraid I can't.'

'That's fine, Sam. Don't worry,' Sunita interpolated— and surely the words had tumbled out just a little too fast. Like they did when she was nervous. 'Could I have a guava and pineapple juice, please?'

'Sounds good—I'll have the same.'

'No problem.'

With that, Sam left the room.

'He clearly doesn't see me as a threat,' Frederick observed.

'There is no reason why he should.'

For an instant he allowed his gaze to linger on her lips and he saw heat touch her cheekbones. 'Of course not,' he agreed smoothly.

Her eyes narrowed, and one sandaled foot tapped the floor with an impatience he remembered all too well. 'Anyway, you came here to solve the mystery. Mystery solved. So your "unofficial" business is over.'

Were her words almost too airy or had he caught a case of severe paranoia from Marcus? 'It would appear so.' He watched her from beneath lowered lids.

'So, tell me more about your official business—the schools project.'

'My brother set up the charity—he believed every child deserves access to an education, however basic.'

It had been a philanthropic side Frederick hadn't even known Axel had had—one his brother had kept private. Because he had been a good man…a good man who had died—

Grief and guilt thrust forward but he pushed them back. The only reparation he could make was to continue Axel's work.

'So, I'm funding and working with a committee to set up schools here. Tomorrow I'm going to visit one of the new ones and meet the children.'

'That sounds incredible—there's so much poverty here, and yet also such a vibrant sense of happiness as well.'

'Why don't you get involved? That would be great publicity for the organisation—I could put you in touch.'

For a second her face lit up, and then she shook her head. 'No. I'm not modelling at the moment and…'

'I'm not suggesting you model. I'm suggesting you get involved with some charity work.'

'I... I don't want any publicity at the moment—'

'Why not?'

'I... Sam and I prefer our life to be out of the spotlight.'

This still didn't make sense. Sunita had thrived in the spotlight, been pulled to it like a moth to a flame. But before he could point that out, the door opened and a waitress appeared with a tray.

'Thank you.' Sunita smiled as the girl placed the drinks on the table, alongside a plate of snacks that looked to range from across the globe. Tiny pizzas topped with morsels of smoked salmon nestled next to crisp, succulent *pakora*, which sat alongside miniature burgers in minuscule buns. 'These look delicious.'

Once the waitress had exited, Frederick sampled a *pakora*, savoured the bite of the spice and the crunch of the batter around the soft potato underneath. 'These are delicious! Sam runs an excellent kitchen.'

'Yes—he and...he has made a real success of this place.'

'You must be proud of him.'

'Yes. Of course.'

'Are you involved with the restaurant?'

'No.'

He sipped his drink, with its refreshing contrast of sharp and sweet. 'So what do you do now? Do you have a job?'

'I...'

Fluster showed in the heat that crept along her cheekbones, the abrupt swirling of her drink, the over-careful selection of a snack.

'I'm a lady of leisure.' Her eyes dared him to challenge her, but he couldn't help it—a snort of disbelief emerged. Sunita had been a human dynamo, always on the go, abuzz with energy, ideas and vibrancy.

'For real?'

'Yes.' Now her fingers tapped on the table in irritation. 'Why not? I'm lucky enough that I can afford not to work—I pay my own way.'

An undercurrent of steel lined her words—one he remembered all too well. 'Just like you did two years ago.'

It had become a standing joke—she'd refused point-blank to let him pay for anything, had insisted they split every bill down the middle. The one time he'd been foolish enough to buy her a gift, she'd handed it back.

I don't like to feel beholden. It's my issue, not yours. Keep it for your next woman. I pay my own way.'

Apparently she still did.

He raised his hands in a gesture of peace. 'Where you get your money from is none of my business. I just can't imagine you doing nothing all day.'

'That's not how it is. I have a very fulfilling life.'

'Doing what?'

'None of your business. You came here to find out why I disappeared. I've told you—I fell in love, I've settled down, and I want to live my life quietly.'

Instinct told him there was something askew with the portrait she painted. Tension showed in the tautness of her body; but perhaps that tension had nothing to do with him.

'My chief advisor will be relieved—he is worried there is some mystery around your disappearance that could damage me.'

For a fraction of a second her knuckles whitened around her glass and then her eyebrows rose in a quizzical curve. 'Isn't that a tad far-fetched? To say nothing of egotistically paranoid?'

'Possibly,' he agreed, matching her eyebrow for eyebrow. 'But it also seems extremely far-fetched to me that you walked away from your career.'

'Well, I did.'

Frederick waited, but it appeared Sunita felt that sufficed.

'So you confirm that your retreat and subsequent dramatic change of lifestyle have nothing to do with me?'

Her glance flickered away and then she laughed. 'We spent one night together two years ago. Do you *really* think that your charms, manifest though they were, were sufficient to make me change my life?'

Put like that, he had to admit it sounded arrogantly self-involved. And yet... 'We spent more than one night together, Sunita.'

A wave of her hand dismissed his comment. 'A publicity stunt—nothing more.'

'OK. Let's play it your way. I can just about buy it that those weeks were all about publicity for you, but what about that night? Was *that* all for publicity?'

These were the questions he should have asked two years ago.

Her gaze swept away from him. 'No. It wasn't. I didn't intend that night to happen.'

'Is that why you left?'

It was as though the years had rolled back—he could almost imagine that they were in that five-star hotel in Paris, where they'd played truant from the glitzy party they'd been supposed to be at. Attraction had finally taken over and—

Whoa! Reel it in, Frederick!

'Yes, that's why I left. I broke my own rules. By sleeping with you I became just another notch on your bedpost—another woman on the Playboy Prince's conveyor belt. That was never meant to happen.'

'That's not how it was.'

'That's *exactly* how it was.' Tawny eyes challenged him.

'And if I'd asked you to stay?'

'You didn't.'

Her voice was flat and who could blame her? The point was that he hadn't. Because it had been easier to believe that she'd never cared, to stick by his *easy come, easy go* motto.

'But this is all beside the point—there was never a future for us. People don't change.' Her voice held utter conviction. 'You were The Playboy Prince...'

'And *you* were very clear that you had no desire for a relationship because you wanted to focus on your career. Then, just weeks later, you met Sam and realised he was the one and your career was no longer important?' It was impossible for Frederick to keep the scepticism out of his voice.

'Yes, I did.'

'So you changed.'

'Love changes everything.'

Damn it—he'd stake his fortune on the sincerity in her voice, and there was that irrational nip of jealousy again.

'So, yes,' she continued, 'I met Sam and I decided to take a break, and the break has extended to a couple of years. Simple. No mystery. That's what you came here to discover.'

Now her tone had lost the fervour of truth—he was nearly sure of it.

'You promise?' The words were foolish, but he couldn't hold them back.

She nodded. 'I promise...'

He studied her expression, saw the hint of trouble in her eyes and in the twist of her fingers under the table.

'No scandal will break over Lycander.'

'Then my work here is done.'

Yet an odd reluctance pulled at him as he rose from the

chair and looked down at her, sure now that there was *more* than a hint of trouble in her eyes. *Not his business.* She'd made a promise and he believed her. He had a country to run, a destiny to fulfil…

'I wish you well, Sunita. I'm glad you've found happiness.'

'I wish you well too.'

In one lithe movement she stood and stretched out a hand, caught his sleeve, stood on tiptoe and brushed his cheek with her lips. Memory slammed into him—her scent, the silken touch of her hair against his skin—and it took all his powers of self-control not to tug her into his arms. Instead, he forced his body to remain still, to accept the kiss in the spirit it was being given—whatever that might be—though he was pretty damn sure from the heat that touched her cheeks that she wasn't sure either.

'I…goodbye.' Once again her hands twisted together as she watched him.

'Goodbye, Sunita.'

He headed for the door, stopped at her audible intake of breath, half turned as she said his name.

'Yes?'

'It…it doesn't matter. It was good to see you again.'

That only confirmed that she had intended to say something else, but before he could respond Sam entered and glanced at them both. 'All OK?'

'Everything is fine.' Sunita's voice was over-bright now. 'Frederick is just leaving.'

Minutes later he was in a taxi, headed back to the hotel. But as the journey progressed doubts hustled and bustled and crowded his brain. Something was wrong. He had no idea what, and it most likely had nothing to do with him. Quite possibly he had the wrong end of the stick. Undoubtedly wisdom dictated that he should not get involved. Sunita was more than capable of looking out for herself, and she had Sam to turn to. But what if Sam was the problem?

Hell.

Leaning forward, he gave the driver Sunita's address.

Damn it all to hell and back! Sunita strode the length of her lounge and resisted the urge to kick a bright red bean bag across the room. Venting wouldn't stem the onrush, the sheer *onslaught* of guilt, the veritable tsunami of distaste with herself.

Why, why, *why* had he turned up? Not telling Frederick for two years had been hard enough—lying directly to Frederick's face was another ballgame altogether. Especially as it was a face that mirrored Amil's—the angle of his cheekbone, the colour of his eyes, the subtle nuances that couldn't be ignored.

The guilt kept rolling on in and her stride increased. *Focus.* Concentrate on all the sensible, logical justifications for her actions.

The decision to keep Amil a secret had been one of the toughest she had ever faced, but it was a decision she still believed to be right. She'd done her research: the Lycanders had a track record of winning custody of their children and hanging the mothers out to dry.

Frederick's father, Prince Alphonse, had fathered five children by four wives; his first wife had died, but he'd fought and won vicious custody battles against all the other three.

Ah, pointed out her conscience, *but Alphonse is dead, and in any case Frederick is Amil's father.*

But Frederick was also his father's son, and who knew what he might do? The scandal of an illegitimate baby was the last thing Lycander's Prince needed at this juncture, and she had no idea how he would react.

She didn't like any of the possible scenarios—from a custody battle to show his people that he looked after his own, to an outright and public rejection of Amil. Well, damn it, the first would happen over her dead body and the second made her shudder—because she knew exactly how awful that rejection felt and she wouldn't put Amil through it.

But the Frederick she'd seen today—would he be so callous?

She didn't know. Her thoughts were muddled by the vortex of emotion his arrival had evoked. Because something had warmed inside her, triggering a whole rush of feelings. Memories had swooped and soared, smothering her skin in desire. Flashes of his touch, of their shared joy and passion…all of that had upended any hope of rational thought or perspective. Just like two years before.

When she'd first met Frederick she'd expected to thoroughly dislike him; his reputation as a cutthroat businessman-cum-playboy had seen to that. But when he'd asked her to dinner she'd agreed to it for the publicity. And at that dinner he'd surprised her. At the next he'd surprised her even more, and somehow, as time had gone on, they had forged a connection—one she had tried oh, so hard to tell herself was nothing more than temporary friendship.

Hah!

And then there had been that *stupid* tug of attraction, which had eventually prevailed and overridden every rule she'd set herself.

Well, not this time.

To her relief the doorbell rang. Amil's arrival would put an end to all this.

She dashed to the door and pulled it open, a smile of

welcome on her face. A smile that froze into a rictus of shock.

'Frederick?'

She didn't know why she'd posed it as a question, since it clearly *was* Frederick. Her brain scrambled for purchase and eventually found it as she moved to swing the door shut, to hustle him out.

Too late.

He stepped forward, glanced around the room, and she could almost see the penny begin to drop—slowly at first, as cursory curiosity morphed into deeper question.

'You have a baby?'

His hazel eyes widened in puzzlement, and a small frown creased his brow as he took another step into her sanctum. His gaze rested on each and every item of Amil's.

'Yes.' The word was a whisper—all she could manage as her tummy hollowed and she grasped the doorjamb with lifeless fingers.

'How old?'

Each syllable was ice-cold, edged with glass, and she nearly flinched. No, she would not be intimidated. Not here. Not now. What was done was done, and—rightly or wrongly—she knew that even if she could turn back time she would make the same decision.

'Fourteen months.'

'Girl or boy?'

'Boy.'

Each question, each answer, brought them closer and closer to the inevitable and her brain wouldn't function. Instead, all she could focus on was his face, on the dawn of emotion—wonder, anger, fear and surely hope too?

That last was so unexpected that it jolted her into further words. 'His name is Amil.'

'Amil,' he repeated.

He took another step forward and instinctively she moved as well, as if to protect the life she had built, putting herself between him and her home.

'Is he mine?'

For an instant it was if the world went out of focus. She could almost see a line being drawn in the sands of time—this was the instant that separated 'before' and 'after'. For one brief instant she nearly took the coward's route, wondered if he would swallow the lie that Amil was Sam's. Then she realised she could not, *would* not do that.

'Yes. He is yours. Amil is your son.'

Now she understood the origins of a deafening silence. This one rolled across the room, echoed in her ears until she wanted to shout. Instead she waited, saw his body freeze, saw the gamut of emotion cross his face, watched as it settled into an expression of anger so ice-cold a shiver rippled her skin.

Panic twisted her insides—the die had been cast and she knew that now, whatever happened, life would never be the same.

CHAPTER THREE

STAY STILL. FOCUS ON remaining still.

The room seemed to spin around him, the white walls a rotating blur, the floor tilting under his feet. Good thing he didn't suffer from seasickness. Emotions crashed into him, rebounded off the walls of his brain and the sides of his guts. His heart thudded his ribcage at the speed of insanity.

A child. A son. *His* child. *His* son.

Fourteen months old.

Fourteen months during which his son had had no father. Anger and pain twisted together. Frederick knew exactly what it was like to have no parent—his mother had abandoned him without compunction in return for a lump sum, a mansion and a yearly stipend that allowed her a life of luxury.

Easy come, easy go.

Yes, Frederick knew what it was like to know a parent was not there for him. The anger unfurled in him and solidified.

'My son,' he said slowly, and he couldn't keep the taut rage from his voice.

He saw Sunita's awareness of it, but she stepped forward right into the force field of his anger, tawny eyes fierce and fearless.

'*My* son,' she said.

Stop.

However angry he was, however furious he was, he had to think about the baby. About Amil. Memories of the horrendous custody battles his father had instigated crowded his mind—Stefan, Emerson, Barrett—his father had treated all his sons as possessions.

'*Our* son,' he said.

The knowledge was surreal, almost impossible to comprehend. But it was imperative that he kept in control—there was too much at stake here to let emotion override him. Time to shut emotion down, just as he had for two long years. Move it aside and deal with what had to be done.

'We need to talk.'

She hesitated and then nodded, moving forward to close the front door. She watched him warily, her hands twisted together, her tawny eyes wide.

'How do you know he's mine and not Sam's?'

The look she gave him was intended to wither. 'I'm not an idiot.'

'That is a questionable statement. But what you *have* shown yourself to be is a liar. So you can hardly blame me for the question, or for wanting a better answer than that. How do you know?'

Her eyes narrowed in anger as she caught her lower lip in her teeth and then released it alongside a sigh. 'Sam isn't my boyfriend. He has a perfectly lovely girlfriend called Miranda and they live together. I asked him to fake it to try and explain to you why I left the modelling world.'

'Is there a boyfriend at all?'

She shook her head. 'No.'

So there had been no one since him. The thought provoked a caveman sort of satisfaction that had no place in this discussion. Sunita had deceived him to his face in order to hide his son from him—now was not the moment to give a damn about her relationship status. Apart from the fact that it meant Amil was his.

Hold it together, Frederick. Shelve the emotion...deal with the situation at hand.

'Why didn't you tell me?'

Sunita started to pace. Her stride reminded him of a caged animal.

'Because I was scared.'

Halting in front of him, she looked so beautiful it momentarily pierced his anger.

'I know how hard this must be for you, but please try to understand I was terrified.'

For an instant he believed her, but then he recalled her profession, her ability to play to the camera, and he swatted down the foolish fledgling impulse to show sympathy and emitted a snort of disbelief.

'Terrified of what? What did I ever do to make you fear me?'

The idea was abhorrent—he'd witnessed his father in action, his delight in the exertion of power, and he'd vowed never to engage in a similar manner. Thus he'd embarked on a life of pleasure instead.

'It wasn't that straightforward. When we split obviously I had no idea I was pregnant. I found out a few weeks later and I was in shock. I did intend to tell you, but I decided to wait until I got to twelve weeks. And then your brother died. I *couldn't* tell you then, so I decided to wait some more.'

Now her expression held no apology, and her eyes met his full-on.

'And?'

'And obviously there was a lot of press at the time about Lycander. I did some research, and it's all there—your father fought custody battles over every one of his children except Axel, and that was only because Axel's mother died before he could do so. Your mother never saw you again, his third wife fought for years before she won the right even to *see* her son, and wife number four lost her case because he managed to make out she was unfit and she had to publicly humiliate herself in order to be granted minimal visiting rights.'

'That was my father—not me.'

'Yes, but *you* had become the Lycander heir. Are you saying your father wouldn't have fought for custody of his grandson? Even if you'd wanted to, how could you have stopped him? More to the point, would you have cared enough to try?'

The words hit him like bullets. She hadn't believed he would fight for the well-being of their child. She'd thought he would stand back and watch Alphonse wrest his son away.

He shook his head. *Do you blame her?* asked a small voice. He'd been the Playboy Prince—he'd worked hard, played harder, and made it clear he had no wish for any emotional responsibilities.

'I would *never* have let my father take our child from you.' He knew first-hand what it felt like to grow up without a mother. All the Lycander children did.

'I couldn't take that risk. Plus, you didn't want to be a father—you'd made it more than clear that you had no wish for a relationship or a child.'

'Neither did you.'

His voice was even, non-accusatory, but she bristled anyway, tawny eyes flashing lasers.

'I changed.'

'But you didn't give me the chance to. Not at any point in the past two years. Even if you could justify your deceit to yourself when my father was alive, you could have told me after his death.'

His father's death had unleashed a fresh tumult of emotion to close down. He'd had to accept that he would now never forge a relationship with the man who had constantly put him down—the man who had never forgiven him for his mother's actions. And on a practical level it had pitchforked him into the nightmare scenario of ascension to the throne.

But none of that explained her continued deceit.

'I read the papers, Frederick. You have had enough to contend with in the past year to keep your throne—the revelation of a love-child with me would have finished you off. You were practically engaged to Lady Kaitlin.'

'So you want my *gratitude* for keeping my child a secret? You've persuaded yourself that you did it for me? Is that how you sleep at night?'

'I sleep fine at night. I did what I thought was right. I didn't want Amil to grow up knowing that he had been the reason his father lost his throne, or lost the woman he loved. That is too big a burden for any child.'

The words were rounded with utter certainty.

'That was not your decision to make. At any point. Regardless of the circumstances, you should have come to me as soon as you knew you were pregnant. Nothing should have stopped you. Not Axel, not my father, not Kaitlin—*nothing*. You have deprived him of his father.'

'I chose depriving him of his father over depriving him of his mother.' Her arms dropped to her sides and a sudden weariness slumped her shoulders. 'We can argue about this for ever—I did what I thought was best. For Amil.'

'*And* you.'

'If you like. But in this case the two were synonymous. He needs me.'

'I get that.'

He'd have settled for any mother—had lived in hope that one of the series of stepmothers would give a damn. Until he'd worked out there was little point getting attached, as his father quite simply got rid of each and every one.

'But Amil also needs his father. That would be me.'

'I accept that you are his father.'

Although she didn't look happy about it, her eyes were full of wariness.

'But whether he needs you or not depends on what you are offering him. If that isn't good for him then he doesn't need you. It makes no odds whether you are his father or not. The whole "blood is thicker than water" idea sucks.'

No argument there. 'I *will* be part of Amil's life.'

'It's not that easy.'

'It doesn't matter if it's easy.'

'Those are words. Words are meaningless. Exactly *how* would it work? You'll disguise yourself every so often and sneak over here to see him on "unofficial business" masked by your charity work? Or will you announce to your people that you have a love-child?'

Before he could answer there was a knock at the door and they both stilled.

'It's my grandmother...with Amil.' Panic touched her expression and she closed her eyes and inhaled deeply. 'I don't want my grandmother to know until we've worked out what to do.'

Frederick searched for words, tried to think, but the enormity of the moment had eclipsed his ability to rationalise. Instead fear came to the podium—he had a child, a son, and he was about to meet him.

What would he feel when he saw Amil?

The fear tasted ashen—what if he felt nothing?

What if he was like his mother and there was no instinctive love, merely an indifference that bordered on dislike? Or like his father, who had treated his sons as possessions, chess pieces in his petty power games?

If so, then he'd fake it—no matter what he did or didn't feel, he'd fake love until it became real.

He hauled in a deep breath and focused on Sunita's face. 'I'll leave as soon as you let them in. Ask your grandmother to look after Amil tonight. Then I'll come back and we can finish this discussion.'

Sunita nodded agreement and stepped forward.

His heart threatened to leave his ribcage and moisture sheened his neck as she pulled the door open.

A fleeting impression registered, of a tall, slender woman with silver hair pulled back in a bun, clad in a shimmering green and red sari, and then his gaze snagged on the little boy in her arms. Raven curls, chubby legs, a goofy smile for his mother.

Mine. My son.

Emotion slammed into him—so hard he almost recoiled and had to concentrate to stay steady. Fight or flight kicked in—half of him wanted to turn and run in sheer terror, the other half wanted to step forward and take his son, shield him from all and any harm.

'Nanni, this is an old friend of mine who's dropped in.'

'Good to meet you.' Somehow Frederick kept his voice even, forced himself to meet the older woman's alert gaze. He saw the small frown start to form on her brow and turned back to Sunita. 'It was great to see you again, Sunita. 'Til later.'

A last glance at his son—*his son*—and he walked away.

Sunita scooped Amil up and buried herself in his warmth and his scent. She held him so close that he wriggled in protest, so she lowered him to the ground and he crawled towards his play mat.

'Thank you for looking after him.'

'I enjoyed it immensely. And thank *you*, Sunita, for allowing me to be part of Amil's life. And yours.'

'Stop! I have told you—you don't need to thank me.'

Yet every time she did.

'Yes, I do. I was neither a good mother nor a good grandmother. You have given me a chance of redemption, and I appreciate that with all my heart.'

'We've been through this, Nanni; the past is the past and we're only looking forward.'

Her grandmother's marriage had been deeply unhappy—her husband had been an autocrat who had controlled every aspect of his family's life with an iron hand. When Sunita's mother had fallen pregnant by a British man who'd had no intent of standing by her, her father had insisted she be disowned.

Sunita could almost hear her mother's voice now: *'Suni, sweetheart, never, ever marry a man who can control you.'*

It was advice Sunita intended to take one step further—she had no plans to marry anyone, *ever*. Her father's marriage had been a misery of incompatibility, bitterness and blame—an imbroglio she'd been pitchforked into to live a Cinderella-like existence full of thoughtless, uncaring relations.

'Please, Nanni. You are a wonderful grandmother and great-grandmother and Amil adores you. Now, I have a favour to ask. Would you mind looking after Amil for the rest of the evening?'

'So you can see your friend again?'

'Yes.'

'The friend you didn't introduce?'

Sunita opened her mouth and closed it again.

Her grandmother shook her head. 'You don't have to tell me.'

'I *will* tell you, Nanni—but after dinner, if that's OK.'

'You will tell me whenever you are ready. Whatever it is, this time I will be there for you.'

An hour later, with Amil fed and his bag packed, Sunita gave her grandmother a hug. She watched as the driver she'd insisted on providing manoeuvred the car into the stream of traffic, waved, and then made her way back up-stairs… To find the now familiar breadth of Frederick on the doorstep, a jacket hooked over his shoulder.

'Come in. Let's talk.'

He followed her inside and closed the door, draping his dark grey jacket over the back of a chair. 'Actually, I thought we could talk somewhere else. I've booked a table at Zeus.'

Located in one of Mumbai's most luxurious hotels, Zeus was the city's hottest restaurant, graced by celebrities and anyone who wanted to see and be seen.

Foreboding crept along her skin, every instinct on full alert. 'Why on earth would you do that?'

'Because I am taking the mother of my child out for dinner so we can discuss the future.'

Sunita stared at him as the surreal situation deepened into impossibility. 'If you and I go out for dinner it will galvanise a whole load of press interest.'

'That is the point. We are going public. I will not keep Amil a secret, or make him unofficial business.'

She blinked as her brain crashed and tried to change gear. 'But we haven't discussed this at all.'

This was going way too fast, and events were threaten-ing to spiral out of control. *Her* control.

'I don't think we should go public until we've worked out the practical implications—until we have a plan.'

'Not possible. People are already wondering where I am. Especially my chief advisor. People may have spotted us at the café, and April Fotherington will be wondering if my presence in Mumbai is connected to you. I want the truth to come out on *my* terms, not hers, or those of whichever reporter makes it their business to "expose" the story. I want this to break in a positive way.'

Sunita eyed him, part of her impressed by the sheer strength and absolute assurance he projected, another part wary of the fact he seemed to have taken control of the situation without so much as a by-your-leave.

'I'm not sure that's possible. Think about the scandal—your people won't like this.' And they wouldn't like *her*, a supermodel with a dubious past. 'Are you sure this is the best way to introduce Amil's existence to your people?'

'I don't know. But I believe it's the right way to show my people that this is *good* news, that Amil is not a secret. That I am being honest.'

An unpleasant twinge of guilt pinched her nerves—*she* had kept Amil secret, *she* had been dishonest. She had made a decision that no longer felt anywhere near as right as it had this morning.

'So what do you say?' he asked. 'Will you have dinner with me?'

The idea gave her a sudden little thrill, brought back a sea of memories of the dinners they had shared two years before—dinners when banter and serious talk had flown back and forth, when each word, each gesture, had been a movement in the ancient dance of courtship. A courtship she had never meant to consummate...

But this meal would be on a whole new level and courtship would not be on the table. Wherever they held this discussion tonight, the only topic of conversation would be Amil and the future.

And if Frederick believed this strategy was the best way forward then she owed him her co-operation.

'Let's get this show on the road.' An unexpected fizz of excitement buzzed through her. She could *do* this; she'd always relished a fight and once upon a time she'd revelled in a show. 'But I need to change.'

'You look fine to me.'

His voice was deep and molten, and just like that the atmosphere changed. Awareness hummed and vibrated, shimmering around them, and she had to force herself to remain still, to keep her feet rooted to the cool tiles of the floor. The hazel of his eyes had darkened in a way she remembered all too well, and now it was exhilaration of a different sort that heated her veins.

Stop.

All that mattered here was Amil and his future. Two years ago she had tried and failed to resist the magnetic pull that Frederick exerted on her—a pull she had distrusted, and this time would not permit. Whatever her treacherous hormones seemed to think.

Perhaps he realised the same, because he stepped backwards and nodded. 'But I appreciate you want to change.'

'I do. You need a show, and a show is exactly what I can provide. Luckily I kept some of the clothes from my modelling days.'

Even if she'd never once worn them, she loved them still. Silk, chiffon and lace, denim and velvet, long skirts and short, flared and skinny—she had enjoyed showcasing each and every outfit. Had refused to wear any item that didn't make her soul sing. And now there was no denying the buzz. This was what she had once lived for and craved. Publicity, notice, fame—all things she could spin and control.

Almost against her will, her mind fizzed with possibility. Amil was no longer a secret, no longer in danger—they could live their lives as they wished. She could resume her career, be Sunita again, walk the catwalks and revel in fashion and all its glorious aspects. Amil would, of course, come with her—just as she had accompanied her mother to fashion shoots—and Nanni could come too.

Life would take on a new hue without the terrible burden of discovery clouding every horizon. Though of course Frederick would be part of that life, if only a minor part. His real life lay in Lycander, and she assumed he would want only a few visits a year perhaps.

Whoa! Slow right down, Suni!

She had no idea what Frederick's plans were, and she'd do well to remember that before she waltzed off into la-la land. She didn't know this man—this Frederick.

Her gaze rested on him, absorbed the breadth of his body, his masculine presence, the determined angle of his stubbled jaw, the shadowed eyes crinkled now in a network of lines she thought probably hadn't come from laughter. Her breath caught on a sudden wave of desire. Not only physical desire, but a stupid yearning to walk over and smooth the shadows away.

A yearning she filed away under both dangerous and delusional as she turned and left the room.

CHAPTER FOUR

FREDERICK CHANGED INTO the suit he'd had delivered to him whilst he was waiting and prowled the flat on the lookout for evidence of Amil's life.

Amil. The syllables were still so unfamiliar—his only knowledge of his son that brief glimpse a few hours earlier. But there would be time—plenty of time—to catch up on the past fourteen months. Provided Sunita agreed to his proposition—and she *would* agree.

Whatever it took, he would make her see his option was the only way forward.

He paused in front of a framed photograph of Sunita and a newborn Amil. He looked at the tiny baby, with his downy dark hair, the impossible perfection of his minuscule fingernails, and the utter vulnerability of him twisted Frederick's gut.

Shifting his gaze to Sunita, he saw the love in her brown eyes clear in every nuance, every part of her body. Her beauty was unquestionable, but this was a beauty that had nothing to do with physical features and everything to do with love.

Perhaps he should feel anger that he had missed out on that moment, but his overwhelming emotion was relief—gratitude, even—that his son had been given something so vital. Something he himself had never received. *His* mother had handed him straight over to a nanny and a few scant years later had disappeared from his life.

For a long moment Frederick gazed at the photo, trying to figure out what he should feel, what he *would* feel when he finally met Amil properly, held him... Panic hammered his chest and he stepped backwards. What if he was like his mother—what if he quite simply lacked the parenting gene?

The click of heels against marble snapped him to attention and he stepped back from the photo, turning to see Sunita advance into the room. For a moment his lungs truly ceased to work as his pulse ratcheted up a notch or three.

Sunita looked... It was impossible to describe her without recourse to a thesaurus. *This* was the woman he remembered—the one who dressed to catch the eye. But it wasn't only the dress with its bright red bodice and gently plumed skirt that showcased her trademark legs. The bright colour was toned down by contrasting black satin panels and silver stiletto heels. It was the way she wore it—she seemed to bring the dress alive. And vice versa. A buzz vibrated from her—an energy and sparkle that epitomised Sunita.

'Wow!' was the best he could do as he fought down visceral desire and the need to tug her into his arms and rekindle the spark that he knew with gut-wrenching certainty would burst into flame. To kiss her senseless...

What the hell was he thinking? More to the point, what part of himself was he thinking *with*?

Maybe he was more like his father than he knew. Alphonse had always put physical desire above all else. If he'd been attracted to a woman he'd acted on that attraction, regardless of marriage vows, fidelity or the tenets of plain, common decency. The last ruler of Lycander had believed that *his* desires were paramount, and it didn't matter who got hurt in the process.

Frederick wouldn't walk that road. He never had—that, at least, was one immoral path he'd avoided.

His business with Sunita was exactly that—*business*. He had an idea to propound, an idea he would not mix with the physical.

'You look fantastic.'

'Thank you. I know it sounds shallow, but it is awesome to dress up again.'

She smoothed her hand down the skirt and her smile caught at his chest.

'You look pretty good yourself. Where did the suit come from?'

'I had it delivered whilst I was waiting.'

'Good thinking, Batman.'

Her voice was a little breathless, and he knew that she was as affected as he was by their proximity. Her scent teased him, her eyes met his, and what he saw in their deep brown depths made him almost groan aloud.

Enough.

Right now he had to focus on the most important factor, and that was Amil. Irritation scoured him that he could be letting physical attraction come into play.

He nodded to the door. 'We'd better go.'

Sunita wanted, *needed* this journey to come to an end. Despite the spacious interior of the limo, Frederick was too...*close*.

Memories lingered in the air, and her body was on high alert, tuned in to his every move, and she loathed her own weakness as much now as she had two years before. She needed to distract herself, to focus on what was important—and that was Amil.

The day's events had moved at warp speed and she was desperately trying to keep up. The truth was out, and it was imperative she kept control of a future that she could no longer reliably predict.

Frederick wanted to be a real part of Amil's life—he had made that more than clear. But at this point she had no idea what that meant, and she knew she had to tread carefully.

The limo slowed down and she took a deep breath as it glided to a stop.

'Ready?' he asked.

'Ready.'

With any luck she wouldn't have lost her touch with the press. In truth, she'd always liked the paparazzi. Her mother had always told her that publicity was a means to measure success, part of the climb to fame and fortune and independence.

They stepped out into a crowd of reporters, the click of cameras and a fire of questions.

'Are you back together?'

'Friends or lovers?'

'Does Kaitlin know?'

'Where have you been, Sunita?'

Frederick showed no sign of tension. His posture and smile were relaxed, his whole attitude laid back.

'At present we have no comment. But if you hold on I promise we will have an announcement to make after dinner.'

Next to him, Sunita smiled the smile that had shot her to catwalk fame. She directed a small finger-wave at a reporter who'd always given her positive press, a smile at a woman she'd always enjoyed a good relationship with, and a wink at a photographer renowned for his audacity.

Then they left the reporters behind and entered the restaurant, and despite the knowledge of how important the forthcoming conversation was a part of Sunita revelled in the attention she was gathering. The simple ability to walk with her own natural grace, to know it was OK to be recognised, her appreciation of the dress and the inner confidence it gave her—all of it was such a contrast to the past two years, during which she had lived in constant denial of her own identity, burdened by the fear of discovery.

The manager beamed at them as he led them past the busy tables, where patrons looked up from their food and a buzz immediately spread. Sunita kept her eyes ahead, noting the dark-stained English Oak screens and latticing that graced the room, the hustle and bustle from the open-plan kitchen where chefs raced round, the waiters weaving in and out, and the tantalising smells that drifted into the eating area.

'As requested, we've seated you in a private dining area where you will be undisturbed. My head chef has arranged a buffet for you there, with samples of all our signature dishes, and there is, of course, champagne on ice—we are very happy to welcome you both here.'

He turned to Sunita.

'I do not expect you to remember me, but when you were a child your mother brought you many, many times to the restaurant I worked in then. Your mother was a lovely lady.'

Memory tugged as she studied the manager's face. 'I *do* remember you. You're Nikhil! You used to give me extra sweets and fortune cookies, and you would help me read the fortunes.'

His smile broadened. 'That is correct—I am very happy to see you here, and I am very sorry about your mother. She was a good woman.'

'Thank you. That means a lot to me. And it would have to her as well.'

It really would. So many people had looked down on

Leela Baswani because she had been a single, unmarried mother, and a model and actress to boot. But her mother had refused to cower before them; she had lived her life and she'd loved every minute of it—even those terrible last few months. Months she didn't want to remember, of watching her mother decline, knowing that soon she would be left alone in the world.

But those were not the memories Leela would have wanted her daughter to carry forth into life. Instead she would remember her as Nikhil did—as a good, brave, vibrant woman.

Nikhil showed them into the private dining room, where a beautifully decorated table laid with snowy white linen held fluted glassware, gleaming cutlery and a simple table decoration composed of an arrangement of glorious white roses.

Sunita looked at them, and then at Nikhil, and a lump formed in her throat. White roses had been her mother's favourite flower—her trademark accessory—and as the scent reached her nostrils she closed her eyes for a second. 'Thank you, Nikhil.'

The manager gave a small bow. 'You are very welcome. Now, both of you enjoy the food. I believe our chef has excelled himself. And I guarantee you complete privacy.'

With one more beaming smile, he left, closing the door behind him.

'I'm sorry about your mother,' Frederick said.

'Thank you.'

'She isn't mentioned in any articles about you except April's most recent one. None of your family is.'

'No. They aren't.'

And that was the way it would stay—she would love to remember her mother more publicly, but to do that would risk questions about her father, and she'd severed her ties with him years before—the man who'd abandoned her before birth and then reappeared in her life only to make it thoroughly miserable.

'Anyway, we aren't here to speak of my family.' He raised an eyebrow and she bit her lip. 'I mean, we are here to discuss Amil's future.'

'We are. But first shall we help ourselves to food?'

She nodded. No way could she hurt Nikhil's feelings, but she sensed there was more to Frederick's suggestion than that. It was almost as if he were stalling, giving himself time to prepare, and a sense of foreboding prickled her skin—one she did her best to shake off as she made a selection from the incredible dishes displayed on the table.

There was a tantalising array of dumplings with descriptions written in beautiful calligraphy next to each platter—prawn and chive, shanghai chicken, *pak choi*… Next to them lay main courses that made her mouth water—Szechuan clay pot chicken, salmon in Assam sauce, ginger fried rice…

The smell itself was enough to allay her fears, and she reminded herself that Frederick had a country to run—other fish to fry, so to speak. Surely the most he would want would be to contribute to Amil's upkeep and see him a few times a year. That would work—that would be more than enough.

Once they were seated, she took a deep breath. 'Before we start this discussion you need to know that I will not agree to anything that feels wrong for Amil. He is my priority here and if you try to take him away from me I will fight you with my last dying breath. I just want that out there.'

There was something almost speculative in his gaze, alongside a steely determination that matched her own. 'Amil is my priority too—and that means I *will* be a real part of his life. That is non-negotiable. *I* just want *that* out there.'

'Fine. But what does that mean?'

'I'm glad you asked that, because I've given this some thought and I know what I believe is best for Amil's future.'

The smoothness of his voice alerted Sunita's anxiety. The presentiment of doom returned and this time her very bones knew it was justified. Spearing a dumpling with an effort at nonchalance, she waved her fork in the air.

'Why don't you tell me what you have in mind?'

His hazel eyes met hers, his face neutral. 'I want you to marry me.'

CHAPTER FIVE

'MARRY YOU?' SUITA STARED at him, flabberghasted. 'That's a joke, right?'

It must be his opening bid in negotiations designed to throw her into a state of incoherence. If so, he'd slammed the nail on the head.

'No joke. Trust me, marriage isn't a topic I'd kid about. It's a genuine proposal—I've thought it through.'

'When? In the past few hours? Are you certifiably *nuts*?'

'This makes sense.'

'How? There is no universe where this makes even a particle of a molecule of sense.'

'This is what is best for Amil—best for our son.'

'No, it isn't. Not in this day and age. You *cannot* play the let's-get-together-for-our-child's-sake card.'

That was the stuff of fairy tales, and she was damned sure that her mother had been right about those being a crock of manure.

'Yes, I can. In the circumstances.'

'What circumstances?' Her fogged brain attempted to illuminate a pathway to understanding and failed.

'If you marry me Amil will become Crown Prince of Lycander after me. If you don't, he won't.'

The words took the wind out of the sails of incredulity. Of *course*. *Duh!* But the idea that Frederick would marry her to legitimise Amil hadn't even tiptoed across her mind. The whole concept of her baby one day ruling a principality seemed surreal, and right now she needed to cling onto reality.

'We can't get married to give Amil a crown.'

'But we can get married so that we don't deprive him of one.'

'Semantics.' *Think*. 'He won't feel deprived of something he never expected to have.' *Would he?* 'Amil will grow up knowing…'

Her voice trailed off. Knowing what? That if his mother had agreed to marry his father he would have been a prince, a ruler, rather than a prince's illegitimate love-child.

'Knowing that he can be whatever he wants to be,' she concluded.

'As long as what he wants to be isn't Ruler of Lycander.'

Panic stole over her, wrapped her in tentacles of anxiety. 'You are putting me in an impossible position. You are asking me to decide Amil's entire future. To make decisions on his behalf.'

'No. I am suggesting *we* make this decision together. I believe this is the best course of action for Amil. If you think otherwise then convince me.'

'He may not want to be pushed into a pre-ordained future—may not want to be a ruler. Why would we burden him with the weight of duty, with all the rules and obligations that come with it?'

'Because it is his *right* to rule. Just as it was my brother's.'

His voice was even, but she saw the shadows chase across his eyes, sensed the pain the words brought.

'Axel wanted to rule—he believed in his destiny.'

'So you believe this is Amil's destiny?' Sunita shook her

head. 'It's too abstract. We make our own destiny and Amil will make his, whatever we decide to do. I want to make the decision that is best for his wellbeing and happiness—you don't need a crown for either.'

'This isn't about need—this is about his birthright. As my first born son he has the right to inherit the Lycander crown.'

'Even though he was born out of wedlock?'

It was the phrase her grandmother had used to describe Sunita's birth, to try and explain why her husband had thrown their pregnant daughter out.

I know it is hard to understand in this day and age, Sunita, but in our family a mixed race child, born out of wedlock, was a stigma. It wasn't right, but it was how my husband felt.'

A feeling shared by others. Sunita could still feel the sting of the taunts her half-siblings had flung at her— nasty, insidious words that had clawed at her self-esteem.

Focus. Frederick watched her, his hazel eyes neutral and cool; he was in control and she quite clearly wasn't. Her thoughts raced round a playground of panic, visited the seesaw, spent time on the slide. Being born out of wedlock would have no impact on Amil's life; it was not a reason to get married.

She forced herself to concentrate on Frederick's answer to her question.

'It makes no odds as long as we legitimise him through marriage,' he said. 'Lycander's rules are complex, but clear on that front.'

Oh, Lord. What was she supposed to do? How could she make a decision like this without the use of a crystal ball? Her mother had believed the right course of action had been to hand Sunita over to her father.

'People can change, Suni,' her mother had said. She'd

stroked Sunita's hair with a hand that had looked almost translucent, the effort of even that movement an evident strain. *'I have to believe that.'*

Sunita understood the uncharacteristic thread of sentimentality in her mother over those final weeks. Leela Baswani had wanted to die believing her daughter would be safe and happy, and so she had allowed herself to be conned again by the man who had already broken her heart. She'd allowed herself to believe that people could change.

Well, she'd been wrong. And so was this.

'This is impossible, Frederick. We can't spend the rest of our lives together.'

The very idea of spending a *week* with anyone made her skin prickle in affront—she could almost feel the manacles closing round her wrists. 'Maybe we should get married, legitimise Amil, and then get a divorce.'

Even as the words left her lips she knew how stupid they were.

'No. I want to give Amil a life with both his parents, and most importantly, if he is to rule Lycander, he needs to live in the palace, be brought up to understand his inheritance. And I need a wife—a true consort.'

This was becoming laughable. 'Really, I am *not* wife material—trust me on this.'

His broad shoulders lifted. 'But you *are* the mother of my child.'

Fabulous. 'So you'll make do with me because I come with a ready-made heir? And this whole marriage idea is because we are convenient?' The idea caused welcome anger—an emotion she could manage way better than panic.

'You don't care about Amil as a person—you only care about him as a commodity.'

'No!' Her words had clearly touched a nerve. 'I care about Amil because he is my son and I believe this is his right. I want him to grow up with two parents. And, believe me, this is hardly *convenient*. I intended to present my people with a wife and heir in a more conventional way.'

'Well, gee, thank you. That makes us feel *really* special.'

But she was the woman who had omitted to mention his son's existence—making her feel special would hardly be anywhere on his agenda.

His raised eyebrows indicated complete accord with her unspoken thought. 'There's no point in hypocrisy. If you expect me to go down on one knee, think again.'

'I don't expect anything—especially not a proposal. I don't want to marry you; I don't want to marry anyone.'

'I appreciate that. Until recently marriage has never exactly been high on my to-do list either. Back in the day I had a business to run and a party lifestyle to maintain. But circumstances have changed. For us both. *We* have Amil. *I* now have a country to run. I need a wife and I need an heir…to show the people of Lycander that I have changed. That I am responsible, that I offer stability, that I can put the principality's needs above my own.'

Sunita tried to equate this Frederick with the man she had known. '*Have* you changed?'

'Yes.' The syllable was bleak in its certainty, but despite its brevity it conveyed absolute conviction. 'You can choose to believe that or not, as you wish. But believe this: I need to get married.'

'Well, I don't. I prefer to be on my own.' She didn't want to be tied to anyone—she wanted to be independent and free to make decisions for herself and for Amil. 'Free.' *In control.*

'I understand that.' His jaw set in a hard line. 'But marriage is the only way to secure Amil his birthright and give him two parents one hundred per cent of the time.'

There was a strange undercurrent to his voice, and she realised just how important this must be to him. According to her research, his parents had split when he was three and his father had won sole custody. After that he'd had a series of stepmothers, none of whom had lasted more than a few years. So perhaps it was little wonder he wanted to give his son the kind of stable family he'd never had. For a moment, compassion for the little boy he had once been touched her and she forced herself to concentrate on the present.

'But it wouldn't be good for Amil to grow up and see his parents in an unhappy marriage.'

'Why assume it will be unhappy?'

'Because…' To her own annoyance, not a single reason sprang to mind that didn't sound stupid. Eventually she said, 'You can't expect me to sign up to a life sentence with a man I don't even know.'

'Fair enough. Then let's rectify that.'

He smiled—a smile of the toe-curling variety, like sunshine breaking through a grey cloudbank. And she couldn't help smiling back. But then the moment was gone and the stormy skies reappeared.

'Rectify it how?'

'Let's get to know each other. Bring Amil to Lycander and—'

'No! Once we are in Lycander I have no idea if we will be subject to Lycander law. Which, as far as I can gather, is *you*.'

The smile was a distant memory now, his face set in granite. 'You don't trust me?'

'I don't trust anyone.' After all, if you couldn't trust your own father, who *could* you trust? His promise to her mother that he would look after Sunita, care for her as only a parent could, had turned out to be a bunch of empty, meaningless syllables.

'So we stay here.'

He raised his hands. 'Fair enough. But I can't be away for too long. I can stay in Mumbai for a few days or... Wait, I have a better idea.' The smile made a return. 'How about we go away for a few days? You and me. Away from the press and the politics and the spotlight.'

'You and me?' Panic and horror cartwheeled in her stomach.

'Yes. You and me. I'll put my money where my mouth is—you said you couldn't marry someone you didn't know, so here's the opportunity to spend time with me. Twenty-four-seven, with no distractions.'

'Be still my beating heart.'

Now his smile broadened and this time she was sure her hair curled.

'I *knew* you'd like the idea. Would your grandmother be happy to look after Amil?'

'If I agree to this, Amil comes with us.' A frown touched her brow and her eyes narrowed in suspicion. 'Surely you want to get to know your son?'

'Of course I do. But before we spend time together as a family, we need to know where we stand. I know he is only a baby, but I want him to have certainty and stability.'

The kind of certainty she guessed he'd never known. Again for an instant she wanted to reach out and offer comfort. *What to do? What to do?* In truth she didn't know. She should close this down now—but was that the right thing for Amil?

Frederick wanted to be a real part of his life, wanted to make him his heir. She couldn't in all conscience dismiss it out of hand. More than that, insane though it might be, there was a tiny part of her that didn't want to. That same tiny part that two years ago had wanted Frederick to ask her to stay, to sweep her into his arms and—

Cue mental eye-roll and a reality check. Fairy tales didn't exist. This was for Amil's sake.

'OK. Two days. I won't leave Amil longer than that.'

'Deal. Where do you want to go?'

Sunita thought for a moment. 'Goa.' That would keep it all in perspective—her parents had spent some time in Goa; they'd been happy there, but that hadn't led to a happily-ever-after in any sense.

'OK. Here's how it'll work. I'll have my people pick up Amil and your grandmother now, and bring them to the hotel. Once we make the announcement about Amil the press will converge. I want my son safe here, under royal security protection.'

She could feel the colour leech from her skin and saw that he had noticed it.

'I don't believe he is danger, but his position has changed. No matter what we decide, there will be more interest in him and his life from now on.'

She inhaled an audible breath. 'You're right. I'll call my grandmother and prepare her.'

Pulling her phone out of her bag, she rose and walked to the opposite end of the room.

Frederick watched as Sunita paced the width of the room as she talked, her voice low but animated, one hand gesturing as the conversation progressed.

It was impossible not to admire her fluidity of movement, her vibrancy. At least she hadn't blown the marriage idea out of the water. But he'd known she wouldn't do that—for Amil she had to consider it. What woman would deprive her son of a crown? Yet unease still tingled in his veins. Sunita might well be the one woman who would do exactly that.

Ironic, really—his chief advisor had a list of women who wanted to marry him, and he'd proposed to the one woman who didn't even want to audition for the part of bride.

No matter—he would convince her that this was the way forward. Whatever it took.

His conscience jabbed him. Really? *Whatever* it took? Maybe that was how his father had justified the custody battles.

Abruptly he turned away and, pulling his own phone out, set to work making arrangements.

He dropped his phone back in his pocket as she returned to the table. 'How did your grandmother take it?'

'With her trademark unflappable serenity. I think she suspected—she may even have recognised you earlier and put two and two together. She'll have Amil ready.' Her chin jutted out at a defiant angle. 'I've asked Sam and Miranda as well.'

She really didn't trust him. 'Do you really think I will take Amil from you by force?'

Silence greeted this and he exhaled heavily.

'If you can't trust my morality then at least trust my intelligence. I want you to marry me—kidnapping Amil would hardly help my cause. Or garner me positive publicity in Lycander. You hid Amil from me for two years. I have more reason to distrust *you* than vice versa.'

'Maybe it's best if neither of us trusts each other.'

She had a point.

'Works for me. Whilst we are away Amil will be in your grandmother's charge, with Sam and Miranda as your back-up. But they remain based in the hotel, and if they go anywhere one of my staff goes with them. Does that work for you?'

'Yes.'

'Good. Once they are safely here I'll announce it to the press. We'll leave for Goa tomorrow, after my visit to the school.'

'Whoa! Hold on.' One elegant hand rose in the air to stop him. 'This is a *joint* operation. So, first off, *I* want to make the announcement. And we are *not* mentioning marriage.'

She drummed her fingers on the table and he could see her mind whir. This had always been her forte—she'd used to play the press like a finely tuned instrument, and had always orchestrated publicity for maximum impact with impeccable timing.

'Prince Frederick and I are delighted to announce that fourteen months ago our son Amil was born. Obviously we have a great deal to discuss about the future, which we will be doing over the next few days. My press office will be in touch with details of a photo opportunity with the three of us tomorrow.'

'Photo opportunity?' Three of us...? The words filled him with equal parts terror and anticipation.

'Yes. Better to arrange it than have them stalk us to try and get one. And I assume you want to spend time with Amil before we go?' She clocked his hesitation before he could mask it. 'Is there a problem?'

'No.' *Liar.*

Her eyes filled with doubt. He racked his brain and realised that in this case only the truth would suffice.

'I don't want to upset Amil or confuse him just before you leave him.'

He didn't want his son to believe on any level that it

was his father's fault that he was losing his mother. Even for a few days.

For the first time since his proposal she smiled—a real, genuine smile—and he blinked at the warmth it conveyed. If he were fanciful, he'd swear it had heated his skin and his soul.

'You won't upset him. Truly. How about we take him to the Hanging Gardens? He loves it there—the press can take their photos and then we can take him for a walk.'

'Sounds great.'

But the warmth dissipated and left a cold sheen of panic in its wake. What if the meeting didn't go well? What if they couldn't connect?

Then he'd fake it. If he could close his emotions down—and he was a past master in the art—then surely the reverse would be true too. 'My school visit is planned for seven a.m., so if we schedule the press for midday that should work.'

'I'd like to come with you to the school. It's a cause I'd love to be involved in, and now...now I can.'

Her smile broadened and it occurred to him that, whilst he couldn't condone what she had done, hiding Amil had impacted on Sunita's life heavily. She'd lost her career, had to subdue her identity and become anonymous.

Sheesh. Get a grip. Any minute now he'd start to feel sorry for her.

The point now was that Sunita would be an asset to the charity.

His phone beeped and he read the message.

'Amil and your grandmother are in the hotel. So are Sam and Miranda. So let's go and face the press.'

And then he'd face the music. He had no doubt his chief advisor had set up a veritable orchestra.

CHAPTER SIX

'YOU'VE DONE *WHAT*?' Marcus Alrikson, hot off a private jet, scooted across the floor of the hotel suite. 'The whole existence of a secret baby is bad enough—but now you're telling me you have proposed marriage!' Marcus paused, pinched the bridge of his nose and inhaled deeply. 'Why?'

Frederick surveyed him from the depths of the leather sofa. 'Because I have a son, and I want my son to live with me *and* his mother. I realise that flies in the face of Lycander tradition, but there you have it. I want Amil to inherit his birthright. The only way to achieve both those goals is marriage.'

'If this marriage loses you the crown he won't have a birthright to inherit.'

'It won't.' Frederick imbued his voice with a certainty he was far from feeling—but he was damned if he would admit that to Marcus. 'This is the right thing to do and the people of Lycander will see that.'

'Perhaps...but that doesn't mean they will accept Sunita or Amil.'

'They will have no reason not to. Sunita has proved herself to be an exemplary mother. And she will be an exemplary princess.'

Marcus shook his head. 'She is a supermodel with a reputation as a party girl. You have no idea what she may or may not do—she would never have made my list in a million years. She is as far from Kaitlin Derwent as the moon is from Jupiter.'

'And look what happened with Lady Kaitlin. Plus, don't you think you're being a little hypocritical? What about *my* reputation?'

'You have spent two years showing that you have changed. The reforms you are undertaking for Lycander are what the people want. You may have been a playboy with a party lifestyle, but you also founded a global business—Freddy Petrelli's Olive Oil is on supermarket shelves worldwide. At least you partied on your own dime.'

'So did Sunita. And her party days were over by the time we met.'

'Sunita has spent two years hiding your son from you,' Marcus retorted. 'There is nothing to suggest she will be good for Lycander and plenty to suggest she will plunge the monarchy straight back into scandal. She could run off with Amil, file for divorce before the honeymoon is over...'

'She won't.'

He couldn't know that, though—not really. He'd known Sunita for a couple of weeks two years ago. Doubt stepped in but he kicked it out even as he acknowledged the sceptical rise of his chief advisor's eyebrow. 'Or at least it's a risk I am willing to take.'

'It is too big a risk. The women on my list are open to the idea of an arranged marriage—they have been brought up to understand the rules. Dammit, Frederick, we *had* this discussion. We agreed that it was important for the Lycander bride to be totally unlike your father's later choices and more in line with his first wife.'

Axel's mother, Princess Michaela, a princess in her own right, had been a good woman.

'We did. But circumstances have changed.'

'Doesn't matter. You plan to present your people with a bride who may well cause a scandal broth of divorce and custody battles.'

'I have no choice—none of this is Amil's fault.'

'I am not suggesting you turn your back on Amil. Provide for him. See him regularly. But do not marry his mother.'

'No.' It was as simple as that. 'I will be a real father to Amil and this is the way forward. I'm doing this, Marcus—with or without your help.'

Silence reigned and then Marcus exhaled a long sigh and sank into the seat opposite. 'As you wish.'

Sunita surveyed her reflection in the mirror, relieved that there was no evidence of the tumult that raged in her brain. Frederick…discovery… Amil… Crown Prince… marriage… Goa….disaster.

There was potential disaster on all fronts—the thought of marriage was surreal, the enormity of the decision she needed to make made her head whirl and the idea of two days in Goa with Frederick made her tummy loop the loop.

A tentative knock on the door heralded the arrival of Eric, the Lycander staff member who had been dispatched to her apartment the previous night.

'Good morning, Eric, and thank you again for getting my things. I really appreciate it.'

'You're very welcome, ma'am. The Prince is ready.'

She followed Eric through the opulence of the hotel, with its gold and white theme, along plush carpet and past gilded walls, through the marble lobby, past luscious plants and spectacular flower arrangements and outside to the limo. There Frederick awaited her, leant against the hood of the car, dressed casually in jeans and a T-shirt, his blond hair still a touch spiked with damp, as if he'd grabbed a shower on the run.

'A limo? Isn't that a touch ostentatious?'

The flippant comment made to mask her catch of breath, the thump of her heart. 'I promised the children a limo after my last visit—they were most disappointed when I turned up in a taxi.'

He held the door for her and she slid inside, the air-conditioned interior a welcome relief against the humidity, with its suggestion of imminent monsoon rain.

'They are amazing kids—they make you feel…humble.'

Sunita nodded. 'I read up on the charity last night. The whole set-up sounds awesome and its achievements are phenomenal. I love the simplicity of the idea—using open spaces as classrooms—and I admire the dedication of the volunteers. I'll do all I can to raise the profile and raise funds. Today and in the future.'

'Thank you. Axel helped set up the charity and donated huge sums after someone wrote to him with the idea and it caught his imagination. I wish…'

'You wish what?' The wistfulness in his voice touched her.

'I wish he'd told me about it.'

'People don't always like to talk about their charitable activity.' She frowned. 'But in this case surely he must have been pretty public about it, because his profile would have raised awareness.'

'It didn't work like that. My father was unpredictable about certain issues—he may not have approved of Axel's involvement. So Axel kept it low-key. Anonymous, in fact. I only found out after his death because someone from the charity wrote with their condolences and their thanks for all he had done. I decided to take over and make it a more high-profile role.'

'Didn't your father mind?'

Frederick shrugged. 'I don't know. He and I weren't close.' His tone forbade further questions. 'Anyway, in the past two years the number of schools has increased three-fold and I've hired an excellent administrator—she isn't a volunteer, because she can't afford to be, but she is worth every penny. The schools are makeshift, but that has saved money and I think it makes them more accessible.'

His face was lit with enthusiasm and there was no doubting his sincerity. Any reservations she'd harboured that this was simply a publicity stunt designed to show that Frederick had a charitable side began to fall away.

This continued when they arrived at the school and a veritable flock of children hurtled towards the car.

He exhibited patience, good humour and common sense; he allowed them to feel and touch the car, and then promised they could examine the interior after their lessons—as long as their teacher agreed.

A smiling woman dressed in a forest-green and blue *salwar kameez* came forward and within minutes children of differing ages and sizes were seated in the pavilion area and the lesson commenced.

Sunita marvelled at the children's concentration and the delight they exuded—despite the open-air arena, and all the distractions on offer, they were absorbed in their tasks, clearly revelling in the opportunity to learn.

'Would you like to go and look at their work?' the teacher offered, and soon Sunita was seated next to a group of chattering children, all of whom thrust their notebooks towards her, emanating so much pride in their achievements that flipped her heart.

She glanced at Frederick and her heart did another turn. Standing against a backdrop of palm trees and lush monsoon greenery, he was performing a series of magic tricks that held the children spellbound. He produced coins from ears and cards from thin air, bringing gasps of wonder and giggles of joy.

Finally, after the promised exploration of the limo, the children dispersed—many of them off to work—and after a long conversation with the teacher Frederick and Sunita returned to the car for their journey back to the hotel.

'Next time I'll take Amil,' Sunita said. 'I want him to meet those kids, to grow up with an understanding of the real world.'

'Agreed.'

The word reminded Sunita that from now on Frederick would have a say in her parenting decisions, but right now that didn't seem to matter. This was a topic they agreed on.

'There's such a lesson to be learnt there—those children want to learn, and it doesn't matter to them if they have computers or science labs or technology. They find joy in learning, and that's awesome as well as humbling.'

'*All* of this is humbling.'

He turned to look out of the window, gesturing to the crowded Mumbai streets, and Sunita understood what that movement of his hand had encompassed—the poverty that was rife, embodied by the beggars who surged to the limo windows whenever the car slowed, hands outstretched, entreaty on their faces. But it was more than that – you could see the spectrum of humanity, so many individuals each and every one with their own dreams and worries.

'You really care. This isn't all a publicity stunt...part of your new image.'

'This is about a continuation of Axel's work—no more, no less. Don't paint me as a good person, Sunita. If it weren't for Axel I would never have given this so much as a thought.'

The harshness of his voice shocked her, jolted her backwards on the seat with its intensity. 'Perhaps, but you were hardly duty-bound to take over—or to come out here and interact with those children like that.' She couldn't help it. 'Axel didn't do that, did he?'

'Axel *couldn't* do that—he needed to be the heir my father wanted him to be.'

With that he pulled his phone out of his pocket in a clear indication that the subject was well and truly closed.

Sunita frowned, fighting the urge to remove the phone from his grasp and resume their conversation, to make him see that he was wrong—in this instance he *was* a good person.

Back off, Sunita.

Right now she needed to remain focused on whether or not she wanted to marry this man—and what the consequences of her decision would be for Amil. And in that vein she needed to look ahead to the photo call, which meant an assessment of the recent press coverage. So she pulled her own phone out of her pocket.

A few minutes later he returned the mobile to his pocket.

'OK. We'll fly to Goa late afternoon, after the photo call and the trip to Hanging Gardens. As you requested I've sorted out a room near your suite for Sam and Miranda.'

'Thank you. I appreciate that.'

Goa! Sudden panic streamed through her and she pushed it down. She was contemplating *marriage* to Frederick, for goodness' sake—so panic over a mere two days was foolish, to say the least. She needed to focus on Amil.

She glanced across at Frederick, wondering how he must feel about taking Amil out. Perhaps she should ask, but the question would simply serve as a reminder of the fact that he had missed out on the first fourteen months of his son's life.

So instead she faced forward and maintained silence until the limo pulled up outside the hotel.

Frederick stood outside the hotel bedroom door. His heart pounded in his chest with a potent mix of emotions—nervousness, anticipation and an odd sense of rightness. In two minutes he would meet Amil. Properly. Terror added itself to the mix, and before he could turn tail and flee he raised his hand and knocked.

Sunita opened the door, Amil in her arms, and he froze. He didn't care that he was standing in the corridor in full sight of any curious passers-by. All he could do was gaze at his son. *His son.*

Wonder entered his soul as his eyes roved over his features and awe filled him. *His son.* The words overwhelmed and terrified him in equal measure, causing a strange inability to reach out and hold the little boy. His emotions paralysed him, iced his limbs into immobility, stopped his brain, brought the world into slow motion.

Determination that he would not let Amil down fought with the bone-deep knowledge that of course he would. He wasn't equipped for this—didn't have the foundations to know how to be a parent, how not to disappoint.

But he would do all he could. He could give this boy his name, his principality, and perhaps over time he would work out how to show his love.

Amil gazed back at him with solemn hazel eyes and again panic threatened—enough that he wrenched his gaze away.

'You OK?' Sunita's soft voice pulled him into focus and he saw understanding in her eyes, and perhaps even the hint of a tear at the edge of her impossibly long eyelashes.

'I'm fine.'

Get a grip.

He had no wish to feature as an object of compassion. So he kept his gaze on Sunita, absorbed her vibrant beauty, observed her change of outfit from casual jeans and T-shirt to a leaf-print black and white dress cinched at the waist with a wide red belt. Strappy sandals completed the ensemble.

'Babababab!' Amil vouchsafed, and a well of emotion surged anew.

'Do you want to hold him?'

'No!' *Think.* 'I don't want to spook him—especially just before the photo call.'

It wasn't a bad cover-up, but possibly not good enough to allay the doubts that dawned in her eyes.

'You won't. He's fairly sociable. Though obviously he doesn't really meet that many strange me—' She broke off. 'I'm sorry. Of all the stupid things to say that took the cake, the biscuit and the whole damn patisserie.'

'It's OK. I am a stranger to Amil—that's why I don't want to spook him.'

His gaze returned to the baby, who was watching him, his eyes wide open, one chubby hand clutching a tendril of Sunita's hair.

'We need to go.'

'I know. But first I have a couple of questions about the press conference and the Kaitlin question.'

Frederick frowned. 'What question would that be?'

'A couple of reporters said, and I quote, that you are "broken-hearted" and that perhaps I can mend the chasm. Others have suggested you would welcome a dalliance with an old flame as a gesture, to show Lady Kaitlin you are over her.'

'I still don't understand what your question is.'

'Two questions. *Are* you heartbroken? *Are* you over her?'

'No and yes. I need to get married for Lycander. My

heart is not involved. Kaitlin understood that—our relationship was an alliance. When that alliance became impossible we ended our relationship. Since then she has met someone else and I wish her well.'

Sunita's expression held a kind of shocked curiosity. 'That's *it*? You were with her for *months*. You must have felt *something* for her.'

Momentary doubt touched him and then he shrugged. 'Of course I did. I thought that she would be an excellent asset to Lycander.'

Kaitlin's diplomatic connections had been exemplary, as had her aristocratic background. She'd had a complete understanding of the role of consort and had been as uninterested in love as he was.

'I was disappointed when it didn't work out.'

'Yes. I see that it must have been tough for you to have the deal break down.' Sarcasm rang out from the spurious sympathy.

'It was—but only because it had an adverse impact on my position as ruler.'

And that was all that mattered. His goal was to rule Lycander as his brother would have wished, to achieve what Axel would have achieved. Whatever it took.

'So all you need to know about Kaitlin is that she is in the past. My heart is intact.' He glanced at his watch. 'And now we really need to go.'

A pause and then she nodded. 'OK. This is our chance to change the mixed reaction into a positive one. An opportunity to turn the tide in our favour.'

'You sound confident that you can do that.'

'Yup. I'm not a fan of bad publicity. Watch and learn.'

One photo call later and Frederick was looking at Sunita in reluctant admiration. He had to hand it to her. By the end of the hour she had had even the most hostile reporter

eating out of her hand. Somehow she had mixed a suggestion of regret over her actions with the implicit belief that
it had been the only option at the time. In addition, she had
managed to make it clear that whilst two years ago Frederick had been a shallow party prince, now he had morphed
into a different and better man, a worthy ruler of Lycander.

No doubt Marcus had been applauding as he watched.

Hell, even *he* had almost believed it. *Almost*.

'You did a great job. And I appreciate that you included
me in your spin.'

'It wasn't spin. Everything I said about you was true—
you *have* worked incredibly hard these past two years, you
have instigated all the changes I outlined, and you *do* have
Lycander's future at heart.'

The words washed over him like cold, dirty water—if
the people of Lycander knew where the blame for Axel's
death lay they would repudiate him without compunction,
and they would be right to do so. But he didn't want these
thoughts today—not on his first outing with Amil.

He glanced down at Amil, secure now in his buggy,
dressed in a jaunty striped top and dungarees, a sun hat
perched on his head, a toy cat clasped firmly in one hand.

'Amamamamam…ma.' Chubby legs kicked and he
wriggled in a clear instruction for them to move on.

Sunita smiled down at her son. 'I think he wants to get
going—he wants to see all the animal hedges. They seem
to utterly fascinate him.'

As they wandered through the lush gardens that
abounded with shades of green tranquillity seemed to be
carried on the breeze that came from the Arabian Sea, and
for a moment it was almost possible to pretend they were
an ordinary family out for the day.

Sunita came to a halt near a topiary hedge, one of many

clipped into the shape of animals. 'For some reason this is his favourite—I can't work out why.'

Frederick studied it. 'I'm not sure I can even work out what it is. I spotted the giraffe and the elephant and the ox-drawn cart, but this one flummoxes me.'

Sunita gave a sudden gurgle of laughter. 'I know what Amil thinks it is. Amil, sweetheart, tell Mu— Tell us what the animal does.'

The little boy beamed and made a *'raaaah'* noise.

Frederick felt his heart turn over in his chest. Without thought he hunkered down next to Amil and clapped. 'Clever boy. The tiger goes *"rah"*.'

'Raaah!' Amil agreed.

And here it came again—the paralysis, the fear that he would mess this up. He'd never managed any other relationship with even a sliver of success. Why would this be different?

Rising to his feet, he gestured around the garden. 'This is a beautiful place.'

'I used to come here as a child,' Sunita said. 'It's one of my earliest memories. I loved the flower clock.'

She pressed her lips together, as if she regretted the words, and Frederick frowned. Her publicity blurb skated over her childhood, chose to focus instead on her life after she'd embarked on her career. Almost as if she had written her early years out of her life history...

'Come on,' she said hurriedly. 'This morning isn't about my childhood. It's about Amil's—let's go to the Old Woman's Shoe.'

Five minutes later Frederick stared at the shoe—actually an enormous replica of a boot. As landmarks went, it seemed somewhat bizarre—especially when the words of the nursery rhyme filtered back to him.

There was an old woman who lived in a shoe.
She had so many children she didn't know what to do.
She gave them broth without any bread,
Then whipped them all soundly and sent them to bed.

'Isn't this a slightly odd thing to put in a children's playground?'

'Yes. But I loved it—I used to climb it and it made me feel lucky. It was a way to count my blessings. At least I didn't live with a horrible old woman who. starved me and beat me!'

At least. There had been a wealth of memory in those syllables, and for a daft moment he had the urge to put his arm around her and pull her into the comfort of a hug.

As if realising she had given away more than she had wanted, she hastened on. 'Anyway, I looked up the rhyme recently and it turns out it probably has political rather than literal connotations. But enough talk. This is about you and Amil. Do you want to take Amil into the shoe? I'll wait here with the buggy.'

The suggestion came out of nowhere, ambushed him, and once again his body froze into immobility even as his brain turned him into a gibbering wreck.

'I think that may be a little bit much for him. He barely knows me.' *Think.* 'We haven't even explained to him who I am.'

The accusation in his own voice surprised him—and he knew it masked a hurt he didn't want her to see. Because it exposed a weakness he didn't want her to know. *'Never show weakness, my son.'* The one piece of paternal advice he agreed with. *'Show weakness and you lose.'* Just as all his stepmothers had lost. Their weakness had been their love for their children—a weakness Alphonse had exploited.

Heat touched the angle of her cheekbones as she acknowledged the truth of his words. 'I know. I'm not sure what you want to do. I don't know what you want him to call you. Dad? Daddy? Papa?'

In truth he didn't know either, and that increased his panic. Sunita stepped towards him, and the compassion in her eyes added fuel to the panic-induced anger.

'But remember, he is only fourteen months old—I don't think he understands the concept of having a dad.'

The words were a stark reminder of her deception.

'Amil doesn't understand or *you* don't?'

The harshness of his voice propelled her backwards, and he was glad of it when he saw the compassion vanish from her expression.

'Both of us. Give me a break, Frederick. Until yesterday it was just Amil and me. Now here you are, and you want to marry me and make Amil the Crown Prince. It's a lot to take in.'

For an instant he empathised, heard the catch in her voice under the anger. But this was no time for empathy or sympathy. Now all that mattered was the knowledge of what was at stake.

'Then take it in fast, Sunita. You chose to hide Amil from me and now you need to deal with the consequences of that decision. Most people wouldn't think they were so bad. *I* am the one who has missed out on the first fourteen months of my son's life. *My son.* I am Amil's father and *you* need to deal with it.'

There was silence, broken only by the sound of Amil grizzling, his eyes wide and anxious as he looked up at Sunita.

Oh, hell. Guilt twisted his chest. What was *wrong* with him? This was his first outing with Amil and he'd allowed it to come to this. Shades of his own father, indeed.

He squatted down beside the baby. 'I'm sorry, Amil. Daddy's sorry.' Standing up, he gestured to the Old Woman's Shoe. 'You take him up. I'll wait here with the buggy. I've upset him enough—I don't want to compound my error.'

Sunita hesitated, but then Amil's grizzling turned to tears and she nodded assent.

'OK.' Leaning down, she unbuckled Amil and took him out. 'Come on, sweetheart. Let's try some walking.'

Frederick watched their progress and determination solidified inside him. He might be messing this up big-time, but he would not concede defeat. At the very least he would give his son the chance to be a prince. Their outing to the Hanging Gardens might be a disaster, but going to Goa wouldn't be.

By the end of their time there Sunita would agree to marry him.

CHAPTER SEVEN

SUNITA LOOKED ACROSS the expanse of the royal jet to where Frederick sat. There was no trace of the man she'd glimpsed mere hours ago in the Hanging Gardens—a man who had exhibited a depth of pain and frustration that had made her think long and hard.

Another glance—he still looked cool, regal and remote, and she couldn't read any emotion or discern what thoughts might be in his mind. Which would make what she had to say all the more difficult.

For a moment she nearly turned craven. *No*. This was the right thing to do and she would do it.

'Frederick?'

'Sunita.'

'Can we talk?'

'Of course.' He pushed his netbook across the table, rose and crossed to sit in the luxurious leather seat next to hers. 'Shoot.'

'I've thought about what you said earlier. About me having to accept that you are Amil's father.'

He raised a hand. 'It doesn't matter. I shouldn't have said what I did.'

'It *does* matter. I don't see how we can even consider a future together until we resolve our past. So I want to say I'm sorry.'

She twisted her hands together on her lap, recalling Frederick's expression when he'd looked at Amil as if his son was the most precious being in the universe.

'I'm sorry you missed out on Amil's first months.'

However justified her decision, Frederick could never have that time back—would never be able to hold his newborn son in his arms, see his first smile, run his finger over his gum to reveal that first tooth.

'I'm sorry.'

'OK.'

'But it's *not* OK, is it?'

'No.' He closed his eyes, then reopened them. 'No. It isn't OK that you hid my son's existence from me.'

'I couldn't take the risk.'

'Yes. You could have. You *chose* not to.'

Rationalisations lined up in her vocal cords but she uttered none of them. Bottom line—he was right. Her choice had meant Frederick had missed out on something infinitely precious.

'Yes, I did. And all the reasons I gave you earlier were true. But it's more than that.'

She inhaled deeply. She had no wish to confide this to him—she wasn't even sure she wanted to acknowledge it herself. But there it was again—the memory of the way Frederick had looked at Amil, the fact that he wanted to be part of his son's life and wanted to create a stable family unit. He deserved a true explanation.

'I thought history was repeating itself. I thought you would be like…' Her voice trailed off, her brain wishing it could reverse track and pull the words back.

'Like who?'

The gentleness of his voice surprised her—gave her the momentum to carry on.

'Like my father. He was a Londoner, on holiday in India

with a group of friends when he met my mother. They fell in love—or so she believed. She fell pregnant and she *did* choose to tell him, and all she could see was a tornado of dust as he disappeared. Straight back, road-runner-style, to his fiancée in London.'

Even now the enormity of her father's selfishness had the power to stun her—he *must* have understood the repercussions. They would have been complex enough in any culture, but in India there had been added layers of complication that transcended even betrayal and heartbreak.

Understanding showed in the expression on Frederick's face. 'That must have been tough for your mother.'

'Yes. It was. It changed the entire trajectory of her life. Her family was horrified and threw her out—she was only nineteen, and she had to fend for herself in a society which by and large had condemned her. And a lot of that is down to my father and his rejection of her—and me. I know we were in different circumstances—you didn't lie to me— but I knew you didn't want children. I didn't want to hear you say the same words my own father had—I didn't want Amil to feel the sense of rejection I did.'

Sunita forced herself to hold his gaze, to keep her tone level. This verged on the excruciating—touchy-feely confidences were not her bag at all.

'It seemed better, easier, less painful, to bring Amil up on my own. I figured what *he* didn't know and *you* didn't know wouldn't hurt anyone.'

There was a silence, and then he reached out, touching her forearm lightly. 'I'm sorry for what happened to your mother and to you. I promise you—I will never reject Amil.'

There could be no doubt as to the sincerity in his voice, and in the here and now she believed he meant every word. But she knew that good intentions did not always turn into actions. Her father must have once believed the empty promises he'd made to make up for his past, to be a good parent.

'It will not happen,' he repeated, as if he sensed her doubts. 'And now let's put the past behind us. I wish you had told me about Amil earlier, but I do understand why you made the choices you did. I believe now that we need to move forward, put the past behind us and focus on our present and our future. Deal?'

He held out his hand and Sunita looked down at it. So perfect—strong, masculine, capable... Capable of the gentlest of caresses, capable of...

Close it down, Sunita.

Too late—images scrambled her mind and for a moment she was unable to help herself. She closed her eyes, let the sensation dance over her skin. But it was more than desire—she knew that this deal signified understanding and forgiveness, and that made her head whirl as well.

Then she opened her eyes and reached out, clasped his hand and worked to still the beat of her heart. 'Deal,' she said. The syllable emerged with way too much violence, and she dropped his hand as if it were burning her. Which in a sense it was.

She looked down, then sneaked a look up at him—had he seen her reaction? Of course he had. It didn't take a forensic degree to know that. Embarrassment flushed her skin even as she couldn't help but wonder if this stupid physical reaction was a mutual one.

Her gaze met his and against all odds her pulse quickened further. His hazel eyes had darkened, the heat in them so intense her skin sizzled as her hormones cartwheeled.

Nothing else mattered except this.

Her lips parted as he rose, and his eyes never once left hers as he held out a hand. Without thought she put her hand in his, and he tugged her up so they stood mere centimetres apart.

Oh, so gently, but with a firmness that neither expected nor brooked denial, his hands encircled her waist and pulled her body flush against his. The feel of him, of the hard, muscular wall of his chest, made her gasp, and she looped her arms round his neck, accidentally brushing the soft skin on his nape.

An oath dropped from his lips and then those self-same lips touched hers and she was lost.

The kiss oh-so-familiar and yet so much more than before; the tang of coffee and the hint of strawberry jam, the sheer rollick of sensation that coursed her blood, made her feel alive and made her want more. He deepened the kiss and she pressed against him, caught in this moment that felt so damn right.

Stop. What the hell was she doing?

She wrenched out of his arms so hard she nearly tumbled over, putting a hand out to steady herself against the back of the chair.

For a moment silence reigned, broken only by the sound of their jagged breathing. Sunita tried to force herself to think through the fog of desire that refused to disperse. She couldn't let herself succumb to him again—she *couldn't*. Two years ago she'd lost her self-respect—now she could lose even more than that. Her attraction was a weakness he could play on—something that might cloud her judgement when she needed it most.

'I'm sorry. That was stupid.'

He ran a hand down his face, almost as if to wipe away all emotion, all desire, and when he met her gaze his expression was neutralised. 'No need to be sorry. That was a *good* thing.'

'How do you figure that out?'

'Because it proves we have physical compatibility. That's important in a marriage.'

His words acted like the equivalent of a bucket of ice-cold water and she slammed her hands on her hips. 'So that kiss was a deliberate ploy? A way to make the marriage more acceptable to me?'

'It wasn't a deliberate ploy, but it wasn't a mistake either. Mutual attraction is a benefit in a marriage. A bonus to our alliance.'

A benefit. A bonus. Any minute now he'd tell her there was some tax advantage to it too.

Sheer outrage threatened at his use of their attraction as a calculated move to persuade her. More fool her for believing he had been as caught up and carried away as she had. This *was* the Playboy Prince, after all.

'Well, I'll bear that in mind, but given that you have found "physical compatibility" with hundreds of women, I'm not sure it counts for much. Now, if you'll excuse me, I'll just go and freshen up.'

Frederick resisted the urge to put his head in his hands and groan. Then he considered the alternative option of kicking himself around the private jet.

Kissing Sunita had not been on the agenda—but somehow her beauty, her vulnerability, her honesty had overwhelmed him, and what he had meant to offer as comfort had turned into the type of kiss that still seared his memory, still had his body in thrall.

Dammit. He would *not* let physical attraction control him as it had his father—that way led to stupid decisions, poor judgement calls and people getting hurt. Yet during that kiss his judgement could have parachuted off the plane and he wouldn't have given a damn.

Then, to compound his original stupidity, he had

morphed into a pompous ass. Words had flowed from his tongue as he'd fought the urge to pull her straight back into his arms and resume proceedings. What an idiot. And then there had been her reference to his past. The truth was, even back then Sunita had been different from his so-called 'hundreds of women'.

He looked up as she returned to the room, her brown eyes cold, her expression implacable as she headed back to her chair and reached down into her bag for a book.

Hell. Now what? This was not going to plan and he didn't know how to retrieve it. Did not have a clue. He was so far out of his comfort zone he'd need a satnav and a compass to find his way back.

'Sunita?'

'Yes.'

'That kiss…'

'I think we've said all that needs to be said about it. As far as I am concerned, I plan to erase it from my memory banks.'

'Fine. But before you do that I want to clarify something. You mentioned my "hundreds of women"—for starters, that is an exaggeration. Yes, I partied hard and, yes, there were women, but not as many as the press made out. But, any which-way, those days are over and they have been for a long time. I was never unfaithful to any woman and I plan on a monogamous marriage.'

Clearly his default setting today was 'pompous ass', so he might as well run with it.

'So you'd be faithful for the duration. For decades, if necessary?'

The scepticism in her tone rankled.

'I am always faithful.'

'But your relationships have only lasted a few weeks

at a time—that's hardly much of a test. Variety was the spice of your life.'

'Very poetic. Let's take it further, then—I believe it's possible to have variety *and* plenty of spice with one woman.'

'Then why didn't you ever try it before?'

Damn. Poetic *and* sharp.

'Because short-term suited me—I didn't want physical attraction to develop into any expectations of marriage or love. I never offered more than I could give and the same goes now. I can offer marriage and fidelity, but not love.'

'I still don't buy it. Most people are faithful *because* of love—if you don't believe in love what would motivate you to be faithful?'

'I will not repeat my father's mistakes. He went through women like a man with a cold does tissues. Any beautiful woman—he thought it was his right to have her, whether he was already in a relationship or not, and it led to a whole lot of strife and angst. So I will not plunge Lycander into scandal and I will not hurt my children or humiliate my wife. That is nothing to do with love—it is to do with respect for my country and my family.'

'OK.'

Sympathy warmed her eyes and the moment suddenly felt too weighted, too heavy, and he cleared his throat. 'I thought you might want to know more about Lycander—after all, it will be your new home and your country.'

'I'd like that. I do remember some of what you told me two years ago. Rolling countryside, where you can walk and smell the scents of honeysuckle and almost taste the olives that you grow. You made the olive groves come to life.' She hesitated, and then asked, 'What happened to your business deal? The one you hoped would go through two years ago?'

Her words caused him to pause. Sunita had been one of the very few people he'd spoken to about his dreams. Ever since he was young he'd been focused on breaking free of his father's money—sick and tired of the constant reminders that he relied on his father's coffers for his food, his clothes, the roof over his head.

Then, at twenty-one, he'd come into the inheritance of a run-down, abandoned olive grove. And as he'd walked around it had been as if the soil itself had imparted something to him, as if the very air was laden with memories of past glories, of trees laden with plump lush olives, the sound and whir of a ghostly olive press.

That was where it had all started, and over the years he'd built an immensely profitable business. Two years before he'd been in the midst of a buy-out—he'd succeeded, and taken his company to the next echelon. That had been the deal he'd been celebrating—the reason he'd handed over the state function to Axel, the reason Axel had died.

Guilt and grief prodded him and he saw Sunita frown. *Focus.* 'The deal went through.'

'So who runs your business now?'

'A board of directors and my second-in-command—I have very little to do with it any more.'

'That must be hard.'

'That's how it is. Lycander needs my attention, and its people need to see that they come first. The principality isn't huge, but we have beaches, we have vineyards, we have olive groves. I know I'm biased, but our olives are the best in the world—they have bite…their taste lingers on your tongue—and the olive oil we produce is in a class of its own. As for our grapes—I believe the wine we produce rivals that of France and Spain. Lycander has the potential to be a prosperous land, but right now it is a vessel of past glories. My father increased taxes, lowered the minimum wage—did all he could to increase the money in the royal coffers without a care for the effect.'

'But couldn't anyone stop him?'

'No. In Lycander, the ruler's word is law—he has the final say on the governing of the land. Of course there are elected advisors, but they have no legislative power and the monarch can disregard their advice. So effectively everything hinges on having a ruler who genuinely cares about Lycander and its people.'

'That sounds like a whole heap of responsibility. For you. *And* to wish upon Amil.'

'It is, but I think it needs to be seen in context. In the past, when everything worked, it was easier—right now it is harder. But I will make sure I set things to rights. I know what needs to be done. I will make the laws fair, I will reduce taxation rates and I'll stop tax evasion. I want the divide between the wealthy and the poor to be bridged. I—'

He broke off at her expression.

'You can pick your jaw up from the ground.'

She raised her hand in admission. 'OK. Busted. I *am* surprised. Two years ago you were passionate about your business, but you didn't mention politics or social beliefs. Now your enthusiasm, your beliefs, are palpable.'

The all too familiar push and pull of guilt tugged within him.

'This isn't about my enthusiasm or my beliefs. It is about Axel—it's about fulfilling a promise. The people and the country suffered under my father's rule. The real reason there was no rebellion was that they knew one day Axel would succeed him, and that kept the unrest at bay. Axel had a vision—one that I *will* make happen.'

That had been the promise he'd made in his very first speech and he would fulfil it.

'What about *your* vison? The way you speak of Lycander—I can hear your pride in it.'

'I never had a vision for Lycander. I had a work hard, play hard lifestyle.'

'But you've changed?'

'Yes, I have.'

But the cost of that had been his brother's life.

Her frown deepened. She leant forward and he could smell her exotic scent with its overtone of papaya, could see the tiny birthmark on the angle of her cheekbone.

'I know you will be a good ruler. Whether you rule because it is your duty or because your heart is in it.'

There was silence. She was close. Way too close. And he had had a sudden desire to tell her the truth about his ascent to the throne—a desire mixed with the longing to tug her back into his arms and damn common sense and practicality.

Neither could happen, so he rose to his feet and looked down at her.

'Thank you. But the point I was trying to make is that I will ensure the principality Amil inherits will be a *good* place, with a strong economic foundation. Of course he will still have much responsibility, but I hope it will not be a burden.'

'What if he doesn't want the job? What if he has other ambitions, other aspirations?'

'I would never force him to take the crown. He could abdicate.' He met her gaze. 'Provided we have more children.'

'More children?' she echoed.

'Yes. I would like more children in order to secure the succession.' After all, there was no hope of his brothers ever having anything to do with Lycander. 'To take the pressure off Amil.'

'Is that the only reason?'

'For now. I haven't really got my head around having Amil yet.'

Right now he was terrified about his ability to parent *one* child—it wasn't the moment for a rose-tinted image of a functional, happy group of siblings.

'Do *you* want more kids?'

Sunita hesitated. 'I don't know…' A small smile tugged her lips upwards. 'I haven't really got *my* head around it all yet either. Until yesterday it was just me and Amil. My happiest memories are of my mother and me—just us. After—'

She broke off, looked away and then back at him, and he wondered what she had been about to say.

'Anyway,' she resumed, 'I'm not sure that the whole "happy family" scenario always works. Are you close to your other brothers?'

'No.'

His half-siblings… Stefan, who loathed all things Lycander, had left the principality as soon as he'd reached eighteen and hadn't returned. The twins, Emerson and Barrett, still only twenty, had left Lycander only days after their father's death and hadn't returned.

There was a definite pattern there, and it wasn't woven with closeness. The way they had grown up had made that an impossibility—their father had revelled in pitting brother against brother in a constant circus of competition and rivalry, and in the end Frederick had retired from the field, isolated himself and concentrated on his own life.

'But that was down to our upbringing. I hope that our children would do better.'

Perhaps it was a fruitless hope—there was every chance he would prove to be as useless a parent as his own parents had been, in which case perhaps a large family was a foolish idea.

But now wasn't the moment to dwell on it.

Relief touched him as the pilot announced their descent to Goa before Sunita could pursue the conversation further.

CHAPTER EIGHT

SUNITA'S EYES STRETCHED so wide she wondered if her eye-balls would actually pop out of her head.

'This is incredible.'

In truth it was beyond incredible—and she hadn't even seen the inside of the villa yet.

The drive itself had been unexpected—their chauffeur-driven car had traversed remarkably peaceful roads until they'd reached an idyllic village seemingly untouched by tourism. Winding lanes had displayed a number of villas draped with greenery, and now they had arrived at Sang-wan Villa.

The Portuguese-built, newly renovated building was nestled amidst verdant grounds where teak and jackfruit trees thrived, giving the air an evocative smell of leather with a hint of pineapple.

Her gaze rested on the structure itself. With its pil-lared verandas and high roof it looked like a vision out of a fairy tale.

The thought jolted her. She needed to remember that fairy tales were exactly that—tales, fiction. And most fairy tales had a dark side, a grim under-story, and the myths they were built on didn't have any happily-ever-afters.

'How on earth did you get it at such short notice?'

'It was closed for maintenance—I made it worth the owners' while to postpone the work.'

A woman walked towards them, a smile on her face, her white and green sari very much in keeping with the verdant backdrop.

'Your Highness. Welcome. I am Deepali and I will be looking after you during your stay. Your staff have been settled in and your suites are ready, if you will follow me. I will show you your rooms and then I thought you may wish to have an evening drink by the pool before dinner. There are menus in your rooms—just call through when you are ready.'

'That sounds wonderful,' Sunita said. 'And thank you so much for making this available at such short notice.'

Minutes later she was looking around a sumptuous suite. 'It's beautiful...'

But it was more than that—it was quirky and cosy, with its warm aura countered by the cool of the tiled floor. The sitting area boasted comfy overstuffed armchairs, where she could imagine curling up with a book and a cup of coffee, or simply gazing at the courtyard outside, resplendent with shrubbery. Two steps led down to the bedroom, where a luxurious wooden bed sprawled against decadent red walls.

Her suitcases had been deposited by a large lacquered wardrobe and she opened one, needing the confidence fresh clothes would give her. A floaty dress with a vivid bird print gave her instant cheer, and as she made her way out to the courtyard she allowed herself to revel in the sound of kingfishers and the sight and scent of the opulent lilies in the ornate pond.

Frederick sat on a recliner chair, a frosted beer bottle on the small table behind him and his blond head slightly tipped back to absorb the rays of the evening sun. Her breath caught as her gaze snagged on the strong line of his throat, the strength of his jaw—Adonis could eat his heart out.

But enough voyeurism...

He turned as she approached and smiled, and for a moment the clock turned back, transported her to two years before, when that smile had quite literally bewitched her, causing her to forget common sense and every promise she'd made herself.

Not this time. This time she had her sensible head on.

So she forced her toes to uncurl and sat down next to him, stretched her legs out and exhaled. 'This is a fabulous place.' She swiped a sideways glance at him. 'And you've surprised me.' *Again.*

'Why?'

'It's not what I expected.'

'What *did* you expect?'

'Something busier—a five-star hotel on the beach, with a nightclub.'

'Is that what you wanted?'

'No.'

'I told you, Sunita, I've changed. Plus, this time needs to be for you and me. No distractions. You wanted to get to know me better. Here I am.'

So he was—and the thought had her reaching for the lime drink she'd ordered.

She needed to focus on the practical—on need-to-know, real-life information.

'I need to know what our marriage would mean on a day-to-day level for Amil. What it will be like for him to grow up in a palace, as a Lycander prince. Right now it feels surreal.'

'The state apartments are a bit more opulent than your

average home, I suppose, but otherwise his childhood will be what we make it.'

'Will he go to a nursery?'

'I don't see why not—there will be a certain level of security arrangements, but I can't see a problem with that.'

'And he'll have friends round to play?'

How she'd craved friendship as a child—but there had been no one. Her mixed race heritage, the fact that she was illegitimate, the fact that her mother was a model, had all combined to make school a miserable place of isolation for her. She knew exactly what a solitary childhood could be like, and she didn't want that for her son.

'Yup. Again, subject to security vetting.'

'Is that how it worked for you?'

She sensed the tension in his body.

'It isn't relevant how it was for me,' he said.

He had to be kidding. 'Of course it is. You are a prince who grew up in a palace. You want Amil to do the same. So, did you make friends, have kids round to play? Were you treated differently?'

Discomfort showed as he shifted on his seat, picked his beer up and put it down again without even taking a sip. 'My life...my younger brothers' lives...weren't as straightforward as I hope Amil's will be. There weren't that many opportunities for us to make normal friends. It was better for Axel, because my father sent him to boarding school, and—'

Whoa! 'That is *not* happening to Amil. I will not send him away.'

'I won't rule that out.'

'Yes, you will. I don't care if every Crown Prince since the Conquest was sent to boarding school. Amil isn't going.'

'That is not why I would do it.' Frustration seeped into

his tone. 'In fact, I didn't say I *would* do it. It is simply a possibility I will consider in the future.'

'*No.*'

His voice tightened. 'Different children thrive in different conditions. Axel was educated at boarding school and it didn't do him any harm. I spent a term there and I loved it.'

'In which case, why did you leave?'

'Because my father changed his mind.'

'He must have had a reason.'

'I'm sure he did.'

Despite the even tone of his voice she could sense evasion.

'Do you know what it was?'

'My father's attitude to my education was a little hit and miss. Axel went to boarding school, but the rest of us... We had tutors some of the time, attended a term of local school here and there, or we ran wild. For my father, education wasn't a priority—in the palace or in the principality as a whole. I will change that, but it will take time—that's why I won't rule out boarding school if it is right for Amil.'

'That is *my* decision.'

'Amil is *our* son. *We* will make decisions about his future. Not you or me. Us—together.'

'And what happens if we don't agree?'

'Then we find a compromise.'

'There is no compromise between boarding school and not boarding school. It's black or white. What happens then?'

'I don't know. But we'll work it out.'

'Those are just words. Neither of us has any idea of how to work things out.'

Which was exactly why this was a terrible idea. Co-parenting sucked.

'Fine. Then let's work it out now,' he said.

'How?'

'You tell me exactly why you are so adamant that boarding school is not an option. The truth. My brother loved his boarding school, and the few months I spent there were some of the happiest times of my life. I will not rule it out without reason.'

'I…' Explanations sucked as well, but she could see that she didn't sound rational. 'I'm scared for him. School was an unmitigated disaster for me—because I didn't fit from day one. I was the only mixed race child in my school, and my mother's status didn't help. Plus, quite often she would pull me out of school to go on shoots with her—she had no one to leave me with, you see. I guess I was an obvious target.'

'Were you bullied?'

Although his voice was gentle she could hear an underlying anger, saw the clench of his jaw.

'No. It was much worse. I was ignored. Some girl decided that the best way to treat someone as low down the pecking order as me would be to pretend I was invisible.'

She could still hear it now. The high-pitched voice, so stuck-up and snobbish, the other girls gathering round to listen. 'It is demeaning to even *acknowledge* a dirty girl like her. So we will ignore her. Are we all agreed?'

'My whole experience of school was miserable. The only saving grace was the fact that it wasn't boarding school—that I could go home to my mother. Amil will be different too. He will be royalty—there will be people who are envious of him. I don't want him to be far away and miserable.'

Though in truth there was even more to it than that. There was her bone-deep knowledge that time was infinitely precious—she had had so few years with her mother, but at least they had had the maximum possible time together.

'I don't want him to be far away. Full stop. He is *my* child—I want to see him grow, and I want to be there for him.'

Frederick's hazel eyes studied her expression with an intensity that made her feel he could read her soul.

Then he nodded. 'OK. You get the casting vote on the boarding school question.'

'Why?' Wariness narrowed her eyes at his capitulation. 'Does it matter?'

'Yes. I need to know that you mean it. That these aren't just words to sweeten the marriage offer.'

'Because you still don't trust me?'

She wanted to—she really did—but how could she when there was so much at stake?

'Let's say it would help if I knew what had changed your mind.'

'You've made me realise why I enjoyed boarding school so much. Why Axel thrived there. It was the opposite to your situation. For us it was an escape from our home life—boarding school was a haven of certainty after the chaos of life at the palace. Somewhere I knew what was what, where I had an opportunity to actually get an education. Our home life was erratic, at best. It won't be like that for Amil.'

Sunita's heart ached at the thought of all those young princes, buffeted by the fallout from their father's chaotic lifestyle. 'No, it won't.'

'And by the time he goes to school I *will* have turned education around in Lycander. Teachers will be better paid, the curriculum will be overhauled in a good way, and there will be more money injected into schools everywhere.'

As if embarrassed by his own enthusiasm, he leant back

with a rueful smile that flipped her heart again. A sure case of topsy-turvy heart syndrome. And it was messing with her head, making the idea of marriage more palatable. *Ridiculous.* Marriage equalled tying herself down, committing herself to a shared life, to a fairy tale ending. The idea hurt her teeth, sent her whole being into revolt.

Only that wasn't true, was it? Horror surfaced at the identification of a tiny glimmer of sparkle inside her that desperately *wanted* a fairy tale ending... Frederick, Sunita and Amil, living happily ever after in a palace. Princess Sunita.

'Penny for your thoughts?' His voice interrupted her reverie.

'They aren't worth it.'

They weren't worth even a fraction of a penny—she had lost the plot and it was time to get it back. This marriage deal wasn't off the table, but there wouldn't be any glimmer of fairy sparkle sprinkled on it.

She looked up as Deepali approached from across the courtyard. 'Your meal is ready. The chef has prepared a selection of traditional Goan food—I trust you will enjoy it.'

Sunita managed a smile even as her brain scrambled around in panic, chasing down that stupid, sparkly bit of her that advocated the ringing out of wedding bells. How had this happened? In a little over twenty-four hours he had somehow persuaded her that marriage was not only a possibility but a sparkly one.

Enough. She had to halt this before this fairy tale place wove some sort of magic spell around her—before that stupid sparkly bit inside her grew.

Frederick studied Sunita's expression as she looked round the dining room. Her eyes skittered over the colourful prints on the white walls, along the simple wooden table, and he could almost hear her brain whirring.

Deepali entered and put their plates in front of them. 'Prawn rissoles,' she said, and Sunita inhaled appreciatively.

'They smell marvellous—and I'm sure they'll taste just as good.'

The middle-aged woman smiled. 'I'll pass on your kind comments to the chef.'

Once she'd gone, Frederick watched as Sunita studied the rissole with more attention than any food warranted, however appetising.

'This looks great.' She popped a forkful into her mouth and closed her eyes. 'Fabulous! The reason why melt-in-the-mouth is a cliché. Cumin, with perhaps a hint of coriander, and…'

But even as she spoke he knew that her thoughts were elsewhere. There was an almost manic quality to her culinary listing, and he interrupted without compunction.

'So,' he said, 'you avoided my earlier question about what you were thinking.'

Her brown eyes watched him with almost a hint of defiance. 'I was thinking how surreal this situation is—the idea that two people who don't know each other at all could contemplate marriage. It's…mad.'

'That's why we're here—to get to know each other.'

'We can't pack that into two days—most people take years.'

'And there is still a fifty per cent divorce rate.'

'In which case we are *definitely* doomed.'

'Not at all. All those people who take years…they try to fall in love, decide they've fallen in love, expect love to last. Every action is dictated by love. They heap pressure on the whole institution of marriage *and* on themselves. Our approach is based on common sense and on us both getting a deal we think is fair. Two days is more than enough time.'

He leant over and poured wine into her glass.

'In days gone by it would have been the norm. Throughout Lycander history, rulers made *alliances*—not love matches.'

'Does posterity say whether they worked?'

'Some were more successful than others, but every marriage lasted.'

Until Alphonse had arrived and turned statistics and traditions on their heads.

'For better or worse?' Sunita sounded sceptical.

'I see no reason why we couldn't be one of the better ones—we'd go in without any ridiculous, unrealistic expectations, with an understanding of what each other is looking for.'

'I don't even know what your favourite colour is.'

'Does it matter?'

'I feel it's the sort of thing one should know before they marry someone.'

'OK. Blue.' He raised his eyebrows. '*Now* will you marry me?'

This pulled a reluctant smile from her, but it came with an attendant shake of her head. 'What sort of blue? Royal blue, because it's on the Lycander flag?'

'Nope. Aquamarine blue.'

'Because…?'

'Does there have to be a reason?'

Sunita tipped her head to one side. 'There usually is.'

'So what's *your* favourite colour?'

'Red.'

'Because…?'

'Because it was my mother's favourite colour—I like to

think it was her way of sticking two fingers up at the world that had branded her a scarlet woman. She always wore something red—her sari would maybe have a red weave, or she'd wear a red flower, or paint her toenails red. And as for her lipstick collection...'

'You must miss her.'

'I do. A lot.' She looked down at her plate and scooped up the last of her rissole. 'Anyway, why aquamarine blue?'

Reluctance laced his vocal cords—along with a sense of injustice that a question that had seemed so simple on the surface had suddenly become more complex. *Get a grip.* If this was a hoop Sunita had constructed as a prelude to marriage then he'd jump through it—he'd do the damn hula if necessary.

'It's the colour of the Lycander Sea. When life in the palace became too much I'd escape to the beach, watch the sea. It put things into perspective. Sometimes it was so still, so calm, so serene it gave me peace. Occasionally it would be turbulent, and then I guess I'd identify with it. As a child I was pretty sure Neptune lived off the coast of Lycander...'

OK, Frederick, that's enough. More than he'd intended in fact. But there was something about the way Sunita listened—*really* listened—that seemed to have affected him.

She watched him now, lips slightly parted, tawny eyes serious, but as if sensing his discomfort she leant back before she spoke.

'OK, next question. Star sign?'

'Leo.'

'Me too.'

'Is that good or bad?'

'I really don't know. We'd need to ask Nanni—she is an avid believer in horoscopes. Though I'm not sure why. I think her parents had her and my grandfather's horoscopes read to see if they'd be a good match, and the astrologer was confident they were compatible.'

'Were they?'

'I don't think they can have been. From what my mother told me my grandfather was a tyrant and a control freak, whereas Nanni is a kind, gentle woman. But Nanni herself never speaks of her marriage—and never criticises my grandfather. And she still believes in horoscopes.'

'What about you? Do *you* believe in horoscopes?'

'I think there may be something in it, but not enough that you can base your life decisions on them—that's the easy way out, isn't it? You can just shrug your shoulders and blame fate if it all goes wrong. It doesn't work like that—life is about choice.'

'Yes…' Bleakness settled on him—his choices had cost Axel his life. 'But life is also about the consequences of those choices. Consequences you have to live with.'

'Yes, you do. But in this case Amil's future is in *our* hands—he will have to live with the destiny *we* choose for him. And that is hard. But it's not only about Amil. It's about us as well. You and me. That's why this marriage can't work.'

Her chin jutted out at an angle of determination.

Frederick frowned—but before he could respond the door opened and Deepali re-entered the room, followed by a young man pushing a trolley.

'Fish *recheado*,' the young man announced. 'Made with pomfret.'

Deepali's face shone with pride. 'This is my son, Ashok—he is the chef here,' she explained.

'I thought you might want to know about the dish,' Ashok said.

'I'd love to.'

Sunita smiled her trademark smile and Frederick saw Ashok's appreciation.

'The pomfret is stuffed with a special paste. I used chillies, cloves, cumin and lemon. It is a Goan dish, but *recheado* means stuffed in Portuguese.' Ashok smiled. 'And there is also Goan bread, freshly baked. Enjoy.'

Frederick waited until the mother and son had left the room and then he looked at Sunita.

'Why not?' he repeated.

CHAPTER NINE

'WHY WON'T THIS marriage work?'

Frederick's voice was even, his question posed as if the topic under discussion was as simple as a grocery list rather than the rest of their lives.

Sunita took a deep breath and marshalled the thoughts she'd herded into a cogent argument throughout the starter. 'Would you have even considered marriage to me if it wasn't for Amil?'

There was no hesitation as he tipped his hand in the air, palm up. 'No.'

To her surprise, irrational hurt touched her that he didn't have to give it even a second's thought. 'Exactly.'

'But you *can't* take Amil out of the equation. If it weren't for Amil you wouldn't consider marriage to me either.'

'I get that. But it's different for you. I don't *need* to marry anyone. You do, and you need it to be the right person—for Lycander's sake. A woman like Lady Kaitlin Derwent. I am the *antithesis* of Kaitlin.'

For an insane moment the knowledge hurt. But she was no longer a child, desperately trying to measure up to her half-sisters and always failing. High academic grades, musical ability, natural intelligence... You name it, Sunita lacked it. But in this case she needed to emphasise her failings with pride.

'I haven't got an aristocratic bone in my body, and I don't have the *gravitas* that you need to offer the Lycander people.'

'You are the mother of my son.'

'Your *illegitimate* son. Plus, I was a model. Your father married or was associated with a succession of models, actresses and showbiz people, and all his relationships ended in scandal. Your people will tar me with the same brush.'

'Then so be it. I agree that you do not have the background I was looking for in my bride, but I believe you will win the people over. In time.'

'I don't think I will.' She inhaled deeply. 'For a start, I want to resume my modelling career—and I can't see that going down a storm with the people.'

Or with him. He masked his reaction, but not fast enough—he hadn't taken that into the equation.

'You don't like the idea either?'

'I neither like nor dislike it. I agree it might be problematic for the people to accept, but it's a problem we can work around.'

'But it doesn't *have* to be a problem. Don't marry me—marry someone like Kaitlin…someone with the qualities to be a true consort.'

Even as she said the words a strange pang of what she reluctantly identified as jealousy shot through her veins. *Jealousy? Really?* She didn't even know who she was jealous of. It meant nothing to her if Frederick married someone else. *Nothing.* As for being jealous of Kaitlin—that was absurd.

Sunita forged on. 'You know I'm right. Tell me about your agreement with Kaitlin. What else did she bring to the table apart from her background?'

'This is not a constructive conversation.'

'I disagree. This isn't only about Amil. This is about us as well. Your life and mine. You want to make me a princess—I deserve to know what that entails, what your expectations are. You said it yourself.'

'What I expected from Kaitlin and what I would expect from you are different.'

Ouch. 'In what way?' Ice dripped from her tone as she forked up a piece of succulent fish with unnecessary violence.

'You are two different individuals—of course I would have different expectations.' Frustration tinged his voice, along with what looked like a growing knowledge that he'd entered stormy waters and was in imminent danger of capsizing.

'Well, I'd like to know what you expected from Kaitlin.' *From your ideal candidate*, her treacherous heart cried out.

'Fine. Kaitlin was brought up for this role—she has dozens of connections, she speaks four European languages, she has diplomacy down pat. I planned to use her as a royal ambassador—she would have played a very public role. I also hoped she would be influential behind the scenes—play a part in turning Lycander round, in shaping policy.'

For Pete's sake! Sunita didn't think she could bear to hear any more. Lady Kaitlin had obviously been on a fast track to royal sainthood, and the role of Lycander princess would have fitted her like a silken glove. Whereas Sunita was more fitted for the lost sock that languished behind the radiator.

The realisation hollowed her tummy and she shook her head in repudiation. 'There you have it. I think you owe it to Lycander to marry someone else.'

Surely she'd made her case? She understood that Frederick wanted to be part of Amil's life, but he *had* to see that Sunita was quite simply not princess material.

'No.' His voice was flat. 'I have already considered everything you've said. And, incidentally, you and my chief advisor are in complete agreement. But you are Amil's mother, and that trumps all other considerations. He is my son. I want him to live with me—I want him to be Lycander's Crown Prince after me. I also want him to live with his mother. So marriage is the only option.'

'No, it isn't. What if I decide not to marry you?' He couldn't actually *force* her to the altar. 'You would still be an important part of Amil's life.'

'Stop!'

'What?' Her stomach plummeted as she saw the expression on his face—weariness, distaste, sadness.

'Don't do this.'

'Why not?'

'Because if you don't marry me I will fight for joint custody.'

Joint custody. The words sucker-punched her. 'You promised that you wouldn't take him from me. You said he needs me.'

'I also told you I will be a real part of his life. What would you suggest? A weekend here and there? He is my son as well.'

'Yes. But you'll marry someone else—have another family.'

'And you think that should make me want Amil less—is that the message you want to give our son?'

'No!'

Damn it—she couldn't think. Panic had her in its grip, squeezing out any coherent thought. All she could think of now was losing Amil for half of his childhood. Of Amil in Lycander with a stepmother—whichever new multilingual paragon of virtue Frederick eventually married—and half-siblings.

History on repeat with a vengeance.

Memories of her own humiliations, inflicted by the

hands of her stepmother and her half-sisters—the put-downs, the differentiation, the horror—were chiselled on her very soul. No way would she risk that for Amil.

'I won't agree to joint custody. I *can't*.'

But she could see his point. She had already deprived him of fourteen months of Amil's life—how could she expect him to settle for the occasional week? Regular phone calls and Skype? Would *she* settle for that? Never in a million years.

She inclined her head. 'All right. You win. I'll marry you.'

It looked as if Princess Sunita was about to enter the land of fairy tales. It was a good thing she knew that happy-ever-afters didn't exist in real life.

CHAPTER TEN

'ALL RIGHT. YOU WIN. I'll marry you.'

The words seemed to haunt his dreams, and by the time the distinctive fluting whistle of a golden oriole penetrated his uneasy repose it was a relief to wake up, hop out of the slatted wooden bed and head for the shower. He could only hope the stream of water would wake him up to common sense.

He had won, and there was nothing wrong with winning—it meant he would have a life with his son, would be able to give Amil his principality. That was *good* news, right?

The problem was Sunita's words had not been the only ones to permeate his sleeping mind. His father's voice had also made a showing.

'Every woman has a price. Find her weakness, exploit it and then you win, Freddy, m'boy.'

He switched off the shower in a savage movement. Time to man up. Yes, he'd won—and that was OK. It was a cause to celebrate—*not* the equivalent of what his father had done. *He* was striving to keep Amil with Sunita full-time. He hadn't destroyed a family—he'd created one. Ergo, he was not his father. It wasn't as if he had *threatened* her with joint custody. It had been the only other option—an option he'd known she would knock back.

Rationally, the facts were undeniable. Sometimes in life you had to choose between the rock and the hard place, and he'd done his best to make the rock a comfortable choice for her. He'd offered her the chance to be a princess—most women would have grabbed the baton and run with it.

End of.

Now it was time to figure out the next step.

He pulled on chinos and a navy T-shirt and headed into the courtyard and the early-morning sunshine.

'Over here.'

He heard Sunita's voice and spotted her sitting under the shade of a tree, simply dressed in a rainbow-striped sundress, sunglasses perched atop her raven hair. Sunlight filtered through the green leaves of the banyan tree, dappling her arms and the wood of the table, lighting up the tentative smile she offered as he approached.

It was a smile that seemed to bathe his skin in the warmth of relief, pushing away any lingering doubts about his actions.

'Hey.'

'Hey…' He sat down opposite and surveyed the array of fruit. 'Wow.'

'I know, right? It's hard to know where to begin!'

'I'm not even sure I can name them all.'

'*Chiku*, papaya, guava, pineapple, *rambutan*. They all taste different and they are all delicious.'

He reached for a *chiku*—a fruit he'd never heard of. 'It looks like a potato.'

'Wait until you taste it.'

He halved the fruit to reveal pinkish flesh seeded with a mere three black seeds. He scooped out a spoonful and blinked at the intense sweetness.

'Better than cotton candy.'

She smiled, and once again relief touched him.

'About last night…' he said. 'I know marriage isn't your ideal option, but I am very glad you said yes.'

'It isn't, but it *is* the best option on the table and I've decided to make the best of it. Perhaps if I'd been more upfront two years ago we wouldn't be in this mess. But we are, and I'll do my best to be positive about the marriage idea.'

'Our marriage doesn't have to be a mess. I think we can make this work. For Amil *and* for us.'

A pause, and then she nodded. 'I'll try. So, what's the next step in Project Marriage?'

There was no room for further doubts or any more discussion with his conscience. Project Marriage was what he wanted and what he believed to be right for them all. Yet for some reason he felt restless, as if the beauty of the surroundings was somehow tainted. This was the sort of place where *real* couples should sit and plan their future—couples foolish enough to believe in the concept of love.

'We need a plan, but I suggest we move this discussion to somewhere else. Is there anything you want to see in Goa? We could hit the beach…visit the old quarter…'

In truth he didn't care—he needed to move, to get on with the business of the day away from this tranquil fairy tale setting that seemed to accuse him of having behaved like his father, however much logic told him he hadn't.

Sunita thought for a moment, her tawny eyes dreamy, as if the question needed deeper consideration than it appeared to warrant.

'I'd like to go to the Dudhsagar Falls.'

There was a nuance in her voice he couldn't identify. 'Any reason?'

For a second she hesitated, then she shrugged. 'My parents came to Goa together and they visited the falls. It's one of the few memories my mother ever shared about them both—she said it was important sometimes to remember the happy memories or they would all crumble to dust.'

She picked up a *rambutan*, rolled the lychee-like fruit almost like a dice.

'I'm not entirely sure what she meant, but I'd like to go somewhere she was happy. Even if that happiness was no more than a mirage.'

He had the feeling that right now Sunita missed her mother—and who could blame her? She was about to step into a whole new world that she didn't want to enter.

'I'm sorry you lost her, Sunita.'

'Me too. But I do feel lucky I had her for the time I did.' She hesitated. 'I don't know the details, but I'm guessing you didn't have much time with *your* mum.'

'No.'

Even before the divorce his mother had spent minimal time with him—at least until the divorce proceedings were underway. Then it had all changed, and even now he could remember the glorious happiness his three-year-old self had felt—not the detail, but the joy that finally his mother wanted his company, would hug him, take him out... And then abruptly it had all ceased. She'd gone before the ink had even dried on the papers. The whole 'loving mother' act had been exactly that—an act undertaken to up her settlement.

'I'm sorry.'

'No need. You can't miss what you've never had.'

The words came out rougher than he'd intended, but he didn't want her compassion. He'd got over his mother's abandonment long ago, buried those emotions along with the rest.

Pulling out his phone, he did a check on the falls, scanned the information. 'The falls it is—I'll speak to Security, see how close they can get us. Looks like the official road is closed off because of monsoon season, but I'm sure we can get something sorted.'

'Actually, I wondered if we could do what my parents did and walk along the railway track to get there. Just us— no security. I know they're discreet, but today I'd like to be just Frederick and Sunita—before we get caught up in the reality of being a royal couple.'

The wistfulness in her voice decided him—alongside the fact that, however much he trusted his staff, it made sense to thrash out the details of this marriage in private. Plus if he was being honest with himself, he too wanted to be 'just Frederick and Sunita' for one day. To put aside the burden of ruling and his complex need for this marriage for one day.

'Sounds like a plan.'

Surprise etched her face. 'You're sure?'

'I'm sure. Tell me the route they took and I'll figure it out.'

She grinned. 'I think they came back on a goods train.'

'We can manage that.'

'The Prince and his future consort hopping on a goods train? I like it.'

Her smile broadened and it caught at his heart, causing a sudden unfamiliar tug of hope that perhaps this might all work out.

Sunita glanced up at the sky, and for the first time in the past forty-eight hours her thoughts slowed down as she absorbed the grandeur of the bright grey monsoon clouds.

Most tourists flocked to India in the summer months, but she loved monsoon—always had, even as a child. Loved the drum of the rain, which brought the country much needed water and succour from heat, and lavished verdant green to the trees and fields.

'It doesn't seem possible that there can be so many different shades of green—it makes me wish I could paint, somehow capture all this.' Her outswept arm encapsulated the winding track, the surrounding green and the skies above. 'Photos never seem to catch the reality of it—they look fake, somehow.'

'Then commit it to memory,' Frederick said, putting out a hand to steady her as she stumbled slightly over an awkward rock.

The touch of his hand against hers almost made her gasp out loud, adding an extra level to her already overcrowded senses. In an almost involuntary movement she clasped her fingers around his.

'Like my mother did. She described this walk to me so many times it almost felt like a story.'

Perhaps a real-life fairy tale, in which a moment of happiness had *not* led to a lifetime of happily-ever-after.

'It's odd to think that they walked here once…maybe took the exact same steps we're taking now.' She turned to him. 'You must feel that a lot as a ruler—the idea of history being always around you. Your ancestors' spirits looking over your shoulders.'

For an instant she'd swear a small shiver shot through him, and understanding smote her. Perhaps for him it was the spirit of his older brother that haunted his every move and decision.

Yet his voice was light as he answered, 'I am more worried about current judgement and the opinion of posterity than the line of my progenitors.'

He slowed as they approached a tunnel, half turning for evidence of any oncoming train.

They stepped inside the dark and now it was her turn to shiver at the dank confines. Water trickled down the damp mossy walls and he tightened his grip on her hand. Without thought she moved closer to the strength of his body.

'It's safe. Even if a train does come through there is ample space as long as we keep to the side.'

Yet suddenly it didn't *feel* safe—though it was no longer the train she was worried about. Frederick was too close, and that proximity was playing havoc with her body.

Did it matter any more? They were to be married—their physical attraction could now be acknowledged. The idea jolted a funny little thrill through her—one she short-circuited instantly. Two years ago physical attraction had lambasted her self-control and her pride. No way would she enter *that* thrall again.

As they emerged into sunlight she dropped his hand, under the pretext of tugging her hair into a ponytail, and then turned to him.

'I think we were talking about current judgement and public opinion—and on that topic we need to decide how to announce our engagement.'

For an instant his gaze locked on her hand and then he nodded. 'I think we keep it low-key. I don't want to announce this as a romantic fairy tale—that would be disingenuous, and way too reminiscent of my father's marriages. Every engagement, every wedding was an extravaganza, with proclamations of eternal love.'

'Did he love *any* of them?'

'According to his own criteria he did—but in reality I believe it was little more than lust and an ability to kid himself.'

'Perhaps he did it for children?'

'My father never did anything unless it was for himself.' His tone was factual, rather than bitter. 'But that isn't the point. I don't want to lie and present our marriage as some sort of perfect love story. I'd rather be honest.'

Sunita stared at him. 'That is hardly the most gripping headline—*Prince Proposes to Legitimise Heir.*' Irrational hurt threatened at his reminder that this was the only reason for their union. Well, so be it. 'I don't believe in fairy tales, but I *do* believe in good publicity.'

'So what would *you* suggest?'

'An old flame is rekindled. Prince Frederick of Lycander and Sunita decide to wed! Both the Prince and his bride profess delight at the prospect of being a real family.' Her pace increased slightly. 'I mean, that is just off the top of my head—I'm sure your spin people can work on it. We don't have to profess undying love, but anything is better than indifference.'

Admiration glinted in his eyes and warmed her.

'I'd forgotten what a natural you are with publicity. You've definitely not lost your touch.'

'Thank you kindly, good sir. Publicity is an incredibly powerful tool. I agree that we shouldn't lie to your people, but what you are doing is a good, principled action for your son—the people should know that. Of course they'll be interested in a bit of fun and glitz and a celebration too.' She glanced sideways at him. 'Fun is important—for all of us. I want Amil's childhood to be full of fun and joy—I want him to have a happy path through life.'

'So do I.'

'Good. Then let's show your people that. Let's make sure the engagement announcement is honest, but happy. We've decided to do this, so we need to make the best of it.'

With impeccable dramatic timing the skies chose that moment to open up, and before Sunita could do more than let out a warning cry the rain sheeted down in a torrential downpour.

Sunita tipped her face up and let it gush over her, revelling in the sheer force of Nature as it provided one of life's essentials.

Mere moments later the rain ceased. Blue skies replaced the grey, and sudden shafts of bright golden sunshine shot down, illuminating the droplets of water that hung everywhere. The smell of wet earth permeated the air and it seemed impossible not to smile.

'It's as if someone switched the tap off and the lights on,' Frederick said, a note of wonder in his voice as he looked round.

'That would be Varuna, the god of water. Nanni says that he listens to what the frogs say, and when they croak enough he gives us rain.'

'I think I'm going to like Nanni.'

'Of course you are.'

'So I take it your mother's family eventually relented and took her and you back in?'

'No...' Sunita sighed, feeling the familiar ache of regret and sadness. 'I wish that was how it had played out, but it didn't. They didn't relent.'

Even when they knew her mother was dying.

Anger was suddenly added to the mix. Her grandfather hadn't even told Nanni that their daughter was ill—hadn't given her the chance to say goodbye.

'I met Nanni for the first time when I was pregnant with Amil.' She glanced across at him. 'I don't expect your sympathy, but when I found I was pregnant I felt very alone.'

His expression hardened slightly, but to her surprise she could see an element of frustrated sympathy in his creased brow. 'So you decided to find your mother's relatives?'

'Yes. My mother had left enough information that it wasn't too hard. It turned out my grandfather had died two years before, and Nanni agreed to see me.'

That first meeting was one she would never forget—her

grandmother had simply stared at her, tears seeping from her brown eyes, her hands clasped as if in prayer. And then she had stepped forward and hugged Sunita, before standing back and touching her face as if in wonder, no doubt seeing not just her granddaughter but her daughter as well.

'She was overjoyed and so was I. She has never forgiven herself for not standing up to my grandfather, for letting my mother go, and I think she sees me and Amil as her second chance.'

'It isn't always easy to stand up to a partner if he or she has all the power. Your Nanni shouldn't be too hard on herself.'

'I've told her that. My mother didn't blame her either. Nanni was totally dependent on her husband—money, clothes, food, everything—and he made sure she knew it. If she had left with my mother he would have cut her off from the rest of her family, her children...everyone.' She paused and then turned to him, willing him to understand. 'I won't *ever* let myself get into that position.'

'You won't. Our marriage will be nothing like that.'

'I understand that, but I did mean what I said yesterday—I intend to resume my career. You saw what happened to your mother, your stepmothers. I've seen what happened to Nanni—I will *not* be dependent on you.'

'You won't be. We can set up a pre-nup.'

'In a principality where your word is law? Any pre-nup I sign wouldn't be worth the paper it was written on.'

'OK. You will be paid a salary that goes directly into your personal account—you can move that into another account anywhere in the world.'

'A salary essentially paid by *you*—one you could stop at any moment?'

His lips thinned. 'You really do not trust me at all, do you?'

There was a hint of hurt in his voice, but it was something she could not afford to listen to.

'I can't trust anyone. Think about it, Frederick. What if I decided to take Amil and leave? Would you still pay my salary? What if you turn out to be like your father? What if you fall in love with another woman?' Life had taught her there could never be too many 'what ifs' in the mix. 'Then I'll need money of my own.'

The easy warmth in his hazel eyes vanished, and now his brow was as clouded as a monsoon sky. 'None of those things will happen.'

'That's what you say *now*, but times change—we both know that.'

A shadow flickered across his face and she knew her point had gone home.

'So I must make sure myself that I have enough money in the bank for whatever life throws at me.'

To ensure there was always an escape route—that she would never be trapped like her grandmother had been, as *she* had been as a child.

'That is non-negotiable.'

'Understood.'

'Also, I want to leave Amil with my grandmother when we go back to Lycander.'

'Why?' The syllable was taut. 'Because you think I will snatch him the minute we land on Lycander soil?'

'No. But I won't risk taking him there until we have worked out how our marriage will be received. Also, I can get things ready for him; it will be a big change for him and I'd like to make his transition as easy as possible.'

The idea of not having Amil with her hurt, but she could not—*would* not—risk taking him to Lycander until she was sure of his reception there.

'I'll come back to Lycander with you, and *then* I'll get Amil.'

'OK. But *we* will get Amil.'

She nodded and then there was a silence, broken by a roar in the not so far distance.

'Dhudsagar Falls,' Sunita said. 'We're close.'

By tacit consent they quickened their pace.

CHAPTER ELEVEN

THE SOUND OF the monsoon-inflated waterfalls pounded his eardrums, but even as Frederick anticipated the sight his brain couldn't banish Sunita's expression, the realisation that she still didn't trust him.

Not that he blamed her—after all, his father had used his wealth and power to grind his wives to dust in the courts. All except his mother, who had played Alphonse at his own game and duped him—an act his father had never forgiven her for. Never forgiven Frederick for, come to that. But he wished that Sunita did not think so badly of him. *Enough.* Her opinion shouldn't matter, and in truth she couldn't judge him more harshly than he deserved. But...

His train of thought was broken by her gasp from next to him. 'Any minute now,' she whispered, as they emerged through a tunnel and onto a railway bridge already populated by a few other visitors.

But they had no interest in Sunita and Frederick— because it was impossible to focus on anything other than the waterfalls, both mighty and terrible. No image could do them justice as the four tiers cascaded and roared in torrents of milky-white water, leaping from the edge of towering cliffs and gusting and gushing down the slippery rock slopes.

The spray drenched him but he didn't move, utterly

mesmerised by the power and glory of Nature's creation, cloaked in a rising mist that mixed with the shafts of sunlight to create a rainbow of light.

'It's beyond description.'

Frederick nodded and moved by awe, on instinct, he reached out and took her hand in his. He wasn't sure how long they stood there, but it was long enough that the other tourists dispersed, long enough that another group came and went.

And then Sunita shook her head, as if coming out of a trance. 'We'd better go.'

He wondered what she'd been thinking all that time—perhaps she'd imagined her parents standing in the same spot, their thoughts and emotions, their hopes and dreams as they'd gazed at the might of the waterfalls.

They continued their trek along the railway tracks in a silence that he instinctively respected until he motioned to the adjacent forest. 'Shall we explore in there—it looks peaceful?'

'Good idea.' She glanced up at him. 'Sorry I've been lost in thought—it was just such an awe-inspiring sight.'

'It was.' He reached into his backpack. 'Time for food—or is that too prosaic?'

'Nope. I'm starving. And this looks idyllic—if a little damp.'

'I've brought a blanket, and if we spread it here, over this branch, we can perch on it.'

'Perfect.'

She accepted the wrapped sandwiches.

'Goan green chutney,' Frederick informed her. 'I promised Ashok to tell you the exact ingredients. Coriander leaves, coconut, chili and a little sugar and salt.'

Sunita took a bite. 'Glorious. That boy is talented.' She

surveyed him. 'So you went to the kitchen yourself? I'm surprised that was allowed.'

'Meaning?'

'Meaning your staff seem to think you shouldn't lift a finger for yourself.'

'I've noticed. I *am* trying to re-educate them—in fact I've given them all the day off today. The problem is my father expected to be waited on hand and foot, and that is what all Lycander staff seem conditioned to do. I even have someone who chooses all my clothes.' He grinned. 'Though, to be fair, Kirsten does a better job of it than I could.'

'Well, for the record, no one is choosing *my* clothes for me. That would drive me nuts. I need to fit my clothes to my mood.'

They ate in companionable silence and then Frederick leant forward, unsure why he felt the need to say his next words, but knowing he had to take heed of the urge to show her that their hopes and dreams didn't have to be built on an altar of falsehood and misunderstanding.

'Sunita?'

'Yes.'

She turned her head and his heart did a funny little jump. Dressed in simple khaki trousers and a red T-shirt, with her hair pulled back in a high ponytail, her features make-up free, she looked absurdly young and touchingly vulnerable.

'I understand why you want to go back to your career, and I understand your need for independence, but let's not go into this marriage expecting the worst. We'll be OK,' he said, even as he realised the ridiculous inadequacy of the words.

'You can't know that.' She lifted her shoulders in a shrug. 'But I appreciate the sentiment.'

'There are some things I *do* know, though. I won't turn into my father.' *Please God!* 'I won't fall in love with someone else and take Amil away from you.'

'You can't know that either.'

'I don't do falling in love, and that will not change. As for Amil, I will not take him from you. You have my word.'

'Words are meaningless.'

Her fierce certainty told him that someone had lied to her with devastating consequence, and increased his need to show her that he would not do the same.

'Sunita, I couldn't do it.' The words rasped from his throat. 'I would have done anything to have a mother. I witnessed first-hand what my father did to his wives, how it affected my brothers. I could not, I *will* not let history repeat itself.'

Her whole body stilled, and then she rose and moved towards him, sat right next to him, so close a tendril of her hair tickled his cheek.

'I'm sorry—I know what it's like to lose a mother through death, but for you it must have been pain of a different type...to know she was out there. And your poor mother... to have lost you like that—I can't imagine how it must have felt. Not just your mother but Stefan's and the twins'.'

For a moment the temptation to let her believe the fiction touched him. To let her believe the false assumption that his mother had been wronged, had spent years in grief and lamenting, that his mother had loved him. After all, he had no wish to be an object of pity or allow the ugly visage of self-pity to show its face.

But as he saw the sympathy, the empathy on her face, he realised he couldn't let her waste that compassion. 'My mother didn't suffer, Sunita.'

'I don't understand.'

'My mother sold me out for generous alimony and a

mansion in Beverly Hills. She played my father like a fine fiddle—conned him into believing she would do anything to keep custody of me, would be devastated to lose me. At the time he was still worrying about his popularity— many people hadn't got over the way he'd married my mother mere weeks after his first wife's death. He wanted to hurt her by taking me away—however, he didn't want to come across as the totally cruel husband again, so he offered her a generous settlement and she skipped all the way to the bank.'

'But…' Disbelief lined her face, along with a dark frown. 'How *could* she?'

'With great ease, apparently. Hey, it's OK. I came to terms with it long ago. I didn't tell you because I want to discuss it, or because I want sympathy. I told you because I want you to know that I could never take Amil from you. I know first-hand that a child needs his mother. From my own experience *and* my siblings'. Stefan, Barrett, Emerson—they have all been devastated by the custody battles and having their mothers torn from them. I would not put you or Amil through it. You have my word, and that word is not meaningless.'

'Thank you.' Shifting on the branch so that she faced him, she cupped his face in her hands, her fingers warm against his cheeks. 'Truly. Thank you for sharing that— you didn't have to. And I do believe that right here, right now, you mean what you promise.'

'But you don't believe I'll make good?'

'I…' Her hands dropped to her sides and, leaning forward, she dabbled her fingers in the soil of the forest floor, trickled it through her fingers and then sat up again. 'I don't know.'

She shrugged.

'Perhaps it's my turn to share now. I told you how my

father left when he found out my mother was pregnant. He promised her that he loved her, that they had a future.' She gestured back the way they'd come. 'Maybe he said those words at the falls. Hell, maybe they even sat here, in this very forest. But that promise meant nothing. And, you see, that wasn't the only promise he made.'

'I don't understand.'

'He came back.' Her eyes were wide now, looking back into a past that he suspected haunted her. 'When my mother found out she was terminally ill she managed to track him down. She had no one else. And he came, and he agreed to take me in. He explained that he was married, with two other daughters, but he promised—he swore that I would be welcomed, that I would have a family, that he would love and cherish me. He said that he was sorry and that he wanted to make it up to her and to me.'

The pain in her voice caused an ache that banded his chest and he reached out to cover her hand in his own, hoped that somehow it would assuage her hurt.

'So, after she died...' Her voice caught and her fingers tightened around his. 'He came to bring me to England— to my new family.'

Perhaps he should say something, Frederick thought. But he couldn't think of anything—couldn't even begin to contemplate how Sunita must have felt. The loss of her mother, the acquisition of a father she must have had mixed feelings about, the total upending of her life. All he could do was shift closer to her, *show* his comfort.

'It didn't work out. Turned out his promises didn't materialise.'

'What happened?'

'My stepmother and my sisters loathed me—I knew that from the instant I walked into the house.'

A house that must have felt so very alien to her, in a country that must have felt grey and cold and miserable.

'In a nutshell, he pitched me into a Cinderella scenario. They treated me like I was an inferior being.' She made a small exasperated noise. 'It sounds stupid, because it is so difficult to explain, but they made me feel worthless. I ate separately from them, my clothes were bought from charity shops, while my half-sisters' were new, I ended up with loads of extra chores so I could "earn my keep", and there were constant put-downs, constant reminders that I was literally worthless.' Another shrug. 'It all sounds petty, but it made me feel like nothing—worse than invisible. I was visible, but what they could see made them shudder.'

'It doesn't sound petty—it sounds intolerable.' Anger vibrated through him, along with disbelief that people could be so cruel. 'Was your father involved in this?'

'He was more of a bystander than a participant. He was away a lot on business. I did try to explain to him that I was unhappy, that I felt my stepmother didn't like me, but he simply said that I must be imagining it or, worse, he would accuse me of base ingratitude. Which made me feel guilty and even more alone.'

No wonder Sunita found it hard to take people at their word. Her own father, who had promised to care for her, had instead treated her like muck and allowed others to do the same.

'I'm sorry. I wish I could turn back time and intervene.'

'You can't change the past. And even if you could perhaps the outcome would be worse. Because in the past I got out, I escaped, and I've come to terms with what happened. I can even understand a little why my stepmother acted as she did. She was landed with a strange girl—the daughter of a woman her husband had been unfaithful with, the woman who probably was the love of his life. The gossip and speculation in the community must have been beyond humiliating for her and my half-sisters. So they turned all that anger and humiliation on to me.'

'That doesn't excuse their behaviour, or explain your father's.'

'I think my father was weak and he felt guilty. Guilty over the way he'd treated my mother…guilty that he had betrayed his wife in the first place. And that guilt translated into doing anything for a quiet life. That worked in my favour later on. I got scouted by a model agency when I was sixteen and my father agreed to let me leave home— my stepmother was happy to see me go, sure I'd join the ranks of failed wannabes, so she agreed. I never looked back and I never went back. I never saw them again. The second I could, I sent my father a cheque to cover any costs he might have incurred over the years. As far as I am concerned we are quits. I don't even know where he is.'

So much made sense to Frederick now—her lack of trust, her fears over Amil, her need to be in control. Admiration burned within him that she had achieved so much, was such an amazing parent herself.

These were all the things he wanted to say, but didn't quite know how. So instead he did what he had promised himself he wouldn't do and he kissed her—right there in the middle of the rainforest, with the smell of the monsoon in the air, and the pounding of the waterfall in the distance. He kissed her as if his life and soul depended on it.

Her resistance was brief—a nanosecond of surprise— and then, as if she too were tired of words, of this walk down a memory lane that was lined with sadness, her resistance melted away and her lips parted beneath his.

He tasted the sweet chili tang left by the sandwiches and heard her soft moan. Their surroundings receded. The call of a hornbill, the rustle of the monkeys in the trees above all melted away and left only them, encased in a net of yearning and need and desire.

He pulled her closer, oblivious of the rustle of the blanket, the unwieldiness of the branch they sat on. Nothing mattered but *this*—losing themselves in this moment of sheer bliss as he deepened the kiss, as her hands slipped under his T-shirt so her fingers covered the accelerated beat of his heart.

Who knew what would have happened if a monkey in the tree above hadn't decided to take advantage and scamper down in an audacious bid for the rucksack. It's insistent chatter and the swipe of an overhanging branch brought Frederick back to reality.

A shout from him, a darting movement from Sunita, and the monkey jumped to safety and jabbered at them in indignation.

They met each other's eyes, hers still clouded with desire, and he managed a smile. 'Well saved.'

Then there were no words. They both simply stood there, and he reached out and took her hands in his.

'What now?' he asked.

'I don't know.' She shook her head. 'Yes, I do. Let's walk. And eat and talk. But let's not talk about unhappy things.'

'That sounds good. Only happy topics—all the way back.' He held her gaze. 'And what happens then?'

She stepped forward, stood on tiptoe, and dropped the lightest of kisses on his lips. 'I don't know,' she whispered. 'I really don't.'

For a moment neither did he. Oh, he knew what he *should* do—he should lock this down now. This physical attraction was too intense, too emotional, and he didn't want intensity or emotion to enter their relationship. This marriage was an alliance and he wanted it to last. Succumbing to physical allure, allowing it too much importance, would jeopardise that.

But today he was just Frederick, not the Playboy Prince or the ruler of a principality who had vowed to fulfil his brother's vision. Today they were Frederick and Sunita.

And so he stepped forward and smiled—a smile that was shamelessly predatory and full of promise. 'Then it's lucky that I know *exactly* what to do.'

'What...?' Her voice was even softer than before, her brown eyes wide.

'We're going to walk to the nearest station and catch a goods train, and then take a taxi back to the villa. Then we're going to resume where we've just left off and this time we are not going to stop.' He paused. 'How does that sound?'

He realised he was holding his breath as she tipped her head to one side, and then she smiled a smile that lit her face and ignited a warmth that spread across his chest.

'That sounds perfect. I just hope the goods train is fast.'

Frederick shook his head. 'Anticipation is half the fun.' He held out his hand. 'Let's go.'

'Anticipation is half the fun.'

Sunita wasn't so sure of that. As they walked alongside the train tracks anticipation streamed through her veins, causing her tummy to cartwheel and her pulse-rate to soar. Was *that* fun?

It was hard to tell—her whole body felt tight with need, a yearning that it would now be impossible to quell, and truth to tell she didn't want to. She glanced down at their clasped hands, at the strength of his profile, the jut of his jaw, the lithe assurance he walked with, the whole time aware of his own scrutiny, the desire that warmed his hazel eyes when they rested on her.

They talked—of course they did. Of films and books and politics…of cabbages and kings…but the words seemed to be filtered through a haze of awareness that glistened in the air alongside the sunlit drops of rain that sparkled from the lush leaves.

Their ascent onto a goods train seemed almost surreal as they travelled amidst the bulky cargo, and she gazed out over the variegated greens of paddy fields, the swoop of the Goan valleys, the shimmering grey of the sky, where clouds swelled and perfumed the air with the promise of rain. All the while, even as her senses stored away Nature's munificent beauty, they also revelled in Frederick's proximity, in the knowledge that soon—soon—they would be together, that for a time at least he would be hers.

Careful!

She must not let this get out of perspective, make it into any more than it was. This was a benefit of their marriage deal—a benefit that could be taken or left at will. This was physical—no more no less—and the only reason she was so on edge was because she hadn't felt like this for two years. Not since that night when all her principles had been abandoned and she'd tumbled into bed with him.

'Hey.'

She turned to see his hazel eyes rest on her face.

'You OK? We don't have to do this, you know? We have a lifetime ahead of us…'

But not like this—not as Frederick and Sunita. Today meant something different—she couldn't explain how she knew it, but she knew with soul-wrenching certainty that this was the case.

'I know, but I want this now, today…' She grinned suddenly. 'There is only so much anticipation a girl can take.'

His answering grin removed all doubts; it was a smile

she remembered from two years ago, boyish, happy, and she hadn't seen it once in the past few days.

'It'll be worth it. I promise.'

And as the train slowed to a stop she had no doubt that this was a promise she could rely on.

Twenty minutes later they arrived back at the villa and alighted from the taxi. She glanced around almost furtively, not wanting to meet Deepali or Ashok or anyone. Hand in hand, they practically tiptoed through the garden… And if Deepali did spot them she remained discreetly hidden and they reached Sunita's bedroom safely.

Once inside, she moved to the window and pulled the blackout shutters closed, then turned and moved towards Frederick with an urgency more than matched by his own as he strode forward and pulled her so she was flush against the hard promise of his body.

'The anticipation was great,' she murmured. 'But now it's got old.'

His laugh held a breathless quality. 'Tell me about it!'

And with that he tumbled her back onto the bed, and after that all coherent thought evaporated as sensation took over. The feel of his lips on hers, his taste, his touch against her sensitised skin—all caused her to moan in unabashed joy. His skin under her fingers, his shudder of pleasure, his voice whispering her name, the shucking of clothes, the urgency and the exquisite gentleness, the awe and the laughter and desire such as she had never known, all created a waving, pulsing sense that carried them higher and higher…

Hours later she opened her eyes, realising that she was being gently shaken awake, a hand on her shoulder. *His* hand. She blinked sleepily, and then sat up as the glorious dream dissipated. Frederick stood back from the bed—fully clothed, she noted with a fuzzy disappointment.

'Hey...' she said.

'Hey. Everyone's back—we need to show our faces before they wonder where we are.'

Sunita blinked, tried to compute why it mattered—they were engaged. Surely he wasn't embarrassed. Properly awake now, she propped herself up on one elbow as a sudden awkwardness descended. 'You should have woken me earlier.'

'I thought I'd let you sleep.' Now a small smile quirked into place. 'We expended a lot of energy.'

'So we did.' For a moment relief touched her—maybe she'd imagined the awkwardness.

'But now the day is over and we aren't "just" Sunita and Frederick any more. We are the Prince and his Princess-to-be and we can't repeat this.'

'This?' she echoed, as a spark of anger ignited by hurt flared. 'Define "this".'

His gaze remained steady. 'We can't sleep together again before the wedding. This engagement needs to be seen as completely different from my father's marriages—I don't want the people to believe it is based on physical attraction alone, that their ruler has been influenced by anything other than the good of Lycander.'

'Of course.'

It made perfect sense, she could see that. Of course she could. She could measure every publicity angle with unerring accuracy. This marriage would not play well with Lycander—she herself had pointed that out. So she understood that they needed to downplay their physical attraction and focus on the real reason for their marriage—Amil.

Yet his words felt like a personal rejection, as though

beneath his common-sense approach lay reserve, a with-drawal.

The knowledge…the certainty that he regretted the day and its outcome, that he regretted 'this', bolstered her pride, gave her voice a cool assurance. 'I understand.'

After all, he'd made it clear enough. Their physical attraction was a side benefit, a bonus to their marriage alliance, and she would not make the mistake of reading any more into it than that.

'I need to get dressed. Shall I meet you in the gardens?'

For a moment he hesitated, and then nodded and headed for the door. Once he was gone Sunita closed her eyes, annoyed to feel the imminent well of tears. Two years before she'd allowed physical attraction to override common sense, and now it seemed she might have done it again. But no more.

She swung herself out of bed in a brisk movement and headed across the room. Pulling open her wardrobe, she surveyed the contents and settled on a black cold-shoulder crop top over floral silk trousers. A quick shower, a bit of make-up and she was good to go.

Once in the gardens, she spotted Frederick in conversation with Eric, saw the hand-over of a package that Frederick dropped into his pocket before he saw her and walked over.

'Shall we have a quick walk before dinner?' he asked.

'Sure.'

They walked into the sylvan glade, skirting the lily pond, where two brilliant turquoise kingfishers dived, their white 'shirtfront' breasts bright in the dusk.

'I wanted to give you this,' he said, and he reached into his pocket and took out the package, undoing it with deft fingers and handing her the jeweller's box inside. 'We can't announce the engagement without a ring.'

She flipped the lid open and gazed inside. The ring had presence; it glinted up at her, a cold, hard, solid diamond. A discreetly obvious ring that knew its own worth—its multi-faceted edges placed it in the upper echelon of the diamond class. A regal ring—perhaps he hoped it would confer a royal presence on her.

Hell, it was the very Kaitlin of rings.

'Did you choose it?'

For a scant instant discomfort showed, but then it was gone. 'No. Kirsten did.'

The woman who chose his clothes. Of course—who better to choose the correct ring for Lycander's bride?

'I asked her to get it done last night. Is there a problem with it?'

'Of course not.'

In an abrupt movement she pulled the ring out and slid it over her finger, where it sat and looked up at her, each glint one of disdain. The ring wasn't fooled—it knew this was not a worthy hand to rest upon.

Sunita glared down at it as she executed an almost painful mental eye-roll. *Note to self: the ring does not possess a personality. Second note: of course I am worthy.*

She summoned a smile. 'Guess we're all set to go.' Even if she couldn't have felt less ready.

CHAPTER TWELVE

Lycander

THE CAR WOUND up the mountain road. Sunita stifled a gasp and Frederick felt a sudden surge of pride as he saw her reaction to Lycander's castle.

'Holy-moly,' she said. 'It's straight out of a fairy tale. Any minute now Snow White will wave at me from a turret or I'll see Rapunzel climb down a tower.'

Something tugged at his heart as he looked at her—something he couldn't identify and didn't particularly want to. Focus on facts…that was the way to go.

'Believe it or not, this castle has been around for centuries. It started out long ago as a wooden fortress and over the years it has been renovated, added to, and here we have it.'

'It's hard to believe I'm going to live there.'

Equally hard to ascertain her opinion on the fact, he thought.

Sunita subsided into silence as they approached the castle and parked in an impressive paved courtyard, complete with fountains, stone lions and an immense marble sundial.

'I'll give you a proper tour later. For now, if it's all right with you, I'll show you to your rooms—I've asked Giselle Diaz, the housekeeper, to get a set of apartments ready.

After the wedding we will move into the state apartments. I'll show you those later—I think you may want to redecorate them.'

Slow down. No need to turn into a tour guide. Come to that, he couldn't help but wonder at the dearth of staff there to greet them. Foreboding touched him—perhaps the no-show was connected to the emergency council meeting he was scheduled to attend right now. Convened to 'discuss'— for that read 'object to'—his marriage.

They reached the apartment suite that would be Sunita and Amil's until the wedding and he scanned it quickly. Clean and polished…welcoming flowers in place. On the surface it all looked fine, but he knew it lacked the extra touches that had abounded the one time Lady Kaitlin had stayed as a Lycander guest. Back then Giselle had been there to greet them, the flowers had been more lavish, the toiletries a tad more luxurious.

Hmm…

'I'll leave you to settle in and I'll be back as soon as I can.'

'Why don't I come with you? My guess is that your council will want to talk to you about our marriage—let's face them together.'

Frederick shook his head. 'I'd rather do it alone. I brokered this marriage—it is my responsibility to explain it to my people.'

A flash of hurt showed in her eyes and then she shrugged. 'As you wish.'

He pushed down the urge to assuage the hurt; this was *his* business and he would deal with it alone.

Fifteen minutes later he looked around the council chamber, which was informally referred to as the tapestry room, due to the needlepoint that lined nearly every centimetre of the walls. The lifework of a princess centuries before, who had toiled whilst her husband had dallied with a string of mistresses.

Each section illustrated a different theme, dominated by war and religion with plenty of fire and brimstone and gore... Presumably it was meant to be an apt backdrop for the discussion of council matters.

'Order!' called one of the council members.

Frederick looked around the table—at Marcus's assessing expression, at the rest of the council's combative stance. 'You requested we meet as soon as I arrived to discuss your concerns. Please enlighten me.'

A middle-aged man rose to his feet. 'This proposed marriage, Your Highness...we do not believe it is a good move.'

'Marcus has kept me apprised of your concerns.' He kept his voice even. 'But this marriage *is* happening.'

'But the people will not like it,' interpolated another council member.

'Sunita is an excellent publicist—I believe she will win them over.'

'How? She is a woman you barely know—a model, the mother of a baby she kept from you—but now that you are on the throne she seems happy to marry you.'

'Shades of your mother...'

'Who said that?' Frederick demanded.

'*I* said it.' The voice came from one of the elder statesmen.

'My relationship with Sunita bears no resemblance to that of my parents.'

'I beg to differ, Your Highness. I was there. Prince Alphonse fell hook, line and sinker for your mother—chased her whilst his wife, the mother of Crown Prince Axel, was dying. Their wedding was an extravaganza pushed forward because the bride was pregnant. Within months of your birth the marriage was floundering; within a few years it had ended in scandal. Your mother played him for a fool.'

White-hot anger roiled inside him. Yet the words were true—a fact he had to face.

'Are you saying that *I* am a fool? What would have happened if you had spoken to my father thus?'

Frederick made a gesture to a guard, who stepped forward without hesitation to a murmur of surprise.

'You would have been marched out and the council would have been shut down until after the wedding.'

He gestured for the guard to stop and rose to his feet.

'But I do not rule as my father did—I have listened to all your concerns and I understand them. Now I tell you this. My marriage to Sunita is to be made in good faith on both our parts. There will be no scandal. There will be no custody battle. This union will endure. This wedding is happening.'

What was he? The Delphi Oracle? But now was no time to exhibit doubt. 'I promise you all that I value your opinion. But you see, ladies and gentlemen, Amil is my son, and if I have a chance to be a father *without* taking my son from his mother then I have to take it. So the wedding will happen and I very much hope to see you all dance at it.'

Further silence, and then Marcus rose to his feet, an enigmatic look on his face. 'I suggest that is the end of this special council meeting.'

As everyone filed out Frederick ran a hand down his face and turned as his chief advisor approached. Frederick shook his head. 'Not now, Marcus. I can't take any more wedding advice.'

The dark-haired man gave a half-smile. 'I wouldn't dare.'

'Now, *that* I don't believe.'

'You should.' Marcus eyed him. 'That is the first time since your ascension to the throne that I have seen you stand up for something *you* believe in.'

'Rubbish. I have stood in this room and fought to convince councillors to support education and tax reform, to close the casinos...'

'I get that. But those were all Axel's policies. This is *your* marriage.'

'Axel would have agreed that I am doing the right thing.'

'Then maybe you and Axel had more in common than I realised.'

For a second his chief advisor's words warmed him— but only for a fleeting second. If Marcus knew the truth he'd never use such words.

Frederick rose to his feet before the urge to confess overcame common sense and tried to rid himself of the grubby feel of deceit.

'Frederick? I'll support you in this, but you will need to make this work. You need to win the public round.'

'I know.'

Luckily, he knew the perfect person to help with that.

Sunita stared down at the diamond ring that sparkled and glistened and weighted her finger. She looked around the apartment that appeared opulent yet felt oppressive, with its heavy faded gold curtains and the bowls of flowers that, though magnificent, emanated a cloying, gloom-laden scent.

These were showrooms—there should be signs and information leaflets to outline the names of the rich and famous who had stayed within these walls, to document the lives of the painters who had created the looming allegorical creations that adorned them.

The furniture was decorative—but the stripes of the

claw-footed chaise longue almost blinded her, and the idea of sitting on it was impossible. As for the bedroom—she'd need a stepladder to get up into a bed that, conversely, seemed to have been made for someone at least a foot smaller than she was.

Well, there was no way she would let Amil live in a showroom, so she needed to make it into a home.

She started to unpack—hung her clothes in the wardrobe, took comfort from the feel of the fabrics, the splash of the colours, every item imbued with memories.

She halted at a knock on the door.

Spinning round, she saw Frederick framed in the doorway, and to her annoyance her heart gave a little pit-pat, a hop, skip and a jump.

'Hi.'

'Sorry, I did knock on the main door.'

'That's fine. How did the meeting go?'

'As well as could be expected. The council understand this marriage. But we need to get the publicity right to prevent a public backlash.'

Sunita moved away from the wardrobe. 'OK. Let's brainstorm.'

Her mind whirred as they moved into the lounge and perched on two ridiculously uncomfortable upholstered chairs.

'We need to make sure the people understand why we have left Amil in India—that it is simply so we can prepare a home for him. I could talk to the local press about my plans to renovate these apartments and the state apartments. I also suggest that before Amil arrives we go on a tour of some of Lycander, so it's clear that I am interested in the country—not just the crown. I won't accept any modelling contracts straight away.'

Even though her agent's phone was already ringing off the proverbial hook.

He rose to his feet, looked down at her with a sudden smile that set her heart off again.

'Let's start now.'

'How?'

'I'll take you on a tour of an olive grove.'

'One of yours?'

For a moment he hesitated, and then he nodded. 'Yes. I'll arrange transport and press coverage.'

'I'll get changed into appropriate clothes for touring an olive grove.' In fact she knew the very dress—a long, floaty, lavender-striped sun dress.

A shot of anticipation thrilled through her.

Stop. This was a publicity stunt—not a romantic jaunt. She had to get a grip. This marriage was an alliance that Frederick had 'brokered'—a word he had used in this very room a mere hour before.

The problem was, however hard she tried—and she'd tried incredibly hard—that anticipation refused to be suppressed by logic or any other device she could come up with.

Perhaps it was simply to do with the glorious weather, the cerulean blue sky, the hazy heat of the late August sun whose rays kissed and dappled the rolling hills and plains of the Lycander countryside. She could only hope it was nothing to do with the man who sat beside her in the back of the chauffeured car.

'So, where exactly are we going?'

'The place where it all started—the first olive grove I owned. It was left to me by a great-uncle when I was twenty-one. I visited on a whim and—*kaboom!*—the whole process fascinated me. The family who lived there were thrilled as my great-uncle had had no interest in the place—they taught me all about the business and that's how Freddy Petrelli's Olive Oil came into being. I expanded, bought up some smaller businesses, consolidated, and now our oil is stocked worldwide.'

'Are you still part of the company?'

'I'm still on the board, but by necessity I have had to delegate.'

'That's pretty impressive—to take one rundown olive grove and turn it into a multi-million-dollar business in a few years.'

'You turned yourself into one of the world's most sought-after supermodels in much the same time-frame. That's pretty impressive too.'

'Thank you—but it didn't feel impressive at the time.' Back then she'd been driven. 'I *needed* to succeed—I would not let my family see me fail. I wanted them to know that they had been wrong about me. I wanted to show them I was my mother's daughter and proud of it.'

At every photo shoot, she'd imagined their faces, tinged a shade of virulent green as they opened a magazine to see Sunita's face.

'That's understandable—and kudos to you for your success. You have my full admiration and, although it may not be politically correct, I hope they choked on envy every time they saw your picture.'

She couldn't help but laugh as a sudden warmth flooded her—it had been a long time since anyone had sounded so protective of her.

Before she could respond further the car came to a halt—and right after that they were mobbed. Or that was what it felt like. Once she had alighted from the car she realised the 'mob' actually consisted of four people—a middle-aged couple, a youth and a young girl—all of whom broke into simultaneous speech.

'The crop has been excellent this year. The olives—they will be the best yet. And last year's olive oil—the gods have blessed it, Freddy!'

'It has been too long, Frederick, too long—how can you have not been here for so long? And why didn't you tell me of this visit earlier? I would have prepared your favourite dishes. Now. Bah… All we have is what I have had time to prepare.'

'Thanks so much for the links to the bikes. Oil, gears, helmets…'

'Frederick, I've missed you! Why haven't you visited?'

There was no mistaking the family's happiness at seeing him, and as Sunita watched Frederick contend with the barrage of comments his smile flashed with a youthful boyishness.

'Pepita, Juan, Max, Flo—I'd like to introduce you to Sunita…my fiancée.'

For a moment the silence felt heavy, and Sunita could feel her tummy twist, and then Pepita stepped forward.

'Welcome, Sunita. It is lovely that Frederick has brought you here. We have all been reading the papers—every article. The little *bambino* looks adorable.'

As she spoke Pepita swept them forward towards a whitewashed villa. Terracotta tiles gleamed in the sunshine and trees shaded the courtyard outside.

'Come—lunch is all ready, Alberto, sort out the drinks. Flo, set the table, Max, come and help me serve.'

'Can I help?' asked Sunita.

'No, no, no. You and Frederick go and sit.'

Within minutes, amidst much debate and chat, food appeared. A bottle of wine was opened, tantalising smells laced the air and Pepita beamed.

'Come and serve yourselves. Frederick, you have lost

weight—I want you to eat. They are not your favourite dishes, but they are still good.'

'Pepita, everything you cook is good.'

Sunita shook her head. 'Nope. Everything you cook is *amazing*.'

It truly was. The table was laden with a variety of dishes. Bite-sized skewers that held tangy mozzarella, luscious tomatoes that tasted of sunshine and basil. Deep-fried golden rounds of cheese tortellini. Freshly baked bread with a pesto and vinegar dip that made her taste-buds tingle. Baked asparagus wrapped in prosciutto. And of course bowls of olives with a real depth of zing.

But what was truly amazing was the interplay between Frederick and the family—to see him set aside his role of ruler, to see him morph back to the man he had been before tragedy had intervened and changed his life path.

There was conversation and laughter, the clatter of cutlery, the taste of light red wine, the dapple of sunshine through the leaves causing a dance of sunbeams on the wooden slats of the table.

Until finally everyone was replete and this time Sunita insisted. 'I'll help clear.'

Frederick rose as well, but Pepita waved him down. 'Stay. Drink more wine. I want to talk to your fiancée alone.'

A hint of wariness crossed his face, but clearly he didn't feel equal to the task of intervention. So, plates in hand, Sunita followed Pepita to a whitewashed kitchen, scented by the fresh herbs that grew on the windowsill. Garlic hung from the rafters, alongside copper pots and pans.

'It is good to see Frederick here,' Pepita ventured with a sideways glance. 'And now he is a father.'

'Yes.' Sunita placed the plates down and turned to face

the older woman. 'I know you must be angry at what I did, but—'

'It is not my place to be angry—this is a matter for you to sort out with Frederick…a matter between husband and wife. I want to tell you that I am worried about him. Since his brother's death we have barely seen him—all he does now is work. I know that he avoids us. There is a demon that drives him and you need to get rid of it.'

'I… Our marriage isn't going to be like that, Pepita…'

'Bah! You plan to spend your lives together, yes? Then that is your job.'

Her head spun as the enormity of Pepita's words sank in. She *was* planning to spend her life with Frederick—her *life*. She wouldn't have another one; this was it.

Closing her eyes, she forced her thoughts to centre, to concentrate on the here and now. 'I'll do what I can,' she heard herself say, wanting to soothe the other woman's worry.

Frederick looked up as Sunita emerged from the house. Her face was slightly flushed from the sun, her striped dress the perfect outfit for a sunny day. Her expression looked thoughtful, and he couldn't help but wonder what Pepita had said—though he was wise enough to have no intention of asking. He suspected he might not like the answer.

Guilt twanged at the paucity of time he had given to this family—people he felt closer to than his 'real' family.

He turned to Juan. 'Is it all right if I take Sunita on a tour?'

'Why are you asking me? It is *your* grove, Frederick— I just tend it for you. Go—show your beautiful lady the most beautiful place in the world.'

Sunita grinned up at him as they made their way towards the fields. 'They are a lovely family.'

'That they are.'

'And it's good to see your royal authority in action.'

'Sarcasm will get you nowhere—but you're right. Pepita wouldn't recognise royal authority if it rose up and bit her. To her I am still the twenty-one-year-old they taught the olive oil business. Right here.'

Sunita gave a small gasp, her face animated as she gazed ahead to where majestic lines of evergreen trees abounded. Olives clustered at the ends of branches clad with silver leaves that gleamed in the sunlight.

'The colour of those leaves—it's like they're threaded with real silver.'

'That's actually the colour of the underside of the leaf. When it's hot the leaves turn light-side up to reflect the sun. When it's cold they turn grey-green side up to absorb the sun.'

'That's pretty incredible when you think about it.'

'The whole process is incredible. The olives are growing at the moment. They won't be ready to harvest for another few months. You should be here for the harvest. It's incredible. The green table olives get picked in September, October, then the ones we use for oil from mid-November, when they are bursting with oil. It is exhausting work. You basically spread a cloth under the trees to catch the olives and then you hit the trees with sticks. The harvest then gets carted off to the mills—which is equally fascinating. But I won't bore you with it now.'

'You aren't boring me. Keep going. Truly.'

Her face registered genuine interest, and so as they walked he talked and she listened. They inhaled the tang of the olives mingled with the scent of honeysuckle carried on the gentle breeze, revelled in the warmth of the sun and the lazy drone of bees in the distance.

It was impossible not to feel at peace here. Impossible

not to note Sunita's beauty—her dark hair shining with a raven sheen in the sunlight, the classic beauty of her face enhanced by the surroundings—and it took all his will-power not to kiss her. That would be a bad move.

She looked up at him. 'I can see why you fell in love with this place—it has a timeless quality.'

'A few of these trees have been here for centuries.'

'And in that time history has played out…generations of people have walked these fields, beaten the trees with sticks, experienced joy and sadness and the full gamut of emotion in between. It gives you perspective.' She gave him a sideways glance and took a quick inhalation of breath. 'Maybe you should come here more often.'

'Because you think I need perspective?'

'Because Pepita misses you.'

'Did she say that?'

'No, but it's pretty obvious. I'd guess that you miss them too.'

'I don't have time to miss them. In the same way I don't have time to come down here—my days in the olive oil industry are over, and I've accepted that.'

'That doesn't mean you can't visit more often.' She stopped now and turned to face him, forced him to halt as well. 'No one would grudge you some down-time. And this place *means* something to you.'

That was the trouble—this place took him off his game, distracted him from his mission, reminded him of a time untainted by guilt, of the man he had once been and could never be again. When Axel had been alive.

Yet he had brought Sunita here today—*why?* The rea-son smacked into him. He'd succumbed to temptation—one more day of 'just Frederick and Sunita'. *Foolish.* 'Just Frederick and Sunita' didn't exist.

'Yes, it does. It represents the past. A part of my life that is over. For good.'

Reality was the crown of Lycander and the path he had set himself. Axel had died—had been denied the chance to rule, to live, to marry, to have children. The only thing Frederick could do now was honour his memory—ensure his vision was accomplished. Ensure the monarchy was safe and Lycander prospered.

'It's time to get back to the palace.'

CHAPTER THIRTEEN

Two weeks later

SUNITA GAZED AROUND the transformed apartments with satisfaction. It hadn't been easy, but the spindly chairs of discomfort, the antique non-toddler-friendly glass tables, the dark gloomy pictures were all gone—and she didn't care if they *were* by museum-worthy artists. Mostly it hadn't been easy because of the intense levels of disapproval exhibited by nearly every single member of staff she'd asked for help.

In truth, Sunita quite simply didn't get it—she hadn't expected instant love or loyalty, but this condescension hidden behind a thin veneer of politeness was both horrible and familiar. It made her feel worthless inside—just as she had in her stepmother's home.

Giselle Diaz, the housekeeper, looked down her aristocratic nose at her, Sven Nordstrom, chief steward, somehow managed to convey utter horror, and the more junior members of staff had taken their cue from their superiors. Whilst they listened to Sunita's instructions, they did so with a frigid politeness that made her quake.

But she'd stuck to her guns, had ransacked the palace for *real* items of furniture, and tucked away in nooks and crannies she'd discovered some true treasures.

Old overstuffed armchairs, ridiculously comfortable sofas…and now she and Amil had a home, a haven.

Sunita gazed at her son. They had brought him back from Mumbai ten days before and he had settled in with a happiness she could only envy. With a smile, he crawled across the floor and she scooped him up onto her lap.

'What do you think, sweetheart?' She showed him two different fabric swatches. 'Do you like this one or this one? For your new nursery when we move to the state apartments.'

'Dabadabad!' Amil said chattily.

'Shall we ask Daddy? That's a good idea, isn't it?'

Frederick would arrive at any moment—every day without fail he was there for Amil's breakfast and tea, and for bedtime. Otherwise he worked.

Ever since the olive grove he'd been distant, as if he'd built a wall of transparent glass that she couldn't penetrate. He was polite, kind and unfailingly courteous, and it made her want to scream. It also made her wonder what demon drove him to spend nigh on every waking hour in the council room, closeted with advisors, lawyers, education experts or engrossed in legal and constitutional tomes that dated back centuries.

Her reverie was interrupted by the familiar knock on the door.

'Come in.'

Frederick entered and, as happened each and every day, her heart fluttered and she noted the lines of tiredness around his eyes and wished she could smooth them away.

'Adadadadaa!' Amil said, and if she'd blinked she'd have missed the smile that lit Frederick's face—one of pure, unaffected joy—before his expression morphed back to neutral.

'Good evening, Amil. And what have you got for tea today?'

'He has lasagne with carrot sticks. Prepared by his very loving, very lovely potential new nanny.'

Satisfaction pumped a fist inside her as she saw his eyebrows snap together—that had at least got his attention.

'Nanny? You didn't tell me you'd chosen one from the list I gave you.'

The list that had chilled her very bone marrow—a list of extremely qualified, excessively expensive women.

'That's because she isn't on the list. But maybe we could discuss this once Amil is in bed.'

'Sure.'

'Then let's get tea underway.'

She headed to the kitchenette and soon had Amil seated in his high chair.

As she did every day, she asked, 'Would you like to feed him?'

He replied as he did every day. 'No. I'm good, thanks. It looks tricky, and I don't know how you manage to get more food into him than ends up elsewhere.'

True enough, meal times weren't the tidiest of processes—and equally true she *had* worked out a dextrous method of spooning in maximum food—but still... She wasn't sure that his reluctance stemmed from fastidiousness. As for worrying that Amil wouldn't get enough to eat, that didn't ring true either—as she had pointed out, he could always have a second helping.

Perhaps he didn't like the idea of being watched and judged.

'I can go into the lounge whilst you feed him, if you like?'

'I'd prefer it if *you* fed him, if that's OK?'

'Of course.'

Only it wasn't OK. Not really.

Just like it wasn't really OK that Frederick didn't engage in bathtime, didn't take Amil onto his lap for his bedtime story. If it were any other man she would suspect that he didn't care, that he was going through the motions. But that didn't make sense. Frederick had fought tooth and nail to be a full-time father to Amil—risked his throne, defied all advice, was willing to take a less than ideal bride.

'Say goodnight to Daddy.'

The little boy gurgled happily and she walked over so that Frederick could give him a kiss.

'See you in a minute.'

Fifteen minutes later she tiptoed from Amil's room and entered the lounge—then stopped on the threshold and cursed under her breath.

Damn. She'd left her sketchbook open on the table—worse, she'd left it open, so she could hardly blame Frederick for sitting there and studying the page.

'Did you do this?'

'Yes.'

There was little point in denial—it wasn't as if he'd believe that *Amil* had drawn a ballroom dress or an off-the-shoulder top.

'They're good.'

'Thank you—they're just sketches…doodles, really. You know how much I love clothes.'

'These look like more than doodles—you've written notes on fabric and cut. How many of these sketchbooks have you got?'

'It doesn't matter.' No way would she confess the number. 'I've always enjoyed sketching and I've always loved fashion. Ever since my mum took me on a photo shoot with her—I loved the buzz, the vibrancy, but most of all I loved the clothes. The feel, the look, the way they could totally transform a person. Sounds mad, maybe, but I think clothes have power.'

His gaze returned to the sketchbook. 'Have you ever thought about fashion design?'

'No.'

That might be a little bit of a fib, but she didn't really want to discuss it. Her sketches were private—she'd never shown them to anyone and she wasn't about to start now.

'It's just a hobby. I think my forte is wearing clothes, not designing them.'

Moving forward, she removed the sketchpad and closed it with a finality she hoped he would apply to the whole topic.

'Anyway I wanted to talk to you about my nanny idea.'

In truth, she wasn't that keen on a nanny—but she could see that if she planned to model and fulfil her commitments as a Lycander consort then it would be necessary.

'Go ahead.'

'I want to give Gloria Russo the role.'

Frederick frowned. 'I thought she worked in the palace kitchens.'

'She does. That's where I met her. I went down there to sort out how it all works—whether I am supposed to shop, or food is delivered, how and where and when I can cook Amil's food... Anyway, Gloria was really helpful.'

Which had made a novel change from every other staff member.

'She only joined the staff recently, but obviously she has been security vetted.'

'So she used to be a nanny?'

'No.'

'All the people on my list have been trained as a nanny—they have extensive qualifications and experience.'

'So does Gloria—she has four grown-up children. And, most important, Amil loves her already.'

'Amil needs a *proper* nanny.'

Frustrated anger rolled over her in a tidal wave—a culmination of being patronised all week and a need to make her own presence felt in a world she didn't fit into. *Again.*

'*Will* you get your royal head out of your royal behind? Gloria will *be* a proper nanny. She knows how to keep him safe and she knows how to provide love and security and fun. She makes him laugh, but she will also make sure he listens. At least agree to meet her and see her with Amil.'

'As long as *you* agree to meet two people from the list. Then we will make the decision.'

'Deal. You'll like Gloria—I'm sure you will. She is kind and she's down to earth and she's fun. Fun is important.' Something Frederick seemed to have forgotten. 'You must remember that—you used to be the Prince of Fun.'

'That was a long time ago.' His tone implied a lifetime rather than mere months.

'Do you miss it? That lifestyle?'

When there had been a different woman in his bed whenever he wanted, and all he'd had to worry about was where the next bottle of champagne was coming from.

'That life feels like it belonged to someone else. So, no, I don't miss it.'

'I know what you mean. My life before Amil seems surreal sometimes, but there are parts of it that I want to retain—I still love clothes, I'm still Sunita.'

Whereas the Frederick of before—apart from the occasional glimpse—seemed to have vanished completely, remorselessly filtered out by grief and the weight of a crown.

'I know that you have taken on a huge responsibility, and of course you need to take that seriously. But there are aspects of the old Frederick that you should keep. The ability to have fun, to laugh and make others laugh.'

'I've had my quota of fun.' He rose to his feet. 'I have a meeting with Marcus now, so...'

'You have to go.'

Sunita bit her lip, told herself it didn't matter. Why should it? Their marriage was an alliance made for Amil's sake—any desire for his company was both ridiculous and clearly unreciprocated.

'Don't forget about tomorrow. We have a family day out scheduled.'

'It's in the diary.' He looked down at her. 'You are sure you don't want to tell me where we're going?'

'Nope. It's a surprise.'

It was an idea she knew the press would love—the fiancée taking her Prince to a surprise destination with their son. A way of emphasising to the people that their Prince and his Princess-to-be had changed and their party lifestyle was well and truly over.

She smiled at him. 'It will be fun.'

For a moment she thought he would return the smile, but instead he merely nodded. 'Goodnight, Sunita.'

'Goodnight.'

There it was again—that stupid yearning to ask him to stay.

Not happening.

The door clicked behind him as her phone buzzed. Her agent.

'Hi, Harvey.'

'Hey, sweetheart. We need to talk.'

Frederick checked the weather forecast as he approached Sunita's apartments. A sunny and cloud-free day—a typical late-summer day in Lycander, perfect for a 'family day out'. The words had an alien twist to them—family days out had been few and far between in his childhood. And now both anticipation and an irrational fear tightened his gut.

Fear at the level of anticipation, and the knowledge that too much of it was tied up in Sunita, was mixed with the fear of messing it up with Amil. Somehow he had to get these fledgling emotions under control—work out which were acceptable, which he needed to nourish to be a good father and which he needed to stifle before they got out of hand.

He could *do* this—he was a past master at emotional lockdown and he would work it out. He would achieve the balanced, calm marriage alliance he wanted.

Pushing open the door, he entered. Sunita smiled at him and his breath caught. *Beautiful*—there was no other word to describe her. She was dressed in flared, delicately embroidered jeans and a simple dark blue sleeveless top, sunglasses perched atop her head and her hair tumbling loose in a riot of waves. Her vibrancy lit the room—a room that she'd made home.

Clutter without untidiness gave it a feeling of relaxed warmth, as did the overstuffed armchairs and sofas that she had commandeered from somewhere in the palace to replace the antique showcase furniture.

'You ready?' he asked.

'We're ready—aren't we, Amil? Look, it's Daddy.'

Frederick turned his head to look at Amil, who waved his favourite toy cat at him in greeting. And then he twisted, placed his hands on the sofa cushion and hauled himself up so he was standing. He turned and—almost by mistake—let go, tottered for a moment, found his balance, and then took a step...and another step...and another until he reached Frederick and clutched at his legs for balance.

He looked down at his son—his son who had just taken his first steps. Amil had a look of utter awe on his face, as the life-changing knowledge had dawned on him—he could walk! Frederick's chest contracted with pride and wonderment as Amil turned and tottered back, with each step gaining confidence, until he reached the sofa and looked to Sunita for confirmation of his cleverness.

Sunita let out a laugh of sheer delight and flew across the room, scooped Amil up and spun him round. 'What a clever boy!' she said as she smothered him in kisses, before spinning to a halt right in front of Frederick.

Something twisted in his chest as he looked at them— a strand of emotion almost painful in its intensity. Sunita's face was slightly flushed, her tawny eyes were bright with happiness and pride, and it filled him with yearning. Like a boy locked out of the sweetshop for ever—doomed always to gaze at the sweets he could never, ever taste.

He forced a smile to his lips and hoped it didn't look as corpse-like as it felt. 'He is a very, *very* clever boy.'

Amil beamed at him and that strand tightened.

Frederick cleared his throat, turned slightly away. 'So, what's the plan?' he asked.

'First up we'll do a little press conference.'

'How can I do a press conference if I don't know where I'm going?'

'You'll have to let me do the talking.' She grinned at him. 'Don't look so worried. There are a million royal duties I am *not* equipped for, but I *am* good with the press.'

The words, though casually stated, held a shade of bitterness, but before he could do more than frown she had headed for the door.

Once in the palace grounds, with a knot of reporters, Amil proudly demonstrated his new ability and she seemed totally at ease.

'Hi, all. I've decided the Prince needs a day off—because even a ruler needs some down-time. So we are off on a family day out—I promise I'll take some pics, which I'll pass on to you. As I'm sure you all appreciate we are still a new family, so we'd appreciate some privacy.'

'And what about you, Sunita? Do *you* deserve a day off? Isn't it true you're headed back to the catwalk?'

'That's the plan—but I'll let you know more about that when I know the details.'

'Don't you feel you should focus on your role as Princess, like Lady Kaitlin would have?'

Frederick felt her tense, sensed her palpable effort to relax. 'Lady Kaitlin and I are two different people, so we are bound to approach the role differently.'

He stepped forward. 'Hey, guys, any questions for me? I'm feeling left out.'

The tactic worked and fifteen minutes later he wound the meeting down. 'OK, everyone, fun though this is, we need to head off.'

Sunita delivered the parting shot. 'Amil, wave to the nice reporters. That would be that one…that one…and that one.'

Not the one who had brought up Lady Kaitlin.

Laughter greeted this, and Sunita smiled. 'Have a great day—and, as I said, the pics will be with you soon!'

Once they were alone, Sunita nodded towards one of the palace cars. 'Hop in. We're off to Xanos Island.' She paused. 'I hope that's OK? Marcus suggested it.'

That surprised him. 'I'd like to take Amil there. Eloise used to take us. Me and Stefan and Axel, and Marcus as well, because he and Axel were best friends.'

'Eloise is Stefan's mother, correct?'

'Yes. She came after my mother, and she truly tried to be a good mother to Axel and me.'

'What happened?'

'Same old story. My father decided to divorce her and it all disintegrated into an awful custody battle. It ended up that she was allowed occasional visitation with Stefan, and only if she agreed not to see Axel or me.'

'That must have been tough on you and Axel.'

'Yes.'

The comprehension that he wouldn't see Eloise again, witnessing Stefan's fury and pain—it had all hurt. The emotions had been painful, until he'd locked the futile grief down, figured out that love could never be worth this type of loss. First his mother, then Eloise—never again.

'But let's not spoil the day—I want to make this a happy memory for Amil.'

'Then let's do that.'

Her smile lit the very air and he forced himself to turn away from it before he did something stupid. Something emotional.

The car slowed down at the small Lycandrian port, and minutes later they boarded the motor boat that would ferry them across. Frederick watched Amil's curiosity and joy at this unprecedented adventure, listened to Sunita as she broke into song and encouraged the Captain to join in.

Closing his eyes, he inhaled the salty tang of the sea breeze, absorbed the sound of her song and the cry of the curlews as they soared in the turquoise blue of the unclouded sky.

Once at the island they alighted and headed over the rocks to the beach, where Sunita produced buckets and spades and a large tartan blanket that she spread out over the sun-bleached sand. Amil sat down and waved a spade with energetic abandon and Sunita grinned as she handed another one to Frederick.

'Right. I thought we'd try and do a sand replica of the

Lycander palace—but I think the hard work may be down to you and me.'

The next hours skated by, and Frederick knew he would add this to his list of happy memories. Preventing Amil from eating sand, building turrets and digging moats, the good-natured bickering over the best way to make the walls secure, Amil walking in the sand, eating the picnic prepared by Gloria—it was all picture-perfect.

'We need to consider Gloria for the role of royal picnic-maker as well as royal nanny.'

'So you really *will* consider her? Give her a fair chance?'

'Of course. But in return I'd like *you* to do something.'

Tawny eyes narrowed. 'What's that?'

'Put a portfolio together and send it to a fashion design college. Or talk directly with an actual fashion house. You said to me that Gloria doesn't need formal qualifications to do the job—maybe you don't either.'

The sketches he'd seen the previous day showed talent—he knew it.

'Those sketches had a certain something about them that I suspect is unique to you—I think you should get them checked out.'

'I'll think about it,' she said, in a voice that was clearly humouring him as she pulled the picnic basket towards her. 'Mmm…chocolate cake.'

Frederick raised his eyebrows. 'Are you trying to change the subject?'

'How did you guess?'

'I'm bright like that. Come on, Sunita, why not send them off? What have you got to lose?'

She looked away from him, out over the dark blue crested waves that sculled gently towards the shore, towards the horizon where a ferry chugged purposefully.

Turning back to him, she shrugged. 'I could lose something precious. Those sketches kept me sane—they were my own private dream growing up. They represented hope that I wasn't totally worthless, not utterly stupid. I don't want to expose them to anyone. I've never shown them to a soul.'

And he understood why—she would have been terrified of the comments from her stepmother or sisters…she would have hoarded her talent and hugged it tight.

'Then maybe now is the time. Don't let them win—all those mean-spirited people who put you down. You've already proved your success to them.'

She shook her head. 'Only through modelling—that's dumb genetic luck, plus being in the right place at the right time. Fashion design requires a whole lot more than that.'

'I understand that you're scared—and I know it won't be easy—but if fashion design is your dream then you should go for it. Don't let them hold you back from your potential. Don't let what they did affect your life.'

'Why not? *You* are.'

He hadn't seen that one coming. 'Meaning…?'

'I think you're scared too.'

'Of what?'

'Of bonding with Amil.'

The words hit him, causing his breath to catch. She moved across the rug closer to him, contrition written all over her beautiful face.

'Sorry. I didn't mean that in a tit-for-tat way, or as an accusation. It's just I see how you look at him, with such love, but then I see how you hold back from being alone with him. You won't even hold him and I don't understand why.'

There was silence, and Frederick knew he needed to tell her. He couldn't bear her to believe he didn't *want* to hold his son.

'Because of dumb genetic luck.'

'I don't get it.'

'When I was eighteen I went to see my mum. I hoped that there had been some mistake—that my father had lied to me, that she hadn't really abandoned me and that there was some reason that would explain it all away. It turned out there was—she explained that she quite simply lacked the parenting gene.'

'She *said* that?'

'Yes.'

Her hands clenched into fists and her eyes positively blazed. 'Is *that* what you're scared of? That you lack the parenting gene?'

His gaze went involuntarily to his son, who lay asleep on the blanket, his bottom in the air, his impossibly long lashes sweeping his cheeks.

He couldn't answer—didn't need to. Even he could hear the affirmation in his silence.

'You don't.' Sunita leaned across, brushing his forearm in the lightest of touches. 'I can see how much you love Amil. You are not your mother *or* your father. You are *you*, and you are a great father—please believe that. Trust yourself. I promise I trust you.' She inhaled an audible breath. 'And I'll prove it to you.'

'What do you mean?' Panic began to unfurl as she rose to her feet.

'He's all yours. I'll see you back at the palace much later. Obviously call if there is an emergency—otherwise the boat will return for you in a few hours.'

Before he could react she started walking across the sand. He looked at his sleeping son. Obviously he couldn't leave Amil in order to chase after Sunita, which meant… which meant he was stuck here.

His brain struggled to work as he watched Sunita disappear over the rocks. If he called after her he would wake

Amil, and that was a bad plan. He stilled, barely daring to breathe as he watched the rise and fall of his son's chest. Maybe Amil would sleep for the next few hours…

As if he should be so lucky.

With impeccable timing Amil rolled over and opened his eyes just as the sound of the boat chug-chug-chugging away reached his ears. He looked round for his mother, failed to see her, and sat up and gazed at his father. Panicked hazel eyes met panicked hazel eyes and Amil began to wail.

Instinct took over—his need to offer comfort prompted automatic movement and he picked Amil up. He held the warm, sleepy bundle close to his heart and felt something deep inside him start to thaw. The panic was still present, but as Amil snuggled into him, as one chubby hand grabbed a lock of his hair and as the wails started to subside, so did the panic.

To be replaced by a sensation of peace, of unconditional love and an utter determination to keep this precious human being safe from all harm—to be there for him no matter what it took.

CHAPTER FOURTEEN

SUNITA GLANCED AT her watch and then back at the sketch-books spread out on the table. Thoughts chased each other round her brain—about Frederick and Amil; she hoped with all her heart that right now father and son had started the bonding process that would last a lifetime.

Her gaze landed back on the design sketches and she wondered whether Frederick had been right—that fear of rejection and self-doubt stood in her way. Just as they did in his. Could she pursue a dream? Or was it foolish for a woman with no qualifications to put her head above the parapet and invite censure? Or, worse, ridicule.

Another glance at her watch and she closed the books, piled them up and moved them onto a shelf. Instead she pulled out a folder—design ideas for the state rooms, where they would move after the wedding.

The door opened and she looked up as Frederick came in, Amil in his arms. There was sand in their hair and identical smiles on their faces. *Keep it cool...don't overreact.* But in truth her heart swelled to see them, both looking so proud and happy and downright cute.

'Did you have fun?'

'Yes, we did.'

'Fabulous. Tea is ready.'

'I thought maybe today *I* could feed him. Do his bath. Put him to bed.'

Any second now she would weep—Frederick looked as if a burden had been lifted from his shoulders.

'Great idea. In which case, if you don't mind, I've got a couple of errands to do. I'll be back for his bedtime.'

Frederick didn't need an observer—especially when Amil lobbed spaghetti Bolognese at him, as he no doubt would. And perhaps she could do something a little courageous as well. She needed to speak with Therese, the snooty seamstress, about her wedding dress.

Lycander tradition apparently had it that the royal seamstress had total input on the design of the dress, but surely the bride had a say as well. So maybe she would show Therese one of her designs.

Grabbing the relevant sketchbook, she blew Amil a kiss and allowed a cautious optimism to emerge as she made her way through the cavernous corridors to the Royal Sewing Room.

A knock on the door resulted in the emergence of one of Therese's assistants. 'Hi, Hannah, I wonder if Therese is around to discuss my dress.'

'She's popped out, but I know where the folder is. I'm sure she wouldn't mind you having a look.' Hannah walked over to a filing cabinet. 'I'll leave you to it.'

With that she scurried to an adjoining door and disappeared.

Sunita opened the folder and stared down at the picture—it was…was… Well, on the positive side it was classic—the designer a household name. On the negative side it was dull and unflattering. There didn't seem to be anything else in the folder, which seemed odd.

She headed to the door through which Hannah had disappeared, to see if there was another file, then paused as she heard the sound of conversation. She recognised Hannah's voice, and that of another assistant—Angela—and then the mention of her own name.

Of course she should have backed off there and then, taken heed of the old adage about eavesdroppers never hearing any good of themselves. But she didn't. Instead, breath held, she tiptoed forward.

'Do you think she knows?' asked Hannah.

'Knows what?' said Angela.

'That that's the dress Therese had designed for Lady Kaitlin—she was dead sure Lady K would marry Frederick. Everyone was, and everyone is gutted she didn't. Even that engagement ring—it was the one they had in mind for Kaitlin. Lady Kaitlin would have been a *proper* princess—everyone knows that. And she would have looked amazing in that dress—because it's regal and classic and not showy. As for Sunita—Frederick is only marrying her for the boy, which is dead good of him. He's a true prince. But Sunita can't ever be a true princess—she'll never fit in.'

Sunita closed her eyes as the flow of words washed over her in an onslaught of truth. Because that was what they were—words of truth. Otherwise known as facts. Facts that she seemed to have forgotten in the past weeks, somehow. She didn't know how she'd started to look at her marriage through rose-tinted glasses. How she had started to believe the fairy tale.

Fact: the sole reason for this marriage was Amil. Fact: Frederick's ideal bride would have been Lady Kaitlin or a woman of her ilk. Fact: fairy tales did not exist.

This must be what her mother had done—convinced herself that a handsome, charming English holidaymaker was her Prince, who would take her off into the sunset and a happy-ever-after. Perhaps that was what her father had done too—convinced himself that he could right past wrongs, that his family would welcome in his bastard child and everyone would live happily ever after.

Carefully she moved away from the door, leaving the folder on the desk, then picked up her sketchbook, and made her way out of the office, back along the marble floors, past the tapestry-laden walls, the heirlooms and antiquities collected over centuries, and back to her apartments.

She took a deep breath and composed her expression—this was a special day for Frederick and Amil and she would not spoil it.

Nor would she whinge and whine—there was no blame to be cast anywhere except at herself. Somehow she'd lost sight of the facts, but she wouldn't make that mistake again.

Entering the room, she halted on the threshold. Frederick sat on an armchair, Amil on his lap, looking down at a book of farm animals with intense concentration as Frederick read the simple sentences, and made all the noises with a gusto that caused Amil to chuckle with delight.

The book finished, Amil looked up and beamed at her and her heart constricted. Amil was the most important factor.

'Hey, guys. Looks like I'm back just in time.' Hard as she tried, she got it wrong—her voice was over-bright and a touch shaky, and Frederick's hazel eyes scanned her face in question.

'You OK?'

'I'm fine.' Walking over, she picked Amil up, hid her face under the pretext of a hug. 'How did tea and bath go?'

'Well, I have spaghetti down my shirt and bubbles in my hair, but we had fun, didn't we?'

'Abaadaaaaada!' Amil smiled and then yawned.

'I'll put him to bed.' Frederick rose and took Amil into his arms. Amil grizzled, but Frederick held on. 'Daddy's putting you to bed tonight, little fella. It'll be fine.'

And it was.

Fifteen minutes later Frederick emerged from Amil's bedroom, a smile on his face, headed to the drinks cabinet and pulled out a bottle of red wine.

Once they both had a glass in hand, he raised his. 'Thank you for today. You were right—I was afraid. Afraid I couldn't be a good parent...afraid I'd hurt him the way my parents hurt me. I thought doing nothing would be better than getting it wrong. Now I really hope that I can be a better parent than mine were, and can create a real bond with my son.'

The words made her happy—truly happy—and she wanted to step forward, to get close and tell him that, show him that happiness. But she didn't. Because close was dangerous—close had landed her in this scenario where she had distorted the facts with perilous consequence.

Perhaps it had been that magical physical intimacy in Goa, or maybe it had been a mistake to confide in him, to share her background and her fears and dreams. Whatever. No point in dwelling on the mistakes. Now it was vital not to repeat them.

So instead she stepped backwards and raised her glass. 'I'll drink to that. I'm so very pleased for you and Amil.'

And she was. But to her own horror, mixed into that pleasure was a thread of misery that she recognised as selfish. Because his love for Amil had never been in doubt—it had simply needed a shift in the dynamic of their relationship. A shift that had highlighted exactly what Sunita was—a by-product, a hanger-on, exactly as she been in her father's family. There only by default, by an accident of birth.

Well, she was damned if she would sit around here for the rest of her life being a by-product.

'Earth to Sunita?'

His voice pulled her out of her thoughts and she manufactured a smile, floundered for a topic of conversation. Her gaze fell on a folder—her plans for the state apartments.

'Would you mind having a look at this? I wanted your opinion before I went ahead.'

She picked up the file, opened it and pulled out the pictures, gazed down at them and winced. Every detail that she'd pored over so carefully screamed happy families—she'd done some of the sketches in 3D and, so help her, she'd actually imagined the three of them skipping around the place in some family perfect scene.

For their bedroom she'd chosen a colour scheme that mixed aquamarine blue with splashes of red. The double bed was a luxurious invitation that might as well have *bliss* written all over it.

She had to face it—her vision had included steamy nights with Frederick and lazy Sunday mornings with a brood of kids bouncing up and down. What had happened to her? This was a room designed with *love*.

This was a disaster. *Love*. She'd fallen in love.

Idiot, idiot, idiot.

Frederick frowned. 'Are you sure you're OK?'

Reaching out, he plucked the pictures from her hand and she forced herself not to clutch onto them. *Think*. Before he looked at the pictures and figured it out. *Think*. Because even if he didn't work it out she couldn't share a room with him—that would take intimacy to insane levels, and Frederick was no fool. He'd realise that she had done the unthinkable and fallen for him.

As he scanned the pictures desperation came to her aid. 'I wondered which bedroom you wanted.'

His head snapped up and his eyebrows rose. He placed

the papers on the table. 'I assumed from these pictures that we would be sharing a room.'

Picking up her wine glass, she met his gaze. 'As I understood it, royal tradition dictates separate bedrooms and I assumed you'd prefer that.' Or at least she *should* have assumed that. 'However, obviously there will be some occasions when we *do* share—hence the design. If you want that bedroom I'll design the second one as mine. But if you don't then I'll take that one and we can discuss how you want yours to be.'

Stop, already. He'd got the gist of it and now she sounded defensive. Worse, despite herself, there was a hint of a question in the nuances of her tone, and a strand of hope twisted her heart. Hope that he'd take this opportunity to persuade her to share a room.

'What do you think?'

He sipped his wine, studied her expression, and she fought to keep her face neutral.

'I think this is some sort of trick question.'

'No trick. It's a simple need to know so I can complete the design. Also, as you know, I'll be giving an interview once the renovations are done, so it depends what you think the people of Lycander would prefer to see. We can pretend we share a room, if you think that would go down better, or…'

Shut up, Sunita.

Just because full-scale panic was escalating inside her, it didn't mean verbal overload had to implode. But she couldn't help herself.

'And then there is Amil to think about. I'm not sure that he should grow up thinking this sort of marriage is right.'

'Whoa! What is *that* supposed to mean? "This sort of marriage"? You say it like there's something wrong with it.'

'There *is* something wrong with it.'

It was almost as if her vocal cords had taken on a life of their own.

'Is this the sort of marriage you want Amil to have? An alliance? Presumably brokered by us? A suitable connection? Perhaps he will be lucky enough to get his own Lady Kaitlin. *Hell.*' She snapped her fingers. 'Perhaps we should get dibs on her first-born daughter.'

'Stop.' His frown deepened as he surveyed her expression. 'What is going on here? We agreed how our marriage would work—we agreed what we both wanted.'

'No, we didn't. I didn't want to get married at all. *You* did.'

'And you agreed.'

'Because there was no other choice.' She closed her eyes. 'There still isn't. But when Amil gets married I don't want it to be like this.'

For her son she wanted the fairy tale—she wanted Amil to love someone and be loved in return and live happily ever after. *The End.*

'There is nothing *wrong* with this.' His voice was urgent now, taut with frustration and more than a hint of anger. 'Amil will see two parents who respect each other, who are faithful to each other, who are polite to each other. There will be no uncertainty, no banged doors and no voices raised in constant anger. He'll have two parents who are there for him—I think he'll take that. God knows, *I* would have. And so would you.'

Touché. He was right. The problem was this wasn't about Amil. It was about her. *She* wanted the fairy tale. Her whole being cried out at the idea of a marriage of civility. Her very soul recoiled from the thought of spending the rest of her life tied to a man she loved who would never see her as more than the mother of his children—a woman he'd married through necessity not choice.

But she'd made a deal and she'd honour it. For Amil's sake. She wouldn't wrest Amil from his father, wouldn't take away his birthright. But neither would she stick around and moon in lovelorn stupidity. The only way forward was to kill love before it blossomed—uproot the plant now, before it sank its roots into her heart.

So she dug deep, conjured up a smile and said, 'You're right. I just had a mad moment.' She gave a glance at her watch. 'Anyway, don't you need to go? I thought you had a meeting about the casino bill?'

He hesitated. The frown still hadn't left his face. 'We'll talk in the morning.'

'Sure.'

Pride kept her cool, enigmatic smile in place as he turned and left the room. Then, ignoring the ache that squeezed her heart in a vicelike grip, she picked up her mobile.

'Harvey. It's me. We need to talk.'

The next morning Frederick approached the door to Sunita and Amil's apartments, forcing his steps to remain measured, forcing himself not to dwell on the previous night's conversation with Sunita. But her words still pummelled his conscience.

I didn't want to get married. You did. There was no choice. There still isn't...

The unpleasant edge of discomfort bit into him.

Shades of his father.

He knocked on the door and entered, glanced around for Amil. Anxiety unfurled as he looked around and saw only Sunita at the table. 'Where's Amil?'

'With Gloria. I need to talk with you.'

Dressed in a simple white three-quarter-sleeved dress, belted with a striped blue and red band, she looked both elegant and remote. The only indication of nerves was the twist of her hands.

Sudden familiarity hit him—she'd had the same stance two years before, when she'd been about to leave. Panic grew inside him and he forced himself to keep still.

'Is anything wrong?'

'No. I've signed a modelling contract. Effective pretty much immediately. We need to discuss the details.'

'Immediately? But you said you wouldn't sign a contract straight away.'

'And I didn't. The first time the offer came in I refused. But now they have upped the ante and agreed to schedule the shoots around my commitments here. I'd be a fool to pass it up.'

A bleakness started to descend…a strange hollow pang of emptiness. 'What about Amil?'

'The first shoot is in India—in Mumbai. I'll take Amil with me. We can stay with Nanni. Thereafter, whenever I can take him I will, or I will leave him in Lycander with you. Gloria will be here, and I will also ask Nanni if she can come and stay.'

She handed him a piece of paper with her schedule printed out.

Frederick frowned. 'This can't possibly have been arranged since last night.'

'No. Harvey was approached a few weeks ago—right after our first press release. The brand had dropped the model they had planned to use due to her lifestyle. They thought of me. I refused—but now I've changed my mind and luckily they still want me.'

'You didn't think to discuss this with me at all?'

'No. Any more than you discuss state business with *me*. Part of our marriage agreement was that I would resume my career as long as I fitted it around Lycander's needs. I understand some people may not approve, but to be honest with you a lot of people won't approve of me no matter what I do. The people wanted Kaitlin. I can't be her, or be like her. I will not try to fit into a box I'll never tick. I spent too many years doing that.'

Frederick knew there were things he should say, things he needed to say, but the words quite simply wouldn't formulate. All he wanted to do was tug her into his arms and beg her to stay—but that was not an option.

Because Sunita didn't want this marriage—she never had. He'd forced it upon her, caught her between a rock and a hard place. Self-disgust soured his tongue, froze his limbs. He was no better than his father. He had ridden roughshod over her wish not to marry him; he'd inveigled and manoeuvred and blazed down the trail he wanted regardless of her wishes. Worse, he'd bolstered himself with pious justifications.

But it was too late to stop the wedding, to release her from their marriage agreement—it would be an impossibility, the impact on Lycander, on Amil, too harsh.

Just Lycander? Just Amil? queried a small voice.

Of course. It made no difference to him. It *couldn't* make a difference to him

Why not?

The small voice was getting on his nerves now. It couldn't because he wouldn't let it. Over the past few weeks Sunita had very nearly slipped under his skin, and that way led to disaster, to pain and loss, to messy emotions that got in the way of a calm, ordered life. That would ruin this marriage before it even got underway.

The silence had stretched so taut now he could bounce off it. One of the terms of their marriage agreement *had* included her right to a career and he would not stand in the way. So he said, 'I understand. You're right to go.'

He looked down at the schedule again, but couldn't meet her gaze, couldn't seem to quell the spread of cold emptiness through his body and soul.

'I'll talk to Marcus—if you need to miss any functions I'll let him know it's OK. I know how important this contract is for you—anything I can do to help, I will.'

'Thank you. I appreciate that.'

He nodded, and yet still that desolation pervaded him, even as that unsquashable small voice exhorted him to *do* something. *Anything*.

But he couldn't. It wasn't in him. So instead he headed for the door.

One week later—Lycander Council Room

Frederick threw the pen across his desk and watched it skitter across the polished wood. Concentration wouldn't come. The words on the document blurred and jumped and somehow unerringly formed into images of Sunita. *Ridiculous.*

Shoving the wedge of paper away, he sighed, and then looked up at the perfunctory knock on the door.

Seconds later he eyed his chief advisor in surprise. 'What's wrong?'

'Nothing. I thought you could do with a break. You've been closeted in here for hours. Days.'

'A break?' Frederick looked at Marcus blankly. 'Since when do you care about me having a rest?'

'Since you gave up on both sleep *and* food. So how about we grab a beer, shoot the breeze…?'

Frederick wondered if Marcus had perhaps already grabbed a few beers—though there was nothing in the other man's demeanour to suggest any such thing.

'Are you suggesting you and I go and have a beer?'

'Yes.'

'Why?'

Marcus shrugged. 'Why not?'

'Because I'm pretty damn sure you'd rather shoot yourself in the foot than have a beer with me.'

Dark eyebrows rose. 'Feeling tetchy?'

Damn right he was. Sunita had been gone for a week and his whole world felt…*wrong*…out of kilter. And he hated it. He loathed it that he didn't seem able to switch these emotions off. However hard he twisted the tap, they trickled on and on. Relentlessly.

'No. Just being honest. So, what gives?'

'I'm your chief advisor, right?'

'Right.'

'So here's some advice. Go after Sunita.'

'Sunita is in Mumbai on a photo shoot—why would I do that?'

'Because I think you love her.'

Frederick blinked, wondered if this conversation was a hallucination. 'Then you think wrong. You *know* all this— we're getting married because of Amil and for Lycander.'

'You can't kid a kidder. But, more importantly, why kid yourself?'

'With all due respect, has it occurred to you that this is a bit out of your remit?'

'Yes, it has.' Marcus started to pace the office, as he had so many times in the past year. 'But I'm talking to you now as Axel's best friend. I know Axel wouldn't want you to throw this away.'

Guilt and self-loathing slammed Frederick so hard he could barely stay upright. 'Hold it right there. You *don't* know what Axel would want.'

'Yes, I do. He'd want you to get on with life. *Your* life.

Right now you're getting on with Axel's life, fulfilling his vision. I think Axel would want you to fulfil your own.'

Frederick searched for words before guilt choked him. He needed Marcus to stop—he couldn't listen to this any more.

'The accident... Axel's death was my fault. *I* should have been in that car. *I* was meant to go that state dinner. I passed it off to Axel.'

'I know.' Marcus's voice was measured. 'Axel was supposed to meet up with me that night. He told me you'd asked him to go because you had a party to go to. To celebrate a buy-out that no one thought you'd pull off.'

A buy-out he now wished he'd never tried for—if he could have pulled out any domino from the cause-and-effect chain he would. Most of all, though, he wished he hadn't chosen a party over duty.

He watched as Marcus continued to stride the floor. 'So why did you take this job with me? Why didn't you tell me you knew the truth?'

'I did what I believed Axel would have wanted. Axel was my best friend—we climbed trees as boys and we double-dated as young men. A few days before the accident he was trying to get up the courage to ask my sister on a date—he'd joke that he wished he had your charm. He cared about you very much, and he wouldn't have wanted you to punish yourself for the rest of your life.'

Marcus halted in front of the desk and leant forward, his hands gripping the edge.

'You didn't know what would happen—you didn't send Axel to his death.'

'But if I had chosen not to party, not to do what I wanted to do, then Axel would be alive now.'

Marcus shrugged. 'Maybe. But it didn't pan out like that. You can't turn the clock back, but you can make the most of your time now. I think you love Sunita, and if you do then you need to go for it—before you lose her. Axel's death should show you how life can change in a heartbeat—don't waste the life you've got. Axel wouldn't want it. And, for what it's worth, neither do I.'

Frederick stared at him. Emotions tumbled around him—poignant regret that Axel had never had the chance to ask Marcus's sister on a date, grief over the loss of his brother, a loss he had never allowed himself time to mourn, and gratitude that Marcus had given him a form of re-demption.

'Thank you.'

There wasn't anything else he could say right now. Later there would be time. Time to grab those beers and sit and talk about Axel, remember him and mourn him. But now…

'Can I leave you at the helm? I need to go to Mumbai.'

'Good luck.'

Frederick had the feeling he'd need it.

Mumbai

•

Sunita smiled at Nanni across the kitchen, listened to the comforting whirr of the overhead fan, the sizzle of *malpua* batter as it hit the heated pan. Ever since Nanni had first made these sweet dessert pancakes Sunita had loved them.

'You don't have to make me breakfast every morning, Nanni, but I do so appreciate it.''

'If I didn't you would eat nothing. And you do not need to stay in with me every night. I am sure there are parties and social events.'

'I'd rather be here.'

Totally true. She didn't want to socialise; she was too tired. Sleep deprivation, combined with the effort it took to work when all she wanted was to be back in Lycander.

Irony of ironies, she wanted to be in a place that had rejected her, with a man who had rejected her. What a fool she was. But she'd be damned if anyone would know it—she'd dug deep, pulled up every professional reserve and hopefully pulled the wool over Nanni's eyes as well.

'You aren't happy.'

So much for the wool pulling endeavour.

Nanni put her plate in front of her; the scent of cardamom and pistachio drifted upward.

'Of course I am. The job is going great, I'm back in Mumbai, Amil is here and I'm with my favourite grandmother.'

'And yet you still aren't happy. You can lie to me, Suni. But don't lie to yourself.'

'Sometimes you *have* to lie to yourself—if you do it for long enough the lie will become the truth.'

Or that was her theory. And, yes, there were holes and flaws in it, but it was a work in progress.

'That still doesn't make it *actual* truth,' Nanni pointed out with irrefutable logic. 'Do you no longer wish to marry Frederick?'

'I have no choice.'

'Yes, you do. There is always a choice—however hard a one it is. If you do not love him, don't marry him.'

'I *do* love him, Nanni. But he doesn't love me.' Tears threatened and she blinked them back.

'How do you know?'

'Because he has made it pretty clear.'

'By action or word?'

'What do you mean?'

'Love is not all about declarations—it is about demonstration. I told your mother how much I loved her repeatedly, but when the time came for me to show that, to fight for her, I failed miserably.'

'But you still loved her, Nanni, and she knew that. She never blamed you—she blamed her father.'

'At least *he* had the courage of his convictions—he did what he did because he believed it to be right. I was a coward—I loved Leela, but not enough to fight for that love. It is one of the biggest regrets of my life, Suni—that I didn't fight for her, for *you*. So all I would say is think about your Frederick, and if there is a chance that he loves you then fight for that chance.'

Sunita stared down at her somehow empty plate and wondered if she were brave enough—brave enough to risk rejection and humiliation. And even if she was...

'I don't fit, Nanni. Even if he loved me I can't live up to Lady Kaitlin.'

'You don't need to live up to anyone—you just have to be yourself. Now, go,' Nanni said. 'Or you will be late for work.'

Frederick approached the site of the photo shoot, where the Gateway of India loomed in the twilight, its basalt stone lit up to create a magical backdrop, the turrets adding a fairy tale element for the photographer to take full advantage of.

The square was cordoned off for the shoot, and he joined the curious pedestrians who had stopped to watch. The people behind the cordon were packing up, so he slipped under the ropes, ignored the protest of a woman who approached

'Sir, I'm sorry, but...' There was a pause as she recognised him.

'I'm here to see Sunita.'

'Is she expecting you?'

'No. I thought I'd surprise her.'

'And you have.'

He spun round at the sound of Sunita's voice; his heart

pounded, his gut somersaulted. She wore a square-necked red dress, in some sort of stretchy material that moulded her figure and fell to her knees in a simple drop.

'Is everything all right?'

'Yes. I want to…to talk.'

She hesitated and then nodded.

'OK. I'm done here. We can go by the wall over there and look out at the sea, if you like.'

'Perfect.'

'Are you sure everything is all right?' Concern was evident in her tone now, as she looked at him.

'Yes. No. I don't know.'

And he didn't—after all, this could be the most important conversation of his life and he could totally screw it up. He could lose her.

'I need to tell you something.'

'Actually, there is something I need to tell you as well.' Her hands twisted together and she looked away from him, out at the boats that bobbed on the murky water.

'Could I go first?' *Before he bottled it.*

She nodded.

'First I need to tell you about Axel. The accident that killed him—*I* should have been in the car. He took my place because I'd decided to go a party—a celebration of a buy-out deal. He not only took my place, he totally covered for me. He told everyone that it had been his idea, that he'd wanted to attend and I'd given up my place.'

Her beautiful brown eyes widened, and then without hesitation she moved closer to him. 'I am so very sorry. I cannot imagine what you went through—what you must still be going through. But please listen to me. It was *not* your fault—you did not know what would happen.'

'I know that, but…'

'But it doesn't help. I understand. I understand how

many times you must think *if only* or *what if?* But you mustn't. I spent years thinking what if my mother hadn't died? What if she hadn't handed me over to my father? What if I could somehow have won his love? My stepmother's love. My sister's love? It made me question how I felt about my mother and it ate away at my soul—like this is eating away at yours. You can't know what would have happened. Axel might have died anyway. Your action wasn't deliberate—you wished Axel no harm.'

'That's what Marcus said.'

'He's a good man.'

'Yes.'

Frederick took a deep breath, looked at her beautiful face, her poise and grace, the compassion and gentleness and empathy in her gorgeous eyes.

'He said something else as well…'

Suddenly words weren't enough—he couldn't encompass how he felt in mere words. So instead he pushed away from the wall, and when she turned he sank to one knee.

'Frederick…?'

He could taste the sea spray, see the expression on her face of confusion, and hope soared in his heart as he took her left hand in his and removed the huge, heavy diamond—a ring chosen by someone else. He delved into his pocket and pulled out a box, purchased earlier from one of Mumbai's many jewellers.

'Will you marry me? For real. Not for Amil, not for Lycander, but because I love you. Heart, body and soul. Because I want to spend the rest of my life with you, wake up with you every morning. I want to live my life side by side with you. I want us to rule together, to laugh together, to live a life full of *all* the emotions. So, will you marry me? For real?'

His heart pounded and his fingers shook as he opened the box and took the ring out.

Her breathless laugh was caught with joy, the smile on her face so bright and beautiful his heart flipped.

'Yes. I *will* marry you. For real. Because I love you. That's what I wanted to tell you. That I love you. I didn't think in a million years that you could possibly love me back, but I wanted to tell you anyway. Heart, body and soul—they are all yours.'

He slipped the ring onto her finger and she lifted her hand in the air, watching the red and aquamarine stones interspersed with diamonds glint in the light of the setting sun.

'It's beautiful. Perfect.'

'I'm sorry about the other ring.'

'It makes this one all the more special. Did I mention I love it? Did I mention I love *you*?'

He rose to his feet. 'You did, but you can say it as many times as you like—those words won't ever get old.'

'No. Though Nanni says we have to back the words up. That love isn't only words—it's actions.' She stepped forward and looped her arms round his waist, snuggled in close. 'You *are* sure, aren't you? Sure this is real?'

'I have never been more sure of anything. I think I loved you from the start—I just couldn't admit it. Not to you, not to myself. You see, I didn't feel I deserved this joy.'

Her arms tightened around him. 'Because of Axel?'

'Partly. But even before that. I had parents who didn't give a damn—a mother who sold me for a crock of gold and a father who saw all his children as pawns or possessions. Love wasn't in the equation. Then I saw how much pain and angst love can cause—saw how losing Stefan tore Eloise apart. It was the same with Nicky, the twins' mother. My parents, who eschewed love, were happy and everyone else who *did* love was made miserable through that love. So I never wanted love to hold me hostage. I could see that emotions led to misery—that life was easier to control without emotion.

'Even two years ago you were different. But then you left, and Axel died, and I froze every emotion in order to cope. When you came back into my life all the emotions I'd bottled up for years kept surging up and I couldn't seem to shut them down any more. I didn't know what to do. I couldn't succumb to them because that was way too scary and it felt *wrong*. Axel died because of me. He'll never have the chance to live and love, have children, so how could it be right for me?'

'I am so very sorry about Axel, but I am sure he wouldn't have wanted you to give up on happiness.'

'I think you're right. Marcus seems sure of that too. And I know that if anything happened to me I wouldn't want *you* to shut your life down. I'd want you to live it to the full.'

'Nothing will to happen to you.' Her voice was fierce. 'And if it did I would never regret loving you.'

Frederick's heart swelled with the sheer wonder that he would share his life with this wonderful woman—and share it for real. The ups and the downs…everything.

He grinned down at her. 'I am so happy it doesn't seem possible. I never believed in my wildest dreams that you would love me too. I was willing to beg, fight—do whatever it took to persuade you to give me a chance to win your love.'

'You won that long ago but, like you, it took me a long time to admit it. I think deep down I knew the day I left you on the island with Amil. I couldn't have done that if I didn't trust you completely. And trust… I always thought that was for mugs and fools. My mother trusted my father once and ended up pregnant and abandoned. She trusted him again and it didn't end well for me. Fool me once, shame on you—fool me twice, shame on me. I figured it was best never to be fooled at all. Which meant the only way forward was never to trust anyone. But I trusted *you*. Even two years ago on some level I trusted you, or I would never have slept with you. But even after the island it all seemed so hard—you were so distant. And I felt like I used to—that I didn't fit. Everywhere I went people compared me to Kaitlin and…'

'You should have told me.'

'I couldn't. After all, you said that Kaitlin was your ideal bride.'

'I'm an idiot.' He cupped her face in his hands. 'I swear to you that you are the only bride I could ever want. Not because of Amil. Not because of Lycander. But because you are you and I *love* you. You make me whole. And if anyone makes any comparisons you send them to me.'

'No need. I've worked out where I've gone wrong—in my assumption that Kaitlin is better than me. She isn't— she is just different. I need to be a princess *my* way. Need to be myself.'

'And I know that means being a model—I will support your career every way I can.'

'About that… I'd better 'fess up. I'm not enjoying it one bit. I miss you and Amil… I miss Lycander. So I will fulfil this contract, but after that I will put a fashion portfolio together and send it off. And I also want to work for Lycander. I want to make it a fashion mecca—maybe set up a fashion show. One day we could rival Paris and London… There are so many options. But, whatever I de-cide, as long as you are by my side I know it will be OK.'

'Ditto.'

As he pulled her into his arms he knew this was the best alliance he could have ever made—because the only thing on the table was love.

* * * * *

THEIR HOT
HAWAIIAN FLING

TRACI DOUGLASS

May there always be warmth in your Hale,
fish in your net,
and Aloha in your heart.

Traditional Hawaiian Blessing

CHAPTER ONE

"Sir, can you tell me your name?" Dr. Leilani Kim asked as she shone a penlight to check her newest patient's eyes. "Pupils equal and reactive. Sir, do you remember what happened? Can you tell me where you are?"

"Get that thing outta my face," the man said, squinting, his words slightly slurred from whatever substance currently flooded his system. "I ain't telling you my name. I know my rights."

"How many fingers am I holding up?" she asked.

"Four." He scowled. "How many am I holding up?"

She ignored his rude gesture and grabbed the stethoscope around her neck to check his vitals. "Pulse 110. Breathing normal. Blood pressure?"

"One-thirty over 96, Doc," one of the nurses said from the other side of the bed.

"Find any ID at the accident scene?" Leilani asked over her shoulder to the EMTs standing near the door of the trauma bay. "Any idea what he's on?"

"Cops got his license," one of the EMTs said, a young woman name Janet. "His name's Greg Chambers. According to the officer who ran his plates, he has a history of DUIs and a couple arrests for meth too."

"Great." It wasn't, in fact, great. It was exhausting

and brought up a lot of memories Leilani would just as soon forget, but that wouldn't be professional, and she couldn't afford to seem anything but perfect these days with the Emergency Medicine directorship up for grabs.

A quick check for signs of distress on the guy—airway, breathing, circulation—all seemed intact and normal. Next, she moved to palpate the patient's torso and extremities. "Do you have pain anywhere other than your head, Mr. Chambers? Can you feel your arms and legs?"

"I feel you poking and prodding me, if that's what you mean." The guy groaned and raised a hand to the bandages covering his scalp. "My head hurts."

"Smashing it into a windshield will do that," Leilani said, finding no evidence of broken bones or internal bleeding on exam. She returned to his head wound. He was lucky. If only the people Leilani had loved most in the world had been so fortunate.

She blinked hard against the unwanted prickle of tears. Must be the exhaustion. Had to be. She never let her personal feelings interfere with her duties.

"Everything okay, Doc?" Pam, the nurse, asked while adjusting the patient's heart monitor.

"Fine. Thanks." Leilani gave her a curt nod, then turned to the paramedics again. "Any other casualties from the accident?"

"Other than the palm tree he hit at forty miles per hour?" Peter, the other EMT, said. "No. No other passengers or vehicles involved, thank goodness. When we arrived, the patient was standing outside his vehicle, texting on his phone. He took one look at us and complained of neck pain before collapsing on the ground claiming he couldn't stand."

"Where's my truck?" Mr. Chambers grumbled.

"Your vehicle is a total loss, sir," Leilani said, hackles rising. People died because idiots like this guy drove under the influence. She checked the laceration on his head.

"No!" He wrenched his arm away from the phlebotomist who'd arrived to take his blood. "You can't take it without my consent. I know my rights."

Energy and patience running low, Leilani fixed the man with a pointed stare. "You keep complaining about your rights, Mr. Chambers, but what about the rights of the other people on the road who just wanted to get home to their family and friends? You put innocent lives at risk driving while intoxicated. What about *their* rights?"

His chin jutted out. "Not my problem."

It will be, if your test results come back positive, she thought, but didn't say it out loud.

Leilani had dealt with her share of belligerent patients during her ten years working at Honolulu's Ohana Medical Center, but this guy took the cake. She turned to Pam. "Call radiology and see if they can get him in for a stat skull X-ray, please. Also, we need a Chem Seven, tox screen and blood alcohol level." Then, to the phlebotomist, "Strap his arm down if needed."

"I'm no addict," the guy yelled, trying to get up and setting off the alarms on the monitors. "Let me out of here."

Several orderlies stepped forward to hold the guy down as Leilani recorded her findings in the patient's file on her tablet.

"How much have you had to drink tonight, sir?" she asked, glancing up.

"Few beers," the patient said, shrugging.

The scent of booze had been heavy on his breath, and Leilani raised a skeptical brow. Based on his delayed reaction times during her exam and his uncoordinated movements, he'd had way more than he was letting on. "And?"

"A couple shots of whiskey."

"And?"

His lips went thin.

Right. Her simmering anger notched higher. The fact someone could be so reckless as to get behind the wheel when they were obviously impaired sent a fresh wave of furious adrenaline through her.

Movements stiff with tension, she set her tablet aside and returned to the bandages on the guy's forehead, peeling them back to reveal a large bruise and several small cuts. She dictated her findings as she went. "On exam there are no obvious skull fractures. Several small lacerations to the forehead and a golf-ball-sized hematoma over the left eye. No obvious foreign bodies seen in the wounds, though we'll need the X-rays to confirm. Sutures aren't necessary, but Pam, can you please clean and dress this again." She glanced over at the EMTs once more. "You said he hit the windshield?"

"Glass starred from the impact."

"Okay. Let's examine your spine next, Mr. Chambers."

"No." He attempted to climb off the bed again. "I want to go home."

"You're not going anywhere until I sign the discharge papers and the police release you from custody," Leilani said, leveraging her weight to hold her uncooperative patient down. People always assumed because she was petite she couldn't handle it if things got rough. What those same folks didn't know was that she was an excellent kickboxer and had already survived way more hardship than most people faced in a lifetime. She was more than capable of fighting her own battles.

"Cops? Aw. Hell. No." The patient gave Leilani a quick once-over. "What are you, ten?"

"Thirty-four, actually." She opened his brace with one hand and carefully palpated his neck with the other, moving her fingers along his spine before cupping his head and turning it slowly from side to side. "No step-offs. Pam please order a stat spinal series as well, since he complained of difficulty walking at the accident scene. Mr. Chambers, were you wearing a seat belt at the time of the accident?"

"Nah. Don't like them. Too confining."

That was kind of the point. Seat belts saved lives. She was proof.

The phlebotomist finished drawing her last vial of blood, then placed a bandage on the patient's arm. "I'll get this right up to the lab, Dr. Kim."

"Thanks." Leilani picked up her tablet once more. "Patient has a possible concussion and will need observation for the next twenty-four hours. Pam, make sure the jail can accommodate that order."

"Will do, Doc," Pam said.

"I ain't going to jail," Mr. Chambers snarled.

"The police might think differently. You caused quite a bit of property damage, from what I've been told, and this isn't your first offense." Leilani rubbed the nape of her neck, her fingers brushing over the scar there. Twenty years since the accident that had changed her life forever, but the memories still brought a fresh wave of pain.

"Police are ready to question the patient whenever you're finished, Dr. Kim," Pam said, hiking her head toward the two uniformed officers standing just outside the door.

"Okay." Leilani turned back to the patient. "Almost done, Mr. Chambers. Just a few more questions."

"Not saying another word," the man said, his scowl dark. "Told you I know my rights."

"Anything I can help with, Dr. Kim?" a new voice said, deep and distracting as hell.

Leilani turned to see Dr. Holden Ross wedging his way between the cops and into the room as Pam was leaving to call in her orders. Ugh. Just what she didn't need. The ER's new locum tenens trauma surgeon barging into her case uninvited. He'd only been here a month, so perhaps he didn't know any better, but it still irked her. She didn't do well with people overstepping her boundaries. She'd worked hard to put up those walls over the years, both professionally and personally. Letting people too close only meant a world of hurt and trouble when they left. And in Leilani's experience, everyone left eventually. Sometimes with no warning at all.

The fact his gorgeous smile filled her stomach with anxious butterflies had nothing to do with it.

She straightened and smoothed her hand down the front of her white lab coat, giving him a polite smile to cover her annoyance. "No. I've got it, thank you, Dr. Ross. Just finishing up."

"Got something you can finish up right here, darlin'." The patient shot her a lewd look and grabbed his crotch.

How charming. Not.

Holden's expression quickly sharpened as he moved to the patient's bedside, his limp drawing her attention once more. She wondered what had caused it before she could stop herself, though it was none of her business. His metal cane clinked against the bedside rails as he glared down into the drunken man's face, his stern frown brimming with warning. "Show Dr. Kim some respect. She's here to save your life."

"I appreciate your concern, Dr. Ross," Leilani said, clearing her throat. "But I've got this. I'm sure there are other patients for you to deal with."

"Actually, I'm just coming on shift." He leaned back, his gaze still locked on the patient. "Fill me in on this guy, so I can take over after you leave."

Darn. He was right. Her shift was over soon, and she needed to get home and rest. Leilani looked over at her colleague again. Holden looked as fresh and bright as a new penny, while she probably looked as ragged as she felt. Add in the fact she seemed irrationally aware of his presence today—not just as a colleague, but as a man—and her stress levels skyrocketed.

The last thing she needed right now was an ill-advised attraction to her coworker.

Distracted, Leilani turned away to futz with her tablet. "What time is it now?"

"Quarter past six," Holden said, moving around the bed to stand next to her. He propped a hip against the edge of the counter, using his cane to take the weight off his right leg. "Your shift ended fifteen minutes ago."

The low hum of the automatic blood pressure cuff inflating on the patient's arm filled the silence. Gossip was already flying amongst the staff about how handsome, intriguing Dr. Ross had ended up at Ohana. Everything from a bad breakup to a good recommendation from some powerful donors. There was one rumor, however, that concerned Leilani the most—that he'd come to their facility at the request of the hospital's chief administrator, Dr. Helen King, and that he was in line for the same directorship she wanted.

Ugh. She shook off the thoughts. None of that mattered at present. She had a patient to deal with. Plus, it was silly to operate off rumor and conjecture. She was a woman of science; she dealt with facts and figures, concrete ideas. Nothing silly or scary like gossip or emotions. Acting on "what-if"s and messy feelings could bring a person to their knees if they weren't careful. Leilani should know.

Pam poked her head into the room again. "Sorry to interrupt, but Dr. Ross, there's a new arrival for you. Female with abdominal pain for the last six hours."

"Duty calls." Holden held Leilani's gaze a moment longer before pushing away from the counter to scan the tablet computer Pam handed him. Leilani found herself unable to stop watching him, darn it. Her curiosity about him was a mystery. Sure, he was charming and would've been just her type, with those dark good looks and soulful hazel eyes. Not to mention he was more than competent at his job, according to the residents on staff. Neither of those reasons was good enough to go poking around into things that were better left unexplored though. Besides, Dr. Ross would hopefully be gone once a suitable replacement for his position was found. Leilani's life was here, in her native Hawaii, and right now her attention was on her career.

There'd be plenty of time for a personal life later. *Maybe.*

Shaking off the odd pang of loneliness pinching her

chest, she continued to complete her documentation while Holden rattled off his orders for Pam.

"Okay. Let's start by running an HCG to make sure the new patient's not pregnant, since she's not had a hysterectomy," Holden said, tapping his tablet screen several more times. "I've added a couple of additional tests as well to get things rolling."

"Thanks, Dr. Ross." Pam took the tablet and disappeared around the corner once more, leaving just the two of them and the patient in the trauma bay again.

Leilani stayed determined to power on through because that's what she did. She was a survivor, in more ways than one. She swallowed hard and rubbed her neck again. The scars reminded her how life could change in a second. There was no time to waste.

Her patient's snores filled the air and she shook the man gently awake. "Mr. Chambers? Can you tell me where you are?"

He squinted his eyes open and scrunched his nose. "Why are you asking me this crap?"

"Because you could have a concussion." She glanced over at Holden and gave a resigned sigh. He obviously wasn't going to leave until she shared the case details with him. Seemed he was as stubborn as she was. Not a good sign. After another resigned sigh, she ran through the details for him. "Single car MVA. Male, twenty-six years old, drove his pickup truck into a tree. Head struck windshield. Denies lack of consciousness. He's alert and—"

"Let me go, dammit!" The patient flailed on the bed and clawed at the neck brace. "Get this thing off me!"

"Combative," Leilani finished, giving Holden a look before returning her attention to Mr. Chambers. "Sir, tell me where you are, and I'll get you something for the pain."

He rattled off the hospital's name, then held out his hand. "Where's my OxyContin?"

"Acetaminophen on the way," she countered, typing the order into her tablet and hitting Send.

"Hell no." The patient struggled to sit up again. "Opioids. That's what I want."

Holden stepped nearer to the patient's bedside again, his face pale. "Calm down, sir."

"Go to hell!" The patient kicked hard, his foot making hard contact with Holden's right thigh.

Holden cursed under his breath and grabbed his leg, "What's he on?"

"Not sure yet. Definitely alcohol, but probably drugs too. Waiting on the tox screen results," Leilani said, scanning her chart notes for an update and finding none yet. "Patient has a hematoma on his forehead and a few lacerations, as you can see. No palpable fractures to the neck or spine, no internal bleeding or injuries upon exam, though I've ordered X-rays to confirm. According to the EMTs, his head starred the windshield, so no air bags either. I'd guess the vehicle was too old."

"Before 1999, then," Holden murmured as he rubbed his thigh and winced.

"Before 1998," Leilani corrected him. "Air bags were required in 1998."

"Sorry to disagree, Dr. Kim, but I researched this during my time in Chicago. Air bags became mandatory in 1999 in the United States."

"Then your research was wrong." Leilani battled a rising tide of annoyance as her grip on her tablet tightened. She of all people should know when air bags became mandatory. The date was seared in her mind for eternity. "It was 1998. Trust me."

"Why are we even arguing about this?" he asked, the irritation in his voice matching her own.

"I'm not arguing. I'm correcting you."

"That would be fine if I was mistaken. Which I'm not."

"I beg to differ. The date was September 1, 1998, to be exact."

She squared her shoulders and held her ground, feeling a strange rush of both energy and attraction. No. Not attraction. She didn't want to be attracted to this bullheaded man. Period. Still, her heart raced and her stomach fluttered despite her wishes. Must be the exhaustion. Had to be. She turned away, incensed, both at herself and Dr. Ross.

"The Intermodal Surface Transportation Efficiency Act of 1991 went into effect on September 1, 1998."

Her words emerged in staccato fashion. Rude? Maybe, but then he'd been the one to insinuate himself into her case without asking. She did a quick internet search to prove her point, then held the evidence on screen before his face.

"See? Every truck and car sold in the US had to have air bags for the driver and front seat passenger."

Holden scanned the information, then crossed his arms, the movement causing his toned biceps to bunch. Not that she was looking. Nope. He narrowed his gaze and studied her, far too perceptively for her comfort. "And you know all that verbatim why?"

Because they would've saved the lives of my family.

She swallowed hard and turned away, not about to share the most painful secrets of her past with a virtual stranger, even though some odd little niggle inside of her wanted to.

Gah! She must be way more tired than she'd originally thought. Sleep. That was what she needed. Sleep and food, because perhaps her blood sugar was low. That could explain her stumbling heart rate. Perhaps could even explain how she seemed hypersensitive to the heat and nearness of him now as they faced off over the span of a few feet. Might also explain her weird sensory hallucinations, like how the scent of his skin—soap and musk—seemed to surround her. Or the way her fingertips itched to touch the shadow of dark stubble just beneath the surface of his taut jaw.

Ugh. Leilani clenched her fists on the countertop, the weight of his stare still heavy behind her. He was waiting on her reply and didn't appear to want to leave until he got it. Fine. No way would she tell him the truth, so she went with a half lie instead. "I watch a lot of documentaries."

"Hmm." He sounded thoroughly unconvinced. "I like those shows too, but that's a lot of random facts to remember for no rea—"

"Radiology's ready for your patient, Dr. Kim," Pam said from the doorway, giving Leilani a much-needed reprieve.

"Thank you," Leilani said as two techs wheeled Mr. Chambers out the door.

Holden still stood there though, watching her closely. "I'll handle him when he's done, Dr. Kim. Go home."

"I'm fine, Dr. Ross." Keeping her gaze averted, Leilani headed for the hallway, thankful to escape. "I've got plenty of paperwork to catch up on before I leave, so I'll still be here to wrap up his case."

* * *

Holden couldn't understand the enigma that was Dr. Leilani Kim and it bothered him.

Figuring people out was kind of his thing these days. Or at least attempting to understand what made them work, before they did something completely unexpected, like shoot up a room full of innocent people.

Frustrated, he ran a hand through his hair before heading down the hall to check on his abdominal pain patient. Each step sent a fresh jolt of pain through his nerve endings, thanks to that kick from Dr. Kim's patient.

He stopped at the nurses' station to grab his tablet and give his right leg a rest. Honestly, he shouldn't complain about the pain, since he was lucky to still be breathing, let alone walking, after an attacker's bullet had shattered his right femur and nicked his femoral artery. He could have just as easily bled out on the floor of that Chicago ER, same as David…

No.

Thinking about that now would only take away his edge and he needed to stay sharp, with a twenty-four-hour shift looming ahead of him. Bad enough he still had that argument with Dr. Kim looping through his head. There was something about her excuse for knowing all those obscure facts about air bags that didn't ring true. And sure, he loved documentaries as much as the next person—in fact, those things were like crack to an analytical nerd like himself—but even he couldn't recite back all the information he'd learned in those films word for word like she had. It was odd. And intriguing. He'd had a good reason for discovering all that information, namely for an article he'd written for a medical journal. But her?

Not that he should care why she knew. And yet, he did. Way more than he should.

Irritated as much with himself as with her, he shook his head and pulled up his new patient's file. The last thing he needed in his life was more puzzles. He already had more than enough to figure out. Like where he planned to live after his stint here in Hawaii was done. Like if he'd ever walk without a cane again. Like when the next attack might occur and if he'd be ready this time or if he'd become just another statistic on the news.

The area around the nurses' station grew more crowded and Holden moved down the hall toward his patient's room and open space. He didn't do well with crowds these days. Preferred to keep to himself mostly, do his work, handle his cases, stay safe, stay out of the way and out of trouble. That was what he focused on most of the time. Which is what made his choice to charge into Dr. Kim's trauma bay so strange. Usually, he wouldn't intrude in another colleague's case unless he'd been called for a consult, but then he'd overheard her arguing with her obviously intoxicated patient and something had smacked him hard in the chest, spurring him into that room before he'd even realized what he was doing.

Holden exhaled slowly and dug the tip of his cane into the shiny linoleum floor. His therapist back in Chicago probably would've said it was related to his anxiety from the shooting. After all, the gunman back in Chicago had been intoxicated too. He'd wanted opioids, just like Dr. Kim's patient was demanding. There was a major difference this time though. No firearm.

He took another deep breath. Yes. That had to be it. Had to explain his weird fascination with finding out more about Dr. Leilani Kim too. The fact she was beautiful, all dark hair and dark eyes and curves for days on end—exactly his type, if he'd been looking—had nothing to do with it.

He definitely wasn't looking.

It was simply the stress of being in a new place, and his posttrauma hypersensitivity to his surroundings. He'd only been here a month, after all. Yep. That was it. Never mind his instincts told him otherwise. Holden didn't trust his instincts. Hadn't for a year now.

Twelve months had passed since the attack on his ER in Chicago. Twelve months since he'd lost his best friend in a senseless act of violence. Twelve months since he'd failed to keep the people closest to him safe.

And why risk getting closer to anyone again when they could be lost so easily?

The tablet pinged with his patient's results and he pulled them up, scrolling through the data. Pregnancy test negative. White blood cell count normal, though that didn't necessarily rule out appendicitis. Amylase and lipase measurements within normal limits. Next steps—an ultrasound and manual exam.

"Hey, Pam?" he called down the hall. "Can you join me in Trauma Three for a pelvic?"

"Yep, just give me a sec to finish up calling the lab for Dr. Kim," she said, holding her hand over the phone receiver.

He nodded, then leaned a shoulder against the wall to wait. Ohana Medical Center was relatively quiet, compared to the busy downtown ER he'd come from in Chicago. Back then he'd loved the constant hustle, but after the shooting, going back to work there had been too painful. So, he'd chosen the locum tenens route instead. And it was that choice that had eventually reunited him with his old friend, Dr. Helen King. In fact, she was the reason he'd ended up at Ohana. He owed her a debt he could never repay, but he'd wanted to try.

Which explained why he was here, in the middle of paradise, wondering how soon he could leave. Staying in one place too long didn't suit him anymore. Staying put meant risking entanglements. Staying put too long made you vulnerable.

And if there was one thing Holden never wanted to be again, it was vulnerable.

A loud metal clang sounded down the hall and his senses immediately went on high alert, his mind throwing up reminders of a different ER, a different, dangerous situation. His best friend lying on the floor, bleeding out and Holden unable to stop it because of his own injuries. His chest squeezed tight and darkness crept into his peripheral vision as the anxiety took over.

No. Not here. Not now. Can't do this. Won't do this.

Pulse jackhammering and skin prickling, Holden turned toward the corner, trying to look busy so no one questioned why he was just standing there alone in the hall. He'd spent weeks after the attack learning how to cope with the flashbacks, the PTSD. Sometimes the shadows still won though, usually when he was tired or anxious. Considering he'd slept like crap the night before, he was both at the moment.

"Sorry for the holdup," Pam said, near his side and breaking through his jumbled thoughts. "Things are a bit crazy right now, with tourist season and all."

He nodded and hazarded a glance in her direction.

Her smile quickly dissolved into a frown at whatever she saw in his face. "You okay, Doc?"

It took him a moment to recover his voice, his response emerging more like a croak past his dry vocal cords. "Fine." He cleared his throat and tried again, forcing a smile he didn't quite feel. "Isn't it always tourist season in Hawaii?"

"It is," said another voice from the staff break room across the hall. Leilani. Crap. He'd been so distracted he'd not even seen her go in there. Adrenaline pounded through his blood. Had she seen his panic attack?

When she came out of the room though, she thankfully gave no indication she'd seen him acting strangely. She just walked past him and headed for the elevators as radiology wheeled out her inebriated patient.

The lingering tension inside Holden ratcheted higher as the patient continued to shout at the staff while they wheeled him back toward the trauma bay. "Pain meds! Now!"

Leilani headed behind the desk at the nurses' station once more. "Let me check the images."

Holden followed behind her, the pain in his leg taking a back seat to his need to prevent a possible calamity if her patient got out of hand again. He reached the nurses' station just as Dr. Kim pulled up the patient's images on the computer. "No embedded glass in his scalp, cervical vertebra appear normal. No damage to the spinal cord or—"

"I'm getting the hell out of here!" A jarring rip of Velcro sounded, followed by a resounding crack of plastic hitting the floor. "And I will take everyone down if I don't get my meds!"

The cops still waiting near the doorway tensed and Holden's heart lodged in his throat.

Oh God. Not again.

Undeterred, Leilani took off for the patient's room. "Time to get this guy discharged."

"Wait!" Holden grabbed her arm. "Don't go in there."

"That's my patient, Dr. Ross." She frowned, shaking off his hold. "Don't tell me how to do my work. We need that bed and he's cleared for discharge. He's the cops' problem now. Excuse me."

She continued on down the hall, signaling to the officers to follow her into the room.

"I want my OxyContin!" Mr. Chambers yelled, followed by a string of curses.

Holden breathed deeply, forcing himself to stay calm, stay present, stay in control.

This isn't Chicago. This patient doesn't have a gun. There are police officers present. No one will get hurt.

From his vantage point, Holden saw the patient sitting up on the side of the bed, his neck brace on the floor. Leilani approached slowly, her voice low and calm.

"Your X-rays were all negative. We're going to release you into police custody."

"Already told you," the patient said, teetering to his feet. "I ain't talking to no cops."

Time seemed to slow as Holden moved forward, his vision blurring with memories of the shooting. So much blood, so much chaos, so much wasted time and energy and life.

Breathe, man. Breathe.

The patient straightened, heading straight for Dr. Kim. The cops moved closer.

Her tone hardened. "I'd advise you to stay where you are for your own safety, sir."

"My safety?" The patient sneered. "You threatening me?"

"Not a threat." Leilani squared her shoulders. "Touching me would not be wise."

"Wise?" The guy snorted, his expression lascivious. "C'mon and gimme some sugar."

The cops placed their hands on their Tasers, saying in unison, "Stand down, sir."

Holden rushed toward the room, his cane creaking under the strain. He couldn't let this happen again, not on his watch. He couldn't fail, wouldn't fail.

Just as Holden shoved between the officers, the patient turned at the sudden commotion and swung. His fist collided hard with Holden's jaw and pain surged through his teeth. He stumbled backward. The cops pulled their Tasers as the patient grabbed Dr. Kim's ponytail. Fast as lightning, she swiveled to face Mr. Chambers, slamming her heel down on his instep until his grip on her hair loosened. Then, as he bent over and cursed, she kneed him twice in the groin. The guy crumbled to the ground and the cops took him into custody.

Over. It's over.

Holden slumped against the wall as time sped back to normal.

While the cops handcuffed Mr. Chambers and read him his rights, Leilani rushed to Holden's side. "You're bleeding."

Confused, he glanced down at his scrub shirt and saw a large splotch of scarlet. Then the ache in his jaw and teeth intensified, along with the taste of copper and salt in his mouth.

Damn.

"Here." Leilani snatched a few gauze pads from a canister on the counter and handed them to him. "Looks like there's a pretty deep gash on your lip and chin." She leaned past him to call out into the hall. "Pam, can you set up an open room for suturing, please?"

"No, no." He attempted to bat her hands away and straightened. "I can stitch myself up."

He was a board-certified trauma surgeon, for God's sake. Though as the adrenaline in his system burned away, it left him feeling a tad shaky. His lip pulsated with pain. At least it was a welcome distraction from the cramp in his thigh. "Seriously, I've got it."

"Don't be silly. It will be easier for someone else to stitch you up." She tugged him out the door and down the hall to the nurses' station once more. "Just let me sign off on Mr. Chambers first so they can get him out of here."

While he waited, he blotted his throbbing mouth with the gauze pads and admitted she was right, much as he hated to do so. He was in no fit state to treat anyone at the moment, including himself. Which brought another problem to mind. "What about the abdominal patient?"

"Let the residents take it. That's why they're here." Leilani finished her signing off on her discharge paperwork, then nudged Holden toward an empty exam room. Behind him, the cops hauled Mr. Chambers, still cursing and yelling, out to their waiting squad car.

Leilani led him into the room Pam had set up, then shut the door behind them. "Take a seat on the exam table and let me take a look at your lip."

He did as she asked, allowing her to brush his hand aside and peek beneath the gauze pad. This close, her warmth surrounded him, as did her scent—jasmine and lily. A strange tingle in his blood intensified. It was far more unsettling and dangerous than any punch to the face. She moved closer still to examine his cut lip and he jerked away, alarmed.

"Don't!" he said, then tried to backpedal at her concerned look. "I mean, *ow*."

He turned away and she walked over to the suture kit set out along with a small vial of one percent lidocaine and a syringe on a wheeled metal tray. "The split is through the vermillion border, so no Dermabond or Steri-Strips. Sutures will give you the best result—otherwise it could pop open again."

Holden stared at his reflection in the mirror nearby to distract himself, frustration and embarrassment curdling within him. He already felt like an idiot after getting punched by her patient. Having her sew him up too added insult to injury. Pain surged through his leg and he gripped the edge of the table.

"Any dizziness?" Leilani asked. "He hit you pretty hard."

"No," Holden lied. He still felt a bit light-headed, but that was more from anxiety than the blow to his face. Needing to burn off some excess energy, he slid off the table and moved to the nearby sink to splash cold water on his face. The chill helped clear his head and after drying off his face with paper towels, he plucked at his soiled scrub shirt. "I should change."

"Hang on." Leilani ran back out into the hall and returned with a clean scrub shirt a few moments later. "Here."

"Thanks." He limped behind the screen in the corner and stripped, tossing the bloodstained shirt on the floor before slipping on the clean one. It was too big and the

V-neck kept slipping to the side, revealing the scar from his second bullet wound through his left shoulder. He fiddled with the stupid thing, glancing up to find Leilani watching him in the mirror on the wall.

He attempted to play off the awkwardness of the situation with a joke. "Checking me out?"

"No." She looked away fast, but not before he spotted a flush of pink across her cheeks. His interest in her spiked again, despite his wishes to the contrary. She was his work colleague. Theirs was a professional relationship, pure and simple. Anything more was definitely off-limits. He made his way back to the exam table as she pulled on a pair of gloves, then filled a syringe with lidocaine.

"People can be unpredictable, can't they?" Leilani said, jarring him back to reality. "Like Mr. Chambers. You think they're going to do one thing, then they do something completely different. Lie down, please." Reluctantly, he did as she asked. The sooner they got this over with, the better.

Leilani moved in beside him again and he did his best to ignore the heat of her penetrating through his cotton scrub shirt, the soft brush of her bare wrist against his skin as she stabilized his jaw for the injection. "Hold still and try to relax. This may burn a bit."

"I know." He did his best to relax and met her intent stare. "Hard being on the receiving end of treatment."

She smiled and his pulse stumbled. "I understand, Dr. Ross. Doctors usually make the worst patients." She leaned back, her gaze darting from his eyes to his left shoulder, then back again. "But you've obviously had treatment before."

He swallowed hard and looked away, anxiety still

shimmering like hot oil through his bloodstream. "Obviously."

"Sorry. I didn't mean to bring up a sore subject." Her hand slipped from his jaw to rest on his sternum, her smile falling. "You're tachycardic."

"I'm fine," he repeated, grasping her hand, intending to remove it from his person, but once her fingers were in his, he found himself unable to let go. Which was nuts. He didn't want entanglements, didn't want connections, and yet, here it was—in the last place he wanted to find one. Which only made his heart beat harder against his rib cage.

Get it together, man.

"Dr. Ross?" she asked, concern lighting her gaze. "Holden? Are you with me?"

The unfamiliar sound of his first name on her lips returned a modicum of his sanity. "Sorry. No, I'd rather not talk about my injuries. Bad memories."

"Okay. No problem. I understand completely. I have a few of those memories myself." Her calm tone, along with the understanding in her eyes, slowly brought his inner angst down to tolerable levels. She pulled her hand from his, then walked over to her tablet on the counter and tapped the screen. "How about some music? What kind do you like? Rock? Country? R & B?"

The change of subjects provided a welcome escape and he grabbed on to it with both hands. He stared up at the ceiling and couldn't care less what she played, as long as it distracted him from the past and her weird effect on him. "Uh…whatever you like is fine."

"Okay." Ukulele music filled the air as she moved in beside him again, a twinkle in her dark gaze as she raised the syringe once more. "I know this situation is uncomfortable for you, Dr. Ross, but the sooner you let me get started, the faster it will be over. I'll even make you a deal. Let me suture you up and I'll take you to a real luau."

"What?" He frowned up at her.

"A luau. You know, poi, Kalua pig, poke, *lomi* salmon, *opihi, haupia* and beer. The works. Plus, you might even get to see a genuine Don Ho impersonator."

"Um…a genuine impersonator?" He gave her a confused look.

She laughed. "Yep. He's the best on the island. Be a shame for you not to get the full Hawaiian experience while you're here. Unless you've already been?"

No. He hadn't been to a luau yet. Hadn't really been anywhere on the island, other than the resort where he was staying and the hospital, to be honest. And sure, he'd planned to take in some sights while he was here, of course, including a luau, but he'd not really made any firm decisions. The fact she'd asked him now, both piqued his interest and set off all the warning bells in his head. "Are you asking me out on a date, Dr. Kim?"

"What?" She stepped back, looking nearly as alarmed as he felt. "No. I just felt bad because my patient punched you and wanted to make you more comfortable, that's all." That pretty pink color was back in her cheeks again, and damn if that unwanted interest in her didn't flare higher.

This was bad. So, so bad.

Luckily, she shrugged and turned away, her tone chilly now. "But I certainly don't want to give you the wrong impression. And I can see now that my asking was a mistake. Forget I mentioned it."

Holden wanted nothing more than to do that, but it

seemed he couldn't. In fact, her invitation now buzzed inside his head like a bothersome fruit fly. He propped himself up on his elbows, feeling completely discombobulated. "I didn't mean to make you uncomfortable."

"Same." She glanced back at him over her shoulder. "I'm not even sure why I mentioned it, to be honest."

The sincerity in her tone helped ease the tension slithering inside him and he lay down flat again, blinking at the ceiling. Seemed they were both rusty at this whole social interaction thing. "I haven't really seen anything since I've been on the island."

"I can give you some suggestions, if you like, since Honolulu's my hometown. My parents own a hotel here," she said, returning to his side, her gaze narrowed as she took his chin again and lifted the syringe. "Okay, here comes the burn."

While the numbing medication took effect, Holden found himself reconsidering her offer. His therapist had told him during their last session back in Chicago that he needed to get out more. She could show him around, perhaps introduce him to some people, broaden his horizons. On a strictly professional basis, of course. Plus, spending more time with her should help lessen the strange heightened awareness he felt around her. Desensitization 101. Taken in those terms, accepting Leilani's invitation made good sense. He blurted out his response before he could second-guess himself. "Okay."

"Okay what?" She frowned down at him.

"Okay, we can go to a luau." His words started to slur as the medication took effect, making his bottom lip ineffective. "Show me some sights too, if you have the time."

Dr. Kim blinked down at him, looking as stunned

as he felt. She seemed to consider it for a long moment before nodding. "Fine. But only as colleagues. Understood?"

He nodded, then exhaled slowly as he tapped his lip to make sure it was numb.

"Good." Her quick smile brightened the room far more than he wished. "Now, no more talking until I get this done. Otherwise, I can't guarantee this will heal symmetrical."

She got to work and he closed his eyes, the better to block her out. He still couldn't quite believe he'd said yes to her invitation. Part of him still wanted to get up and get the heck out of there, but the other part of him knew she was right. It was easier for someone else to stitch him up.

CHAPTER TWO

LEILANI STILL COULDN'T quite believe what had happened with Holden Ross. What had she been thinking, offering to take him sightseeing, let alone to a luau? Ugh. She didn't date coworkers. Didn't date anyone really these days, truth be told. Sure, she'd had relationships in the past, but nothing that had worked out long term. And the past six months or so, socializing had taken a back seat with the directorship position on the line.

But this wasn't really socializing, was it? He was new in town and she was being hospitable, that's all.

Like a good neighbor.

A neighbor you'd like to get to know a whole lot better.

Flustered, Leilani turned to face the counter.

This was so not like her to get all giddy over a man. Especially a potential rival for the job she wanted. Never mind there was something wildly compelling about him. Like the flash of panic in his eyes when she'd asked about his previous injuries.

Unfortunately, his reaction was all too relatable—the gut-wrenching terror, the uncertainty of being bruised and battered and broken and alone. If it hadn't been for the kindness and patience and fast thinking of the medical staff the night of the accident, she wouldn't be here today.

The old injury at the base of her neck ached again, reminding her of those who'd saved her, after the rest of her family had been lost. And that was probably exactly why she should be avoiding Holden Ross like the proverbial plague, instead of escorting him around her island as his tour guide. Maybe she could find some way out of it. Work usually gave ample excuses. There was bound to be a case or two requiring her assistance, right? Leilani ripped open the suture kit and pulled out a hemostat.

The music streaming from her tablet on the counter switched to a different song, this one slow and sweet and filled with yearning. Her own chest pinched slightly before she shoved the feeling away. She had nothing to yearn for. She had a great life. A good career. Adoptive parents who loved her and supported her decisions. A new house. A pet who adored her—U'i, her African gray parrot.

And sure, maybe sometimes she wished for someone special to share it all with. She'd get there when she was ready.

If you're ever ready...

She was taking her time, that was all. Being cautious. Never mind she still woke up with nightmares from the accident sometimes. She'd get over it. All of it.

Someday.

"No one told me you're a ninja," Holden said, his words wonky due to his numb lip.

"Those skills come in handy more often than you know." She opened a 6–0 suture and grabbed the curved needle with the hemostat to align the vermillion border with one stitch. Once that was done, she switched to a 5–0 absorbable suture for the rest. "Just four or five more then we're done."

"Internal?" he asked, though the word came out more like "ee-turtle."

"No damage to the orbicularis oris muscle that I can see, so all external." She tied off another stitch, then grabbed a couple more gauze strips off the tray, soaking them in saline before carefully pulling down his bottom lip. "Let me just check the inside to make sure there aren't more lacerations hidden in there."

The salt water dripped down his chin to the V-neck of his scrub shirt.

"Oops. Sorry." Leilani grabbed a tissue from the tray and dabbed at the wet spot, doing her best not to notice his tanned skin and well-defined muscles. Sudden, unwanted images of her kissing from his neck to collarbone, then down his chest, lower still, made her mouth go dry…

"Dr. Kim?" Holden said, yanking her back to reality. *Oh God.*

Mortified, she tossed the tissue back on the tray then gave him a too-bright smile. "Almost finished."

He frowned, then looked away, the movement giving her another glimpse of the scar on his left shoulder. She gave herself a mental shake. His body and his wounds were none of her business. That was the exhaustion talking, making her nerves hum and her curiosity about him soar. She continued with the sutures, berating herself. *Focus, girl. Focus.*

The song on her tablet switched again, this time to a sweeping, sexy guitar concerto.

Holden blinked up at the ceiling, looking anywhere but at her. "That's pretty."

"One of my favorites." Leilani tied off another stitch then started on the next.

He waited until she was finished before asking, "Where'd you learn to fight?"

It took her a minute to figure out his slurred question. "Oh. You mean with Mr. Chambers? I kickbox. I've taken classes since I was fifteen."

"Wow." Then, out of the blue, he reached up and cupped her face. Her pulse stumbled.

"What are you doing, Dr. Ross?" she managed to squeak out.

"That guy pulled your hair hard," Holden said, gently tilting her head to the side.

"I'm fine. Really." Her breath hitched at the intensity of his gaze.

Oh goodness.

The romantic music washed around them, and unexpected heat gathered in her core. Not good. Not good at all.

Holden Ross was the last man she should get involved with. He was her colleague. He was strictly off-limits. He was far too tempting for her own good. Any connection she felt to him needed to be severed, any awareness currently scorching her blood needed to be doused. End of story. She couldn't risk allowing him closer.

Can I?

Blood pounded in her ears and forbidden awareness zinged over her skin. She ignored the first and tamped down the last before forcing words past her suddenly dry throat. "Thank you, Dr. Ross. Now, let's finish these stitches and get you on your way."

"Holden," he said.

"I'm sorry?" She held the needle poised over his lip for the last stitch.

"Call me Holden."

"Okay." Leilani placed her thumb on his chin to pull slight tension and her finger along his chiseled jawline to steady her hand.

"So, you're native Hawaiian then?"

"Please try not to speak." She sat back. "And yes. Born and raised. My parents own a resort in town."

She could hear the sadness in her own voice and as perceptive as he was, she had no doubt he'd hear it too. Despite all the love and joy her adopted family had given her, part of her would always miss the ones who'd gone. The pain of the accident had never truly faded. Nor had the fear of losing someone else she cared for. She tied off the last stitch, then sat back with relief. "All done."

He sat up and looked in the mirror on the wall again. "Nice job, Dr. Kim."

"Thanks." She began cleaning up from the procedure. "There are more clean scrub shirts on the rack in the hall, if you want to grab a different size."

"Will do." He grabbed his cane and limped toward the door, then turned back to her once more. "Thanks again."

"No problem." Leilani watched him walk away, feeling that riptide of interest tugging at her again and knowing that if she gave in, it could pull her right under. And drowning in the mysteries of Dr. Holden Ross was not part of her plans.

The following morning, after his shift, Holden drove his rental car through the streets of Honolulu toward the

Malu Huna Resort and Spa, the steady, hypnotic beat of the windshield wipers almost putting him to sleep. His current residence was only fifteen minutes outside of downtown but driving in the rain after work wasn't exactly his favorite thing.

He pulled into a handicapped parking spot near the entrance to the hotel then stared in through the front windows at the breakfast crowd filling the lobby of the resort. The unusual, crappy weather actually suited his mood far better than the cheerful tropical decor inside the place, but if he wanted to get to his room, he had to traverse the maze of tourists and guests filling the tables in the lobby.

After a deep breath, he cut the engine and grabbed his cane, before glancing at himself one last time in the mirror. The numbing medication in his lip had long since worn off and his lower jaw and into his teeth ached. Eating would be a joy for a while. Not that it mattered. He ate his meals alone in his room most of the time anyway, avoiding the other guests. No sense ruining everyone else's time in paradise with his gloomy attitude.

With a sigh, he got out of the car, then hobbled toward the entrance, his head down to keep the rain off his face. The automatic doors swished open and a gust of warm air swept around him, scented with maple and bacon from the food-laden coffers of the all-you-can-eat buffet in the dining room. His traitorous stomach growled, but Holden didn't stop to fill a plate. Just kept his eyes focused on the elevators ahead as he made a beeline through the lobby. Since the shooting, he had a hard time spending long periods with large groups of strangers. He found himself too distracted, always scanning the room for danger.

His therapist back in Chicago had urged him to build up his tolerance slowly. So far, Holden hadn't tried that suggestion out, preferring his own company to constantly being on guard for the next attack.

Weaving through groups of tourists dressed in shorts and T-shirts and sandals, he felt more out of place than ever in his wrinkled scrubs, his name tag from work still pinned crookedly on the front pocket. He excused himself as he sidled by a quartet of women bedecked with leis and sun hats and nearly collided with a potted palm tree for his trouble.

The lobby of the Malu Huna looked like a cross between a *Fantasy Island* fever dream and a Disney movie in Holden's estimation—with its rattan furniture, gauzy white curtains and golden pineapple design inlaid in the shiny tile floor. There was even a parrot behind the front desk, squawking at the people passing by. Holden glanced over at the bird as he waited for his elevator. An African gray, if he wasn't mistaken. One of his roommates back in college had had one. Smart as a whip and quick learners. They'd had to be careful what they said around the bird because it picked up words like crazy, especially the bad ones.

Holden punched the up button again.

"Dr. Ross?" a voice called from across the lobby and his heart sank. The owner.

The elevator dinged and the doors whooshed open.

So close and yet so far.

He considered making a run for it but didn't want to be rude.

Forcing a weary smile, he turned to face the Asian man who bustled over to him from the dining room. The shorter guy beamed up at him now, his brightly colored Hawaiian shirt all but glowing beneath the recessed overhead lighting. "Won't you join us for breakfast?"

Holden glanced at the roomful of people and his stomach twisted hard. "Oh, I'm not really hungry."

Once more, his stomach growled loud, proving him a liar.

The hotel owner raised a skeptical brow, his grin widening. "Your body says otherwise. Please, Dr. Ross? We'd love to show you our hospitality during your stay." He gave Holden a quick once-over. "You look as if you could use a good meal. Come on."

Before he could protest, the man took his arm and guided him across the lobby. Familiar panic vibrated through his bloodstream and he looked over the man's head out the rain-streaked windows toward his car. It was only breakfast. He could do breakfast.

Sit. Eat. Talk.

Except the idea of making conversation with strangers made his spine kink.

Sure, he talked to patients all day long, but that was different. At the hospital, he had a plan, a specific purpose. Those things made it easier to shove his anxiety to the back of his mind. Small talk, however, required interest and energy, both of which Holden was running critically low on at the moment.

A year ago I could talk with anyone, party with the best of them.

But now, postattack, his social skills had vanished, leaving him feeling awkward and weak. He hated feeling weak. Weak meant vulnerable. And vulnerable was something Holden never wanted to be again.

He made one final valiant attempt at escape as the hotel owner dragged him thorough the dining room and a maze of packed tables. "Honestly, I can just order room service. I'm tired and grubby and probably won't make good company anyway, Mr….?"

"Kim," the man said, stopping before a table where two women sat. "Mr. Kim. But you can call me Joe. Please, sit down, Dr. Ross."

"Holden," he mumbled, staring at the woman across the table from him. Dr. Kim stared back, looking about as happy to see him as he was to see her. "Please, call me Holden."

She'd mentioned her parents owned a hotel in town while she'd stitched him up, but he'd been so focused on ignoring her and all the uncomfortable things she made him feel, that he'd let it go in one ear and out the other.

Now he felt like an even bigger idiot than before. "Uh, hello again."

"Hello," she said, fiddling with the napkin in her lap. "Are you going to sit down?"

Sit. Yes. That sounded like a marvelous idea, especially since his thigh was cramping again. With less grace than usual, he pulled out the empty chair and slid into it, stretching out his aching leg as he hooked his cane over the back of his seat.

Mr. Kim, Joe, was still smiling at him, as was the woman beside him, presumably Mrs. Kim.

Trying his best to not flub up again, Holden extended his hand to the older woman. "Dr. Holden Ross. Pleasure to meet you."

"Same." Mrs. Kim's dark gaze darted between Leilani and Holden. "You work with my daughter?"

"Yes. I'm filling in temporarily at Ohana Medical Center." He sat back as a waitress set a glass of water in front of him. "Trauma surgery."

"Excellent," Mrs. Kim said. "You and Leilani must work together a lot then. Funny she's never mentioned you."

Leilani, who was quieter than he'd ever seen her before, stared down at her plate of food. "I'm sure I mentioned him, Mom."

"He'll have the buffet," Joe said to the waitress, ordering for Holden. "And it's on the house."

"Sure thing, Mr. Kim," the waitress said, walking away.

"No, no," Holden protested. "I can get this. My locum tenens position comes with a food allowance, so…"

"Locum tenens?" Mrs. Kim said, leaning closer to him. "Tell me more about that, Dr. Ross. Sounds fascinating."

"Holden, please," he said, eyeing the crowded buffet table nearby and longing for the peace and quiet of his hotel room. "I…uh…"

"Hey, guys." Leilani's calm voice sliced through his panic. "Leave the poor man alone. He's just worked a long shift. He needs coffee and a nap, not the third degree. Right, Dr. Ross?"

He swallowed hard and managed a nod.

Leilani poured him a cup of coffee from the carafe on the table and pushed it toward him. "Busy at the ER?"

"Yeah." Talking about work helped relax him and as he stirred cream and sugar into his cup, he told them about the cases he'd seen and the funny stories he'd heard from the staff and soon he'd even answered the questions the Kim's had asked him without locking up once. The whole time, he found himself meeting Leilani's gaze across the table and marveling at the sense of peace he found there.

Whoa. Don't get carried away there, cowboy.

His peace had nothing to do with Leilani Kim. That was absurd. They barely knew each other. It was the routine—talking about work—that calmed his nerves. Nothing else. Nope.

"Well, this has been fun," Mrs. Kim said once he'd finished, pushing to her feet. "But my husband and I need to get back to work at the front desk."

Joe looked confused for a minute before his wife gave him a pointed look. "Oh right. Yeah. We need to get to work. You kids stay and have fun. Lani, be sure to invite him to the luau next Friday." He shook Holden's hand again. "See you around the resort."

Holden watched them walk away, then turned back to Leilani. "So, this is the resort your family owns?"

"Yes." She gave him a flat look, then cocked her head toward the buffet. "Better get your food before they start tearing the buffet down."

CHAPTER THREE

LEILANI EXHALED SLOWLY as Holden hobbled away toward the food line. If she'd left five minutes earlier, she would've missed her parents trying to play matchmaker again, this time with the last man on earth she should be interested in.

They were colleagues, for goodness' sake. She didn't date people from work.

No matter how intrigued she might be by Holden's tall, dark and damaged persona.

Part of her wanted to get up and leave right then, but manners dictated she stay at least until he returned with his plate. They did have to work together, after all. She didn't want things to be awkward—or more awkward than they already were—between them.

So, she'd wait until he got back to the table, then make her polite excuses and skedaddle. For once, Leilani was grateful for the long shift ahead of her at work. Twenty-four hours to keep her busy and away from dwelling more on her encounter the day before with Holden. But first, she planned to hit the gym for a good martial arts workout.

She rolled her stiff neck, then sipped her water. Even tired as she'd been, her sleep had been restless, her dreams filled with images of dealing with combative, intoxicated Mark Chambers again. Those moments then had quickly blurred into memories of the long-ago accident that had taken the lives of her parents and brother. Mixed in were flashes of Holden, changing his scrub shirt, the scar on his shoulder, the wary look in his warm hazel eyes as she'd stitched up his lip. The rough scrap of stubble on his jaw that she'd felt even through her gloves as she'd held his chin, the clean smell of shampoo from his hair, the throb of his heart beneath her palm as she'd dabbed the saline solution from his chest…

"So," he said, shaking her from her thoughts as he straddled the chair across from her and set a plate of scrambled eggs, toast and bacon on the table in front of him. "You honestly don't have to stay if you don't want to. I can tell you'd like to leave."

Leilani did her best to play it off. "Don't be silly. I just have a busy day ahead."

He sat back as the waitress returned to fill a cup of coffee for him. The server gave Holden a slow smile filled with promise and a strange jab of something stabbed Leilani's chest. Not jealousy, because that would be insane. She had no reason to care if another woman flirted with Holden. He was a coworker, an acquaintance. That was it.

Holden continued to watch her as he stirred cream and sugar into his coffee, his gaze narrowed. His skeptical tone said he saw right through her flimsy excuse. "Well, don't let me keep you. I wouldn't be here either if your dad hadn't dragged me in."

She frowned at him. It was true she'd planned to leave soon enough, but that didn't mean he shouldn't want her to stay. A niggle of stubbornness bored into her gut, and she accepted a refill on her coffee from the waitress. At Holden's raised brow she said, "I've got a few minutes."

He took a huge bite of eggs and lowered his gaze. "Don't stay on my account."

"Are you always this jovial, Dr. Ross?" she snorted.

"No. Most of the time I eat alone in my room," he said, devouring half a piece of bacon before glancing at her again. This time, his stoic expression cracked slightly into the hint of a smile. "Sorry. Out of practice with socializing."

A pang of sympathy went through her before she could tamp it down. Seemed they were in the same boat there. She sipped her coffee while he finished off his plate, then sat back in his seat. ER doctors learned to eat fast, at least in Leilani's experience, since you never knew when you'd be called out for the next emergency. Leilani wasn't sure where he put all that food, since there didn't appear to be an inch of spare flesh on him. A sudden, unwanted flash of him with his shirt off in the exam room flickered through her mind before she shook it off.

Nope. Not going there. Not at all.

With a sigh, she finished the rest of her coffee in one long swallow, then stood. "Right. Well, I really do need to go now. Have a nice rest of your day, Dr. Ross."

Holden wiped his mouth with a napkin, then gave a small nod. "Your shift at the hospital doesn't start until two. It's only 9:00 a.m. now."

"What?" Heat prickled her cheeks as he caught her in a lie. Outrage mixed with embarrassment inside her and came out in her blunt response. "I wasn't aware my schedule was your concern, Dr. Ross."

He downed another swig of coffee. "It's not. Helen mentioned it earlier."

At the reminder of Ohana's head administrator, Leilani's breath caught. Reason number one billion why she shouldn't be spending any more time than was necessary with this man. Not with Holden potentially vying for the same job she wanted. "Dr. King told you my schedule? That seems odd."

"Not really. She mentioned it in relation to some project she wants us both to work on." Leilani opened her mouth to respond, but he held up a hand. "Before you ask, she didn't give me any details yet. Said she wanted to discuss it with you first, as the acting director." He exhaled slowly, his broad shoulders slumping a bit, and he gestured toward her empty chair. "Look, I'm sorry if I was grumpy before. Please, don't rush off on my account. It's actually kind of nice to have someone to talk to besides myself."

Much as she hated to admit it, Leilani felt the same. Sure, she had friends and her parents, but they weren't physicians. She couldn't talk shop with them like she could another doctor. Not that she really planned to discuss cases with Holden Ross, unless a trauma surgeon's skills were needed, but still. Torn between making her escape and being more enticed by his offer than she cared to admit, Leilani slowly took her seat again. "You don't get out much?"

"No. Not since…" Holden's voice trailed off, and that haunted expression ghosted over his face once more before he hid it behind his usual wall of stoicism. He cleared his throat. "Working locum tenens has a lot of advantages, but creating bonds and connections isn't one of them. Maybe that's why I like it so much."

"Wow. That sounds a bit standoffish."

"Not really." He shook his head and frowned down into his cup. "Just smart."

Huh. Leilani sat back and crossed her arms, studying him. Having been through a nightmare herself with the accident, she recognized the signs of past trauma all too well. Something horrible had definitely happened in his past—she just wasn't sure what. Given his limp and the wound she'd spied on his left shoulder, she'd bet money a bullet had been involved. That was certainly enough to ruin anyone's outlook on their fellow humans and relationships.

Before she could ask more though, he shifted his attention to the windows nearby and the gray, overcast day outside. "Does it rain a lot here?"

"Not really," she said, the change in subject throwing her for a second. "But it's March."

"And March means rain?"

"In Honolulu, yes. It's our rainiest month." Leilani held up her hand when a server came around with a coffeepot again. Too much caffeine would upset her stomach. "Why?"

"Just interested in the island." The same waitress from earlier stopped back to remove Holden's dishes and slid a small piece of paper onto the table beside his mug. From what Leilani could see, it had the woman's phone number on it. Holden seemed unfazed, taking the slip and tucking it into the pocket of his scrubs before reaching for the creamer again. The thought of him having a booty call with the server later made Leilani's gut tighten. Which was stupid. He was free to see anyone he liked, as was she. She wasn't a workaholic spinster, no matter what her parents might say to the contrary. Leilani had options when it came to men and dating. She was just picky, that's all. She had standards.

Holden must've caught her watching him because he said, "I promised to check on the waitress's son later. The kid's got what sounds like strep throat."

Uh-huh. Sure.

She managed not to roll her eyes through superhuman strength. His social life was of no concern to her. She flashed him a bland smile. "Nice of you."

He shrugged. "So, what are you rushing off to this morning? If you don't mind me asking."

Her first response was a snarky one that yeah, she did mind. But then she caught a hint of that lonely sadness and wariness in his eyes again and she bit back those words. She didn't want to get friendlier with Holden Ross, but darn if there wasn't something about him that kept her in her seat and coming back for more. She could lie and make up a story, but what was the point? So she went with the truth instead. "I was going to do my daily workout."

"Oh?" Holden perked up a little at that. "I've been meaning to try the hotel gym, but with my crazy schedule at work, haven't made it there yet. Mind if I tag along, just to see where it is? Then I'll leave you alone, I promise."

Alarm bells went off in Leilani's head. She already felt way more interested in this guy than was wise. Spending more time with him would only put her at risk of that interest boiling over into actually liking him and the last thing Leilani wanted was to open herself up to getting hurt again. Even the possibility of letting someone close to her heart, to be that vulnerable again, honestly filled her with abject terror.

"Let the man go with you, *keiki*," her father said from where he was helping clean up a nearby table, and Leilani tensed. Jeez, they were really on snooping patrol today. "Show our guest the gym."

She glanced over at her father and gave him a look. Her dad just shook his head and moved on to another section of tables to clean. They thought she was being ridiculous and maybe she was, but she needed to do things on her terms. Stay in control. Control was everything these days.

Holden chuckled and gulped more coffee. "Kiki?"

"Keiki," she corrected him. "It means child in Hawaiian."

Ever since they'd adopted her, the Kims had always called her that. First, because that's what she'd been. A scared fourteen-year-old kid with an uncertain future. Now it was more of a pet name than anything.

Leilani exhaled slowly before pushing to her feet again, her good manners too ingrained to refuse. "Fine. If you want to come with me, you can. Get changed and meet me in the lobby in fifteen minutes. Don't be late, Dr. Ross."

Holden's smile widened, his grateful tone chasing her from the restaurant. "Wouldn't dream of it, Dr. Kim."

The workout facilities at Malu Huna were much like the rest of the resort—clean, spacious and well-appointed—even if the decor was a bit much for his Midwestern sensibilities. More golden palm trees decorated the tile floor here and large murals of the famous Hawaiian sunsets bedecked the walls. There were neat rows of treadmills and stair-climbers, weight machines, stationary bikes and even a boxing area, complete with punching bags and thick mats on the floor.

Holden followed Leilani as she headed for those workout mats, her snug workout clothes clinging to her curves in all the right places. Not that he noticed. He was here to release some tension, not to ogle his colleague. No matter how pretty she was. It had been too long since he'd been with a woman, that was all. The slip of paper with the phone number the waitress had given him flashed in his mind. He hadn't lied to Leilani earlier, but he hadn't been entirely truthful either. He had spoken to the waitress a few days prior about her sick kid and offered to see him, but then the waitress had also asked him out. At the time, he'd declined because he'd been tired and busy and not up for company. But now, with loneliness gnawing at his gut again, maybe he should give the server's invitation second thoughts.

Leilani strapped on a pair of boxing gloves, then turned to face him once more.

Holden stopped short. "Are you going to hit me?"

"Not unless you provoke me." She raised a dark brow at him.

He snorted. "Remind me not to get on your bad side."

"Don't worry. I will." She grinned, then turned to face the heavy bag. "Well, this is the gym. Enjoy your workout."

Looking around, he considered his options. Treadmill was out, with his leg. So were the stair-climbers as they put too much pressure on his still-healing muscles. Stationary bike it was then. He hobbled over and climbed onto one, setting his course to the most difficult one, and began to pedal. Soon his heart was pumping fast, and sweat slicked his face and chest, and he felt the glorious rush of endorphins that always came with a hard work-out. Near the end of his course, Holden glanced over to where he'd left Leilani on the mats and found her work-ing through what looked like kickboxing moves with the punching bag.

Her long hair was piled up in a messy bun atop her head now and her face was flushed from exertion. Her toned arms and back glistened with perspiration beneath the overhead lights as she walloped the heavy bag over and over again. Jab, hook, cross, uppercut. Sweep, cross, kick. Jab, cross, slip. Front kick, back kick. Roundhouse kick. Repeat. Holden found himself entranced.

Once his bike program was done, he moved back over to where she was still dancing around the bag, her movements as coordinated and graceful as any prima ballerina. Even the hot pink boxing gloves didn't de-tract from Leilani's powerful stance. She looked ready to kick butt and take names. On second thought, just forget the names.

His gaze followed her fists driving hard into the bag. Then he couldn't help continuing to track down her torso to her waist and hips landing finally on her taut butt in those black leggings.

Whoa, boy.

Yep. Dr. Leilani Kim wasn't just pretty. She was gor-geous, no doubt about that. He glanced back up to find her staring at him, her expression flat.

Oops. Busted.

"You know how to fight," he said, for lack of any-thing better.

She steadied the swinging bag, then punched one glove into the other, blinking at him. "I do. Very well.

Years of training, remember? I'm not afraid to use those skills either."

"I remember you taking down that patient. Don't worry. Point taken." Holden stepped back and chuckled. Back before the shooting he'd been into boxing himself, but he hadn't tried since his injury. He turned to head back to his bike but stopped at the sound of her voice.

"You box?"

"I used to," Holden said, looking back at her over his shoulder. He gestured to his right leg. "Haven't since this though."

"Want to give it a try now?" she asked, tapping the tips of her gloves together. "Be my sparring partner?" Her gaze dipped to his cane then back to his eyes. "I'll take it easy on you."

Whether or not she'd meant that as a challenge didn't matter. He took it as one. The pair of black boxing gloves she tossed in his direction helped too. He caught them one-handed, then narrowed his gaze on her. For the first time in a long time, he wanted to take a chance and burn off a little steam. "Fine."

He strapped on the gloves, then moved back over, setting his cane aside before climbing atop the mat to stand beside Leilani.

"We can stick to bag work, if it's easier on your leg."

"Sparring's fine." He finished closing the Velcro straps around his wrists, then punched his fists together. "Unless you're scared to face off against me?" His tone was teasing. It felt easy to tease her. He didn't want to think about why.

Leilani snorted. "Right. You think you can take me?"

"I think you talk big, but you look pretty small."

"Them's fighting words, mister." She moved several

feet away and faced him before bending her knees and holding her gloves up in front of her face. "All right, Dr. Ross. Show me what you got."

Holden smiled, a genuine one this time, enjoying himself more than he had in a long, long time. "My pleasure, Dr. Kim."

They moved in a small circle on the mat, dodging each other and assessing their opponent. Then, fast as lightning, Leilani struck, landing a solid punch to his chest. He gave her a stunned look and she laughed. "Figured you already had a split lip. Didn't want to damage that handsome face of yours any further."

That stopped him in his tracks.

She thinks I'm handsome?

The reality of her words must've struck Leilani too because the flush in her cheeks grew and she looked away from him. "I mean, I'm taking pity on you. That's all."

Pity. If there was one word sure to set Holden off, it was that one.

All thought of keeping away from Leilani Kim went out the window as he went in for the attack. Apparently still distracted by what she'd said, she didn't react fast enough when he charged toward her and swept his good leg out to knock her feet from under her. Of course, the movement unbalanced him as well, and before Holden knew it, they were both flat on the mat, panting as they tried to catch their breaths in a tangle of limbs.

He managed to recover first, rising on one arm to lean over her. "I don't need your pity, Dr. Kim."

She blinked up at him a moment, then gave a curt nod. "Understood."

"Good." He pushed away to remove one of his gloves

and rake a hand through his sweat-damp hair. "Are you all right?"

"Other than my pride, yes." She sat up next to him and removed her gloves too, several strands of her long, dark hair loose now and curling around her flushed face. "I didn't mean to insult you with what I said, by the way. It was just trash-talking."

"I know." He released a pent-up breath, then wiped off his forehead with the edge of his gray Ohana Medical T-shirt. "The whole pity thing is still a touchy subject for me though, with my leg and all."

"Sorry. I should've realized." She got up and walked over to a small fridge against the wall to pull out two bottles of water, then returned to hand him one. Leilani sat back down on the mat and cracked open her water. "What exactly happened, if you don't mind me asking?"

He gulped down half his bottle of water before answering, hoping to wash away the lump of anxiety that still rose every time someone asked about his injury. He did mind, usually, but today felt different. Maybe because they were the only ones in the gym, and that lent a certain air of intimacy. Through the windows across the room, he could see a bit of the gloom outside had lifted and weak rays of sunshine beamed in. Maybe it was time to let some of his past out of the bag, at least a little. He shrugged and fiddled with his gloves once more. "I got shot. Shattered my femur."

"Yikes. That's awful." Leilani grabbed the white towel she'd tossed on the floor nearby when they'd first arrived and wiped off her face. He glanced sideways at her and did his best not to notice the small bead of sweat tickling down the side of her throat. Tried to stop the sudden thought of how salty that might taste, how warm her skin might be against his tongue.

Wait. What?

He looked away fast as she wrapped the towel around her neck, then faced him once more.

"So," she said, her clear tone cutting through the roar of blood pounding in his ears, not from anxiety this time, but from unexpected, unwanted lust. "Is that when you took the bullet to your shoulder as well?"

Holden nodded, not trusting his voice at present, then drank more water. He didn't want Leilani Kim. Not that way. She was his coworker. She was just being nice. She was drinking her water too, drawing his attention to the sleek muscles of her throat as they worked, the pound of the pulse point at the base of her neck, the curve of her breasts in that tight sports bra.

Oh God.

Move. He needed to move. He started to get to his feet, but Leilani stopped him with a hand on his arm. "I'm sorry that happened to you. I know what it's like to be in a situation where you feel helpless and alone."

The hint of pain in her tone stunned him into staying put. From what he could see, she'd had a fairy-tale life here in paradise, raised in this wedding cake of a hotel.

"How's that? And please, call me Holden," he said, more curious than ever about this enigmatic, beautiful woman. To try to lighten the mood, he cracked a joke. "You get hit by a pineapple on the way to surf the waves?"

Her small smile fell and it felt like the brightening room darkened. She shook her head and looked away. "No. More like hit by a truck and spent six months in the hospital."

"Oh." For a second, Holden just took that in, unsure what else to say. Of course, his analytical mind wanted to know more, demanded details, but he didn't feel comfortable enough to do so. Finally, he managed, "I had no idea."

"No. Most people don't." She sighed and rolled her neck, reaching back to rub her nape again, same as she had the other day in the ER with that combative patient. Then she stood and started gathering her things. "Well, I should go get ready for work."

Of all people, Holden knew a retreat when he saw one. He got up as well, reaching for his cane to take the weight off his now-aching leg. Doing that foot sweep on Leilani hadn't been the most genius move ever, even if his whole side now tingled from the feel of her body briefly pressed to his.

He grabbed his water bottle and limped after her toward the exit, pausing to hold the door for her. Before walking out himself, he looked over toward the windows across the gym one last time. "Hey, the sun's out again."

Leilani glanced in the same direction, then gave him a tiny grin. "Funny how that works, huh? Wait long enough and it always comes back out. See you around, Holden."

"Bye, Dr. Kim," he said, watching her walk away, then stop at the end of the hall and turn back to him.

"Leilani," she called. "Anyone who leg-sweeps me gets to be on a first-name basis."

CHAPTER FOUR

The ER at Ohana Medical Center was hopping the following Wednesday and Leilani was in her element. She was halfway through a twelve-hour shift, and so far she'd dealt with four broken limbs, one case of appendicitis that she'd passed on to a gastro surgeon for removal, and two box jellyfish stings that had required treatment beyond the normal vinegar rinse and ice. The full moon was Friday and that's when the jellyfish population tended to increase near the beaches to mate. There weren't any official warnings posted yet, according to the patient's husband, but that didn't mean there weren't jellyfish present. They were a year-round hazard in Hawaii.

So yeah, a typical day in the neighborhood.

Leilani liked being busy though. That's what made emergency medicine such a good fit for her. Kept her out of trouble, as her parents always said.

Trouble like thinking about that gym encounter with Holden Ross the week prior.

She suppressed a shiver that ran through her at the memory of his hard body pressed against hers on that mat, the heat of him going through her like a bolt of lightning, making her imagine things that were completely off-limits as far as her colleague was concerned.

Since that day, they'd passed each other a few times in the halls, both at the hospital and at the hotel, but hadn't really said more than a friendly greeting. Just as well, since time hadn't seemed to lessen the tingling that passed through her nerve endings whenever he was near. In fact, if anything, the fact they'd taken a tumble on that mat together only seemed to intensify her awareness of him. Which probably explained why she was still hung up on the whole thing. Leilani tried never to let her guard down but Holden had somehow managed to get around her usual barriers.

Boundaries were key to her maintaining control. And control required no distractions.

Distractions led to accidents and accidents led to…

Shaking off the unwanted stab of sorrow in her heart, she concentrated on the notes she was currently typing into her tablet computer at the nurses' station. The EMTs had just radioed in with another patient headed their way and she wanted to get caught up as much as possible before taking on another case.

As she documented her treatment for the latest jellyfish sting patient—visible tentacles removed from sting site, antihistamine for mild allergic reaction, hydrocortisone cream for itching and swelling, ice packs as needed—she half listened to the commotion around her for news of the EMTs arrival with her next patient. She'd just closed out the file she'd been working on when the voice of the sister of one of her earlier patients, a guy who'd broken his arm while hiking near the Diamond Head Crater, broke through her thoughts.

"Doctor?" the woman said, coming down the hall. "I need to ask you something."

Leilani glanced over, ready to answer whatever questions the woman had, then stopped short as the woman headed straight past her and made a beeline for Holden, who'd just come out of an exam room.

He glanced up at the buxom blonde and blinked several times. "How can I help you, ma'am?"

"My brother was in here earlier and I'm concerned he won't take the prescription they gave him correctly, even after the other doctor explained it to him. She was Hawaiian, I think, and—"

"Dr. Kim is the head of Emergency Medicine. I'm sure the instructions she gave him were clear." Holden searched the area and locked eyes with Leilani. "But if you still have concerns, let's go see if she has a few moments to talk to you again, Mrs....?"

"Darla," the woman said, batting her eyelashes and grinning wide.

Leilani bit back a snicker at her flagrant flirting.

"And it's Miss. I'm single. Besides, I'm old-fashioned and prefer a male doctor."

Holden's expression shifted from confused to cornered in about two seconds flat. Darla didn't want medical advice. She wanted a date. Leilani would've laughed out loud at his obvious discomfort if there wasn't a strange niggle eating into her core. Not jealousy because that would be stupid. She had no reason to care if anybody flirted with Holden. It was none of her business. And it wasn't like men hadn't tried to flirt with Leilani in the ER either. It was another occupational hazard. No, what should have bothered her more was the woman doubting her medical expertise. Shoulders squared, she raised a brow and waited for their approach.

Holden cleared his throat and stepped around Darla to head to the nurses' station and Leilani. "Dr. Kim is one of the best physicians I've worked with. She's the person to advise you and your brother on his medications, as she's familiar with his case." He stopped beside Leilani at the desk, tiny dots of crimson staining his high cheekbones. "Dr. Kim, this lady has more questions about her brother's prescription."

Leilani gave him a curt nod, then proceeded to go over the same information she'd given to Darla's brother an hour prior. Steroids weren't exactly rocket science, and from the way the woman continued to focus on Holden's backside and not Leilani, it seemed Darla could have cared less anyway. Finally, Darla went on her way and Leilani exhaled slowly as the EMTs radioed in their ETA of one minute.

Showtime.

Refocusing quickly, she grabbed a fresh gown and mask from the rack nearby and suited up, aware of Holden's gaze on her as she did so. Her skin prickled under the weight of his stare, but she shook it off. The incoming patient needed her undivided attention, not Dr. Ross.

"What's the new case?" Holden asked, handing his tablet back to the nurse behind the desk. "Need help?"

"Maybe," Leilani said, tying the mask around her neck. "Stick close by just in case."

"Will do." He took a gown and mask for himself, then followed her down the hall to the automatic doors leading in from the ambulance bay. His presence beside her felt oddly reassuring, which only rattled her more. She was used to handling things on her own. Safe, secure, solo. That's how she liked it.

Isn't it?

Too late to stew about it now. The doors swished open and the EMTs rushed in with a young man on a gurney. Leilani raced down the hall next to the patient as the EMT in charge gave her a rundown.

"Eighteen-year-old male surfer struck in the neck by his surfboard," the paramedic said. "Difficulty breathing that's worsened over time."

They raced into trauma bay two and Leilani moved in to examine the patient, who was gasping like a fish out of water. "Sir, can you speak? Does it feel like your throat is closing?"

The kid nodded, his eyes wide with panic.

"Okay," Leilani said, keeping her voice calm. "Is it hard to breathe right now?"

The patient nodded again.

"Are you nodding because it hurts to talk or because you can't?" Holden asked, moving in on the other side of the bed once the EMTs got the patient moved from the gurney.

"I…" the kid rasped. "C-can't."

"No intubation, then," Holden said, holding up a hand to stop the nurse with the tracheal tube. "Dr. Kim, would you like me to consult?"

Nice. The other trauma surgeons on staff usually just commandeered a case, rarely asking for Leilani's permission to intercede. Having Holden do so now was refreshing, especially since she'd asked him to stick close by earlier. It showed a level of professional respect that she liked a lot. Plus, it would give her a chance to see firsthand how he handled himself with patients. For weeks now, the nurses had been praising his bedside manner and coolness under pressure. About time Leilani got to see what she was up against if they were both vying for the directorship.

"Yes, please, Dr. Ross." She grabbed an oxygen tube to insert into the kid's nose to help his respiration. "Okay, sir. Breathe in through your nose. Good. One more time."

The kid gasped again. "I c-can't."

Leilani placed her hand on his shoulder. "You're doing fine. I know it hurts."

Holden finished his exam then stepped back to speak to relay orders to the nurse taking the patient's vitals. "We need a CTA of his neck and X-rays, please. Depending on what those show, I may need to do a fiber-optic thoracoscopy. Call ENT for a consult as well, please."

"Where's my son?" a man's voice shouted from out in the hall. "Please let me see him!"

After signing off on the orders, Holden moved aside to let the techs roll the patient out of the trauma room, then grabbed Leilani to go speak to the father. "Sir, your son was injured while surfing," Holden said, after pulling down his mask. "He's getting the best care possible between myself and Dr. Kim. Can you tell me your son's name?"

"Tommy," the man said. "Tommy Schrader. I'm his father, Bill Schrader."

"Thank you, Mr. Schrader." Leilani led the man down the hall to a private waiting room while Holden headed off with the team to complete the tests on the patient. "Let's have a seat in here."

"Will my boy be all right?" Mr. Schrader asked. "What's happened to him?"

"From what the EMTs said when they brought your son in, Tommy was surfing and was struck in the throat by his surfboard. He's got some swelling in his neck and is having trouble breathing." It was obvious the man cared deeply for his son and it was always hard to give difficult news to loved ones. In her case, they'd had to sedate her after delivering the news about her family's deaths. At least Tommy was still alive and getting the treatment he needed.

"When I got the call from the police, I panicked. I told Tommy the surf was too rough today, but he didn't listen." Mr. Schrader scrubbed his hand over his haggard face. "All kinds of crazy things went through my mind. I've never been so scared in all my life."

"Completely understandable, Mr. Schrader. But please know we're doing all we can, and we'll keep you updated on his progress as soon as we know more. They're doing X-rays and a CT scan on him now to determine the extent of damage and the next steps for treatment." She patted the man's shoulder, then stood. "Can I get you anything to drink?"

"No, no. I'm good. I just want to know my son will be okay."

"He's in the best hands possible," Leilani said. "Let me go check on his status again and I'll be right back."

"Thank you," Mr. Schrader said. "I'm sorry I don't know your name."

"Dr. Kim." She gave him a kind smile. "Just sit tight and I'll be back in as soon as we know more."

"Thank you, Dr. Kim," Mr. Schrader said.

Leilani left him and headed up to radiology to check in with Holden. She'd no more than stepped off the elevators when he waved her over to look at the films.

"See how narrow this is?" Holden asked her, pointing at the films of the kid's trachea. "There's definite swelling in his airway. In fact, given that there's maybe only one or two millimeters open at most, it's starting to close off completely. There should be a finger's width all the way up."

Definitely not good, especially since the airway normally narrowed at that point anyway, right before the vocal cords. Which brought up the next issues.

"What about his voice box?" she asked.

"That's my concern," Holden said, the grayish light from the X-ray viewer casting deep shadows on the hollows of his cheeks and under his eyes. "Looks like the surfboard made a direct hit on that area. The voice box could've been broken from the impact. It's a high-risk injury in a high-risk area of the body." He shook his head and leaned in closer to the films. "At least this explains his trouble breathing."

"Are you going to operate?" Leilani asked.

Holden exhaled slowly. "No, not yet. Hate to do that to a kid so young. My advice would be to treat him with steroids first and see if the swelling goes down. Watch him like a hawk though. If conservative treatment doesn't work, then I'll go in with the thoracoscopy."

"Agreed." Leilani stepped back and smiled. Working with Holden felt natural, comfortable. Like they were a team. "Best to keep him in the ER then for the time being. That way if he needs emergency assistance, we're there."

"Yep. Let's do it."

She and Holden rode back down to the trauma bay with the medical team and Tommy, then called his father into the room.

Holden and Leilani exchanged looks, then she nodded. He stepped forward to take the lead. "Mr. Schrader, I'm sorry to tell you this is a very, very serious situation. Your son's airway is currently compromised due to swelling from the surfboard strike. It's possible his voice box had been damaged. If that's the case, it could have long-term effects on his speech."

"Oh God." Mr. Schrader moved in beside his son and took the kid's hand. "I told you not to go surfing today. I was so worried."

"I know," Tommy managed to croak out, clinging to his dad's hand. "Sorry."

"Our biggest concern though, at this point," Holden continued, "is that if his larynx—his voice box—is too badly damaged, your son runs the risk of losing his ability to breathe. We need to keep him here at the hospital, in the ER, for at least the next twelve hours for observation. That way if his condition worsens, we can rush him into surgery immediately, if needed. I'd also like to get a consult from one of the throat specialists on staff to get their opinion."

"Whatever you need to do," Mr. Schrader said. "I just want my son to be okay."

"Great. Thank you." Holden stepped back and glanced at Leilani again. "Both Dr. Kim and I will check on Tommy periodically through the night to keep an eye on him then."

"Yes, we will. You won't be alone." Leilani leaned in to place the call button in the kid's hand and give him a reassuring smile. Once upon a time, that had been her in a hospital bed—scared and unsure about the future. "And if you feel your breathing gets worse at any point, you just press that button and we'll rush back in right away, okay?"

Tommy gave a hesitant nod.

"Someone will always be here for you, Tommy," Holden said, meeting Leilani's gaze. "I promise. We're not going to let anything else happen to you."

The kid swallowed, then winced.

"Don't worry. We'll be in here checking on you so often you'll get sick of seeing us." Leilani winked, then headed toward the door with Holden. "Promise."

"And I'll be here too, son," his dad said, pulling up a chair to the beside.

She and Holden walked back to the nurses' station, discarding their masks and gowns in the biohazard bin and stopping to wash their hands at the sink nearby. His limp seemed less pronounced today, though he still used his cane to take the weight off his right leg.

She glanced over at him and smiled as she soaped up, then rinsed off. "You handled that case well."

"Thanks." He smiled, then winced, tossing his used paper towels in the trash and reaching up to touch the sutures in his lower lip.

"Stitches bothering you?" she asked, leaning a bit closer to inspect his wound. "Looks like it's healing well."

"I'm fine. It just stings a bit when I forget it's there," he said, holding up a tube of lip balm. "This helps though."

"Glad to hear it." Leilani turned away from the cherry flavored lip balm he held up. That was her favorite flavor. And now, for some reason, her mind kept wondering what his kisses would taste like with cherries in the mix. Ugh. Not good. Not good at all. She stepped back and looked anywhere but at him. "So, I should probably get back to work on another case then."

"Yeah, me too." He fiddled with the head of his cane, frowning slightly. "Hey, um, I meant to ask you about the luau."

"Luau?" she repeated, like she was channeling her pet parrot. Her pulse kicked up a notch. Damn. She'd been hoping he'd forget about all that. Apparently not. She forced a smile she didn't quite feel and flexed her fingers to relax them. Considering she'd just been having inappropriate thoughts about this man—her coworker—if she was wise, she'd get the heck out of there as soon as possible. Unfortunately, her feet seemed to have other ideas, because they stayed firmly planted where she was.

At least he seemed as awkward as she felt about it all, shuffling his feet and fumbling over his words. It was actually quite endearing… Leilani's heart pinched a little at the sweetness, before she stopped herself.

Keep it professional, girl.

"The other day, last week, uh," he said, keeping his gaze lowered like he was a nervous schoolkid and not a highly successful surgeon. "Anyway, I think your dad mentioned the luau at the hotel and I'd seen some flyers on it too, and I wondered if you still wanted to take me." He hazarded a glance up and caught her eye. "Not that I'll hold you to that. I just…" He exhaled slowly and ran his free hand through his hair, leaving the dark curls in adorable disarray.

No. Not adorable. No, no, no.

But even as she thought that, the simmering awareness bubbling inside her boiled over into blatant interest without her consent. Damn. This was beyond inconvenient. Of all the men for her to be interested in now, it had to be Holden Ross.

He huffed out a breath, then cursed quietly before straightening and meeting her gaze head-on as his words tumbled out in a rush. "Look. I don't get out much and I'd like to see some sights while I'm here, and since you offered the other day, I thought I'd take you up on that, if the offer…if it still stands. Not a date, because I don't do that. Just as two people, colleagues…" He hung his head. "I'm off tomorrow and Friday."

Leilani blinked at him a moment, stunned. Blood thundered in her ears and she turned away to grab her tablet from behind the desk, needing something, anything, to keep herself busy, to keep herself from agreeing to his invitation and more. Because for some crazy reason that's exactly what she wanted to do.

Think, girl. Think.

Saying yes could lead to a friendship between them beyond work, could lead to those uncomfortable tingles of like for this guy going a whole lot further into other *l* words. Not *love*, because that was off the table, but another one with a capital *L. Lust.* Because yeah, Holden really was just her type. Tall, dark, gorgeous. Smart, funny, sexy as all get out.

So, she should definitely say no. He was her coworker, her potential rival.

Except that would be rude. And she just couldn't bring herself to be rude to him. Maybe it was that haunted look in his eyes she spied sometimes. Maybe it was his obvious awkwardness around commitment.

I don't date.

Well, neither did she at present. Or maybe it was the

air of brokenness about him that called to the same old wounded parts in her.

Whatever it was, she didn't want to turn him down, even though she should.

There was one problem though.

She looked back at him over her shoulder as she brought up the next patient's information on her screen. "Malu Huna's luaus are only on Friday nights. And I have to work tomorrow. If you wanted to see the sights on Friday," she said, taking a deep breath to calm her racing nerves, "then I guess we could. It will make for a long day though. Are you sure you're up to that?"

"I am if you are," he said, his cane clinking against the desk as he moved closer. "I'll double up on my pain pills so I'm ready for anything."

Ready for anything.

Damn if those words, spoken in that deep velvet voice of his, didn't conjure a whole new batch of inappropriate thoughts. The two of them on the beach, holding hands and running into the waves together, lying in the sand afterward, making out like two horny teens, the feel of that dark stubble on his jaw scraping her cheeks, her neck, her chest, lower still…

Oh boy. I'm in trouble here.

Heat stormed her cheeks and she swiveled to face him, not realizing how close they were until it was too late. Her hand brushed his solid, warm chest before she snatched it away. Holden's hazel eyes flared with the same awareness jolting through her, before he quickly hid it behind a frown.

"Look, if you don't want to—"

"No, it's fine. I promised you and I always keep my word." She focused on the file on her screen again, trying in vain to calm her whirling thoughts. This was so not like her. She never went gaga over men. Yet here she was, blushing and stammering and acting like an idiot over the last man on Earth she should be attracted to. And yet, she was. Much as she hated to admit it.

Gah! Images of them lying together on that mat in the hotel gym zoomed back fast and furious to her mind. No. If she was going to get through this with her sanity and her heart intact, she needed to think logically about it. She'd show him her island home, not just the tourist sights, but her favorite spots too. Besides, it might give her a chance to find out more about his relationship with Dr. King and his real motives for being here in Hawaii. Taken in that light, she'd be a fool not to take him up on his offer, right? She took a deep breath, then set her tablet aside. "Fine. We'll tour the town, then end with the luau. Meet me in the lobby at the hotel at 8:00 a.m. the day after tomorrow and don't be late."

Holden opened his mouth, closed it, then he smiled—the slow little one that made her toes curl in her comfy white running shoes. Ugh. No more of that. She turned away to head into her next exam room as his surprised tone revealed an equal amount of shock on his part. "Uh…okay. Eight o'clock on Friday it is."

Four hours later, Holden was finishing up his shift by checking for the last time with Tommy Schrader. The kid was lucky. The steroids had helped reduce the swelling in his larynx and it didn't look like the thoracoscopy would be necessary after all.

When Holden arrived upstairs to Tommy's room, several of the kid's surfer friends were there, along with Tommy's father. Tommy was holding court like a king

on his throne from his hospital bed, sun-streaked shaggy
blond hair hanging in his face and his voice like gravel in
a blender. But the fact the kid was speaking at all was a
minor miracle. His injury could've been so much worse,
and Holden was glad such a young guy wouldn't carry
lifelong scars from his accident.

Unlike Holden himself.

He cleared his throat at the door to the hospital room
to announce his presence. "Sorry if this is a bad time.
Just wanted to check in on my patient one more time
before my shift is over." He limped into the room with
his cane and smiled at Mr. Schrader and the new guests.
"Tommy's very lucky."

"Dudes, you have no idea," Tommy rasped out, smiling at Holden, then his friends. "They were gonna stick a
camera up my nose and down my throat and everything."

"Whoa," his friends said, both as shaggy and sun-
burned as Tommy. "Man, that's gnarly. You were gonna
be awake for that?"

"Patients are usually awake for thoracoscopy, yes,"
Holden confirmed as he reached Tommy's beside and
leaned closer to examine the kid's throat. The swelling
was greatly reduced, even from the last time Holden
had checked him about an hour prior. He'd be fine to
discharge.

He straightened and turned to Mr. Schrader, who was
sitting on a chair near the window. "Your son appears to
be healing just fine now, though Dr. Kim will continue
to check on him for the remainder of his stay. I don't
imagine there'll be any lingering effects, but I'll leave
orders to discharge him with another round of steroids
and some anti-inflammatory meds too. Then have him
check in with your family physician in two weeks."

"Sounds good." The father shook Holden's hand. "Thanks so much, Doc. Now that I know my son's gonna be all right, once I get him home I'll make sure his older brothers keep an eye on him too. And try to talk him out of surfing so close to a full moon again."

Holden grinned and turned back to Tommy. "Listen to your dad. Take care, Tommy."

"Thanks, Doc. *Mahalo*," the kid said, shaking Holden's hand too. "I'll be sure to thank the pretty lady doc too. You guys make a good team. She your girlfriend?"

"Son," Mr. Schrader said, his voice rife with warning. "Don't mind him, Dr. Ross. That's all him and his friends think about these days when they're not surfing. Girls."

"I'll pass along gratitude to Dr. Kim," Holden said, dodging the uncomfortable questions and ignoring the squeeze of anxiety in his chest it caused. "Take care, all."

"*Mahalo*, Doc!" Tommy called again as Holden walked from the room to the nurses' station down the hall.

He should feel relieved to have another successful patient outcome under his belt, but now all he could think about was Leilani and their upcoming date on Friday.

Wait. Scratch that. Not a date.

He hadn't lied when he'd told her he didn't do that. Life was too unpredictable for long-term commitments. The shooting had taught him that. Nothing was permanent, especially love. So now he chose short, sweet, no strings attached affairs. No deeper, messy, scary emotions involved, thanks. No connections beyond the physical. No chance to have his heart ripped out and shredded to pieces. Because that's what he wanted.

Isn't it?

Not that it mattered. He and Leilani Kim were work colleagues, nothing more. Best to keep his head down and focus on his work, then move on when this stint ended. That was the safest bet. And Holden was all about safety these days.

She'd show him around the city, then take him to the luau at the resort, as promised. That's all. Nothing more. And sure, he couldn't stop thinking about the feel of her beneath him on that stupid gym mat, the sweet jasmine and lemon scent of her hair, the warm brush of her skin against his and…

Oh God.

He was such an idiot. What the hell had he been thinking to bring up her invitation to the luau? He hadn't been thinking, that was the problem. Or more to the point, he'd been thinking with his libido and not his brain. Memories of her dressed in those formfitting leggings and tank top at the gym that day, how she might wrap those shapely legs of hers around him instead, and hold him close, kiss him, run her fingers through his hair. He shuddered.

No. No, no, no.

With more effort than should be necessary to concentrate, Holden finished electronically signing off on his notes on the Tommy Schrader case, then left instructions for his discharge for Leilani before handing it all over to the nurse waiting behind the desk.

"Dr. King asked to see you upstairs in her office when you have a moment, Dr. Ross," the nurse said.

"Thanks." Probably about that project she'd mentioned to him before. He took a deep breath, then headed for the elevators. The clock on the wall said it was nearly time for him to leave. Good. He'd see Helen, then head back to the ER to hand off his cases to the next physician on duty before going back to the hotel for some much-needed sleep.

Besides, talking to Helen should be a good distraction from his unwanted thoughts about Leilani. The elevator dinged and he stepped on board then pushed the button for the fifth floor, where the administrative offices were located.

He had to get his head on straight again before Friday. Hell, if he was really serious about keeping to himself, he'd cancel the whole day altogether. Given the surprised look on her face when she'd offered to show him around, she'd probably be glad to be rid of him as well. But then if he did cancel, she might take it the wrong way, and the last thing he wanted was to offend her. They still had to work together, after all.

You guys make a good team.

Tommy's words from earlier echoed through his head. The worst part was, they were true.

Working with Leilani on that case had felt seamless, effortless, *right.*

Which was just wrong, in Holden's estimation.

He didn't want partnerships anymore, professionally or personally. Getting too close to people only made you vulnerable and weak, especially when they could be taken from you so easily.

Ding!

The elevator doors swished open and Holden stepped out into the lobby on the administrative floor. Thick carpet padded his footsteps as he headed over to the receptionist's desk in the middle of the plush leather-and-glass sitting area.

"Hi. Holden Ross to see Helen King, please," he said,

feeling out of place and underdressed in his shift-old scrubs and sneakers.

"Dr. King's been expecting you, Dr. Ross." She pointed down a hallway to her left. "Last door on the right."

"Thanks." He gave the woman a polite smile, then headed for the office she'd indicated. The other times he'd met with Helen here in Hawaii, it had been outside the hospital, either at her home near Waikiki or at the fancy restaurant she'd taken him to on his first night in the city. Other than that, he'd never been up here, since regular old human resources was in another building entirely, half a block down from the medical center. He made his way to the end of the hall and stopped to admire the amazing view from the floor-to-ceiling glass wall beside the office before knocking on the dark wood door.

"Come in," Helen called from inside, and Holden entered the office.

For a moment, he took in the understated elegance of the place. It was Helen to a T, no-nonsense yet comfortable. "Wow, this is a big step up from Chicago, huh?"

Helen chuckled, her husky voice helping to soothe his earlier anxiety. "It doesn't suck. Please come in, Holden. Have a seat."

He did so, in a large wingback leather chair in front of her desk that probably cost more than his rent back home. As always, Helen's desk was spotless, with stacks of files neatly placed in bins and every pen just so. "The nurse downstairs said you wanted to see me?"

"I wanted to see how you're settling in," she said, sitting back in her black leather executive chair that dwarfed her petite frame. With her short white hair and sparkling blue eyes, she'd always reminded Holden of a certain British actress of a certain age, who took no crap from anyone. "We haven't talked in a few weeks. How are you liking things here at Ohana?"

"Fine." He did his best to relax but found it difficult. He and Helen had been friends long enough for him to suspect this wasn't just a social call. They could've gone to the pub for that. "The facilities are top-notch and the staff is great."

Better than great, his mind chimed in as he recalled Leilani.

Not that he'd mention his unwanted attraction to his coworker to Helen. The woman had been trying to get him married off since they'd worked together back in Chicago. If she even suspected a hint of chemistry between him and Leilani, she'd be all over it worse than the Spanish Inquisition.

"Glad to hear you like it." Helen steepled her fingers, then watched him over the top of them, her gaze narrowed, like M getting ready to assign her best secret agent a new kill. "But do you like it enough to consider staying?"

"What?" Holden tore his gaze away from the stunning views of the ocean in the distance and focused on Helen once more, his chest tightening. He frowned. "No. I'm locum tenens."

"I know," she said, sitting forward to rest her arms atop her desk. "But what if you weren't."

The low-grade anxiety constantly swirling in his chest rose higher, constricting his vocal cords. "But I am. You know I don't want to get tied down to anywhere. Not yet."

Maybe not ever again.

Helen blinked at him several times before exhaling slowly, her expression morphing from confident to concerned. "I'm worried about you, Holden. You've been on your own since the shooting, jetting off to a new place every few months, no connections, no home."

"I'm fine," he said, forcing the words. "Look, I thought you called me here to talk about that project you mentioned, not dissect my personal life."

"Are you fine though?" Her blue gaze narrowed, far too perceptive for his tastes. She sighed and stood, coming around the desk and leaning her hips back against it as she changed the subject. "Well, all that aside… Fine, let's discuss the project then."

Holden released his pent-up breath, his lungs aching for oxygen, and stared at the floor beneath his feet. Helen had saved his life after the shooting. Stitching up his wounds and staunching his blood loss until the orthopedic surgeons could work their magic on his leg and shoulder. Without her, there was a good chance he would've ended up six feet under, just like David.

An unexpected pang of grief stabbed his chest. Even a year later, he still missed his best friend like it was yesterday. The funeral. The awful days afterward, walking around like a zombie, no emotions, no light, no hope.

Still, he was here. He was coming back to life slowly, painfully, whether he wanted to or not. Like a limb that had fallen asleep, pins and needles stabbed him relentlessly as the emotions he'd suppressed for so long returned. Maybe that was why he felt so drawn to Leilani—her vibrant spirit, the sense that perhaps in some weird way she understood what he'd been through, how she made him feel things he'd thought he'd never feel again.

Plus, he owed Helen a debt he could never repay. That's why he was here in Hawaii. Why he was here now. She'd saved his life and his leg. The least he could do was hear her out. He cleared his throat, then asked, "What kind of project is it?"

"Twofold, actually." Helen clasped her hands in front of her. "First, our national accreditation is coming up for renewal next year and we need to make sure all of our security policies are up-to-date for the ER. I'd like you to help with that."

Holden swallowed hard and forced his tense shoulders to relax. "I can do that."

"Good." Helen glanced out the windows then back to him again. "Secondly, you know I'm looking for a new director of emergency medicine, yes?"

"Yes," he said. "But I'm here as a trauma surgeon."

"True. But you've got the experience and the temperament to head a department, Holden." She crossed her arms. "You were on track to run the ER back in Chicago, before the shooting."

He had been. That was true. But those ambitions had died along with David that day. He didn't want to be responsible for all those people, for all those lives. What if he failed again?

"I don't want that anymore. I'm happy with the temporary stint." His response sounded flat to his own ears and his heart pinched slightly despite knowing he couldn't even consider taking on a more permanent role. "Besides, Dr. Kim is doing a great job as temporary director. Why not offer it to her?"

"She's in the running, to be sure," Helen said before pushing away from the desk and walking over to the windows nearby. "But I like to keep my options open.

And it's been nice having you here, Holden. I won't lie. We're friends. I know you. Trust you. Dr. Kim seems more than competent and her record at Ohana is outstanding, but every time I try to get to know her better, she shuts me down. I'm not sure I can work with someone I don't know and trust implicitly."

Holden had noticed Leilani deftly skirting his questions around her past too. Then again, he had no room to talk. He hadn't told her anything about what had happened to him either.

He exhaled slowly and raked a hand through his hair. He didn't like the idea of spying for Helen, no matter how much he owed her. Maybe he should cancel Friday, just so it wouldn't come back to bite him later, one way or another. Shut down any semblance of something more between him and Leilani before it ever really started. The fact he seemed more drawn to her each time they were together scared him more than anything, to be honest, and Holden was no coward. But damn if he wanted to open himself up to a world of hurt again, and some hidden part of him sensed that getting closer to Leilani would bring heartbreak for sure.

"I don't feel comfortable spying for you," he said bluntly. "Not on a colleague."

"No," Helen said, giving him a small smile. "I didn't imagine you would. Well, that's fine. Just keep an eye out during the project. If you see anything you think I should know about, let me know. Oh, and I haven't talked to Dr. Kim about it yet, so keep it under your hat, until I do. Okay?"

"Okay." Seemed an odd request, but an innocent one. "No problem. Anything else?"

"Nope. That's it." Helen walked back around her desk

and took a seat. "I've got work to do, so get out of my office."

He chuckled and stood, his cane sinking into the thick carpet as he leaned his weight on it. "Let me know when it's safe to mention the project to Leilani. I'll be out until the weekend."

Helen gave him a quizzical look at his use of Dr. Kim's first name, and he kicked himself mentally. Then she winked and grinned as he hobbled toward the door.

"Enjoy your days off," she called after him.

"Thanks," he said, gritting his teeth against the soreness in his thigh. He needed to finish up his shift, then get back to the hotel, take a shower, rest, recharge, decide whether to cancel on Friday or spend the day with the one woman who'd somehow gotten under his skin despite all his wishes to the contrary.

"Oh, and Holden?" Helen called when he was halfway into the hall.

"Yeah?" He peeked his head back inside the office.

"Don't stay cooped up your whole time here in Hawaii," she said, as if reading his thoughts. "Get out and live a little. Trust me—you'll be glad you did."

Holden headed back down the hall and over the elevators, unable to shake the sense of fate weighing heavy on his shoulders. Too bad he didn't believe in destiny anymore. One random act of violence had changed all that forever.

Still, as he headed back down to the ER his old friend's words kept running through his head, forcing him to reconsider canceling his Friday plans with Leilani.

Get out and live a little. Trust me—you'll be glad you did...

CHAPTER FIVE

At seven fifty-eight on Friday morning, Leilani stood behind the reception desk at her parents' resort, feeding her parrot, U'i, and wondering if it was too late to fake a stomach bug to get out of her day with Holden.

"Who's a pretty bird?" U'i squawked, followed by a string of curses in three languages—Mandarin, Hawaiian and English.

Leilani snorted and fed him another hunk of fresh pineapple. She'd had him as a pet since right after the accident and loved him with all her heart, even though he acted like a brat and swore like a sailor sometimes. Considering he was sixteen and African grays typically lived as long as humans, U'i was definitely in his terrible teen years.

"More," he screeched when she wasn't fast enough with the next hunk of fruit. He took it in his black beak, then held on to a slice of orange with one foot while cocking his head at her and blinking his dark eyes. "Thanks, baby."

"You're welcome, baby," she said in return, scratching his feathered head with her finger and grinning. "Mama loves you."

"Mama loves you," U'i repeated, before devouring his treat.

"Hey," a deep male voice said from behind her, causing her heart to flip.

Leilani set aside the cup of fruit she'd snagged from the breakfast buffet in the dining room, then wiped her hands on the legs of her denim shorts before turning slowly to face Holden. *Too late to run now*, she supposed. She gave him a smile and prayed she didn't look as nervous as she felt. "Hey."

In truth, she'd spent the last twenty-four hours seriously questioning her sanity for offering to be Holden's tour guide today. Sure, she wanted to get to know him better, but that was a double-edged sword. Getting to know him better risked getting to like him better. And liking him even more than she did now was a definite no-no, considering she melted a little more inside each time she saw him.

Like now, when he was standing there, looking effortlessly gorgeous in a pair of navy board shorts and a yellow Hawaiian shirt that rivaled any of the loud numbers her dad wore. The open V of his collar beckoned her eyes to trail slowly down his tanned chest to his trim hips and strong, sexy, tanned calves. God. How was that even possible? Their schedules at the hospital were nuts. Who had time to soak up the sunshine? Apparently, Holden did, since he looked like he'd walked straight off a "hot hunks in paradise" poster.

He shuffled his feet and switched his cane from one side to the other, making her realize she'd been staring. Self-conscious now, she turned back to her pet and fed him another chunk of pineapple from the cup.

"Who's your friend?" Holden asked.

"This is U'i," she said, leaning in to kiss the bird's head.

"Huey?" Holden asked, stepping closer to look at the parrot, who was eyeballing him back.

"No. *U'i*," Leilani corrected him. "No *h*. It means *handsome* in Hawaiian."

"Ah." He reached up toward the bird, then hesitated. "Does he bite?"

"Only if he doesn't like you." She snorted at Holden's startled expression, then took pity on him, holding out the fruit cup toward him. "Here, feed him some of this. U'i's never met food he didn't like."

Sure enough, her traitorous pet snagged the hunk of melon from Holden's fingers, then gave him an infatuated coo that Leilani was lucky to hear even after a half hour of cuddles and tummy rubs. Seemed Holden's considerable charms worked on more than just her.

"African gray, right?" Holden asked, bravely stroking a finger over U'i's head.

"Correct." Leilani smiled despite herself. "You a bird fan?"

"A friend of mine back in med school had one. Smart as a whip and snarky too."

"Yep, that's my guy here." She gave her beloved pet one more kiss, then stepped away fast. Holden moved as well, causing his arm to brush hers, sending tingles of awareness through her already overtaxed nervous system. "So, are you, uh, ready to go?"

"Whenever you are," Holden said, stepping back and giving her a too-bright smile. "Doubled my pain meds, so lead onward."

For the second time since their conversation in the ER

on Wednesday, the thought popped into her head that maybe he was as nervous about all this as she was. After all, he'd been stammering and shifting around as much as her, his frown still fresh in her mind. She'd assumed it was because he didn't really want to spend time with her, but now she wondered if it went deeper than that.

"Did you get Tommy Schrader released okay—the surfboard patient? He was doing much better the last time I checked. He told me *mahalo*."

"Yep. He was doing much better when I discharged him. Gave him your scripts too. I'm glad there wasn't any permanent damage to his voice box." She wiped her hands off again and tossed away the empty fruit cup before walking back around the desk and beckoning for Holden to follow her. Well, regardless of how he felt about things, they were both stuck together for the day now. Correction, day and evening, since they had the luau tonight after their day of sightseeing. Then they could go back to their separate lives. Leilani glanced at the clock on the wall again. Five after eight. Man, it was going to be a long day at this rate.

Okay. At least she had a full itinerary to keep them busy. First though, a few questions. She glanced at his cane, then back to his eyes. "How are you with walking?"

"Fine, I think," he said, adjusting his weight. "Like I said, I took my pain meds this morning and have another dose in my pocket in case I need it later. Actually, I think the exercise might do me good. My physical therapist back in Chicago is always on me to move more. Says it's the only way I'm going to get full function back and lose this someday." He waggled his cane in front of him.

"I may need to take breaks every so often, but I'm looking forward to a day in the fresh air."

"Okay then. Great." She started toward the front entrance, slowing her usual brisk pace to make it easier on Holden. "I thought we could start at North Shore, since the beach there is a bit less crowded than Waikiki and you can get to Diamond Head easy enough on your own with it being so close to the hotel.

"We can maybe grab a quick breakfast at one of the stands at North Shore too, then go see Honolulu's Chinatown markets, stop by the Iolani Palace downtown and visit the USS *Arizona* memorial, then end the day by hiking to Manoa Falls. It's short and mostly shaded, so it shouldn't be too tough for you. That should get you plenty hungry for the luau tonight when we get back to the hotel."

"Sounds great. Let's roll," he said, climbing into the hotel shuttle Leilani had commandeered just for their use today, then holding his cane between his knees. He seemed more relaxed now than she'd ever seen him, and Leilani had to admit she found him more attractive by the minute. "I'm all yours."

At his words, that darned awareness simmering inside her flared bright as the sun again, and she said a silent prayer of thanks that she was sitting down, because she doubted her wobbly knees would've supported her. There was a part of her that wished more than anything that were true, that he was hers, and if that wasn't terrifying, she didn't know what was.

She turned out of the hotel parking lot and wound her way through town before merging onto the H1 highway heading north, allowing the warmth from the sunshine and fresh air breezing in through the open windows to ease some of her tension away. His comment had been innocent enough and the fact that she instantly took it as more spoke to her own loneliness and neglected libido than anything else. Traffic thinned as they left the city behind. For his part, Holden seemed content to just stare out the window at the passing scenery, dark sunglasses hiding his eyes from her view.

Good thing too, since they were passing right by the spot where the accident had happened years ago. Man, she hadn't even thought about that when she'd been planning the itinerary for today, which only went to show how torn and twisted she'd been about this whole excursion. Now though, as they neared the junction of H1 and H2 and she veered off toward the right and the H2 highway, Leilani spotted a sign for the outlet mall close by and gripped the steering wheel tighter. They'd been going there that day, shopping for back-to-school clothes for her and her brother, when the accident happened. Her mouth dried and her chest ached as she held her breath and sped past the spot where they'd skidded off the road after impact, their station wagon tumbling over and over down into the ravine until finally landing on its roof, the wheels still spinning and groaning, the smell of gasoline and hissing steam from the radiator as pungent now as they'd been that long-ago day when Leilani had been trapped in the back seat, upside down, gravely injured, screaming for help while her loved ones died around her…

"Uh, are we in a huge hurry?" Holden said from the passenger seat, drawing her back to the present. "Speedometer says we're pushing eighty."

Crap.

She forced herself to take a breath and eased her death

grip on the steering wheel. Throat parched, her words emerged as little more than a croak. "Sorry. Lead foot."

Holden watched her closely, his gaze hidden behind those dark glasses of his, but all the same, Leilani could feel his stare burning. Her cheek prickled from it and she focused on easing her foot off the accelerator to avoid the unsettling panic still thrumming through her bloodstream. It was fine. Things were all fine now. She was safe. They were safe.

"Everything okay?" Holden asked after a moment. "You look a little pale."

"No. It's fine." She took a few deep breaths as a couple of cars passed them. "Driving on the freeway bothers me, that's all."

His full lips turned down at the corners. "You should've said something earlier. If this is making you uncomfortable, we can go somewhere else. I can see the beach myself another time."

"No, it's fine." She kept her eyes straight ahead, afraid that if she looked at him, he'd see all the turmoil inside her. "Look. There's a sign for the Dole Plantation."

Holden looked toward his window then back to her. "Should we go there instead?"

"Nah." She shrugged, releasing some of the knots between her shoulder blades. "It's pretty and all, but not very exciting."

"Not very exciting isn't always a bad thing," he said, shifting to face front again.

The hint of sadness in his voice made her want to ask him more about his injuries, but after her flashbacks a minute ago, now didn't seem like the best time. Instead, she drove on toward the beach and, hopefully, something to keep them busy and away from dangerous topics. The rest of the forty-minute trip passed without incident, thankfully.

Sure enough, the beach was lovely. Fewer people and beautiful stretches of sand and surf for miles. They grabbed acai bowls in Haleiwa Town, then headed over to Ehukai Beach Park and the Banzai Pipeline to watch the surfers shred some waves.

They snagged some seats atop a wooden table in one of the picnic areas lining the sandy beach and had excellent views of the massive waves crashing toward the rocks just offshore.

"Man, that's impressive," Holden said around a bite of granola, coconut and tangy acai berries. "Look at that. How big do the waves get here?"

"Up to twenty-five feet during the winter. We're at the tail end now, with it being March, but they can still get pretty big." She chuckled at a small boy running out into the surf. "Check him out. Can't be more than five and already fearless."

"Wow." Holden stared wide-eyed as the child held his own on the big waves right next to the adults. "That's amazing."

"Yeah. I remember being his age and coming here with my dad. I learned to swim not far from here at the Point." Sadness pushed closer around her heart before she shoved it away. "Those were good days."

"Really?" He blinked at her now, suitably impressed. "So, you can hang ten with these guys then?"

She laughed around another bite of food. "Back in the day, sure. It's been years since I surfed though, so probably not now. Though they say it's like riding a bike. You never really forget."

"Hmm." He finished his food, then tossed his trash in

a nearby receptacle, scoring a perfect three-pointer. He swallowed some water from his bottle, the sleek muscles working in his throat entrancing her far more than they should. "Well, I certainly won't be doing much surfing these days with my leg."

He rubbed his right thigh again, tiny whitish scars bisecting his tanned skin. From a distance they weren't as visible, but this close she could see them all. The questions she'd been putting off rose once more, but before she could ask, he slid down off the table and toed off his walking shoes. "Think I'll take a gander down the beach, if you don't mind."

"No. Go for it." She watched him head off, then finished her breakfast before standing to throw her own trash away. It was a beautiful spring day, not too hot or too cold, the scent of salt and sand filling the air. Above her, seagulls cried and leaves of the nearby banyan trees rustled in the breeze. She'd used to love coming here as a kid, building sandcastles with her brother, or cuddling on her mom's lap beneath the blue sky. She wrapped her arms around herself and kicked off her sneakers, venturing down to the water's edge to dip her toes in the bracing Pacific waters.

Lost in thought, she didn't even hear Holden return until he was right next to her on the wet sand, his cane in one hand and his shoes dangling from the fingers of the other. His dark hair was tousled and the shadow of dark stubble on his chin made her want to run her tongue over it, then nuzzle her face into his neck. She swallowed hard and stared out at the horizon and the surfers balancing on the crests of the waves rolling in. "How was your walk?"

"Good. Needed to stretch my legs after the car ride." He took a deep breath in and glanced skyward. "Hard to imagine your dad out here though. Never thought of Joe Kim as a surfer."

"Oh, he's not," she said without thinking, then stopped herself. Too late.

Holden was looking at her again, reaching up to lower those sunglasses of his so his hazel eyes were visible over the tops of their rims. "I'm confused."

A few weeks ago, she would've walked away, shut down this conversation with him. But now, today, she felt tired. Tired of pushing him away, tired of keeping up her walls so high and strong, tired of running. Leilani sighed and shook her head. "The Kims aren't my real parents. They adopted me after my family was killed in a car accident twenty years ago."

"Oh," Holden said, his voice distant as he took that in. After a few moments, he seemed to collect himself and stepped closer to her to block the breeze. "I'm sorry. That must've been horrible."

"It's okay," she said out of habit. Years of distancing people took their toll. "I mean, it happened a long time ago, when I was fourteen. I've moved on." And she had, at least in most areas. Work. School. Anywhere that didn't require true intimacy. Speaking of intimacy, Holden's body heat penetrated the thin cotton of her pink tank top and made her crave all sorts of things that were best left alone. She moved away and headed back toward their car. "We should probably get going if we want to make our eleven-thirty ticket time at Pearl Harbor."

He lingered on the beach a moment before limping after her. "Right. Sure."

* * *

Three hours later, Holden sat on the hard bench seat in the Navy boat shuttle beside Leilani on their way to the USS *Arizona* Memorial, glad for a break to rest his sore leg. Not that he would've missed anything from their day. They'd already spent time at several of the other sites within the World War II Valor in the Pacific National Monument, including touring the USS *Bowfin* Submarine Park, the Pearl Harbor Aviation Museum, and the USS *Missouri* Battleship Memorial, as well as walking through the visitors center, the Road to War Museum, and the Aloha Court. Neither of them had said much since leaving the North Shore.

Holden had spent much of the time trying to wrap his head around what Leilani had shared with him. Being a teenager was hard enough without losing your entire family. He couldn't imagine what she must've gone through back then, the grief, the loss. That certainly explained the pain he saw flashing in her dark eyes sometimes though. Also explained why she'd known so much about that seat belt law in the ER that day.

He'd wanted to ask her more about what had happened, but then she'd not really seemed open to it on the ride to Pearl Harbor. Once they'd gotten inside the park there'd been films to watch and audio tours, and now Holden had no clue how to broach the subject with her again.

Of course, then there was the fact that coming here, to the site where so many had lost their lives in another act of violence brought all of his own pain rushing back to the forefront. December 7, 1941, was a long time ago, and he hadn't expected it to affect him as much as it did, but there'd already been several times when he'd nearly lost it.

The first time had occurred when they'd toured the Attack museum, which followed the events from Pearl Harbor through the end of World War II, and he'd seen the delicate origami crane by Sadako Sasaki, a young girl of only two when the bomb had been dropped on Hiroshima. Her goal had been to fold a thousand cranes during her time in the hospital for her injuries, which according to Japanese legend meant she'd then be granted a wish, but she'd only made it to six hundred and forty-four before her death at the age of twelve. Holden's chest still squeezed with sadness over her loss. Her family had donated the sculpture to the museum in the hopes of peace and reconciliation.

The second time had been during the film they'd watched before boarding the shuttle to tour the USS *Arizona* Memorial. Hearing the servicemen and women and the eyewitnesses to the event talk about their fallen comrades and the horrific things they'd seen that day had taken Holden right back to the shooting in Chicago—the eerie quiet in the ER after the gunman had opened fire broken only by the squeak of the attacker's shoes on the tile floor, the metallic smell of the weapons firing, David's last desperate gasps for air as he'd bled out on the floor beside Holden, and the helpless feeling of knowing there was nothing he could do to stop it.

He forced himself to take a deep breath and focused out the open window on the gentle waves lapping the sides of the shuttle. The scent of sea and the light jasmine shampoo from Leilani's hair helped calm his racing pulse. This wasn't Chicago. They were safe here.

They docked a few minutes later and got out to traverse the new ramps that had been installed the previous year for visitors to the monument. The other passengers were quiet too, almost reverent at they stood before the iconic white stone structure. According the audio narration both he and Leilani were listening to through their headphones, it was built directly over the site of the sinking of the battleship *Arizona* in 1941 and to match the ship's length, to commemorate the lives lost that day.

Ahead of them in line was a group of six older men, dressed in hats and sashes from World War II. Some were in wheelchairs or walked with canes, like Holden. All of them were visibly shaken the moment they entered the memorial. Holden himself had goose bumps on his arms at the thought of the brave soldiers who'd perished that day with no warning, no chance to escape. He felt their panic, knew their fear, understood their need to protect others even at the cost of their own lives.

Lost in his thoughts, he barely noticed when the narration ended and Leilani put her hand on his arm. He leaned heavily on his cane, swallowing hard against the lump in his throat, and finally met her gaze. Her expression was both expectant and worried and he realized she must've asked him something. He removed his headphones and swiped a hand over his face. "I'm sorry?"

"I asked if you were all right," she whispered. "You look like you're going to pass out."

"I'm fine," he said, though he wasn't. Thankfully, a cool breeze was blowing in through the openings in the sides and ceiling of the stone monument, cooling him down a bit. At her dubious look, he gave her a wan smile. "Really. But could we just stand here a minute?"

"Sure." She moved them out of line and over to the railing, where the breeze was stronger, and the shade helped too. As the other patrons in their tour group made their way up toward the front of the memorial, where the names of all the people lost that day were etched into the stone, Leilani leaned her arms on the railing beside him and gazed out over the water. "Every time I come here it hits me. How fragile and precious life is. How quickly it can be taken from you." She shook her head and looked at the horizon. "Not that I should need the reminder."

"True." He watched the group of veterans approach the wall of names, most of them openly crying now, and he blinked away the sting in his own eyes. He never talked about the shooting with people he didn't know. It was still too raw. But for some reason, Leilani didn't feel like a stranger anymore. In fact, today he felt closer to her than he had anyone in a long, long time. He rubbed the ache in his right thigh and exhaled slowly before saying, "I shouldn't need the reminder either. Not after what happened in Chicago."

She looked sideways at him then, her tone quiet. "Is that where you were injured?"

He nodded, absently fiddling with the head of his cane. "There was an attack in the ER where I worked."

Leilani frowned and shifted to face him, the warmth of her arm brushing his. "Someone attacked you?"

Holden took a deep breath then dived in, afraid that if he stopped he wouldn't get it all out, and right now it felt like if he didn't get it all out at once, he'd choke. "A shooting. Gunman looking for opioids. Guy needed his fix. Came in, got past the security guards and opened fire when we refused to give him anything."

"Oh God. Holden, I'm so so—" she started, but he held up a hand.

"I tried to stop the guy. Well, me and my best friend,

David. We tried to take him down before he could hurt anyone, but we failed. I failed." He swallowed hard and forced himself to continue. "Took a bullet to my right thigh. Shattered my femur but missed my femoral artery, luckily. David was applying a tourniquet to my leg to stop the bleeding when the gunman shot him point-blank in the back. He died instantly. The bullet that pierced his heart tore through my left shoulder as it exited his body. I lay there, bleeding beneath my best friend's body, until help arrived. Longest hour of my life. I thought I would die too. For a long time, I wished I had."

Silence fell between them for a long moment. Leilani reached over and took his hand, lacing her fingers through his before giving them a reassuring squeeze. "How long ago did it happen?"

"Almost a year." The group of veterans at the stone wall turned to make their way out of the memorial arm in arm, a brotherhood forged by grief and remembrance. Holden used his free hand to swipe at the dampness on his own cheeks, not caring now what people thought about him crying in public. Hell, almost every person in the place had tears in their eyes it was that moving.

He took another deep breath, then hazarded a glance over at Leilani. "I don't tell many people about that."

She nodded, staring at the lines of people going in and out. "I understand. I don't talk about the accident much either."

Her hand was still covering his, soft and strong and steady, just like the woman herself. He had the crazy urge to put his arm around her and pull her into his side, bury his nose in her sweet-smelling hair, hold her close and never let her go.

Whoops. No.

He wasn't staying here in Hawaii. He never stayed anywhere long these days. Leilani deserved a relationship that would last forever, not a fling with a broken man like him. She deserved better than he could give. So he kept to himself and pulled his hand away before he couldn't anymore. They still had the rest of the day to get through and the luau tonight. Best to keep things light and not mess it up by bringing his libido into the mix.

They got back in line and saw the carved names of the people who'd perished, then they rode back to the shore on the shuttle before exiting the park and making their way back to their vehicle. A strange sense of intimacy, a heightened connection, had formed between them after their mutual confessions about their past, but Holden refused to make it into anything more than it was. No matter that his heart yearned to explore the undeniable chemistry between them. Leilani was off-limits, same as before. They could be friends, good friends even, but not friends with benefits.

Nope.

Now, if he could just get his traitorous body on board with that plan, he'd be all set.

"So, where are we going next?" he asked, once they were back in the car. He swallowed another pain pill, gritting his teeth against the lingering bitterness on his tongue, then forced a smile. They couldn't have a future together, but that didn't mean he couldn't savor the rest of the day.

"Figured we'd hit Honolulu Chinatown next, get some lunch, then head to the Iolani Place before hiking to Manoa Falls to round out the day." She grinned over at him before starting the engine and pulling out of their parking spot. "Sound good?"

"Sounds great," he said, ignoring the way his stomach somersaulted with need now every time he looked at her. He'd enjoy their time together, remember today and move on when it was over. No heartache, no emotions, no vulnerability. Because that's what he wanted.

Isn't it?

Except as they merged back onto the H1 highway toward Honolulu once more, the warmth in Holden's chest told him that quite possibly he'd already gotten far more attached to his lovely Hawaiian colleague than he'd ever intended, and the realization both thrilled and terrified him.

CHAPTER SIX

AFTER WANDERING AROUND the markets and arts district of Chinatown and enjoying a yummy late lunch of dim sum and noodles at the Maunakea Marketplace, they'd hit the Iolani Palace in downtown Honolulu before heading to a residential street just past Waakaua Street. Leilani parked near the curb and got out. It had been a while since she'd spent a day just enjoying all that her hometown of Honolulu had to offer, and she had Holden to thank.

She should also thank him for opening up to her about the shooting and for not pressing her about the car accident that had killed her family. In fact, she wanted to thank him for a lot of things, not the least of which was for helping her to relax and just breathe again.

Honestly, Leilani couldn't remember the last time she'd had such a fun, relaxing day.

No. Not relaxing. That wasn't the right word, given that her adrenaline spiked every time Holden brushed against her or leaned closer. More like exhilarating. She'd had an exhilarating day with him. Good thing the short hike to the falls would help to burn off some of her excess energy. Otherwise she just might tackle him and kiss him silly, which was unacceptable.

Leilani waited on the curb while Holden got out of the passenger side of the car, then hit the button on her key fob to lock the doors before they slowly started down the sidewalk toward the trailhead. He limped along beside her, looking better than he had back at the *Arizona* Memorial. When she first turned and saw him looking gray and desolate as a stormy sky, her immediate thought had been he was seasick. But then she'd seen the pain and panic in his eyes and feared an anxiety attack was on the way.

So she'd steered him over to the side of the space and heard his harrowing tale. Funny, but she'd always felt a bit isolated after the accident, as if she'd been the only person to experience such a violent and immediate loss. But hearing Holden speak about the attack in his ER made her realize that she wasn't as alone as she'd thought. Of course, she'd had twenty years to adjust to the past. For Holden it was still fresh, not even a year had passed.

Knowing what he'd been through made her want to reach out and hold him close, keep him safe from harm and soothe his wounded soul. Except she wasn't sure she could stop herself there, instead falling deeper into like or lust or whatever is was that sizzled between them.

She wasn't ready to go there, not now. Not with him.

Am I?

No. It would be beyond stupid to get involved with the guy. He was only there temporarily, and even if he wasn't, he was her biggest rival for the job of her dreams—which she needed to remember to ask him about too. Amidst all the fun they'd had, she'd forgotten earlier, but now she needed to remember her true purpose for today. Find out more about him and why he was here, so she'd know better how to handle the promotion competition at work.

The fact that he looked adorable and smelled like sunshine was beside the point.

"It's only about a half mile ahead to the start of the trail. Will you be okay?" she asked, giving him some side eye as they continued up the sidewalk.

"I'm good," he said, flashing her a quick crooked grin that did all sorts of naughty things inside her. "I took my other pain pill while we were in Chinatown, so I should be set for the next six hours at least."

"Great."

"Yeah."

They continued a while longer in companionable silence, dappled light through the palm fronds above creating patterns on the ground beneath their feet. The neighborhood was quiet and peaceful, just the occasional yap of a dog or the far-off rush of the ocean filling the air around them. The tang of freshly mowed grass tickled her nose and a pair of zebra doves waddled across the paths not far ahead of them.

"Did I ask you about Tommy Schrader?" Holden asked at last.

"Yeah, you did," she said, chuckling. "This morning back at the hotel."

"Right. Sorry." He looked away. "Thanks for today, by the way. All the places you've taken me to have been great."

"You're welcome." She pointed to the right and a sign for the trailhead. "There's so much more to see too. Besides Diamond Head, if you get the chance you should check out the snorkeling at Hanauma Bay. The zoo and aquarium in Waikiki are nice too. Oh, and Kualoa Ranch on the windward coast. It's beautiful, with a private nature reserve, working cattle ranch, as well as the most amazing zip line ever."

"Cool. I'd love to see it sometime." He closed his eyes and inhaled deep. "Maybe we can take another day trip together."

Her chest squeezed and she gulped. She'd like nothing better, so the answer was no.

When she didn't respond right away, he hurriedly said, "Or not. I'm sure I can find my way on my own. I didn't mean to—"

"No, no. It's fine." Liar. Leilani felt lots of things at the moment—excited, scared, nervous, aroused—but *fine* definitely wasn't one of them. Still, she'd gotten so used to blowing off people's concern over the years it was hard to shift gears now. "I mean, I appreciate the offer, but I'd have to check my schedule and things are a bit crazy right now at the hotel too, so my parents need my help sometimes in my off hours and…"

He gave her a curious look. "The Kims seem like good people. You were lucky to have them adopt you."

Glad for the change of subject, Leilani took the bait. "Yeah, they're awesome. They were friends of my parents, actually. It was easier for me to adjust to living with them than it might've been if they were strangers."

He nodded and continued beside her onto the wide, black, gravel-covered trail into the rain forest surrounding the waterfall. "Like I said before, I can't imagine how hard that must've been for you, losing your family. And at that age too. Being a teenager is hard enough as it is."

"True." The light was dimmer in here with the thick foliage and the temperature had dropped. Leilani shivered slightly and was surprised when Holden moved closer to share body heat. The scent of dirt and fresh growing things surrounded them, and the low hum of the waterfall ahead created a sense of privacy. She'd not gone into detail about the accident with Holden earlier at the beach, but with everything he'd shared with her about the shooting, she felt like, for the first time in a long time, she could open up with him too.

They crested a short hill and reached the falls. One hundred and fifty feet tall, the water cascaded down the granite walls behind it, shimmering with rainbows in the sun. She looked over at him, her pulse tripping a bit at his strong profile, his firm lips, so handsome, so kissable. He was almost as dazzling as the falls themselves. To distract herself she asked the most mundane thing she could think of. "Why'd you go into emergency medicine?"

Holden shrugged. "I always loved science as a kid and wanted to know how things worked, especially things inside the body. I'm a natural problem solver and detail oriented. But I'm also restless and a bit hyperactive, so I needed to choose a specialty that took that into consideration. Trauma surgery ticked all the boxes for me." He smiled, his teeth white and even in the slight shadows from the trees around them, and the barriers around her heart crumbled a bit more. "What about you?"

"Well," she said, moving her ponytail aside to reveal the scar on her neck. "See this?"

He leaned in closer, his warm breath tickling her skin. She suppressed another shiver, this one having nothing to do with the temperature and everything to do with the man beside her. "Wow. Is that from the accident?"

"It is." Leilani took a deep breath, then exhaled slowly before diving in. "We were on our way to the outlet mall, of all places. It was a sunny day and hot. The sky was blue and cloudless. Weird how I remember that, right?"

"Nah." Holden took her arm to pull her aside to let another couple pass them on the trail. "I remember all the details about the shooting. What people wore, what the room smelled like, how the floor felt sticky under my cheek. It's what trauma does to people's memories."

She nodded, then continued down the trail once the other people had passed. "Anyway, our car was an older model. When the other driver T-boned us, it sent us through the guardrail and down into a ravine. Car flipped over three times before landing on the roof, from what the police report says." She blinked hard against the tears that threatened to fall. "My brother and parents died instantly." They stopped under a natural canopy of tree trunks entwined over the trail, and Leilani rested back against their solid weight for support. "I was the only one left alive."

"Oh God." Holden stepped closer and took her hand this time, holding it close to his chest. The steady *thump-thump* of his heart beneath her palm helped ground her and kept her from getting lost in the past again. "I'm so sorry, Leilani. How in the world did you survive?"

"Sheer luck, I'm pretty sure." She gave a sad little laugh. "Both my legs were broken, but I was awake the whole time. I still have nightmares about it sometimes."

"I bet."

After another deep breath, she continued. "The scar on my neck is from a chunk of glass that lodged there. It nicked the artery but kept enough pressure until help arrived. Otherwise I would've died like the rest of my family. The only reason I'm here now is the paramedics and the ER staff who helped me that day. So that's why I went into emergency medicine. Because of their compassion and to pay my debt to them."

"Wow." He slowly slid his arm around her and pulled her into a hug. She didn't resist, too drained from telling her story and, well, it just felt too darned good being this close to him at last. He rested his chin on the top of her head and said again, "Wow."

The stroke of his fingers against her scalp felt so good it nearly hypnotized her.

"That's why you knew about the seat belt laws, isn't it?" he asked after a moment, his voice ruffling the hair at her temple.

"Yeah," she said, pressing her cheek more firmly against his chest. "Seat belts and air bags would've made all the difference."

They stood there, wrapped in each other's arms and their own little world, until more people came down the trail and they had to step aside to allow them through. Once separated, neither seemed to know where to look or what to do with their hands.

For her part, it took all Leilani's willpower not to throw herself back into Holden's arms. But then, thankfully, her good old common sense kicked in, along with the warning bells in her head, telling her that no matter how tempting it might be to throw caution to the wind, she couldn't do that. Couldn't let him in because he'd either be leaving soon or possibly taking the job she wanted if he stayed. Both of which would only break her heart. And she'd had more than enough heartache for one lifetime.

Hoping for some time and space to get her head clear again, she started back down the trail toward the car, then waited for him to follow. "We should get back to the hotel so we can shower and change before tonight."

Holden stared at his reflection in the full-length mirror in his room early that evening and hoped he was dressed appropriately for a luau. Honestly, he had no idea what you wore to a party on the beach. Swim trunks, maybe, but that seemed a bit too relaxed.

He'd opted instead for a fresh Hawaiian shirt, this one in a pale turquoise color with small palm trees and desert islands on it and a clean pair of jeans. Flip-flops on his feet, per Leilani's advice, since it was the beach after all, and sand was everywhere.

His mind still churned through everything that had happened that day, all he'd seen, and the things he and Leilani had told each other. He still couldn't quite believe he'd confided in her about the shooting. He never really talked about it with anyone, outside of his therapist back in Chicago and occasionally with Helen. But telling Leilani about what had happened had felt different today. Scary, yes, but also strangely cathartic and right.

Maybe it was because of what she'd gone through with that awful car accident, but she'd never once made him feel judged or forced him to go further with his story than he was willing. The fact that she'd also confided in him had made the exchange even more special. From working with her the past month, he knew she was almost as guarded as he was when it came to letting other people close, so for her to open up with him like that meant something.

Then, of course, there was that hug at the waterfall.

Couldn't deny that had been nice. Amazing, actually. And sure, it was ill-advised, given he had no busi-

ness starting anything with Leilani. Holden never knew
where he'd be from month to month, let alone year to
year. Beginning a relationship only to move thousands
of miles away wasn't fair to anyone.

Trouble was though, his heart seemed to have other
yearnings where Leilani was concerned.

She was smart, sweet and made every nerve ending in his body stand at attention. But there was also a
wealth of vulnerability lurking beneath her sleek, shiny
exterior. Sort of like him. She'd been through things,
dealt with pain most people never experienced, and yet
she was still standing. That took guts. It also took a lot
out of a person. Made them more resilient, yes, but at
a cost. He absently rubbed the ache in his chest, then
grabbed his cane.

Enough stewing over things that would never happen anyway.

He left his room and headed down to the lobby, where
he was supposed to meet Leilani. Dinner was served at
sunset, she'd said, but there were plenty of other things
to see before then. It was going on seven now and the
sun was just nearing the horizon. People milled about
the lobby, most heading out toward the beach behind
the hotel where the luau would take place. He'd chosen his outfit well, considering lots of other guys were
wearing similar things. The ladies mainly had on casual
dresses or skirts and a few had tropical flowers pinned
in their hair. From somewhere outside the strains of ukulele music drifted through the air, and the general mood
of the place was festive and fun.

Being taller than most people at six foot four did have
its advantages, and over the tops of the people's heads,
he spotted Leilani waiting for him against the wall near

the exit to the beach. He started that way, only to find his path blocked by one of the hotel staff, a pretty Polynesian girl dressed in a traditional hula outfit.

"Aloha," she said, giving him a friendly, dimpled smile. She reached up and hung a lei made of black shiny shells around his neck, then kissed his cheek. *"Pōmakia'i."*

Blessings. He'd managed to pick up a few native words during his stay in Honolulu and he smiled down at the woman. Lord knew Holden and Leilani could use all the good fortune they could get.

"Pōmakia'I," he said in return.

He stepped around the woman and continued on toward the far wall, stopping short as he got his first full look at Leilani tonight.

Seeing her earlier today in shorts and a tank top or as she was usually dressed at work in scrubs was one thing. Seeing her tonight in a short, colorful sarong-style dress made of native tropical print purple and white fabric was, well... *Stunning.* Her sleek black hair was loose, streaming down her back like shimmering ink, and that strapless dress hugged her curves in all the right places, ending above her knee and revealing just enough of her tanned legs to give a guy all kinds of wicked fantasies.

She looked over and spotted him, then smiled, waving him over. He blinked hard, trying to clear his head of images of them hugging near the waterfall, of him pulling her closer, kissing her, holding her, unwinding that dress of hers and covering her naked body with his and driving her wild with passion until she was begging him for more...

Whoa, Nelly.

He ran a finger under his collar, wondering when the

temperatures had gotten so warm. His pulse pounded and his blood thrummed with need, and man, oh, man—he was in serious trouble here.

"Holden," she called, "over here." The slight impatience edging her tone cut through his haze of lust, spurring him into action at last. He slowly limped through the people to where she stood near the open doorway. At least the spark of appreciation in her eyes as she took in his appearance made him feel a bit less awkward. She liked him too. That much was obvious. Too bad they couldn't explore it. If he'd had more time here, then maybe, just this once…

Helen's offer of the directorship position flashed back in his mind.

No. He couldn't take that job. Leilani wanted it. She'd be damned good at it too. Better than him, probably.

But if it gave me more time here in paradise…

"You look great," she said, her words a tad huskier than they'd been before. Or maybe that was just his imagination. Either way, the compliment headed straight southward through his body. "Like you belong here."

"Thanks," he managed, doing his best not to get lost in her eyes. "You look beautiful."

Pretty pink color suffused her cheeks before she looked away and gestured toward the outside. "Thanks. Shall we?"

He followed her out onto the cement patio, then down the stairs to the large grassy gardens spanning the distance between the hotel and the beach beyond. A line of palm trees designated the border between the two. Rows and rows of long tables and chairs had been set up for people to sit and eat, and along each side were buffet tables piled high with all sorts of food. Beyond those were other activities, like spear throwing and craft making. She led him through it all—the men weaving head wreaths out of coconut leaves, the women making leis, the young guys offering to paint temporary tattoos on the cute girls. All the hotel staff seemed to be participating, all dressed in native Hawaiian outfits—grass skirts for all with the women's being longer than the men's, elaborate neck pieces and headdresses, leis everywhere. It was walking into another world and Holden found himself completely enchanted.

"This is awesome," he said, accepting a leaf crown from one of the men weaving them. "I had no idea it would be so elaborate."

Leilani showed him a huge fire pit, where a whole pig was roasting beneath enormous banana leaves. The smell was so delicious, his stomach growled loudly. Lunch seemed way too far away at that point and he thought he could probably eat half that pig all by himself. "Don't worry," she said, as if reading his thoughts. "They've got more inside in the kitchen."

"Good, because I'm starving."

"Me too." She laughed, then took his arm, tugging him toward the front of the area, where a stage had been set up and currently a quartet of local musicians played a variety of Hawaiian music. That explained the ukuleles he'd heard earlier. Holden spotted Leilani's dad behind the stage and waved to him. Joe waved back. Leilani pulled Holden out of the way of a racing toddler, then kept her hand on his bare forearm, the heat of her searing his skin and bringing his earlier X-rated thoughts back to mind. They stopped near the best table in the bunch, front row, center stage. "This is where we're sitting for dinner and the show."

"Really?" He raised his brows. "Pays to know people in high places, huh?"

"It does." She winked, then pointed back to where the pig was roasting. Two burly staffers in native costumes had pulled away the banana leaves and were raising the whole roast pig up in the air with a loud grunt. The crowd applauded and Leilani leaned in close to whisper, "C'mon. Let's eat."

Didn't have to ask him twice. After loading up their plates with Kalua pig and barbecue chicken and *lomi* salmon and poi and fresh pineapple, they made their way back to the table just as Leilani's father took the stage as MC for the evening.

"Aloha! Welcome to the weekly luau at the Malu Huna Resort. Please help yourselves to the wonderful food and enjoy our entertainment this evening. Mahalo!"

The band started up again, joined by hula dancers, and Holden dug into his food with gusto. "This. Is. Amazing," he said around a bite of tangy, salty *lomi* salmon. The cold fish mixed with ripe tomatoes and onions was just the right foil for the sweeter pork and chicken. "Thanks for inviting me tonight. And thanks again for today."

"You're welcome." She smiled at him over the rim of her mai tai glass. "I love my hometown and am always glad to share it with others."

"It's great here. Seriously." He swallowed another bite of food, this time devouring a spoonful of poi. It was a bit like eating a mouthful of purple cream of wheat mixed with fruit. Not bad at all. Next he tried more pork and nearly fainted from the goodness. "Man, why does food never taste this amazing back on the mainland?"

Leilani snorted. "Probably because you didn't hike all over an island back in Chicago."

"True." He continued munching away as the band played on and more dancers joined them onstage. They were picking tourists from the crowd as well, but he kept his head down to avoid eye contact and not be chosen for humiliation. Finally, he'd had enough to eat and sat back, rubbing his full stomach and smiling lazily. "I don't think I've felt this full in forever."

"There's still haupia for dessert, don't forget." Leilani said, still eating. "Can't miss that."

"Nope." He sat back as a server cleared his empty dishes, then hobbled over to grab himself a plate of said haupia. It looked a bit like cheesecake without the crust, served on top of more banana leaves. He brought back two slices, one for himself and one for Leilani, then took a bite. It was good—creamy like cheesecake, but a burst from the coconut milk that was pure Hawaii. "Wow, this is really good too."

"Told you." Leilani finished her food at last, then pushed her plate aside and pulled her dessert over. "Speaking of Chicago, how exactly to you know Helen King?"

Holden almost choked on his bite of haupia but managed to swallow just in time. "She was a visiting surgeon at the hospital where I worked. We got to know each other there."

She saved my life.

He kept that last bit to himself, figuring he'd already told her more than enough about the shooting and there was no need to ruin the night by bringing it up again. "Why?"

"Just wondered." She shrugged, then watched the

dancers for a bit. "I'm interested in the directorship position, you know."

Ah. So that's where this was headed. He wanted to tell her she had nothing to worry about, but then he couldn't really. Could he? Even if he didn't take the offer Helen had made him, there was the other issue of Helen not feeling like she knew Leilani well enough to trust her with that much authority yet. Maybe her temporary stint as director would become a full-time gig, maybe it wouldn't. Either way, Holden planned to be gone before then anyway. He tried to play it off with humor instead. "I kind of figured, since you're doing the job already and all."

"Has she offered you the job?" Leilani asked bluntly.

Yes.

"No," he lied. Helen had brought the subject up, but he'd turned it down. No need to bring that up either, right? Leilani watched him closely, her dark gaze seeming to see through to his very soul and for a moment he felt like a deer in headlights. Maybe he shouldn't have lied. If he told her the truth now though, that might be the end of all this, and he really didn't want it to be over. Not yet. He looked away, toward the stage, without really seeing it. "Why do you ask?"

"No reason," she said, the weight of her gaze resting on him a bit longer before moving away. "I just…" She sighed, then faced the stage as well, her tone turning resigned. "Listen, Holden. About what happened at the waterfall earlier. I don't want you to get the wrong idea. I like you. You're a good doctor, but I'm not looking for anything more, okay? We can be friends, but that's it." She took another bite of her haupia then pushed the rest aside. "And as friends, I'd appreciate a heads-up if you decide to pursue the directorship, all right?"

"All right." He was still trying to wrap his head around the swift change of subjects and how she'd sneaked in the bit about the waterfall into the mix, like he wouldn't notice that way. Of course, his analytical mind took it one step further, making him doubt the connecting and chemistry he'd felt between them earlier. He shouldn't care and yet, he did. In fact, her words stung far more than he wanted. Which was silly because he didn't want that either.

No strings, no relationships. That was his deal.

Isn't it?

Holden hung his head, more confused now than ever. Maybe it was the fact she'd beat him to the punch that bothered him. Usually he was the one stressing that there'd be nothing long-term. Yep, that had to be it.

He shoved aside the lingering pang of want inside him and brushed his hands off on his jeans, doing his best to play it all off as no big deal—when inside it felt like a very big deal indeed. "If I decide to go after the directorship, I promise I'll let you know. And don't worry about earlier. Look, we shared some personal things, hugged. That was all," he said, trying to sound way more unaffected than he was. "No harm, no foul."

The band cleared the stage, replaced by a line of men with drums. Torches were lit around the area and the same big, burly guys who'd been weaving crowns and throwing spears earlier took the stage. A hush fell over the crowd as Leilani's father announced the fire dance. Much as Holden wanted to see it though, a strange restlessness had taken up inside him now and he needed to move, needed to get out of there and get some fresh air.

Get his mind straight before he did something crazy like pull Leilani into his arms and prove to her that he didn't care about the job, to show her that their hug earlier really had meant something, no matter how much she denied it. Talk about fire. There was one raging inside him now that refused to be extinguished no matter how hard he tried.

Onstage, the male dancers stomped and grunted and beat their chests in a show of strength and dominance over the flames surrounding them. Holden pushed to his feet and grabbed his cane, feeling like he too was burning up from the emotions he'd tried so long to suppress after the shooting, but that Leilani had conjured back to life all too easily.

"I need to walk," he said to her before sidling away through the tables toward the beach beyond, one hand holding his cane and the other clenched at his side in frustration. "Be back in a bit."

CHAPTER SEVEN

LEILANI SAT AT the table for a few minutes, brain buzzing about what to do. He'd not really answered her question about the job, but she'd told him point-blank where she stood with that, so yeah. She'd put her cards on the table, careerwise. The next move there was up to him.

Emotionally though, there were still a lot of things she hadn't told him.

Things like if he'd have kissed her at the waterfall, she'd have let him. Would have allowed him a lot more than kisses too, if she were honest. An old, familiar lump of fear clogged her throat before she swallowed hard against it. Much as it terrified her to admit, she wanted Holden, plain and simple. If she were honest, she'd wanted him for a while now. That certainly explained the awareness sparking between them whenever he was around. She sipped her mai tai and tried to focus on the dancers onstage, but it was no use. All she could seem to think about now was him. About how well they'd worked together on the surfboard kid's case. About how adorable he'd looked that morning, awkward but adorable. About all the things he'd shared with her that day and how he'd made her feel less alone. About how he'd kept up with her, even though it had been hard with his leg. About how he'd not given up or given in.

He was kind and smart and more than competent as a surgeon. And truthfully, she'd always been a sucker for men with brains and brawn. Not to mention his dreamy hazel bedroom eyes.

Gah!

A waitress came by and replenished Leilani's drink, but she barely noticed now. All she could think about was the hug they'd shared earlier at the waterfall. The feel of him in her arms, the heat of his body warming her, the thud of his heart beneath her ear, steady, strong, solid.

The long-standing walls around her heart tumbled down even further.

Holden had lived through horrific events, just like her. He understood her in a way no other man ever had. And he didn't treat her differently because of what she'd been through either, whereas all the past men she'd been with had acted like she was made out of fragile china or something once they knew about the accident. Leilani wasn't breakable, well, not to that extent anyway.

She resisted the urge to rub the uncomfortable ache in her chest—yearning mixed with apprehension.

The trouble was Holden made her vulnerable in a whole new way. Part of her wanted to put as much distance as possible between them, let him go his way and stick to her own solitary path. But the other part of her longed to go after him, to find him on the beach and tell him that she didn't want forever, but she'd sure as hell take right now.

He made her want to take risks again. And that was perhaps the scariest thing of all.

Also, the most exhilarating. She couldn't remember the last time she'd felt so alive.

As the fire dancers reached a fevered pitch onstage, a volcano of feelings inside Leilani finally erupted as well, making her feel reckless and wild. She wasn't ready for a relationship with Holden, that was true. Relationships meant ties and connections and all sorts of other terrifying things that could rip out a person's heart and shatter it into a million pieces.

But a fling...

Well, flings were another beast entirely. If he agreed, a fling meant they could have their cake and eat it too. Given that Holden would most likely be moving on to another locum tenens position and the fact he'd flat out told her he wasn't interested in a relationship either, meant he might be game for an affair. He hadn't ruled that out at all.

She downed the rest of her mai tai in one gulp then stood. Desire vibrated through her like a tuning fork and adrenaline fizzed through her bloodstream. As the fire dancers' performance ended to thunderous applause and her dad took the mic again to introduce the Don Ho impersonator, Leilani weaved her way through the tables and headed for the beach in search of Holden.

Once she was past the light of the torches at the edge of gardens, it took her eyes a minute to adjust in the twilight. At first she didn't see him, then she spotted Holden near the shore, silhouetted by the full moon's light, his cane in one hand, his flip-flops in the other.

Heart racing in time with her steps, Leilani kicked off her own shoes, then rushed down toward the water, toward Holden, her mind still racing with discordant thoughts.

He wants you. He doesn't want you. It's all in your head. It's all in your heart.

Whatever the outcome, she had to try. Felt like she'd die if she didn't.

Leilani stopped a few feet behind Holden, hesitating before saying, "I lied."

For a moment he didn't turn, just stood there, staring out over the Pacific as the stars twinkled above. She lived and died in those few seconds. Then he turned to face her, his gaze dark in the shadows surrounding them. "About what?"

Feeling both brave and terrified at the same time, she stepped closer and forced herself to continue. She didn't do this, didn't run after men, didn't pursue her feelings. But tonight, with Holden, she couldn't stop herself. She wanted him and she'd have him, if he wanted her too. "I lied, earlier." She fumbled for her words. "I mean not about long-term things. I don't do those either. Not after the accident. But I do want you. I mean I want to be with you."

Damn. This was harder than she'd imagined. She took a deep breath and forced the rest out before she couldn't say it at all, grateful the darkness hid her flaming cheeks. "Do you want to have an affair with me?"

Yikes. Way to be blunt, girl.

Holden blinked at her a minute, unmoving, looking a bit stunned. She couldn't really blame him. Her statement had been about as romantic as a foot fungus. But then he moved closer, tossing his shoes aside along with his cane, to cup her cheeks in his hands. His expression was unreadable in the shadows, but the catch in his breath made her own heart trip.

Then he bent and brushed his lips over hers, featherlight, before capturing her mouth in a kiss that rocked her to her very soul. Forget romantic. This was mind-blowing, astounding, too much yet not enough. Would never be enough.

Oh man, I'm in trouble here.

He broke the kiss first, the crash of the waves against the shore mixing with their ragged breaths and the far-off crooning of the Don Ho singer belting out *Tiny Bubbles*. For the first time in a long time, Leilani felt more than just a sense of duty, more than pressure to succeed, more than the low-grade sadness of loss and grief.

She felt needed and wanted, and it made her head spin with joy.

Before she could think better of it, she slid her arms around Holden's neck and pulled him in for a deeper kiss.

Holden got lost in Leilani—her warmth, the taste of sweet pineapple and sinful promise on her tongue, her soft mewls of need as she pulled him closer, so close he wasn't sure where she ended and he began. His lower lip stung where the stitches pulled, but not enough to make him stop kissing her. He pulled her closer still, if that were possible.

Then the doubt demons in his brain crept forward once more. He shouldn't be doing this, shouldn't be holding her like this. He was broken and battered, inside and out, and didn't deserve a woman like her, a woman who was as sunny and vibrant as the island around her. A woman who'd overcome the darkness in her past to forge a bright new future for herself.

A future he wouldn't be around to share.

He summoned the last remnants of his willpower

and pulled away—only a few inches, enough to rest his forehead against hers as they both fought to catch their breath. His hands were still cupping her cheeks, her silky hair tangled between his fingers, and her skin felt like hot velvet to his touch. But he had to let her go. It was the right thing to do.

He wasn't staying. He couldn't stay. He'd been running so long—running from risk, from commitment, from the past—he didn't know how to stop. Leilani deserved so much more than he could give, even temporarily.

"I—" he started, only to be silenced by her fingers on his lips.

"An affair. That's all," she said, her voice hushed as the waves crashed nearby. "No strings, no pressure. I want you, Holden. For however long you'll be here."

The words made his pulse triple, sending a cascade of conflicting emotions through him—astonishment, excitement, want, sadness. That last one especially threw him for a loop. She was offering him exactly what he'd said he wanted. No strings attached. Just sex, fun, a fling. But for reasons he didn't want to examine too closely, the thought of a casual romp with Leilani made his chest pinch with loneliness.

She pulled back slightly, far enough to look up into his eyes, her own dark gaze as mysterious at the ocean beyond. "I know it's crazy. I just…" She hesitated, shaking her head. "I like you, Holden. And this chemistry between us is amazing. Be a shame not to explore that, right? Especially if we both know the score."

Right, his libido screamed in response, but he needed time to sort all this through to make sure he made the best decision. Because the last thing he wanted to do was screw things up between them. They still had to work together during his time here. If things went south between the sheets, it could have direct impact on their professional relationship, if they weren't careful.

And Holden was nothing if not careful these days.

The reminder was like a bucket of cold water over his head. He took a deep breath and tried again to speak, "Listen, I—"

Her dad called out from the garden area in the distance. "Lani? If you're out there, Mom and I could use some help in the kitchen."

With a sigh, she stepped back, letting her hands slide from around his neck and down his chest before letting him go completely. His nerve endings sizzled in their wake and his fingertips itched to pull her close once more, but instead Holden forced himself to turn away and pick up his cane and shoes.

"Be right there," Leilani called back, staring at him in the pale moonlight. The question in her gaze prickled his skin. "Just think about it, okay? When's your next shift at the hospital?"

"Sunday," he said, shaking the sand from his flip-flops to avoid looking at her. Because if he looked at her now, there was every chance he'd throw caution to the wind entirely and carry her back to his room to make love right then and there.

"Good. That gives us a couple days to think this through. I'm working then too." After a curt nod, she started back toward the hotel. "We'll talk again then."

Holden stayed where he was, watching her walk away and wondering when in the hell he'd lost complete control of his senses because damn if he didn't want to say yes to an affair.

CHAPTER EIGHT

LEILANI SAT IN her tiny office at the hospital two days later, working her way through a backlog of paperwork that had stacked up over the last week or so while she'd been too busy in the ER. Today was slower, so she'd decided to tackle some of it while she could.

Well, that and she needed a distraction for the constant replays of her kiss with Holden on the beach and her brazen invitation for them to have an affair.

You shouldn't have done that, the commonsense portion of her brain warned.

The thing was though, Leilani had spent her whole life up to this point doing what she *should* do. For once, she was ready to go with what she *wanted* to do. And what she wanted was Holden Ross.

Even if the whole idea of opening up with him like that pushed every crazy button inside her.

A one-night stand was one thing but having to get up the next morning and see that person at work was entirely another. Of course, there wasn't any specific rule against dating coworker's in Ohana policies. She'd checked. But there was still the possibility that things could go wrong. And the last thing she wanted was to mess up her good reputation here by getting chewed up and spit out by the rumor mill. At least that's the excuse she was going with.

Truth was she was scared and looking for an opportunity to back out of the whole thing. Perhaps that explained why she'd been avoiding him since Friday night. Making heated suggestions in the moonlight was one thing. Looking that person in the eye again in broad daylight was quite another. So she'd kept her head down and her nose to the grindstone since their kiss. Because of that, she hadn't really seen Holden much at all since Friday night.

They'd passed each other in the lobby of the hotel twice, her on her way in, him on his way out. Between the crowds and her parents' watchful gazes behind the front desk, neither of them had said more than a basic greeting. And today, they'd both been so busy working and had barely had two seconds to say hello, let alone get into anything deeper.

So yeah. Pins and needles didn't begin to describe what she felt, trying to figure out what to do. Thus, she purposely put herself in paperwork hell to keep her mind off things best forgotten. She rubbed her temple and concentrated again on the requisition form nurse Pam had filled out for the monthly supply order in the ER.

She'd just ticked off the charge for two crates of gloves when a knock sounded on her door. Without looking up, she called, "Come in."

"Dr. Kim," Helen King said, "do you have a moment?"

Leilani's heart stumbled. She swiveled fast on her chair to face the hospital administrator, wincing inwardly at the mess her office was in at the moment. She stood and quickly cleared away a pile of folders and binders off the chair against the wall, then swallowed hard, forcing a polite smile. "Yes, of course. Please, have a seat."

"Thank you." The older woman, looking crisp and professional as always, shut the door behind her and sat on the chair Leilani had just cleared for her. Her short white hair practically glowed beneath the overhead florescent lights and her blue gaze was unreadable, which only made the knot of anxiety inside Leilani tighten further. Beneath her right arm was tucked a large black binder.

"I wanted to speak to you about a project that needs done here in the ER," Dr. King said. "I'd like you and Dr. Ross to work on it together."

Right.

Leilani nodded. She'd forgotten about Holden mentioning that with everything else going on. "Absolutely. Whatever you need, Dr. King."

"Good." The older woman sat forward and crossed her legs, placing the thick binder on her lap. "As you know, we're preparing for our JCAHO recertification next year and part of that is reviewing all the security protocols in the emergency medicine department. Since you've been with us for nearly a decade and are interested in moving into the directorship role for the department in the future, this would be a great opportunity to show me your leadership skills."

"Absolutely."

"Great. I'll send you more information on what needs be done and the deadlines. I've asked Dr. Ross to assist you because he handled a similar project at a different facility, and I believe he'll be able to provide good insight on the project. I've already spoken with him about it and he's on board with assisting you in any way he can. I'll need the project completed by the end of next month." She handed the heavy binder to Leilani, who needed both hands to support its weight. "The current protocols are in there."

"Okay. Wonderful." Leilani set the thing aside on her desk, then stood when the hospital administrator did. "Is that all?"

"Yes. That's all for now." Dr. King walked to the door and stepped out, then leaned her head back in. "And thank you, Dr. Kim. I look forward to your completed results. It will go a long way toward helping me decide the best candidate for the directorship position."

Leilani stood there a moment longer after Dr. King had left, wrapping her head around her new assignment. One month wasn't a long time for a project of that size, especially when both she and Holden had other job duties to attend to as well. But if it meant impressing Dr. King and potentially winning her the directorship, Leilani would get it done.

Of course, that meant another mark in the "Don't sleep with Holden column," since the last thing she wanted was for a potential drama between the sheets to jeopardize their new project together. And Holden and Dr. King were good friends too. Couldn't forget that. If things with their fling went south, then that could impact her chances at the new job as well.

Ugh. Things were getting way too complicated way too fast.

As she sank back into her chair, her chest squeezed with disappointment.

Her whole body still thrummed each time she pictured them together on the beach, the feel of his hard muscles pressing against her soft curves, the taste of salt and coconut in his kisses, the low growl of need he'd given when she'd clung to him tighter…

Sizzling connections like that didn't come along very often. Plus, she liked spending time with him, talking to him, just being around him. Their day sightseeing together had been one of the best she'd had in a long, long time. But was exploring that worth losing the future she'd planned for herself?

Feeling more on edge than ever, she pushed to her feet and headed for the door. She needed to move, to think, to organize the jumbled thoughts in her head before she and Holden spoke again.

But she barely made it through the door before she collided with six foot four inches of solid temptation, wearing soft green scrubs and a sexy smile on his handsome face.

"Hey," he said, his voice a tad hesitant. "I was just coming to talk to you. I'm on break."

Hands off, her brain whispered, even as her ovaries danced a happy jig.

"Good. Because I need to talk to you too. Dr. King came to see me about the project."

She gestured him into her office, then closed the door behind him. Perhaps discussing work would keep her errant brain on track. Except as he passed her, the smell of soap from his skin and his citrusy shampoo drifted around her and her chest squeezed with yearning before she tamped it down. He took a seat in the chair vacated by Dr. King, then set his cane aside.

"Well, on the bright side, the work should go faster with two of us working on it, at least," he said.

"True." She leaned her hips back against the edge

of her desk and crossed her arms over her lab coat and stethoscope. "I want to do a good job, since she said this will help her decide who gets the directorship position." Her gaze narrowed on him, trying to read past his usual stoic expression. "Are you sure you're not considering the job yourself? Tell me the truth, Holden."

A muscle ticked near his tense jaw and he frowned down at the floor. "I'm not planning on taking the job, no."

Good. One less thing to worry about.

Then he stood and stepped toward her and the desire she'd tried so hard to keep on low simmer since Friday rolled over into full boil again.

"Can we talk about something else now?" he asked, his rough, quiet tone sending molten warmth through her traitorous body. "Like Friday night."

Leilani squeezed her eyes shut and took a deep breath. "Yes."

When he didn't answer right away, she squinted one eye open to find him watching her with a narrowed gaze, his expression quizzical now, as if he was trying to figure her out. Finally, he took one more step closer and slid his arm around her waist, his hand resting on her lower back as she placed her palms on his chest. That same spark of attraction, of need, flared to life inside her, urging her to throw caution aside and live again, to take what she wanted from Holden and enjoy the moment because it would all be over too soon. She inhaled deep and hazarded a look up into his eyes, noting the same heat there, feeling the pound of his heart under her palms.

"If we're doing a project of this size, it would mean a lot of hours, a lot of time spent together," he said, his words barely more than a whisper. His hold on her tightened, causing her to bump into his chest. Her eyes fluttered shut as he bent and brushed his lips across hers before trailing his mouth down her cheek and jaw to nuzzle her neck and earlobe. "I haven't been able to think about anything but you since Friday."

She shivered with sensual delight, craving his touch more than her next breath, but that small part of her brain that was terrified of getting too close demanded she set boundaries up front. "Me neither," she panted. "But whatever happens, we can't let it interfere with work."

"Never," he vowed, his breath hot against her throat. "I promise you this thing between us will stay between the sheets. I won't let it get out of hand."

"I won't either," she said, not knowing or caring if it was true or not. All she wanted right now was his mouth back on hers. That's when she noticed his stitches were gone. "You got them out?"

"I did. Removed them myself earlier today." He chuckled. "Good as new thanks to you, Doc."

He kissed her again then, deep and full of passion. When he finally pulled away, she felt bewitched and bewildered and all kinds of bothered. Holden straightened his scrub shirt, then gave her a sexy smile before grabbing his cane. "What time does your shift end?"

"Four," she managed to say past the tightness in her throat. "You?"

"Six." He headed for the door, then turned back to her with a wink. "Come to my room for dinner. Number 1402. Eight o'clock. Don't be late."

Holden stood before the doors leading out to his room's balcony later that evening, wondering exactly what had possessed him to be so bold earlier in Leilani's office. Maybe it was the fact he hadn't been able to stop thinking about her since their kiss on the beach. Maybe it was the fact that after that day they'd spent together and sharing their most traumatic moments in life, he felt the bond between them even more strongly than before.

Whatever it was, he was now on a collision course of his own making.

He turned slightly to look back over his shoulder at the small table set for two in the corner of his junior suite, set up by room service and complete with a white linen tablecloth and a bottle of champagne chilling in the ice bucket. The lights were lowered and the single candle at the center of the table flickered in the slight breeze drifting through the open doors, casting a soft glow around the room. The scent of surf and sea surrounded him, as did the occasional notes of music floating in from a party somewhere on the shore. All of it should've soothed him.

But Leilani was due to arrive any minute and Holden felt ready to jump out of his skin from a mix of nerves and excitement. Now he'd made the decision to pursue an affair with her, he was second-guessing himself. Was this the right choice? Yes, he wanted her more than he'd wanted any woman in a long, long time, perhaps ever. And yes, she'd already made it clear that this was only a temporary thing, that she didn't do forever. Usually he was the one saying those words, and honestly, he wasn't sure how he felt about that. His analytical brain said he should be relieved. Leilani had taken the guesswork out of it all, taken the burden off him by offering a no-strings-attached affair.

Instead though, he felt torn.

Which was stupid, because a guy like him who was too scarred both inside and out to settle down for long had no business wanting more than a few nights in paradise. He should be happy with what he got because it could all disappear in the blink of an eye anyway.

Then there was the fact they'd now be working on that project for Helen together. And while he'd agreed days ago to do it, even before Leilani knew about it, now he was feeling a bit off-kilter about it. The fact he should've thought it through better in the first place bugged him. Going over security measures in the ER would be triggering for him, regardless of whether they addressed a mass shooting scenario. But really, how could they not, since that type of violence was on the rise nationwide. Not to address it would be wrong.

But at the time of the meeting with Helen, he'd been eager to please and wanted to help in any way he could to repay her for saving his life back in Chicago. The fact she'd tried to pressure him about the directorship position didn't help either. Now he had firm proof from Leilani that she wanted the job, and he wouldn't go near it, even if Helen wanted otherwise. Leilani deserved the position. He scrubbed a hand over his face, then fiddled with the hem of his black T-shirt. No sense getting worked up about it now. He had bigger things to deal with at present.

Get out and live a little. Trust me—you'll be glad you did...

Helen's words echoed through his head again and made him wonder if perhaps his old friend had assigned them both to this security project as a way of bringing him and Leilani together.

He snorted and shook his head. Nah. He was just

being paranoid now. Helen knew how squirrelly he was about commitment after the shooting, how he didn't want to stay in one place too long or form deep attachments. She wouldn't try to play matchmaker now to get him to stay in Hawaii.

Would she?

A knock sounded on his door while that thought was still stewing in his mind, making his heart nosedive to his knees. His pulse kicked into overdrive and his mouth dried from adrenaline, like he was some randy teen before the prom. No. Honestly, it didn't matter what Helen may or may not have intended. Both he and Leilani were consenting adults and they'd both made the choice to be here tonight. They were the engineers of their fates, at least in this room.

After a deep breath, he wiped his damp palms on the legs of his jeans, then limped barefoot over to the door to answer, his trusty cane by his side.

Leilani stood in the hall, shuffling her feet and fiddling with her hair, looking as wary and wired as he felt. She'd worn jeans too, soft faded ones that hugged her curves and made his fingertips itch to unzip them. Her emerald green top highlighted her dark hair and eyes to perfection and contrasted with the pink flushing her cheeks. The V-neck of her shirt also gave him a tantalizing glimpse of her cleavage beneath and suddenly it seemed far too warm for comfort.

Holden resisted the urge to run a finger beneath the crewneck of his T-shirt and instead stepped back to allow her inside. "Hey. Come on in."

"Thanks." She gave him a tentative smile as she brushed past him, the graze of her arm against his sending a shower of sparks through his already-overtaxed nervous system and notching the want inside him higher. Leilani stopped at the end of the short entry hall and stared at the table set up in the corner. "Are we eating here?"

"Yeah," he said, limping up to stand behind her, close enough to catch a hint of her sweet jasmine scent. Her heat and fragrance lit him up like neon inside, and his body tightened against his wishes. To distract himself, he concentrated on dinner. "Uh, I thought after a busy day, it might be nice to just chill and relax. Is that okay?"

She exhaled slowly, then turned to face him with a smile as dazzling as the stars filling the cloudless night above. "It's perfect, actually. Thank you for thinking of it."

"My pleasure." Holden grinned back, imagining all the ways he'd like to pleasure her, with his mouth and hands and body. He cleared his throat and gestured toward the love seat against one wall. "Make yourself comfortable. There's champagne I can open if you want some."

"What are we having for dinner?" She walked over to the table and lifted one of the silver domes covering their plates, then the other before turning back to him. "Salads?"

"I figured it would be healthy and—"

And would keep for a while in case we didn't eat right away and ended up in bed first.

He didn't say that last part out loud, but then, it turned out he didn't have to, because next thing he knew, Leilani had kicked off her sandals and was heading back toward him, the heat in her eyes heading straight to his groin.

"Good. Because there's something else I'm hungry for right now…" She reached out and traced a finger down his cheek, his neck, his chest, lower still. "And it isn't food or booze."

Before he could rethink his actions, he let his cane fall to the floor and pulled her into his arms, kissing her again like he'd been wanting to since their encounter in her office earlier, since the night at the beach, since eternity. It started out as a light meeting of their lips, but soon morphed into something deeper and more intense. Leilani sighed and ran her hands up his pecs to his shoulders, then threaded her fingers through his hair, making him shiver as she pulled his body flush to hers. "How's your lip?"

"Never better." He whispered the words against the side of her neck, licking that special spot where throat met earlobe—the one that made her sigh and mewl with need. Holding her felt like the most natural thing in the world. Even when she slipped her hands beneath his T-shirt and tugged it off over his head, exposing the scar on his left shoulder from the shooting. Usually, he kept it hidden, a dark reminder of a dark day, but now with Leilani, he wanted her to see it all, every part of him, the good, the bad, the damaged and the whole. In fact, the only thing he was thinking about now was getting Leilani naked too, and into his bed—over him, under him, any way he could have her.

She leaned back slightly to meet his gaze. "Sure you don't want to eat now?"

"Oh, I want to eat all right," he growled, grinding his hips against hers and allowing her to feel the full extent of his arousal. "I plan to lick and taste every inch of you, sweetheart."

She snorted, then wriggled out of his arms to take off her shirt and toss it aside, revealing a pretty pink lace bra that served her breasts up to him like a sacred offering. He reached out a shaky hand to run the backs of his fingers across the tops of their soft curves.

Then Leilani undid the clasp, letting the straps fall down her arms before allowing the bra to fall to the floor, where she kicked it away with her toe.

Oh man.

His mouth watered in anticipation. Man, he couldn't wait to find out if she tasted as delectable as she looked, all soft and pink, with darker taut nipples.

Unable to resist feeling her skin against his any longer, Holden slipped one arm around her waist, tugging her close so her breasts grazed his bare chest.

Exquisite.

Then he went one step further, cupping one breast in the palm of his hand, his thumb teasing her nipple as he nuzzled the pulse point at the base of her neck, sliding his tongue along her collarbone. Her moan and answering shudder was nearly his undoing. He smiled, savoring the moment. "You like that?"

Her response emerged as more of a breathy sigh. "Yes."

"Good." Holden dropped to his knees, ignoring the protests from the muscles in his right thigh, and kissed her belly button, her stomach, the valley between her breasts, before taking one pretty pink nipple into his mouth.

"Holden," Leilani groaned, her nails scraping his scalp. "Please, don't stop."

"Never," he murmured, kissing his way over to her other nipple to lavish it with the same attention, his fingers tweaking it as he licked and nipped and sucked until she writhed against him, her head back and her expression pure bliss. Normally, he'd be unable to stay in such a position long, given his leg, but there was something about being with her that made his pain disappear.

The only thing that mattered now was this night, this moment, this woman.

Steering her by the hips, Holden managed to get them to the bed. His leg would protest the effort tomorrow, he was sure, but for now all he wanted was to get them both naked and to bury himself deep inside her. He'd stocked up on condoms in the nightstand, just in case.

Once Leilani's knees hit the edge of the mattress, she tipped back onto the bed, and he crawled atop the mattress over her. She ran her fingers up and down his spine, making him shudder again. It had been so long, too long, since anyone had touched him like this, since he'd allowed anyone close enough to try. And now that he had, he couldn't get enough.

Before he took his pleasure, however, he wanted to bring Leilani there first. Needed to see her come apart in his arms as he licked and kissed and suckled every square inch of her amazing body. To that end, he worked his way downward from her breasts, his fingers caressing her sides, her hips, before slipping between her parted thighs to cup the heat of her through her jeans.

"Holden," Leilani gasped, arching beneath him. "Please."

"Please what, sweetheart?" he whispered, nuzzling the sensitive skin above her waistband. "Tell me what you want."

"You. I want you," she panted, unzipping and pushing down her own jeans before kicking them off, leaving her in just panties. "Please. You're killing me."

He chuckled, ignoring the throb of his erection

pressed against the mattress. He was determined to make all this last as long as possible. He parted her thighs even more and positioned himself between them, then slowly lowered her panties, inch by torturous inch, until she was completely exposed to him. The scent of her arousal nearly sent him over the edge again, but Holden forced himself to go slow.

After kissing his way up her inner thighs, he leaned forward and traced his tongue over her slick folds. Leilani bucked beneath him and would've thrown him off the bed if he hadn't been holding on so tight. Tenderly, reverently, he nuzzled her flesh, using his lips and tongue and fingers to bring her to the heights of ecstasy over and over again. When he inserted first one, then two fingers inside her, preparing her for him, she called out his name and he didn't think he'd ever heard a sweeter sound in his life.

"Holden! Holden, I…" Her breath caught and her body tightened around his finger as she climaxed in his arms. This was what he'd been imagining for days, weeks. Hearing her call out for him and knowing that he was responsible for that dreamy look on her gorgeous face.

Once her pleasure subsided, he kissed his way up her body, stopping to pay homage to her breasts again before leaning above her and smiling at the sated expression on her face. She gave him a sleepy grin, then pulled him down for another deep kiss. Her hand slid down his chest to the waistband of his jeans, then beneath to take his hard length in hand.

He could have orgasmed just from her touch, but he wanted more. Tonight, he wanted to be inside her. Tonight, he wanted everything with Leilani.

Summoning his last shreds of willpower, he captured her wrist, pulling her hand away from him and kissing her palm before letting her go. "If you touch me now, sweetheart, it'll all be over and I want this to last as long as possible."

"Me too," she said, touching his lips. "Make love to me, Holden."

No need for her to ask twice. He grabbed a small foil packet out of the nightstand drawer while kissing her again, then climbed off the bed to remove his jeans and boxer briefs, putting the condom on before returning to her side. Supporting his weight on his forearms, he leaned above her once more, positioning himself at her wet entrance, then hesitating. "You're sure about this?"

"Absolutely," she said, pulling him down for an open-mouthed kiss.

Holden entered her in one long thrust, holding still then to allow her body to adjust to his size. Leilani began to move beneath him, her hips rocking up into his and he withdrew nearly to his tip before thrusting into her once more. She was so hot and tight and wet, everything he'd imagined and so much more.

Pain jolted from his leg all too soon however, and he couldn't hide his wince.

She must have seen it because, before he knew what was happening, she rolled them, putting him flat on his back with her over him. He'd thought having her beneath him was hot. Having her above him like that though, with the moonlight streaming over her beautiful face as she rode them both to ecstasy drove his desire beyond anything he'd ever imagined. Soon they developed a rhythm that had them both teetering on the brink of orgasm again far too soon.

"Oh," Leilani cried. Her slick walls tightened around him, her nails scratched his pecs and her heels dug into the side of his hips, holding him so close, like she'd never let him go.

Then she cried out his name once more, her body squeezing his, milking him toward a climax that left Holden stunned, breathless and boneless and completely drained in the best possible way.

He might've blacked out from the incandescent pleasure, because the next time he blinked open his eyes, it was to find Leilani laying atop his chest, drawing tiny circles with her fingers through the smattering of hair on his pecs. He stroked his fingers through her silky hair and for those brief seconds, all seemed right with the world. In fact, Holden never wanted to move again.

Finally though, Leilani raised her head slightly to meet his gaze, her chin resting over his heart as she flashed him a weary smile. "That was incredible."

"It really was," he said, the remnants of his earlier excitement dissolving into warm sweetness and affection. Then his stomach rumbled, reminding him of the dinner they'd neglected. She giggled and he raised a brow at her. "How about a picnic in bed?"

She rolled off him before he could stop her and rushed across the hotel room naked to grab one of the giant Caesar salads topped with crab and lobster before rushing back to bed. They got situated against the headboard, under the covers, then she handed him a fork and napkin before digging into their feast first. "My favorite kind of picnic."

CHAPTER NINE

THE NEXT MORNING Leilani blinked her eyes open and squinted at the sunshine streaming in through the open doors to the balcony. It took her a minute to realize that she wasn't in her own room. The warm weight around her waist tightened and a nose pressed into the nape of her neck, close to the scar there.

Holden.

She yawned, then snuggled deeper into his embrace, not wanting to get up just yet, even though she was scheduled for another shift later that day. Her body ached in all the right ways and sleepy memories of the night before drifted back. Honestly, after their first round of lovemaking, she'd expected to have been worn out. But man, there was something about Holden that kept her engine revved on high. The guy definitely knew what he was doing between the sheets.

Not to mention his stamina. They'd ended up having sex twice more. Once in the bed and again in the bathtub, just before dawn. Afterward, they'd finally fallen asleep together, wrapped in each other arms.

Being with him had been amazing. Awesome. Enlightening.

She'd expected his past and injuries to maybe cause

issues, but they'd found ways to make it work. In fact, some of the new positions they'd tried were better than she'd ever imagined. Plus, it was as if telling each other about their worst moments in life had opened them both up to just be present now and enjoy the moment. It was refreshing. It was energizing. It was addictive.

A girl could get used to that.

Except she really couldn't. Leilani sighed and slowly turned over to face a still-snoozing Holden. He would be gone soon, no matter how easy it might be to picture him now as a steady fixture in her life. Besides, she'd been the one to lay the ground rules between them at the start of all this. She couldn't be the one to change them now.

Could I?

She reached out and carefully ran her fingers along the strong line of his jaw, smiling at the feel of rough stubble against her skin. His long, dark lashes fanned over his high cheekbones and the usual tension around his full lips was gone. He looked so relaxed and peaceful in sleep she didn't want to wake him. Then she spotted the scar on his left shoulder and couldn't stop herself from touching that too. The thought that he might have died that day, been taken away before she'd ever had a chance to work with him, to know him, to…

Whoa, girl.

She stopped that last word before it fully formed, her chest constricting.

Nope. Not going there at all. No ties, no strings. That was their deal.

The happiness bubbling up inside her wasn't the *l* word. It was satisfaction.

Yeah. That was it. And sure, she liked Holden. Liked talking to him, liked working through cases with him.

Liked the way he looked, the way he smiled, the way he smelled and tasted and…

"Hey." His rough, groggy voice wrapped around her like velvet, nudging her out of her head and back to the present. "What time is it?"

"Early," she said. From the angle of the early-morning sun streaming in, it couldn't have been much past six, she'd guessed. "You've got time before your shift. We both do."

"Good." He stretched, giving her a glorious view of his toned, tanned chest before propping himself up on one elbow to smile over at her, all lithe sinew and sexy male confidence. "How do you feel this morning?"

"Fine." The understatement of the century. Heat prickled her cheeks despite her wishes. "And you?"

"Leg's a bit sore after the workout last night, but otherwise, I'm excellent." He pulled her closer and she snuggled into his arms, tucking her head under his chin.

"We should try and get some more sleep while we can," she said against the pulse point at the base of his neck.

"Hmm." He kissed the top of her head and her whole body tingled, remembering how he'd felt moving against her last night, moving within her. The feel of his lips on hers, the taste of him on her tongue. If he hadn't mentioned his leg hurting, she might've climbed atop him again for round four and give him something nice to dream about.

As it was, she lay there until his soft snores filled the air, letting her mind race through what was becoming more undeniable to her by the second. Somewhere between the hospital and their day touring the island and their post-luau beach kiss, she'd gone way past *like* with this guy. In truth, she'd fallen head over heels for Holden.

Her muscles tensed and she took a few deep breaths to force herself to relax.

Love was a four-letter word where Leilani was concerned. Yes, she loved her adopted parents and U'i. But what she felt for Holden was different—deeper, bigger, stronger. And so much scarier.

She didn't want to love him. He'd be gone soon, and she'd be left to pick up the pieces, the same as she had after her family had died.

Unfortunately, it seemed her heart hadn't gotten that memo though, dammit.

She fell into a restless sleep, dreaming she was back on the highway heading for North Shore, then down in a ditch with Holden trapped and with her having no way to help him. She'd woken with a start, thankful to find him still asleep.

Leilani eased out of bed to shower before heading back to her room to have breakfast alone and get ready for her day. She'd hoped time and space would help her forget about her foolish thoughts of things with Holden being about anything more than mutual lust, but that pesky *l* word continued to dog her later as she started her shift at the hospital as well.

At least the ER was busy, so there was that.

"I haven't gone for a week and a half," the middle-aged black woman said, perched on the end of the table in trauma room three. "Tried mineral oil, bran cereal, even suppositories my family doc recommended. Nothing."

Leilani scrolled through the woman's file, frowning. "Well, I see here you're on a couple of different pain medications. Constipation is a common side effect with those. Are you drinking lots of water?"

"I'm trying," the woman said. "But my stomach's cramping and it hurts."

"Yes, it can cause a lot of pain. We can do an enema here today and see if that helps." She made a few notes on her tablet, then walked over to a drawer and pulled out a gown to hand to the woman. "Put that on and I'll be back in shortly to do an abdominal exam, Mrs. Nettles."

Leilani stepped back out into the hall and closed the door before walking over to the nurses' station. Pam was there, typing something into the computer behind the desk. She glanced up at Leilani, her gaze far too perceptive.

"Hey, Doc." Pam smiled. "You look awfully refreshed for a Monday. What'd you do over the weekend? Have a hot date or something?"

"What? No." Leilani frowned down at her tablet screen. "I'm probably going to need an enema for the patient in Room Three."

Pam snorted. "Way to change the subject. Dr. Ross seemed to have a bounce in his step too when I saw him a few minutes ago."

Leilani prayed her cheeks didn't look as hot as they felt. "Well, good for him. That has nothing to do with me."

"Uh-huh." Pam sounded entirely unconvinced. "Well, I think two people as great as you guys deserve happiness where you can find it."

"Thanks so much," Leilani said, her tone snarky. "But can we focus on patients, please?"

"Sure thing, Doc." Pam finished on the computer then came around the counter. "Heard you and Dr. Ross are going over the security protocols. That's good, since your loudmouth MVA patient showed up here again last night. We've all been a bit on edge since."

Her gaze flew to Pam's. "Mr. Chambers came back?"

"Yep," Pam said, gathering supplies for the enema patient onto a tray. "Claimed he still had pain and wanted more drugs."

"Did you call the police?" Leilani asked, concerned.

"No. One of the guards got him out of here." Pam snorted and shook her head. "But the guy was shouting the whole time about how we hadn't heard the last of him."

Damn. That wasn't good news. She had a bad feeling about that guy.

"If he shows up again, please text me right away, okay?" Leilani said, heading back toward room three with Pam by her side. "Let's finish examining Mrs. Nettles."

Hours later, Holden sat in Leilani's office, going over the safety polices for the ER. So far it hadn't been triggering at all, he was happy to say. In fact, it had all been about as exciting as watching paint dry. If it hadn't been for her nearness and the enchanting way she blushed each time their gazes caught, he probably would've dozed off a while ago. As it was, he couldn't stop thinking about their night together. Or the fact she'd been gone when he'd woken up again.

Usually, he would've been fine with that. Save them both the morning-after awkwardness. But being with Leilani last night had felt different. Seemed the more time he had with Leilani, the more he wanted. Which was not good.

He'd agreed to her terms. A fling, nothing more. He wouldn't go back on that promise now.

She didn't do relationships and he was the last guy in the world anyone should get involved with. There were too many shadows still lurking from his past, too many demons he still had to conquer from the shooting before he'd be good company long-term for anyone. Some days he wondered if he'd ever be victorious over them and get back to the man he was before the shooting. Not physically—since his physical therapist assured him his mobility would only improve with enough time and hard work—but emotionally. When he was with Leilani though, she made him feel like he could heal the darkness inside him, could open his heart and love again. Truthfully, after being with her, getting to know her better, he felt pretty invincible all around. But that was just the endorphins talking. He knew better than anyone what a lie that false sense of security was, that false high of connection that made you believe in rainbows and miracles and love…

Whoa, Nelly.

This wasn't love. They'd had one night together. Things didn't happen that fast.

Do they?

"Okay," she said, glancing over at him. "We've knocked out most of the updates, and I put this one off until the end, but it's probably the most important. I understand if you'd like me to handle this one on my own."

"The active shooter protocol." He raked his hand through his hair and shook his head, hoping to expel the sudden jolt of anxiety bolting through him. He'd been expecting this, and still it took his breath away. He pushed to his feet to pace. He could do this. It was important. It could save lives. "No. I can handle it. What's the current protocol?"

"It's pretty basic," she said, her expression concerned as she looked away from him and back to the black binder in front of her. "The last time this was revised was three years ago and the problem has only gotten worse since then. This only lists sheltering in place and calling the police."

"Both of those are good, but it's not enough." Holden walked from one side of the ten-by-ten office to the other, then back again. His therapist back in Chicago had told him talking about what happened was good for him, better than keeping it all bottled up inside. Didn't mean it was easy though. Especially now, when he was still trying to process all his feelings from last night with Leilani. Still, this was a chance to create some good out of the tragedy he'd suffered. It's what David would've wanted. Perhaps he could find some closure too. Helen's suggestion that he help Leilani with the project made more sense taken in that light.

He took a deep breath, then began to talk his way through the problem while Leilani took notes. "We need to check out the Homeland Security website. They've got lots of good information and videos there to help us get the staff trained properly." He'd watched them all hundreds of times since the incident in Chicago, searching for reasons to explain why the shooting had happened and how to make sure it never happened again.

"Run, hide, fight are the three options basically. In the ER we've got both soft targets and crowded spaces to contend with." As he went over the whole "see something suspicious, say something" issue, Leilani gave him a worried look. He stopped his pacing and frowned. "What?"

"Nothing." She shook her head and scowled down at the paper again. "Pam mentioned that my patient from a few weeks ago, Greg Chambers, showed up here again last night asking for more pain meds."

"Did he make threats?" Holden asked, tension knotting between his shoulder blades.

"No." Leilani sighed. "Just lots of shouting and being generally disruptive. I told Pam to let me know immediately if he shows up again."

"Make sure to tell her to phone the cops too." He clenched his fist around the head of his cane. "The shooter in Chicago was after drugs. All the staff need to be trained on how to handle those situations, so they don't escalate into something much worse. If we'd had the proper training back in Chicago, then…" His pulse stumbled at that and he leaned his hand against the wall for support. Dammit. The last thing he needed was a panic attack. Not now.

"Okay," Leilani said, getting up and guiding him back into his seat. She stayed close, crouching beside him, stroking his hair and murmuring comforting words near his ear to keep the anxiety at bay. Slowly, his breathing returned to normal and his vision cleared. The ache in his chest warmed, transforming from fear to affection to something deeper still…

No. No, no, no.

He didn't love Leilani. They'd only known each other a few weeks, hadn't spent more than a few days together, had only had one incredible night. None of that equaled a lifelong partnership. It was just the stress of this moment, wasn't it?

Except…

Holden took another deep inhale to calm his raging pulse and caught the sweet jasmine scent of her shampoo. Damn if his heart didn't tug a little bit further toward wanting forever with her.

"Hey," Leilani said, standing at last and moving back to her seat. "I think I can find enough information on the internet to handle this section of the protocol from here. How about I put it together and then you can go over it all later to make sure I didn't miss anything?"

He appreciated her concern, but needed to keep going, if for no other reason than if he didn't, he'd have nothing else to think about other than the fact he'd gone and done the last thing in the world he ever wanted to do—fall in love with Leilani Kim. And if that wasn't a disaster waiting to happen, he didn't know what was. He swallowed hard, then shook his head. "No. Let's keep going."

"Are you sure?" She cocked her head to the side, her ponytail swinging behind her.

"I'm sure."

They spent the next few hours watching videos online and reading PDF manuals, coming up with training programs and protocols for the staff. It would take a while to implement everything, but at least they knew what needed to be done and that was half the battle.

The knots that had formed between Holden's shoulder blades eased slightly and he sat back as a knock sounded on the door to Leilani's office.

Pam stuck her head inside. "Sorry to interrupt, guys, but the EMTs called. They've got a new case coming in. Toddler caught in the midst of a gang incident."

"Be right there," Holden said. "What's the ETA?"

"Five minutes out," Pam said before closing the door once more.

"I'll help," Leilani said. "I could use a break from all this stuff too."

They moved out into the bustling ER again, and Holden tugged on a fresh gown over his scrubs and grabbed his stethoscope from behind the nurses' station while Leilani did the same. They met up again near the ambulance bay doors to wait.

The knots inside Holden returned, but in his gut this time. Hurt kids were always the worst. Plus, there was also the unresolved, underlying tension of the situation with Leilani. He cared for her, far more than he should. Love made you vulnerable, and that led to heartache and pain in his experience.

An ambulance screeched to a halt outside and the EMTs rushed in with the new patient.

"Two-year-old girl, bullet fragments in left lower leg from a drive-by shooting," the paramedics said as they raced down the hallway toward the open trauma bay at the end. The little girl was wailing and squirming on the gurney.

"Please, help my daughter," the mother cried, holding on to her daughter's hand. "I tried to take cover, but it all happened so quick."

"She's in good hands, ma'am. I promise," Leilani said, glancing from the woman to Holden then back again. "Can you tell me your daughter's name?"

"Mari," the mother said. "Mari Hale."

Holden helped the EMTs transfer the child to the bed in the room, then moved in to take her vitals. "Pulse 125. BP 102 over 58. Respirations clear and normal." The little girl gave an angry wail and reached for her mom, who was fretting nearby as the cops arrived to take her statement. Holden placed a hand gently in the center of the little girl's chest and smiled down at her. "It's okay, sweetie. I promise we're going to take care of you."

Leilani moved in beside him to examine the wound to the little girl's leg. "One four-centimeter laceration to the left inner calf. On exam, her reflexes are normal and there doesn't appear to be any nerve damage or broken bones."

"Okay." Holden stepped back and slung his stethoscope around his neck once more as the nurses moved in to get an IV started. "Let's get X-rays of that left leg to be sure there's no internal damage and to visualize the foreign material lodged in there." He called over to the mother, who was speaking to the cops near the entrance to the trauma bay. "Ma'am, does your daughter have any allergies or underlying conditions we need to know about?"

The mother shook her head. "Will she be okay?"

"We'll do everything we can to make sure she is." Holden typed orders into his tablet for fluids and pain medications for the child, then waited while the techs wheeled the table out of the room and down the hall to the X-ray room. The mother went along, taking her daughter's hand again and singing to her to keep her calm.

Depending on how deeply the bullet fragments were embedded in the child's leg and where, would determine whether he could do a simple removal here in the ER of if she'd need more extensive surgery upstairs in the OR.

"You okay?" Leilani asked, her voice low.

"Yes," he said. Shooting cases always brought up painful memories, but he was a professional. He pushed past that to do his job and save lives. The fact that Leilani thought maybe he wasn't all right chafed. He turned away to talk to the cops instead. "What happened?"

"According to the mother, it was two rival gangs settling a dispute," one officer said.

"Gangs?" Holden scrunched his nose. "They have those in Hawaii?"

"Yep," the second officer said. "Not as bad as they were back in the nineties, but a few are still here. The mom and kid live in Halawa. Lots of the gang activity centered there these days."

Holden glanced sideways at Leilani for confirmation.

"The tourism board likes to keep it under wraps as much as possible, but unfortunately, it's true," she said. "The housing projects in Halawa are filled with low-income families looking for a way out. Gangs exploit that and use it to their advantage. And every once in a while there are turf wars."

"And this poor kid got caught up in one," the first officer said.

"Is the mother involved with the gangs?" Holden asked.

"No," the second officer said. "Just in the wrong place at the wrong time."

Holden knew all about that. "Did you catch the people who did this?"

"Not yet," the second officer said. "Neighbors generally don't want to get involved for fear of retaliation. The mother gave us descriptions of the men who opened fire though, so at least we've got that to go on."

"What about her and her daughter then?" Leilani asked, frowning. "Will they be safe when they go home?"

"Hard to say," the first officer said. "We'll add extra patrols for the next week or so, but that's about all we can do, since we're understaffed as it is at the moment."

Deep in thought, Holden exhaled slowly to calm the adrenaline thundering through his blood. The last thing he wanted to do was patch the kid up only to send her and her mother right back into a war zone.

The radiology techs wheeled the little girl back in a few minutes later. Both she and her mother were a bit calmer now, which was good. Holden pulled the films up on his tablet and assessed the situation. None of the fragments were too deeply embedded. He could remove them in the ER and send them on their way. Good for the little girl, bad for their situation at home.

Leilani peeked around his arm to see the images. "Thank goodness the damage is only superficial."

"Yes," he said quietly. "But I hate to discharge them until the guys who did this are caught."

"Then don't." She shrugged. "Say we need to keep her overnight for observation. I can make arrangements upstairs for a room with a foldout bed so the mom can stay with her."

"Are you sure?" He gazed down into her warm brown eyes and his heart swelled with emotion. The fact that they were on the same wavelength with the kid's case only reinforced the connection he felt for her elsewhere too. Which filled him with both happiness and trepidation.

Leilani nodded, and Holden turned back to the patient and her mother. "Right. I'll need to perform a minor surgery here in the ER to remove the bullet fragments still lodged in your daughter's leg, then we'll want to keep her at least overnight to make sure she doesn't develop any clots from the injury. Pam, can you get the procedure room set up for me?"

"Sure thing, Doc," Pam called, walking out into the hall.

"And I'll walk you through all the forms to sign and answer any questions you might have," Leilani said, guiding the mother toward the door. She glanced back once at Holden and gave him a small wink, then led the woman from the room.

Holden smiled down at the little girl. He couldn't do anything about the gangs out there, but he could keep her safe in the hospital, at least for tonight. Plus, helping his young patient and her mother gave him a break from stewing over the mess in his personal life. He took the little girl's hand and rested his arms on the bedside rail. "Don't worry, sweetie. We're going to take good care of you and your mom."

CHAPTER TEN

THE NEXT MORNING Holden was at the nurses' station, working through documentation on the charts from the patients he'd treated through the night. His mind wasn't fully on the task though, with part of it upstairs with little Mari Hale and her mother on the third floor. The two-year-old had come through the procedure to remove the bullet fragments from her leg nicely and there shouldn't be any lasting effects. He hoped that both the patient and her mother had gotten a good night's sleep in the peace and safety of the hospital.

Another part of his brain was still lingering on thoughts of Leilani. He'd missed sleeping with her last night, holding her close and kissing her awake so they could make love again. His body tightened at the memories of how amazing she'd felt in his arms, under him, around him, her soft cries filling his ears and the scent of her arousal driving his own passion to new heights.

But he shoved those thoughts aside. He was at work now. People needed him here. He needed to clear his head and get himself straightened out on this whole affair. No matter what his feelings were for Leilani, the thing between them was temporary because that's what she said she wanted. He refused to pressure her into anything she didn't want.

Period. Amen.

In fact, it was probably a good thing she'd been busy too since last night, dealing with her own cases and the security paperwork in her office, for them to have seen much of each other after dealing with the little girl. Images of her from their day on the town popped into his head. She'd been so happy, so relaxed and in her element as she'd showed him around the island. He honestly couldn't remember when he'd had a better day, or better company. It was almost enough to make him want to stick around Hawaii for a while...

"Hey, Doc," Pam called to him from her desk nearby. "Dr. King wants to see you again."

With a sigh, he finished the chart he was working on, then shut down his tablet and stood. Helen probably wanted to check in on their progress on the project. "Be right back then."

"Happy Monday, Doc," Pam said, chuckling as he headed for the elevators.

The ride to the fifth floor was fast, and the receptionist waved him into Helen's office even faster. She looked perfectly polished, as usual, which only made Holden feel more unkempt. He patted his hair to make sure it wasn't sticking up where it shouldn't, then took a seat, setting his cane aside and folding his hands atop his well-worn scrubs. "Good morning."

"Morning," Helen said from behind her desk, watching him over the rims of her reading glasses. She set aside the papers in her hands, then leaned forward, resting her weight on her forearms atop the desk. "So,

Holden. Have you given any more thought to staying here in Honolulu?"

He had, yeah. But not for the reason Helen hoped, so he fibbed a bit. "Not really. I've been busy."

"Hmm. Working with Dr. Kim, I suspect," she said. Well, it was due to Leilani, but not because of the project. "I've heard gossip that you two have been spending more time together."

He took a deep breath and stared at the beige carpet beneath his feet. Damn the rumor mill around this place. "I'm staying at the resort her parents own. We're bound to run into each other on occasion."

"Uh-huh." His old friend's tone suggested she didn't buy that for a minute. Helen sat back and crossed her arms, her gaze narrowing. "After everything you've been through, you deserve to be happy."

He hid his eye roll, barely. "Is this going to be some kind of pep talk? Because I really don't have time for it this morning. I need to get back to work."

"You know me better than that." Helen laughed. "I'm not a rainbows and sunshine kind of person."

Nah, she really wasn't. That's probably why they were such good friends. Helen told it like it was. A trait Holden appreciated even more after the shooting, when people treated him like he'd shatter at the slightest bump. Still, the last thing Holden wanted was relationship advice. "So, what is it you needed to see me about then?"

"I want you to think seriously about taking a permanent trauma surgeon position, Holden. That's what I want." When he didn't say anything, she continued. "Look, you turned down the directorship job, and I respect that. Having had a chance to go over Dr. Kim's credentials again, I think you're right. She is a better fit for the job. But that doesn't mean I can't use your skills elsewhere. You could stay in Honolulu, build a new life for yourself here. I can already see a change in you for the better since you arrived. You're more relaxed, less burdened by the past."

Holden took a deep breath and stared out the windows at the bright blue sky. Helen was right—he did feel better. Even his leg wasn't bothering him so much—well except for after his night with Leilani…

"Here," Helen said, handing him a job description. "At least look at what the job entails before you turn it down. I've added the salary I'm willing to pay in the corner there too, as an enticement."

Shaking off those forbidden thoughts, he focused on the paperwork. It was a good offer, with way more money than what he was making now, higher even than what he'd made back in Chicago. Plus, the benefits were great too. And it would allow him to put down roots again, if he wanted. Allow him to continue exploring this thing with Leilani too, if they both agreed.

But he wasn't quite ready to take the plunge yet. "Can I think about it for a few days?"

"Of course," Helen said, smiling. "Take as long as you need. I'm just glad you didn't flat out say no again. Now, get back to work. My next appointment should be here soon."

"Thanks." He hobbled to the door and opened it, stepping out into the hall before turning back. "I really do appreciate the offer and you're right. Staying in Honolulu would be nice."

He'd just closed the door and turned toward the elevators when he nearly collided with Leilani. He put his hand on her arm to steady her, then dropped it fast when he took in her stiff posture and remote expression. Not sure how to react, he fumbled his words. "Oh…uh…hi."

She blinked at him a moment before sidling around him, her tone quiet. "I have an appointment with Dr. King. Excuse me."

Leilani walked into Dr. King's office with her heart in her throat, Holden's words still ringing in her ears.

I really do appreciate the job offer and you're right. Staying in Honolulu would be nice…

Thoughts crashed through her brain at tsunami speed. When she'd first seen him in the hall, before he'd spotted her, she'd been happy, smiling, excited to be near him again. Then her brain processed his words to Dr. King. What job offer? The directorship? Did he want to stay in Honolulu? Did he want the same job she did? He'd said he didn't, but maybe he'd lied. Maybe he wanted to keep her off balance. Maybe he'd only slept with her as a distraction.

Wait. What?

No. Her heart didn't want to believe that, refused to believe that. But damn if those good old doubt demons from her past didn't resurface and refuse to be quiet. She ignored Holden's befuddled stare and fumbled her way past him and into Dr. King's office, closing the door behind her. She flexed her stiff fingers, more nervous now than her initial interview for the directorship position.

"Dr. Kim, please sit down." Dr. King gestured to a chair in front of her desk. "I wanted to ask you for an update on the security protocols for the ER."

Right. Okay. So, it wasn't about the job.

Why would it be, if she's already offered it to someone else? her mean mind supplied unhelpfully.

Leilani forced a smile she didn't feel and concentrated on explaining the pertinent details of the plans she and Holden had been working on downstairs earlier. "They're coming along well. We've worked through most of them already. The only one with substantial changes is the active shooter policy and I'm working on coming up with a substantial training protocol for the staff we can implement soon."

"Excellent," Dr. King said, fiddling with some paperwork on her desk, not looking at Leilani. "We'll need the details solidified by the end of the month to add to the rest of our recertification packet."

"I'll make sure it's completed." She swallowed hard, wondering if she should just come right out and ask about the directorship. Torn as she was about her feelings for Holden anyway, it would be better to know the truth up front so she could nurse her wounds in private. Her heart, her future, everything seemed to be on the line. If he'd lied, then she needed to know. Hurt stung her chest, but she shoved it aside. This was business. She had no right to be upset with Holden for taking the position out from under her. They were technically still rivals, after all. And the fact that she'd fallen for him anyway was entirely on her. Her heart pinched, but she pushed those feelings down deep. Personal feelings had no business in professional life. Honestly, if she'd been faced with the same choice, she would've made the same decision as Holden, wouldn't she?

Except no, she wouldn't have. Because she loved him, even though she shouldn't. It was so stupid. He'd never once said he wanted anything more than sex from her. She'd gone into their fling with her eyes wide-open and set the rules herself. No strings attached. The fact she wanted more now was her problem, not his.

Doing her best to stay pragmatic despite the monsoon of sadness inside her, Leilani cleared her throat and raised her chin. "Have you made a decision on the directorship position?"

"What?" Helen King looked up and seemed distracted. "Yes, I have, actually, Dr. Kim." Before she could say more, however, the phone on her desk jangled loudly, cutting her off. She held up a finger for Leilani to wait as she answered. "Yes, Dr. King speaking. What? Hang on." She covered the receiver and said to Leilani, "I'm sorry, I need to take this. Can we continue this later, Dr. Kim?" At Leilani's reluctant nod, Dr. King smiled. "Good. Have the receptionist pencil you in for another slot on your way out. Excuse me."

Right. Leilani left the office and headed back out to schedule her appointment then down to the ER, still stewing over things in her mind. She hadn't gotten the answers she needed from Dr. King, so it was time to be a big girl and confront Holden directly.

Determined, as soon as the doors opened and she stepped off into her department, Leilani made a beeline toward the nurses' station, her adrenaline pumping hotter with each step. "Where's Dr. Ross?"

Pam glanced up at her, her gaze a bit startled, and she took in Leilani's serious expression. "Exam room two. Stomach flu case. Everything okay, Doc?"

"Peachy," she said over her shoulder as she headed down the hall toward where Holden was working. She knocked on the door, then opened it to find him performing an abdominal exam on a middle-aged man. "Dr. Ross, can I speak with you a moment, please?"

"Uh, sure. Let me just finish with this patient first."

"I'll be waiting outside," she said, ignoring the curious look the nurse working with Holden gave her.

"It won't take long," he said.

Several minutes passed before he limped out of the room and followed Leilani down the hall to a quiet, deserted waiting area. "Is something wrong? Is it the little girl from last night?"

"No. The last time I checked in on her, Mari was fine." Leilani crossed her arms, her toe tapping on the linoleum floor to burn off some excess energy. "Want to tell me about your meeting with Dr. King?"

His stoic expression grew more remote, telling her everything she needed to know. "Uh, no, Not really. Why?"

"Because it would have been nice to have a heads-up that you were taking the directorship job I wanted." Her anger piqued at his audacity, standing there looking shocked and innocent when he'd gone behind her back to swipe the job out from under her. She should've known better than to trust him. Letting people into your heart only caused you pain in the end. And yet Holden Ross had gotten past all her barriers. Dammit. She wasn't sure who she was more furious with—him or herself. "That's the offer you were thanking her for, wasn't it?"

"No." The confusion in his eyes quickly morphed to understanding. "Leilani, that's not what happened."

"So, she didn't offer you the directorship?"

"No, she did, but I turned it down."

She couldn't stop her derisive snort. "You turned it down? I don't believe you."

A small muscle ticked near his tight jaw. "Well, it's the truth. She asked me weeks ago about it and I told her I didn't want it. Told her I thought you should have it. She agreed."

"Excuse me?" she said, battling to keep her voice down to avoid feeding the rumor mills any further. "Then what offer were you thanking her for upstairs? And why would she ask for your opinion anyway?" Then a new thought occurred, as bad as the previous ones. "Wait a minute. Have you been spying on me for her?"

The more she thought about it, the more it made sense. All that time they'd spent together, the day touring the island, the cases they'd worked together, their night in each other's arms. All of it was a lie.

He cursed under his breath, crimson dotting his high cheekbones now. "No." He raked his hand through his hair again, something he did when he was stressed, she'd noticed. Well, she'd be stressed too if she'd been caught in a lie. "I mean, originally Helen did ask me about you because she said she knew so little about you, but all I told her was that you were more qualified for the directorship than me."

"Damn straight I am," she said, on a roll now, hurt driving her onward, completely ignoring the fact he'd all but said Leilani was getting the job. This was about far more than work now, as evidenced by the crushing ache in her heart. She'd loved him, dammit. Opened up to him. Trusted him. And look what it got her, more pain and sorrow, just like she'd feared. "So, I'm just supposed to believe you now, that everything that happened between us wasn't just some ploy to keep tabs on me for your friend?"

"Is that what you think? The kind of guy you think I am?" That knocked him back a step and pain flashed in his hazel eyes before being masked behind a flare of indignation. He turned away, swore again, then shook his head, his expression a blend of resignation and regret. "Well, I guess that works out just fine then, doesn't it? I'm glad to know the truth because that makes my decision a hell of a lot easier." He wasn't trying to keep his voice down now, and the other staff started noticing them at the end of the hall.

"You want to know about my meeting with Helen King? Fine. For your information, Leilani, the job I was referring to upstairs wasn't the directorship. It was a permanent trauma surgeon position. Not that it's any of your business. And if you don't believe me then there's nothing else I can say. I thought what we shared together the past few weeks, the connection between us, spoke for itself, but I guess I was wrong. I was so stupid to think this would work, to think there might be something more between us than a fling. You said you don't do relationships? Well, neither do I. Especially with a woman who's so afraid to let anyone in that she pushes everyone away."

"Me?" She stepped closer to him, her broken heart raging inside her. "You're the one who's always running. Always hiding from your past. Don't talk to me about trust when you flat out lied to me."

"I have never lied to you, Leilani," he said, the words bitten out. "I—"

Whatever he'd been about to say was silenced by what sounded like a firecracker going off near the front entrance to the ER. The loud bang was followed in short order by screaming and people running everywhere.

Leilani started down the hall toward the nurses' station. "What's happening?"

Holden grabbed her arm and hauled her back. "I don't know, but I do recognize that sound. It's gunfire."

CHAPTER ELEVEN

TIME SEEMED TO slow and speed up at the same time as Holden's mind raced and his blood froze. Shooting. Screams. Sinister flashbacks nearly drove him to his knees. Another ER, another gunman. David, bleeding out on the tile floor as Holden lay beside him, too injured himself to help.

Oh God. Not again. Please not again.

"Holden!" Leilani shouted, struggling to break his hold on her arm. "Let me go! We've got to help those people!"

He wasn't expecting the punch of her elbow to his stomach and he doubled over, releasing her as he struggled to catch his breath.

"Wait!" he called as she ran off toward the front entrance, toward danger. "Leilani!"

"Use the emergency phone to call the police," she shouted to him before disappearing around the corner.

Damn.

Blood pounded loud in his ears, making it hard to hear as he dialed 911. After relaying the info to the dispatcher, he hung up, then swallowed hard and hobbled toward the corner, his breathing labored from the anxiety squeezing his chest. If anything happened to

Leilani, he'd never forgive himself. Regardless of what she thought of him now, he couldn't lose her, not like he'd lost David. He couldn't fail this time.

But what if you do...?

Teeth gritted, he pressed his back to the wall, the coolness shocking to his heated skin. He feared the shooter might be one of the gang members who'd shot the little girl upstairs, come to finish off the job. But as a male voice yelled, he realized it wasn't a gangbanger at all. He recognized that voice. Greg Chambers, the guy who'd punched him a few weeks back. The man Leilani had warned him about the day before in her office.

"Give me my opioids and no one gets hurt," the guy snarled. "Or don't and die."

Reality blurred again, between the ER in Chicago and now. The other shooter had wanted drugs too and he'd made the same threat. Made good on that threat too. Dammit. Holden cursed under his breath. The police were on their way, but what if they didn't make it in time? They hadn't been able to save David. No. It was up to him.

His analytical mind kicked in at last, slicing through the panic like a scalpel. Berating himself and "what if" thinking wouldn't help anyone now. Action. He needed to move, needed to find a way to take down Greg Chambers before he hurt anyone else.

Run. Hide. Fight.

Those were the words Homeland Security drilled into the heads of everyone who encountered an active shooter situation. Running was out, since the gunman was already here. Hiding would be good for those in the lobby, but not for Holden. He was the one person here who'd been through this before. He was outside the current hot zone and in the best position to surprise the attacker and possibly take him down and disarm him before the cops arrived.

More shots rang out, followed by screams and crying.

The unbearable tension inside Holden ratcheted higher as precious seconds ticked by.

Think, Holden. Think.

Eyes closed he rested his head back against the wall and thought through what he knew. Greg Chambers was an addict. He liked alcohol and drugs. Chances were good he'd be intoxicated now, since no sober person would attack an ER. If he was lucky, the guy's reflexes and reaction time would be affected by whatever substances were in his system. Holden could use that, if he could sneak up on the other man. He glanced down at his cane and winced. Hard to be stealthy with that thing. Which meant he needed to leave it behind.

Okay. Fine.

He set the cane aside, then took another deep breath, listening. Greg Chambers was still talking, but Holden was too far away to understand what he was saying. Then another voice, clear and bright, halted his heart midbeat. Leilani. As fast as his pulse stopped, it kicked back into overdrive again. If the bastard harmed one hair on her head...

Move. Now!

Holden hazarded a peek around the corner and spotted the shooter with his back toward the hallway. Saw Leilani near the nurses' station, hands up as she faced down the gunman while the people behind her cowered on the floor. She was so brave, so good, so beautiful and honest and true and he realized in that moment he'd do anything to keep her safe.

Even risk his own life.

After one more deep breath for courage, Holden inched his way toward the front entrance, doing his best to stay as silent as possible. His right leg protested with each step, but he pressed onward, knowing that if he didn't act now, it might be too late.

"Shut up, bitch!" Greg shouted, aiming his gun at Leilani again. "Sick of your talking. Give me my damned drugs before I blow your head off!"

"I can't do that, sir," she responded, her voice calm and level. Her dark gaze flicked over to Holden then back to the shooter, faster than a blink, but he felt that look like a lifeline. She'd seen him, knew he was coming to help. Leilani continued. "The police are on their way. Let these people go and put your gun down. You can't win here."

"Shut up!" Chambers yelled, his tone more frantic now as he looked around wildly. "I ain't going to jail again. I can't."

In the far distance, the wail of sirens cut through the eerie quiet in the ER. Holden spotted the two security guards near the automatic doors. One was down and bleeding. Holden couldn't see how badly. The other guard was kneeling beside him, trying to help his wounded comrade. Both guards' guns were at Chambers's feet, probably kicked there as the gunman had ordered.

"Give me the opioids and let me the hell out of here," Greg screamed again, waving his weapon around. "Do it, or I'll open fire. I swear I will. Ain't got nothing left to live for anyway."

He took aim at Leilani, at point-blank range.

"Bye, Lady Doc," Greg Chambers said. "You had your chance."

The snick of the trigger cocking echoed through Holden's head like a cannon blast. Adrenaline and desperation electrified his blood and he forgot about planning, forgot about strategy. Forgot about everything except saving the woman he loved.

Holden charged, wrapping his arm around Chambers's neck from behind and jerking him backward along with his weapon, sending the bullets skyward. He wasn't sure what was louder, the bullets firing from the semiautomatic or the screams from the people crouched in the lobby. Florescent bulbs shattered and chunks of ceiling tile rained down.

The muscles in his right thigh shrieked from the strain, but Holden held on, knocking the gun from Greg Chambers's hands, then flipping the smaller man over his shoulder and tossing him flat on his back on the floor. Tires screeched outside the front entrance and sirens screamed inside as the Honolulu PD SWAT team raced inside and took control of the gunman.

"Get off me!" the guy screamed, fighting and wrestling to get free as the cops handcuffed him and hauled him to his feet, reading him his Miranda rights as they walked him out the door. "I ain't going to jail!"

The adrenaline and shock wore off, and Holden slumped back onto his butt on the floor, breathing fast as he started to crawl toward the injured security guard near the door.

"Doc, we need help over here!" Pam called from behind him. "She's been hit."

His chest constricted and his heart dropped to his toes. Holden swiveled fast, his leg cramping with pain, to see Leilani slumped on the floor against the front of the reception desk, a blotch of crimson blooming on the left arm of her pristine white lab coat. She looked pale. Too pale.

No. Please God, no!

"Leilani," he said, reaching her. She frowned and mumbled something but didn't open her eyes. David had looked like that too, just before he'd lost consciousness. He'd never woken up again.

No. No, no, no. I won't fail this time. I can't fail this time. Please don't let me fail this time.

His hands shook as he carefully slipped her arm from the lab coat then pushed up the sleeve of her shirt. From the looks of it, the bullet had passed clean through. It had also passed perilously close to her brachial artery. Years of medical training drowned out his anxiety and emotional turmoil and spurred him into action once more. "Check her vitals. Order six units of blood on standby, in case she's hypotensive. We need an O2 Sat and X-rays to see the damage. Let's move, people."

While the residents dealt with the wounded guard and the other patients, Holden stuck by Leilani's side. He held her hand as they raced toward trauma bay one, refusing to let go, even as Helen King ran into the room and took over.

"Holden, tell me what we've got," she said as she did her own exam of Leilani's wounds. He recited back what he knew and what he'd ordered, all the while still clutching her too-cold fingers. When he was done, Helen came over and put her hands on his shoulders, shaking him slightly. "You're in shock, Dr. Ross. I've got her. Go and sit in the waiting room. You look like you're ready to pass out. You saved the lives of a lot of people today. You're a hero. Now go rest and talk to the cops."

Pam took Holden's arm and led him back toward the front entrance and helped him into a chair. He couldn't seem to stop shaking. "I can't lose her," he said to Pam. "I can't."

"She's in the best care possible, Doc. You know that." Pam shoved a cup of water into his hands before heading back toward the trauma bay. "I'll keep you posted on her condition."

A while later the cops took his statement, then left him alone with his thoughts. Holden tipped his head back to stare at the bullet holes in the ceiling and swallowed hard against the lump in his throat.

You saved the lives of a lot of people today. You're a hero.

Helen's words looped in his head but rang hollow in his aching heart.

He didn't want to be a hero. He just wanted Leilani alive and well again.

Leilani blinked her eyes open slowly, squinting into the too-bright sunshine streaming in through the windows of her room at the hotel. Except…

She frowned. The windows were on the wrong side of the room. And where were the curtains? And what was that smell? Sharp, antiseptic. Not floor cleaner or bleach, but familiar, like…

Oh God!

Head fuzzy from pain meds, memories slowly began to resurface.

Gunshots, Holden tackling the shooter, shouting, screams, a sharp burst of pain then darkness…

She moaned and tried to sit up only to be held down by the IV, tubes and wires connecting her to the monitors beside her bed. Her left arm ached like hell and her mouth felt dry as cotton.

"Welcome back, Dr. Kim," a woman's voice said from nearby. Leilani blinked hard and turned her head on the pillow to see Dr. King at the counter across the room. "How are you feeling?"

"Like crap," she mumbled, trying to scoot up farther in her hospital bed and failing. The whole scenario brought back too many memories from after the car accident for her comfort. "What's going on? Where's Holden?"

"He's fine. Should be returning to your bedside shortly," Dr. King said, moving to check the monitors attached to the blood pressure cuff and the pulse ox on Leilani's finger. "I made him go home to sleep and shower. Otherwise he hasn't left your side since the surgery."

"Surgery?" The beginnings of a headache throbbed behind Leilani's temples as she tried to recall more about what had occurred in the ER. "I had surgery?" She glanced down at the bandages wrapping her left bicep. "Who operated?"

"Yours truly." Dr. King smiled, then adjusted the IV drip settings on the machine. "Holden was a bit too close to the situation to handle it. And he was exhausted after taking down that gunman."

That much Leilani did remember. Considering what he'd been through, his actions had taken a tremendous amount of courage. He'd been a hero, saving her and countless other people. She ached to hold him and thank him for all he'd done, to beg him to forgive her for accusing him of stealing her job. He hadn't stolen anything. Except her heart.

"Anyway, I had to make sure you healed up nicely. Can't have my new Director of Emergency Medicine less than healthy." Dr. King stood near the end of the bed as Leilani took that in. "If you still want the position, that is."

"I…" She swallowed hard. "Yes, I want it. But what about Holden?"

"What about him?" Holden said from the doorway. Limping in, he set his cane aside, then took a seat in the chair at her bedside. "You look better now. Not so pale."

"Her vitals are good," Dr. King said. "And her wound is healing nicely. I'm just going to pop out for a minute. Dr. Kim, we can discuss your new position further once you're back to work."

An awkward silence descended once the door closed behind Dr. King, leaving Leilani and Holden alone in the room.

"So, I guess I should thank you," Leilani said at last.

"For what?" Holden frowned.

"For saving my life."

He gave a derisive snort. "I didn't save anything. In fact, I'm the reason you got shot in the first place. After all the research I did into active shooter situations, I should've known better than to tackle a man with a weapon."

"What?" Now it was her turn to scowl. "You're kidding, right? I don't remember everything that happened in the ER, but I do remember you taking that guy down. If anyone's at fault for me getting shot, it's Greg Chambers. You were a her—"

Holden help up a hand to stop her. "Please don't say hero. That's the last thing I am."

Leilani ignored the pain in her left arm this time and shoved higher in her bed to put them closer to eye level. "Well, whatever you want to call yourself, you saved a lot of lives down there and I'm grateful to you." She exhaled slowly and fiddled with the edge of the sheet with her right hand. "And I'm sorry."

"Sorry?" His expression turned confused. "What do you have to be sorry for?"

"For accusing you of stealing the directorship job. That was stupid of me. I should have believed you." She shook her head and gave a sad little chuckle. "I don't know why I didn't, except that I've been a mess emotionally since the luau and then that night we spent together and I took it out on you, and…" She shrugged, looking anywhere but at him. "I'm sorry."

"It's okay. I haven't exactly been thinking clearly myself since that night." He sighed and glanced toward the windows, giving her a view of his handsome profile. His hair was still damp from his shower and his navy blue polo shirt clung to his muscled torso like a second skin. Leilani bit her lip. He really was the most gorgeous man she'd ever seen, even with the dark circles under his eyes and the lines of tension around his mouth. She longed to trace her fingers down his cheek and kiss away his stress but didn't dare. Not until they hashed this out between them.

"Look, Leilani." His deep voice did way more than the meds to ease her aches and pains. "I know we agreed to just a fling, but the thing is, I don't think I can do that anymore."

"Oh." Her pulse stumbled and the monitor beeped

loud. Apparently, she'd misread the situation entirely. Just because she'd fallen head over heels for the guy didn't mean he felt the same for her. She should have kept her barriers up, should have known better. "Don't worry about it," she said, doing her best to act like it wasn't a big deal and failing miserably as tears stung the back of her eyes. Leilani blinked hard to keep them at bay, but her vision clouded despite her wishes. "We can go back to just being colleagues. Probably better that way since we'll be working together permanently."

"Yeah," he said absently. Then his attention snapped to her and his scowl deepened. "No. That's not what I meant."

"You mean you're not taking the trauma surgeon job?" she asked, confused.

"No. I am. I just… I don't want to be your friend, Leilani." Holden reached through the bedrail to take her hand, careful of her injuries. "What I mean to say is that I want to be way more than just your friend." He sighed and stared down at their entwined fingers. "I know I promised to just have a fling, no strings attached, but I can't do that anymore because I fell in love with you."

Stunned, she took a deep breath, her pulse accelerating once more. "Uh…"

"No. Let me finish, please." He exhaled slowly, his broad shoulders slumping. "You were right. I was running. I've been running since I left Chicago. Too afraid of getting hurt again to settle down anywhere. I never wanted to get that close to anyone again. Losing my best friend, David, nearly killed me, even more than the bullets did." He gave her fingers a gentle squeeze. "But then I met you. You were so full of life, so vibrant and smart and funny and kind. You were everything I didn't know

I needed. You healed me, from the inside out. Showed me I could laugh again, love again. So no, I can't go back to just having a fling with you, Leilani Kim. Because I want more. So much more. If you'll have me."

She sniffled, her tears flowing freely now. "You're the one who healed me, Holden. I thought I'd gotten over the accident that took my family all those years ago, but I'd just walled myself off, thinking that not caring too deeply would keep me safe. All that did though was make me lonely. You opened my heart again." She laughed, then winced when the movement hurt her arm. "I love you too, Holden Ross."

"You do?" His sweet, hesitant smile made her breath catch.

"I do."

He leaned closer to brush his lips across hers, and she let go of his hand to slip her fingers behind his neck to keep him close.

"I'm glad you're staying in Hawaii," she said at last, after he'd pulled back slightly.

"Me too." He nuzzled his nose against hers. "Does this mean we're officially dating?"

"I believe it does, Dr. Ross," Leilani said, winking. "The rumor mill will be all abuzz."

"Good, Dr. Kim." Holden kissed her again. "Give them something new to talk about."

CHAPTER TWELVE

One year later...

"WHAT DO WE have coming in?" Leilani asked, tugging on a fresh gown and heading toward the ambulance bay entrance.

Nurse Pam was waiting there for her, already geared up. "Per the EMTs, it was a rollover accident on the H1. Family of five. ETA two minutes."

Not exactly how she'd expected to spend the morning of her wedding day, but the ER had been short-staffed and as Director of Emergency Medicine, it was her duty to fill in when needed. Besides, it helped her stress levels to keep busy, since all the planning was done and all she had left to do was show up and marry the man of her dreams.

First though, it seemed like an ironic twist of fate that the last case she worked as a single woman was a rollover. Her biological family hadn't survived their similar accident, but today, she planned to do all she could to ensure history did not repeat itself.

Two ambulances screeched to a halt outside and soon the automatic doors whooshed open as five gurneys were wheeled in by three sets of paramedics. The

trauma surgeon on call—not Holden, thank goodness—
and a resident took the mother and son and the son's
girlfriend. Leilani and another resident took the father
and the daughter.

"You're in good hands, sir. Just lie still and let us do
all the work, okay?" she said to the father as they raced
for an open trauma bay. Then she focused on the EMT
racing along on the other side of the gurney. "Rundown,
please."

"Car rolled five times. Wife was driving," the EMT
said.

"I just remember coming around the bend and that
other car slammed into us. Then rolling and rolling."

"It was so scary," the daughter said as they transferred
her to a bed adjacent to the one her father was on, her
voice shaky with tears. "My first car accident. With the
four people I love most."

Leilani's heart squeezed with sympathy. Twenty-one
years ago, she'd experienced her first car accident too.
Worst day of her life. Funny how life worked, because
now—today—would be the best day ever. Once her shift
was over, of course. She rolled her left shoulder to ease
the ache in her bicep, then began taking the father's
vitals while the resident working alongside her in the
trauma bay did the same with the daughter.

"Do you remember what happened, sir?" Leilani
asked the father.

"I remember my life flashing before my eyes," he
said, his voice husky with emotion. "I remember glass
flying and people screaming, then everything stopped.
I'm just glad we're all still alive."

"Me too, sir," she said, swallowing against an unexpected lump of gratitude in her throat. "Me too."

"Patient is complaining of abdominal pain," the resident called over to Leilani. "I'd like to get an ultrasound to rule out internal injuries or bleeding."

"Do it," Leilani said before continuing her own exam on the father. "Where are you experiencing pain, sir?"

"My neck is killing me." He lifted his arm to point at his throat, then winced. "My chest hurts too. How are my wife and son? His girlfriend?"

"As far as I know, they're doing fine, but I'll be sure to check on that for you as soon as we get you set up here." She finished checking his vitals and rattled them off to Pam to enter into the computer, then carefully removed the plastic neck brace the EMTs had applied and examined the man's neck while a tech wheeled in an ultrasound machine for the daughter. "After you finish with that patient, I'll need a cardiac ultrasound over here too for the father, please. He's complaining of chest pain and has a history of high blood pressure and arteriosclerosis. Rule out any issues there, please. While we wait, let's see if CT can work him in for an emergency C-spine. I'm concerned about intracranial bleeding or neck fractures."

"Sure thing, Doc," Pam said, setting the tablet aside. "Keep an eye on your time too, Dr. Kim. Don't want to be late for your big day."

"I will. Thanks." She smiled at the nurse, then turned back to her patient. "Sir, we're going to get some tests done on you to make sure there are no underlying conditions going on I can't see on exam. Some films of your neck and head and also an ultrasound of your heart." She looked up as two techs came in to wheel her patient to radiology for his CT scan. "While you're doing that, I'll check in on the status of your family members, okay?"

"Okay." The father reached out and grasped Leilani's hand. "Thank you, Doctor."

"You're most welcome," she said, smiling.

The EMTs were still hanging out in the hall when she headed toward the other trauma bay to check on the mother and son and his girlfriend. One of the EMTs stopped her and showed her a picture he'd snapped at the accident scene of the mashed-up SUV lying on its side in a ditch. "The way that car looked, I'm surprised they all walked away. It's a miracle," the EMT said.

"It is." Leilani nodded, then headed for trauma bay two. "But miracles are what we specialize in around here."

She was living proof of that. She was also proof that you could not only survive the worst thing possible, you could thrive after it. Thanks to her wonderful adopted family, and Holden, who'd taught her how to love again. Her heart swelled with joy as she walked into the room where the son and his girlfriend were now sitting up and chatting while his mother gave her statement to a police officer. They appeared bruised and a bit rattled, but nothing too serious.

"I drive that route every day from our house," the mother said to the cop. "We were on our way home to watch a football game. That didn't work out so well." She sniffled. "When I saw that other car coming at us, I didn't know what to do. I didn't want him to hit us head-on, so I swerved to the left and my poor husband took the brunt." She looked up and spotted Leilani, her expression frantic. "Is he okay? Is my husband okay? I never wanted our day to end like this."

"He's fine, ma'am," she reassured the woman. "We're

running a few tests to rule out any broken bones or bleeding internally."

The woman bit back a sob and reached over to take her son's hand. "Oh thank God. I'm so grateful we're all okay."

"Me too, ma'am. Me too." Leilani pulled the resident aside and got the scoop on the three patients in the room before they wheeled the father past the door of the room heading back to trauma bay one, and she excused herself to check in on her patient once more.

While Leilani went over the images, the ultrasound tech performed a cardiac ultrasound and Pam cleaned and bandaged up the lacerations on the man's hand. Of the five passengers in the car, the father seemed to be the one most badly hurt, but the CT had ruled out any fractures in his neck or bleeding in his head, which was great. The man would be sore for sure for a few days, but otherwise should make a full recovery, barring anything abnormal on the cardiac ultrasound.

"Everything looks fine, Doc," the tech said a few minutes later, wiping the gel off the patient's chest. "No abnormalities seen."

"Perfect." Leilani moved aside so they could wheel her portable machine back out of the room. "All right, sir. Looks like you're banged up a bit, but otherwise you'll be fine. I checked on the rest of your family as well, and they're all doing fine too. You all are very lucky."

The daughter, who'd been cleared to move about freely, jumped down and walked over to take her father's hand. Soon, the rest of the family entered to join them in the trauma bay.

"How are you, honey?" the mother asked her husband, kissing his cheek.

"My neck still hurts," he said, then held up his other hand. "And this got messed up a bit. But otherwise, I'm fine." He chuckled. "Remind me never to ride with you again though."

The mother promptly burst into tears and he pulled her down closer to kiss her again.

"I'm kidding," the father said. "You handled that situation better than I would have. I love you so much. It's fine. We're all fine, thanks to you."

Leilani checked the time, then backed out of the room while the family gathered around each other, hugging and laughing and saying prayers of thanks. Tears stung the backs of her eyes, as an unexpected feeling of completeness filled her soul. That's how it should have been for her family all those years ago. It hadn't been, but now at least she'd been able to give that gift of a future to another family. Circle of life indeed.

After finishing up the discharge paperwork for her patients, she checked the time, then discarded her gown and mask into a nearby biohazard bin.

Speaking of futures, it was time to get on with hers.

Holden stood on the beach in front of the Malu Huna Resort as a warm breeze blew and the waves lapped the shore behind him. Joe Kim stood beneath an arbor adorned with palm fronds, tropical flowers and white gauzy fabric that flowed in the wind, ready to marry off his adopted daughter. He'd gotten ordained just for the ceremony. Leilani's mother was passing out leis to the guests as they took their seats. Now all Holden needed was his bride.

He shifted his weight slightly, his bare toes sinking deeper into the sand. His leg hurt less and less these days, thanks to all the outdoor activities available in and around Honolulu. He loved hiking and swimming and had even tried his hand at surfing. The warmer temperatures helped too. And of course, having the woman he loved by his side while he did all those things was the biggest benefit of all. In fact, he'd left his cane inside the hotel today—as he was doing more and more often now. He'd stop and get it though, before the reception, since there would be dancing involved later.

They'd decided on a casual, traditional Hawaiian wedding and he was not upset with it. His white linen pants and shirt were certainly more comfortable than some tuxedo monkey suit, that was for sure. Especially with the great weather. Blue skies, sunshine, a perfect day in paradise.

Hard to believe that a year ago he couldn't wait to get out of this place. Now he couldn't ever imagine calling anywhere else home ever again. He and Leilani had moved into her—now *their*—newly remodeled house three months prior, and things were pretty magical all around as they started their new life together. But even with the great beachfront abode, it wasn't the location so much as the people.

Once they'd told the Kims about their relationship, they had taken him in like a prodigal son. Family like that was something to appreciate and Holden didn't take one day of it for granted.

Same with Leilani. They'd both wanted to go slow, explore their relationship before diving into anything permanent too fast. Given their collective past, it was understandable. But now they were both ready to take the leap.

Holden glanced over and caught sight of his own parents sitting in the first row and flashed them a smile. They'd flown in from Chicago and were loving all Hawaii had to offer. Maybe someday they'd move down here too. He'd like that. As the guests' chairs filled in and the ukulele band they'd hired to play for the ceremony finished a sweet rendition of "Somewhere Over the Rainbow," a hush fell over the crowd. Holden looked up to see his bride at last at the end of the white satin runner covering the aisle of sand between the rows of bow-bedecked folding chairs.

He couldn't stop staring at her, his heart in his throat and his chest swelling with so much love he thought he might burst from the joy of it. She looked amazingly beautiful in a strapless white gown that was fitted on top, then flowed into a silken cloud around her legs, the breeze gently rustling the fabric. Like an angel. His angel, who'd been heaven-sent to teach him how to live and love again, who'd filled his life with so much purpose and meaning and emotion.

The band began "Here Comes the Bride" and the guests stood as Leilani slowly made her way toward Holden, her long dark hair loose beneath the woven crown of flowers on her head and her eyes sparkling with happiness.

She was everything he'd ever dreamed of and nothing he deserved, and his life was infinitely better because she was in it. He planned to tell her as much in his vows. They'd each written their own, but no matter what she said today, it would never mean as much to him as the moment she'd told him she loved him for the first time that day in her hospital room.

Music floated on the jasmine-scented breeze and Leilani reached his side at last.

Before the ceremony began, while the guests were settling into their seats again, Holden leaned closer and whispered for her ears only, "You look spectacular and I'm the luckiest man in the world. I love you, Leilani Kim."

Her smile brightened his entire universe as she beamed up at him. "I'm pretty lucky myself, Holden Ross. I love you too."

He leaned in to kiss her, but Leilani's father cleared his throat. Chuckles erupted from the assembled guests. Holden winked down at his wife-to-be instead, unable to keep the silly, lovesick grin off his face. "Ready to do this thing, Doc?"

"So, so ready," she said, slipping her hand in his as they turned to face her father.

* * * * *

THE SPANIARD'S
STOLEN BRIDE

MAISEY YATES

CHAPTER ONE

DIEGO NAVARRO HAD a bad habit of breaking his toys.

It had started with a little wooden truck when he was a boy. He hadn't intended to break it, but he'd been testing the limits, running behind it while he pushed it down on the ground.

He'd ended up falling on top of it and splitting his lip open, as well as popping the wheels off his favorite possession.

His mother had picked him up and spoken softly to him, brushing the tears from his face and taking the pieces of the truck into her hand, telling him it was okay.

His father had laughed.

He'd pushed Diego's mother aside and taken the toy from her hand.

Then he'd thrown it into the fire.

"When something is broken," he'd said darkly, "you must learn to let it go."

Those words had echoed in Diego's head later. When his mother was dead and his father stood emotionless over her body, laid out for burial before the funeral.

Diego hated his father.

He was also much closer to being his father than he would ever be to resembling his sweet, angelic mother, who had been destroyed by the hands of the man who had promised to love her.

Her hands had been gentle. Diego's were weapons of destruction.

All throughout his life he had demonstrated that to be the truth.

In a fit of frustrated rage after his mother's death, he had burned down his father's shop at the family *rancho*. His father had known he'd done it, and Diego had wondered if the old man would finally kill him too. Send him to the devil, as he had sent Diego's mother to the angels.

It had been worse. His father had simply looked at him, his dark eyes regarding him with recognition.

To be recognized by a monster as being one of his own had been a fate near death. At least then.

Diego had spent the next few years accepting it. And daring the darkness inside of him.

His father gave him a sports car for his eighteenth birthday. Diego crashed it into a rock wall on a winding road. If he had spun another direction before the accident he would have simply plummeted into the sea, and both he and the car would have sunk down to the ocean floor.

It would have been a mercy. For him to die young like that. Before he could create the kind of damage he had been seemingly destined for.

But no. He had been spared.

His mother, sweet and worthy, had not been. Reinforcing his faith in nothing other than the cruelty of life.

While he seemed to create a swath of destruction around him, Diego had thus far been indestructible himself.

It was the things he touched that burned. That broke.

Like Karina.

His one and only attempt at human connection.

His brother, Matías, was a good man. He always had been. Just as Diego had been born with a darkness in him, Matías seemed to have an innate morality that Diego could never hope to understand, much less possess.

Once he had realized that, he had isolated himself from his brother as well.

But he had met Karina. Pretty, vivacious and exciting.

She had lived life harder and faster than he had. Embracing all manner of mood-altering substances and wild sex. For a hedonist such as himself, she had been a magical, sensual embodiment of everything he hoped to lose himself in.

He had married her. Because what better way to tie his favorite new toy to him forever than through legal means?

Sadly, he had broken her too.

She had been beautiful. And he regretted it.

More than that, he regretted the life lost along with hers. The only innocent party in their entire damaged marriage.

But he was not heartbroken. He did not possess the ability to suffer such a thing.

His heart had already been broken. Shattered neatly, like his mother's bones when she had fallen off her horse after his father had shot her.

The only good thing about that was, now that it was done, it could not be done again.

Now there was only the destruction he caused the world to concern himself with.

And truly, he did not concern himself with it overmuch.

He carried those losses on his shoulders. Felt the weight of them. Like a dark and heavy cloak.

It was his nature. And he had grown to accept it.

He took a long drink of the whiskey in his hand and looked around the room. He was back at Michael Hart's impossibly stuffy New England mansion, playing the game that the older man demanded he play before they entered into any kind of business deal.

While Diego had a reputation as more of a gambler than a businessman, the truth of the matter was, he had not made his billions in Monte Carlo. He was a brilliant investor, but he made sure to keep his actions on the down low. He preferred his outrageousness in the headlines, not his achievements.

He wanted a piece of Michael Hart's company. But more than that…

He was fascinated by the man's daughter.

The beautiful heiress Liliana Hart had fascinated him from the moment he had first seen her, over two years ago. Delicate and pale, with long, white blond hair that seemed to glow around her head like a halo.

She was lovely, and nothing at all like the stereotype of an American heiress. No sky-high heels and dresses that made the wearer look most suited to dancing on poles.

She was demure. Lovely. Like a rose. He wanted to reach out and touch her, though he knew that if he did, he was just as likely to bruise her petals as anything else.

But he was not a good man. He was selfish and vain. He was also competitive. And at the moment he and his brother were being pitted against each other by their grandfather for the inheritance of the family *rancho*.

They had to marry to get their share or forfeit entirely.

Matías was too good to rush out and pluck a wife out of thin air simply for financial gain.

Diego wasn't too good for anything. He would happily marry a woman for financial gain. And if on top of it, Liliana made his blood pound in a way no other woman ever had.

The money was an aside. The real attraction was besting his brother, and debauching Liliana.

And if Michael Hart was willing to give her up in trade for his investment in the company and solve the issue of his inheritance along with it?

Diego would chance bruising her.

He would be more annoyed with his *abuelo* if the old man's edict hadn't given him the excuse he'd needed to pursue the beautiful jewel of a woman who had captured his eye from the first.

He saw a flash of pink by the library door, and he realized it was Liliana, peeking inside, and then running away.

A smile curved his lips. He knocked the rest of the whiskey back, and then excused himself from the gathering, striding out with confidence, enough that no one asked where he was going.

No one dared question him.

He saw her disappear around the corner, and he followed, his footfall soft on the Oriental rug that ran the length of the hall.

There was a door slightly ajar, and he pushed it open, finding that it was another library. And inside, standing behind one of the wingback chairs, her delicate hands resting on the back, was Liliana.

"Ms. Hart," he said. "We have not had a chance to say hello to each other tonight."

Her face went scarlet. He found it so incredibly appealing. She always blushed when they talked. Because she found him beautiful. He was not a man given to false humility. Or indeed, humility of any kind.

God had made him beautiful, and he well knew it. But God had also made vipers beautiful. The better to attract their prey.

The fact he knew the weapons at his disposal was more necessity than vanity.

That Liliana found herself under his spell would make this so much easier.

"Mr. Navarro. I didn't realize... That is... I don't make a habit of attending my father's business parties."

"You attended our business dinner only a few weeks ago."

She looked down. "Yes. That's different."

"Is it? I'm tempted to believe that you're avoiding me, *tesoro*."

"What does that mean?" she asked.

"Treasure," he said, taking a step toward her.

"And why would you call me that?"

He paused, midstride. She was not exactly what she appeared. Or perhaps she was. There was an openness to her. A lack of fear that spoke most certainly of inexperience. At least, inexperience with men like him.

Are there men like you? Or just monsters?

"It is what you are, is it not? Certainly, you are a treasure to your father."

"If by that you mean a commodity."

A smile curved his lips. "Well, money is the way of the world."

"It would be nice if it weren't."

"Spoken like a woman who has always had it." It wasn't the first time he'd stolen time away to speak with Liliana. He found himself drawn to her like a magnet. And no amount of pursuing other women had dampened his interest in her.

"I prefer books," she said, those delicate fingers curling around the chair, as if she were using it to brace herself.

"I prefer to experience life, rather than hiding away in a dusty library with only fantasy to entertain me."

She surprised him by rolling her eyes. "Yes. A man of action. I prefer to pause and learn about the world, rather than simply wrapping myself up in my own experiences."

"I didn't realize you were socially conscious," he said.

"A terrible detraction from my charms. Or so I'm told."

He took another step toward her. "Who has told you this?"

"My father."

"He is incorrect," Diego said. "I find it fascinating."

"Well. In that case. All of my personal issues of self-worth are solved."

"I'm glad I could help."

They stared at each other and he felt something. Heat. But something deeper. He was well acquainted with sexual attraction, and much in defiance of his typical fare, Liliana had an innocence about her that should not appeal to him. But did.

Still, he could appreciate the fact that his appetite—jaded from years of gluttony—was interested in something a bit different.

Something softer, sweeter.

She was like a ripe strawberry. And he wanted badly to have a bite.

But that thing beneath it... That current that made him feel as though he was being drawn to her against his will; that he could not quite understand.

She looked away, and her glossy hair caught the firelight, shimmering orange, as though the flames had wrapped themselves around the silken strands.

He closed the distance between them, and she did not turn to look his way. He reached out, brushing her curls to one side, his fingertips brushing the delicate skin of her neck.

"You are truly beautiful, Liliana. Do you know that?"

She looked at him, those blue eyes guarded. "Men have told me that before. Usually when they want something from my father."

"Is that so?" It was on the tip of his tongue to tell her that he wanted something from her father too. That he wanted her. But he held it back.

"My father is a powerful man."

"So am I, *tesoro*." He placed his hand on her hip and felt a jolt beneath his touch. "Believe me when I tell you that I do not require anything to help bolster that. I need a hand up from no one. My money is my own, and my power is my own."

"Is it?" she whispered.

"What do you think of that?"

She reached up, as though she were going to touch his face, and then she jerked her hand away. "Your power's all your own?"

"Perhaps at the moment some of it is with you."

She jerked away from him suddenly, almost tipping toward the fireplace before he caught her around the waist and sent them both stumbling back against the rock fireplace. His chest was pressed against her breasts, and she was breathing hard, those blue eyes locked with his.

"Sorry," she said, breathless.

She began to wiggle, trying to get out of his hold.

"You don't really want to escape me," he whispered.

"I have to. I was avoiding you."

"And I found you."

"Don't you want to know why?"

There was something in her voice, a catch in her tone that made him find he did want to know. He released his hold and took a step back. And that was when he noticed the sparkling diamond on her left hand.

"Why, Liliana?" he asked.

"I told you, a great many men have seen me as a way to get to my father."

"So you did."

"And, well... One of them presented him with an offer that neither of us could refuse."

"Is that so?" he asked, his voice rough, raging heat and fire and fury burning inside of him. "That is so interesting, as your father did not indicate as much to me."

"Were you bartering with my father for my body as well?"

"Yes," he responded.

He did not tell her that he had been offering her father money, and not the other way around. That he wanted her most of all.

"You're not different," she said, turning away from him. "Which is good to know."

"It doesn't matter. I doubt we'll ever see each other again."

She laughed softly. "We probably will. Christmases. Birthdays. That sort of thing."

"Why would we see each other then?"

"Because, Diego. I'm about to become your sister-in-law. I'm marrying your brother."

CHAPTER TWO

SHE WAS GETTING MARRIED. She could hardly believe it.

Liliana had spent her life being cosseted and protected in her family's sprawling estate in the US. While she had done a bit of traveling, it had always been under the watchful eye of her father and the au pair he had chosen to keep her company.

This was the first time in her life she'd felt like she wasn't being hovered over.

She had been in Spain now for two weeks with her fiancé, Matías.

Fiancé.

It was so very strange.

She had spent more time talking to…

She swallowed hard, curling her hands into fists as she sat down on the edge of the bed in her room.

She tried not to think of those piercing, dark eyes. That rakish grin that looked like dangerous enticement.

Truly, Matías and Diego Navarro looked so much alike it shouldn't make one bit of difference to her which one she married. They were both devastatingly handsome. And by all accounts, Matías was a much better man than his brother. Not that she knew much about them. She refused to allow herself to search the internet for information about Diego, as much as she had wanted to. But he radiated an air of danger that Matías simply did not.

That was the problem. There was something more than looks driving that strange connection she had felt to Diego from the moment she had first set eyes on him two years earlier. She'd heard people describe attraction in terms of being struck by lightning.

She'd met Diego Navarro and it had been as if a black fire had been lit inside her. Burning slowly, growing, over the course of all that time.

Matías was a good man. A man that her father wanted to do business with. And why shouldn't she...

Why shouldn't she do exactly as he asked?

After all, she was the reason he had lost the love of his life. The reason her fragile, beautiful mother had died in childbirth.

She had to be the daughter her mother would have wanted. A daughter who was worth the loss her father had sustained. A daughter who made him happy. A daughter who was enough.

And so she did her best.

She had always known that her father would have a hand in choosing her husband.

She had accepted it with grace and dignity. The only time she had ever mouthed off, the only time she had ever allowed the witch rolling around in her mind to escape, was in conversation with Diego.

There was no point thinking about him now.

He had not offered for her.

But he might have.

She closed her eyes and sighed.

She heard footsteps in the hall and her heart rate quickened. She sat there on the edge of the bed, praying that it wasn't Matías.

There was no reason to believe that it should be.

Two weeks she had been here, and he hadn't so much as kissed her.

He had been solicitous beyond the point of reason. Constantly putting parasols over her head in the sun and worrying over her pale skin in the heat. Like she was a scoop of ice cream that might melt into a puddle.

She might be free of her father, but her fiancé had taken up the charge of overprotective presence easily enough.

Today had been the first time he had given her a bit of breathing room. There had been an accident with one of the horses on the *rancho* and a stable boy, and Matías had been consumed with the care of the boy since it had happened. As a result, Liliana had finally been given a few hours free to wander the *rancho* without someone clucking after her like a hen.

That was what was so funny. He was more like a protective older brother than he was a fiancé. At least, how she would imagine a fiancé would be.

And she was grateful for it. Which was another bad sign, she imagined.

She had never seen a married couple together. She didn't know how her parents had been, but the way that her father talked about her mother made her believe that theirs had been a passionate love. That when she had died his heart had been ripped from his body and sent to the grave right along with her.

She couldn't imagine having a connection like that with another person.

Much less Matías.

She didn't think she wanted one like that, really.

The footsteps passed by and she let out a sigh of relief. She wasn't ready to be physical with him. Which was foolish, as they were going to be married very soon. They would have to be physical then. They should kiss. *Something.* They should do something.

The idea didn't disgust her—it was just that she found…

When she closed her eyes and thought of kissing Matías, inevitably, his sculpted, dark features transformed. Into more dangerous ones.

Diego.

She had never—not in all her life before setting eyes on that man—indulged in childish infatuations. Having always had a sense that her father was going to arrange her marriage, she had known there was no point.

She wasn't a fairy-tale princess. Prince Charming wasn't going to come for her.

Prince Acceptable was going to be selected for her.

And so there had never been a crush. Never been a fantasy.

Until *him*.

She wondered if it could be called a crush or a fantasy. This dark, terrible feeling that made her want to do something reckless and awful. Something the Liliana she'd been raised to be would never consider.

Diego was the worst possible man for her to have developed a connection to. The worst possible man to be fixated on now.

Her father wanted her to do this and she'd poured all of her energy, all of her life, all of herself, into doing what he asked.

Liliana felt compelled to be a counterpoint to death. And that was a very heavy weight to carry. But she was alive. Her mother was dead.

Could she complain about anything being too heavy when she *lived*?

But you'll live your whole life without ever touching him...

"It doesn't matter!"

She hadn't meant to say that out loud, but it burst from her mouth and she looked around, hoping her voice didn't draw attention to her.

It didn't matter. *He* didn't matter.

She'd made her choices. She could have been a rebellious daughter. She could have pushed back against her father's edicts. His demands she learn etiquette and deportment instead of going on to university. His pronouncement that she'd play hostess when he had businessmen over.

His long-standing proclamation he would choose her husband.

But when she thought of rebelling against him...

It made her cold all over.

Her father was her only family. The only person in the world who loved her.

How could she push back against that? How could she test that?

Maybe someday Matías would love her.

The idea didn't fill her with any sense of joy.

She stood from the bed and paced across the large bedroom. The *rancho* was opulent, but she had spent her life surrounded by opulence. It was nothing new, and suddenly, she despised her own jadedness on that score.

So many people would be grateful to marry Matías. To be made his princess, for all intents and purposes. To be the lady of the *rancho*, and have all these beautiful lands, this incredible hacienda and the horses that came with it.

And she could find nothing, no sense of excitement, no sense of triumph inside of her.

Nothing at all.

She stood at the window, brushing the curtains to the side and looking out at the well-manicured lawn. The pale moonlight spilled over the rippling grass, the slight breeze making it look like water rather than earth. Making her feel as though she could open the window and dive straight down into the depths and swim far, far away from all of this.

Suddenly, she saw movement. Not the shift of a blade of grass, but a shadow, moving across the grounds. She didn't know what possessed her, only that she unlatched the window, opening it and the screen along with it, leaning out slightly so that she might get a better look at whatever was below.

And then, the dark shadow was closer to the house, and she could see for sure what it was.

A man.

There was a man out on the grass, moving around. She should call someone. For in all likelihood someone clearly sneaking through the property was not staff, and was not supposed to be here at all.

Perhaps he was one-half of a pair of ill-fated lovers. In which case, she didn't want to call anyone.

Her own love life was, if not ill-fated, then severely stunted, and she was hardly going to damage anyone else's.

But the figure kept coming closer to the house, and when he began to scale the side of the building, using the ornate molding and the window ledges as footholds, she stood frozen, watching him.

She should scream. She should call out for help. But she didn't. She simply stood. With the window open, as if she were inviting him in. He kept moving closer, and closer. And then he looked up, and she saw dark, glittering eyes just barely visible in the moonlight.

Still. She didn't move. Still, she stood without making a sound.

It wasn't until he climbed to her window, and wrapped his arm around her waist, one hand holding tightly to the molding up above, his eyes clashing with hers, that she screamed.

"Now we must hurry," he said, that voice low and far too familiar. "Because you have caused a scene."

She found herself being jerked from the window, suspended above the ground, terror roaring through her veins.

She clung to the man, because she had no choice. She would fall to her... Well, perhaps not her death, but her certain maiming if she did not cling to those strong, broad shoulders, her breasts pressed against the chest so solid it seemed to be made of stone rather than flesh.

But he was hot. Hot in a way that only flesh and blood could be.

He had spoken.

And she *knew*.

Knew exactly who held her in his arms.

"I have a helicopter waiting," he whispered. "Are you holding on to me?"

"Y-yes."

"Good," he responded.

He let go of her and she wrapped her arms more tightly around his neck, as he made startling time scaling down the side of the house. She gave a short prayer of thanks when her feet connected with the grass, but it was short-lived as she found herself being picked up and hauled away quickly.

She heard voices, shouting, and she looked over his

shoulder to see dark figures standing in her bedroom window. Clearly responding to the scream.

"We will escape before he manages to mobilize. Believe me. I was hardly going to plan a kidnapping that I could not execute. I'm far too vain for such a thing."

"For kidnapping?"

"For *failed* kidnappings. I would only ever engage in a successful one." He bustled her into a car waiting at the edge of the lawn and drove them to the edge of the woods, taking her out of the car again, hauling her around like she was a sack of nightgown-wearing potatoes.

"Why exactly are you kidnapping me?" she asked, as she hung limp over his shoulder.

It was strange, she imagined, that she wasn't fighting him. That she wasn't screaming or pitching a massive fit, trying to escape his hold.

But she didn't want to. Not even a little bit. Not in the slightest. She found that she wanted to…see where he was going. Because hadn't it been Diego she had just been thinking of?

And she had to ask herself why she had stood there with the window open if she truly didn't want to be taken.

And so she let him carry her into the woods, across to a clearing, where there was indeed a helicopter awaiting them. He hauled her up inside easily, depositing her in the seat and buckling her before taking his position at the controls.

"You pilot…helicopters?"

"We don't have time to talk."

He fired up the rotors, and they began to gain speed. Just as she saw lights in the distance, they lifted off from the ground, above the trees, and away.

She couldn't hear, not over the sound of the engine and the propellers, but then he put a headset on, and placed one on her head as well. She adjusted it.

"Can you hear me?"

His voice came over the speakers and into her ears. "Yes," she responded.

"Excellent."

"Did you want to make conversation now?" It seemed strange, all things considered.

"I thought we might pick up where we left off when last we spoke," he said.

"Did you? Well, it might be a slightly different conversation, Diego, as when last we spoke we were in my father's library. And today we are in a helicopter, with you having kidnapped me from my fiancé's home."

"You will not marry him."

Her heart kicked into gear, slamming into her breastbone. "I won't?"

"No," he said, his voice dark and decisive.

"He's going to come for me."

"I'm not going anywhere that he will be able to trace us. My brother and I are not close. Believe me when I tell you he has no idea of all the residences I own. Nor the aliases they are listed under."

"Aliases…"

"What did you think of me, *tesoro*? That I was simply misunderstood? And that was why I was the black sheep of the Navarro family? No. I am not misunderstood. Not in the least. In point of fact, I am rather well understood. I'm not a good man."

"That is not…overly comforting, considering I'm now hurtling through the air with you."

"It was not intended to be a comfort. I'm simply

making sure that you are aware of the position you find yourself in."

"What position is that?"

"You're going to marry *me* now, Liliana."

Something hot and reckless jolted through her, a lot like fear, but with a hard edge to it that thrilled her as much as it repelled her.

"You can't just… How can you possibly think that I would agree to that?"

"Don't be silly, *tesoro*. I have all the ammunition I could possibly want. Did you honestly think I would go to all this trouble without hedging my bets? I was not counting on my charm to sway you."

If only he knew. Before this moment, he could have climbed through the window and seduced her, likely so easily it would be humiliating.

She had never kissed a man. Not truly. The chaste exchanges she'd had with Matías were nothing like a real kiss, and the idea of Diego's lips kept her awake at night.

Indeed, they had been keeping her awake this very night. And he had no idea. Of course not.

But now… Now she was seeing him in a slightly different light.

She looked at him, his face cast in sharp relief by the glow of the control panel in front of him. High, hard-cut cheekbones, a cruel, sculpted mouth, nose straight like a blade.

Oh, dear heaven, she was no less attracted to him now than she had been before. There was perhaps something wrong with her. And she wasn't entirely certain there was anything that could be done about it. She wasn't entirely certain there was anything she would want to do about it. Because she had never felt anything like this. Nothing quite so dangerous, nothing quite so exhilarating. Her life had been lived entirely to please her father. Entirely to live up to the memory of her mother.

Lusting for dark and dangerous men fit nowhere in that. But Diego had swept into her father's house like an undeniable force. Indeed, he had swept into her bedroom tonight like one as well. And at the moment there was nothing she could do.

She was being whisked away, after all. She could hardly leap from the helicopter.

And the fact that he made her stomach sink, made it swoop like a butterfly whose wings had been torn, one that was falling out of the sky, toward its inevitable demise... Well, right now there was nothing she could do about that.

"If you truly wanted to marry me, you could have spoken to my father," she said, her voice small.

"You don't understand," Diego said. "I must prevent my brother from marrying you." He turned to face her for a moment, his lip curled into a sneer. "If he marries you, then he gains the inheritance of the ranch. I want you, and I want the *rancho*. My marriage ensures that I get it. And that is why you must marry me. The fact that I have fantasies of tearing that virginal nightgown from your body is only a bonus."

His words rolled over her like a poison. He didn't want her, not really. He didn't want to marry her because he had any finer feelings for her. He wanted to marry her because of an inheritance.

Matías wanted to use her as well, wanted to use her to forge an alliance with her father, and apparently, to get an inheritance. But that didn't bother her. Because when it came to Matías, she had only been following her father's orders.

Her feelings for Diego had nothing to do with orders.

"If my brother has had you, that makes no difference to me. In fact, I shall take a great joy in wiping your memory of him from your mind."

She realized what he meant, though it took a moment, and shock rolled over her.

She had not been with Matías. But she wasn't going to tell him that. She didn't know why, but for the moment it felt like a small bit of power.

He said that he didn't care, but the fact he had mentioned it made her think that perhaps he did.

And so she said nothing. She simply sat with her hands folded, staring straight ahead into the darkness as she was taken further and further away from any kind of certainty and deeper into this madness of Diego's making.

CHAPTER THREE

DIEGO WATCHED HIS captive closely as they walked from the helicopter toward his home. If she was expecting that there would be anyone here who might become sympathetic to her plight and offer her assistance, she would be sadly mistaken. He had taken pains to clear his house of all the usual staff, leaving it stocked with everything they would need to get through the next period of time without drawing attention to them.

He paused at the beginning of the walkway that led up to the old manor that looked near consumed by ivy where it was pressed deep into a rocky hillside.

He extended his gloved hand, and she took it, and he could feel her delicate fingers, could feel the heat of her body through the black leather.

He felt a bit like Hades, leading Persephone down into the underworld.

Some men might be consumed with guilt at that easy comparison. The idea that they might be the devil himself.

Diego suffered from no such guilt.

Diego did not suffer from a conscience at all.

Liliana was silent, and she looked like a very small ghost shrouded in her white nightgown, her pale hair blowing in the breeze.

"Where are we?"

"On a private island," he said. "Near enough to Spain, but far enough as well. This is mine. And no, my brother does not know."

"It's… It looks rather English."

"The English like Spain," he said. "At least, they like to get drunk in Spain."

"Is that what *you* like about Spain?"

"I *am* Spanish, *querida*."

"Of course," she said, her cheeks coloring slightly.

How funny that she could be embarrassed over making a faux pas with him. Her kidnapper. How charming that she would care at all.

"I take that as a compliment on the proficiency of my English," he said. His lips curved into a smile. "But not as much of a compliment on my character."

"Were you looking for compliments on your character, Diego? Because if so, you might have stopped short of the kidnapping."

He chuckled. "I was not. It is delightfully freeing when you don't care about your own morality. If you just sink into turpitude, I find that it has a very warm embrace. And there are a host of fabulous side effects. A lack of caring what anyone thinks. Least of all your own conscience."

"Some of us don't live exclusively for ourselves," she said softly.

"Your father?" He wondered if the poor creature imagined her father to be a good man. Why wouldn't she? She was… She was sweet. And in this world that was a rare and precious thing. A thing he was going to destroy. He should care about that. He found he didn't. "What a fantastic paragon for you to live for."

He began to walk more quickly, drawing her into the

entryway of the house, and pressing his thumb against the door to unlock it. "My thumbprint only, *tesoro*," he said.

"Does that include getting out as well?"

He laughed. "You know it does. Again, I would not conduct a kidnapping without being thorough."

"I suppose I should appreciate that as a commentary on my fortitude and ingenuity."

"I feel that you should be flattered by this entire caper."

"Should I?"

"Indeed. I've gone to quite a lot of trouble to procure you."

"More due to the relationship with your brother than anything to do with you."

"Yes. But if I did not find you enticing in your own right then I would simply have held on to you until the date on my grandfather's great edict expired."

"Lucky me."

"Many women would say that you were lucky. Being fought over by the Navarro brothers as you are."

"And yet, I feel more like a wretched hen between the jaws of two posturing dogs."

"Or, a precious gem being traded amongst thieves. Pick your metaphor, *tesoro*. I would pick the more flattering of the two."

"I don't have the motivation. Flattered or not, I remain kidnapped."

"Perhaps you will in time." He brought her inside, closing the door behind them. The lock clicked with a delicious, satisfying finality.

"What are you going to do with me?" For the first time, she looked afraid. No, more than afraid—terrified. And two things dawned on him in that moment.

That she had not looked truly frightened this entire time, which was an oddity. She seemed to have accepted her kidnapping with a remarkable aplomb. She had not fought him. In fact, she had clung to him, long after her safety had depended on it.

She had opened the window for him.

Something about that kicked masculine triumph through his veins. She did not hate him. That much was clear.

Or perhaps, she did not care for his brother. It didn't matter to him which it was. Not in the least. The fact that it was either was good enough.

The second was that she looked out of her mind with fear at the moment, and he did not care for that. Another revelation. He could not recall much caring about the feelings of another. Not ever.

Or at least, not in quite some time.

"I already told you," he said. "I intend to marry you."

"Are we alone here?" She backed up against the wall, her pulse thundering at the base of her throat.

Diego frowned and walked toward her, marveling as she shrank away from him, turning herself near inside out to avoid him. He reached out, pressed his thumb against that delicate hollow there. It felt like a frightened bird against his touch, fluttering, trying to escape.

"What do you think I will do to you?"

"You have already kidnapped me. I fear that any number of indignities can't be too far away."

He dropped his hand quickly. "I have never once forced myself on a woman. I would hardly start with you."

"Why do you say it like *that*?"

"Because you want me."

"I want you? You kidnapped me. Do you honestly

think that I'm panting after you now that you've stolen
me out of my bedroom window?"

He lifted a brow and shrugged one shoulder. "A bedroom window you opened for me. That makes your protests slightly weak."

"I didn't know it was you."

"Did you not?"

Her shoulders went rigid. "I did not."

"It is moot. I saw the way you looked at me at your
father's house. You wanted me then. You want me now.
I would take absolutely no pleasure in forcing you. I
would much rather you had to lower yourself to beg
for what you want. Taking it from you would make it
far too easy on you."

Her lip curled and she raised her hand, pulling it
back as if she meant to strike him. He didn't stop her.
He merely stood, ready for her strike. And she of course
didn't land the blow.

It did not surprise him. Not in the least.

"A word of advice, *tesoro*," he said. "If you're going
to make threats you had best be prepared to follow
through. I am not a man who makes idle threats, and
therefore, you do not want to be the kind of woman
who makes them. Not in my presence. If you're going
to hit me, you best do it hard. If you're going to tempt
my retribution, then it had better be worth it."

She said nothing. She simply stood there, shaking
like an indignant leaf, her rage and fear barely suppressed. "Would you like to go to your room?"

"I'll have my own room?"

He sighed heavily, feigning exasperation. "Of course
you will have your own room. I already made it clear
that I do not intend to force myself on you."

"You just intend to force marriage on me."

"Naturally." He said it as if it were the most obvious thing in the entire world.

"You make no sense."

"I'm a villain. I don't have to make sense."

He turned away from her and they began to walk up the long staircase and down a winding corridor, leading her to the chamber he had selected expressly for her.

Truly, the entire house had been chosen for her. The entire island.

There was something classic about it. Classic, and yet wild. He had appreciated it from the moment he'd set eyes on it last week. From the moment he had decided on his course of action.

The chamber that he had selected for her, had had furnished and decorated and filled with beautiful clothes, had been chosen specifically with her in mind. He had imagined how she might react to it. Had imagined the delight she might take in the way the soft mattress molded itself around her body, in the way the soft fabrics felt against her skin.

Instead, when she saw the room, her expression was blank.

"Is it not to your liking?"

"As jail cells go, I imagine it's quite a beautiful one."

"There is a library," he bit out. "Just through that door."

"Do you think this is a movie? And that you can buy away my ire with books?"

"You told me you liked books," he said.

"Books *and* freedom. Perhaps I should have added that last part."

"Sadly, in this instance, you may have one, but not the other."

He began to walk away, his heart thundering hard,

rage he did not quite understand beginning to spike in his system.

"How do you expect that you'll force me to marry you?" she asked. "I can't do anything about the fact that you have me in this house, but you cannot make me say vows."

He paused, bone-deep satisfaction rolling through him. "I already told you, *tesoro*. I have thought of absolutely everything."

"What have you thought of?"

"You told me that you live for other people. For your father. Well, I know things about Michael Hart that would destroy your girlish fantasies of the man you call father. I can ruin him, Liliana. His reputation, his fortune. I can reduce it all to dust."

"How? My father is a good man."

"Your father is a criminal, who has made the same mistake a great many idiotic criminals make. He has built his power upon legitimacy. For my part? I am a criminal who would lose nothing if the world were to find out."

"You could be arrested for kidnapping me."

"Could I? Do you suppose I am not prepared to bribe officials in Spain and in the United States to make sure that is not so? You mistake me for a man with limits."

"The man that I knew back at my father's home… He was not a monster."

"Yes," Diego said, advancing toward her. "He was. The monster is always there, Liliana, and make no mistake." He reached out, grabbing hold of her hand and forcing it down onto his chest, over his heart. "Understand this. No matter how civil I may seem, the monster is always there. When I'm smiling at you, the monster is there. Right there," he said, pounding her hand against him now. "Do not ever forget it."

Her eyes went wide, and for a moment he thought he might have succeeded in terrifying her. Then her face relaxed, a clear decision having taken place inside her.

"As seduction bids go," she said, her voice wobbly, "this is not a good one."

She was tough, was Liliana. Never as fragile as she appeared.

"At what point did you begin to believe this was a seduction? If I had wanted to seduce you, I would have done so back at your father's home. I could have. We both know. The moment you told me you were to marry my brother I could have had you on the floor. I can sense how badly you want me. But it's not enough. It's not permanent enough for my purposes. And that's why I didn't. I wanted insurance. And I found it. Your father has been scamming those who invest in his company. And I have the proof. Not only that, there are rafts of harassment allegations from a great many female employees. All buried. Covered up by his money. But the only person who possesses the power to pay more than he does is me. I have my finger poised on the kill button, Liliana, and he would be a fool to think I won't press it."

"He… He couldn't have."

"Oh, but he could have. And did."

"If you draw attention to yourself…"

"My reputation as a gambler, womanizer and reprobate will be compromised?"

She shrank in on herself, clearly realizing that she was defeated.

"I recommend that you get a good night's sleep. For we are to be married as quickly as possible."

"How?"

"I have already begun the paperwork for a license. It requires only your signature and then it is poised to be processed. After which I have arranged for an officiant to come and speak our vows to us. I am a traditionalist at heart. I could have simply had us married over the computer, but I find technology so cold."

"I don't think it's technology. I rather think it's your heart."

He laughed. "No, darling. I don't have a heart."

"I just felt it beating."

"You just felt the monster. Trying to escape."

CHAPTER FOUR

LILIANA WAITED UNTIL she was certain that Diego was asleep. Or, if not asleep, then not roaming the house. She needed to figure out if there was some method that she could use to contact the outside world.

In all likelihood, there wasn't.

And in fact, Diego would probably be insulted if she voiced that to him. "No, *tesoro*," she intoned in a deep voice, "I would not be so sloppy as to leave an accessible landline."

She blew out a breath and sneaked out of the bedroom, padding down the hall and then down the stairs. She knew there had to be an office down there. And perhaps, if she could find that, there would be a phone. A fax machine. Something.

She could hardly believe she had been kidnapped only a few hours ago. She felt as if it had been days. She felt as if she had been wearing this nightgown for her entire life.

She had looked in the closets and seen there were other clothes, but she hadn't been able to bring herself to put any of them on. Not even an alternate nightgown. It was too strange. She was not going to take something offered to her by a kidnapper and a blackmailer.

Her heart twisted.

That was the most difficult thing. That part of her had felt something for Diego. That she had thought there had been some mystical connection between them from the moment they'd met two years ago. And it had been a lie.

It's just the monster trying to get out.

If this was him with his monster buried, then she really wouldn't like to see him with the monster out.

She picked around the furniture downstairs, tip-toeing to one closed door after the other. Some rooms were empty, others holding dusty furniture that gave her some measure of hope. It was entirely possible he hadn't scoured the place for methods of communication.

The man who put the thumbprint reader on the door didn't look for a phone?

She ignored her mouthy inner bitch and pressed on.

She was crouched down below the desk when the door to the study opened.

"What exactly are you doing?"

She popped up, banging her head on the furniture, so hard that a white light burst behind her eyes. She rubbed at it furiously, whimpering as she tried to stand.

Suddenly, strong arms had come around her, were holding her close, pulling her against his body. "Do not hurt yourself," he growled.

Heat spread through her like a fire, the strength in his hold shocking. She forgot to breathe, her head swimming, her body going weightless and floaty. From not breathing. Not from the look in those dark, stormy eyes. Not from staring down at those sculpted lips and wondering how it would feel if they…

She took a step back, stumbling slightly, but finding balance when she was some distance from him.

"Do not startle me," she bit out.

"It was not my intention to startle you. Why are you snooping around?"

"I need to talk to my father."

He laughed. "All you had to do was say so."

"You're going to let me talk to my father?"

"I imagine you have questions for him. It behooves me that he answer them. Because I am not lying to you. I know that you wish I were. But if you need to hear it from your father himself, then by all means."

He held his cell phone out to her, and she took it, feeling suspicious. "I'm not even sure what time it is there."

"Does it matter? You have been kidnapped, after all."

"You're not worried that my father is going to call the police?"

"My brother already has."

"And you're not worried…"

"So concerned for my feelings, *tesoro*. It is admirable, and a bit touching, but there really is no need. I am more rock than man."

"Unsurprising."

She dialed her father's number, feeling self-conscious with Diego standing there staring at her. Her head still throbbed.

"Hello?"

"Father," Liliana said. "I've been kidnapped."

"How much money does he want?" her father asked, his voice clipped and tight, but not as surprised as she would've thought.

"I… He wants to marry me."

"Are you having a last-minute fit about marrying Matías?"

"*No,*" she protested. "I'm not having a fit. I'm currently a victim of a crime."

"What?"

"I was kidnapped. I told you. From Matías's house."

"*Who* has taken you?"

"Diego. Diego Navarro."

The silence on the end of the phone suddenly became weighted. Tense. "What does he want?"

"To marry me," she reiterated. "It's complicated. But he said… He said I had to."

"Why did he say that?" The fact that her father didn't sound shocked concerned her more than just about anything else.

"He said he knows things about you. Things that could ruin you. He said… He said that he can destroy you. Your reputation. Your fortune. Everything. If it's not true…"

"You must stay with him," her father said. "You must give him what he asks for."

Liliana felt like the world had dropped out from beneath her feet. "I… You can't truly expect for me to marry my kidnapper?"

"One Navarro should be the same as the other. In any case, this one is much more dangerous."

"He *kidnapped* me."

"Has he harmed you?"

"I have been terrorized," she said, ignoring the flare of amusement in Diego's eyes when she said the word.

Honestly, she wanted to hit him.

"Has he put his hands on you in any way?" her father pressed.

"Other than when he carried me out of my bedroom window, no," she admitted, reluctant to do so, because it was clear that somehow that seemed to absolve Diego from taking her against her will.

"I cannot tell you I have no reason for concern," her father said. "I can only tell you that if you don't wish to lose absolutely everything we have… You must marry him."

"But I…"

"Your mother dearly loved our life together. She loved the company that she and I built together. To lose it would destroy her."

But she's dead. Liliana wanted to scream. She couldn't. So she didn't. Instead, she simply hung up the phone. With numb fingers, she handed it back to Diego.

"I assume he did not give you the answer that you required."

"No."

"I told you that you would not care for the answer."

Her mind was spinning. "I don't believe that you want a wife," she said finally.

"Why exactly?"

"I don't believe you want fidelity."

"Well. I've never tried it for too terribly long. But I have managed it for a couple of years, at least."

That admission surprised her. "Really?"

"It is not my past that is open for discussion. However, continue."

"I'll marry you," she said. "I will marry you for exactly as long as we have to stay married. But then, I want money. To go and live my own life. I want to be free. Of you and of my father. Let his empire stand but help me be free of it. And once you don't need me anymore…you can be free of me."

She felt exhilarated. She had never conceived of doing anything quite so reckless. Of figuring out a way to tilt the scale so that she might benefit. Freedom. Not just from her father, but from a husband.

Finding out that her father could do such a thing to her. That he could manipulate her as he was doing now, so easily. Even as he was revealing himself to be a villain, bringing up her mother's death. A death she had no control over. But one that she felt an immense amount of guilt over all the same. It was sobering. And immensely painful.

It made her reckless. It made her want something different. Made her want something more.

"I will not be satisfied with the marriage in name only," he said, his obsidian eyes dark on hers.

She was afraid his gaze would burn right through her, and that his touch would reduce her to ash. What would it be like to be naked with someone? Naked with him.

It would be so overwhelming. So intimate. So impossibly close.

She'd spent her whole life feeling close to no one. The very idea made her tremble.

She shrank back. "You said you wouldn't force yourself on me."

"And I won't. But I'm making it very clear, that while I may agree to a marriage with an end date, and while I have absolutely no issue providing you with a settlement, I do expect what I want. As I said, if I did not wish to marry you I would have simply kept you away from Matías. But I want you." He moved closer to her, reminding her of a large, dangerous cat. "I have wanted you from the moment I first laid eyes on you. Wanted to spoil all that innocent beauty that you carry around with you so effortlessly." He didn't move nearer to her. Didn't touch her. And yet she felt him. As if his words had reached inside of her. "Do you know what I mean by that?" he asked.

She was trembling. From the inside out. And frankly,

she didn't quite know what he meant by that. But she refused to look so foolish.

"I suppose you're a man. And you can't help yourself."

"Oh, it goes so far beyond me being a man and you being a woman. If it was only that, I could satisfy it with anyone. But you... You, Liliana, have bewitched me from the moment I first laid eyes on you and I find that unacceptable. I do not want without having. It is not in my nature."

What difference would it make? Really. She had been willing to sleep with Matías. But then, she had been planning on staying married to him, but truly, she had already been planning on being with a man she didn't love. Why not this one?

And you want him.

She ignored that voice.

The fact of the matter was the idea of being with him didn't... It didn't disgust her. And she was...curious. It was funny how she felt profoundly uncurious when it came to Matías. But there was something about Diego. A spark that was between them... Or at least, it lived inside of her. And it fascinated her. It made her want to know more. More about sexual attraction. About the reasons why people lost their minds in the pursuit of physical satisfaction. She understood it on a cerebral level.

She had read a great many books that depicted the acts. The feelings of lust.

And when the writing was particularly evocative she could feel those things resonating inside of her. She could imagine what it would feel like to have them for another person.

But this was different. Reckless. When those feelings were contained to a fantasy there was a safety in them.

But she was here, alone with Diego. And there was nothing to stop him from grabbing hold of her and having his way with her now.

That was the real trouble.

All those bold proclamations he'd made... Ultimately, he was right.

She did want him.

At least, she thought she did.

There was a layer of safety, of gauze between the sexual words she had read, and the experience itself. At least, she assumed so. You could read about the flavor of a peach, and get a sense for it, but it didn't truly capture the way it felt to bite into the fruit. The thickness of the skin, the texture of the pulp. The way the juice felt as it ran down your chin. You could read about all those things, and not really understand. Words didn't leave you full—they didn't change things inside of you in the same way.

She had a feeling that the physical act would be something else entirely.

But if this was the start of her independence, if this was the beginning of the life that she would create for herself, then perhaps it was exactly the right time, and Diego was exactly the right man to begin this sort of exploration with.

A man that she chose—ignoring the fact that he had kidnapped her and demanded that she sleep with him—because she wanted him, and not because her father had selected him as a worthy husband.

As justifications went, it might be a little bit thin, but she was willing to go with it. And anyway, her options were limited. That was the simple fact of the matter.

The deal that Diego was offering was infinitely better than the... Well, the other deal he was offering.

Wherein her family was disgraced, they lost all of their money, and she found herself without shelter and her father's home, and without the shelter of a husband. Because Matías would have no need to marry her if her father's business no longer mattered.

There was the matter of the inheritance, but he could find any number of women to help with that.

And Diego would simply kidnap a different one.

"You have a deal," she said, tilting her chin upward. "But there is a condition. You're not touching me until after our marriage vows are spoken."

He laughed, a dark, dangerous sound that rolled over her like a tide. "Oh, that is not too difficult a thing, *tesoro*. We are to be married in the morning."

She blinked. "How?"

"I told you. I have left nothing to chance. And really, it is morning now."

"I don't have a gown."

"But you do. I'm very solicitous like that. I took the liberty of choosing exactly what I wished to see my bride in."

"That's...creepy. Do you know that?"

"Hmm." He made a thoughtful noise. "I have kidnapped you out of your bedroom window, in spite of the fact that you were set to marry my brother. In spite of the fact that you have likely spent the past two weeks in his bed. I have been obsessed with you from the moment that I saw you and plotted a way to make you mine. Obviously I'm a bit creepy. And I've made my peace with it. Hence the kidnapping and arranged speedy marriage. Do you honestly think that pointing it out is going to shame me?"

"You're..."

"A monster? I called myself that only moments ago. Why exactly do you think that will insult me."

"A *criminal*," she said.

"I've been called worse. If you've ever a mind to find out exactly what, feel free to peruse the internet."

"I don't have access to it."

"I didn't say it would be *easy* for you to peruse the internet. I just said that you could."

"Perhaps I'm not that interested in you, Diego. If I was going to fight for internet access I would go online shopping instead of googling you."

"There is no need for you to online shop. Everything you could possibly want is already here."

"You don't know my taste."

He reached out, gripping her chin between his thumb and forefinger. "That's where you're wrong. I know everything about you. Everything. I've looked at every photograph that exists of you that's been published in public. I made a study of you every time I went to your father's house. Every item of clothing in that closet fits you. Believe me. I have made a study of your curves."

A shiver went down her spine. She should be mortified. Furious. And on some level, she was. But there was more. She felt... She didn't even know. She had never been someone's focus. Not like this. And while she knew he had other reasons for taking her, while she knew it served him in other ways, the fact remained that she did matter. He wanted her. Matías didn't want her. He didn't care. He certainly wouldn't have kidnapped her out of the bedroom window. He simply would have found another woman. Diego made it sound as if he couldn't. It was...

For a woman who had felt almost invisible for most of her life it was intoxicating in a way it should not be.

Perhaps her father had been right to protect her

all this time. Maybe her natural inclination was to be drawn to darkness.

But you have no way of turning on the light, so you might as well accept it. You might as well live in it.

She didn't see that she had another choice. Not now. Why fight when she couldn't win?

"We need to sign an agreement," she said.

"You're not really in a position to be making demands," he said, his voice dry.

"Yes," she said, "I am. I have something you want."

"By that you mean your body?"

"Yes. My body—" she tried to speak without trembling "—and my acquiescence to being your wife. I think I'm in a fantastic position to be making demands."

"By all means, list them."

"I want assurance that you will give me a settlement." She named a sum. Outrageous. She was certain that he would tell her she could jump straight off the hillside manor and into the sea.

"Double it," he said. "I'm a man of means, *tesoro*. I will hardly leave my ex-wife without access to designer clothing."

"Generous of you," she responded.

"Not at all. Of course, you should receive a healthy payment for time spent in my bed."

Heat lashed her cheeks. "Don't make it sound like that. You're not paying for...for that."

"Am I not? I find I would pay quite handsomely for access to that space between your thighs."

She gritted her teeth, well aware that he was trying to be inflammatory. Or maybe, he wasn't trying. Maybe it was simply who he was. But the man she had met at her father's house had been a damn sight more charming than the one who stood before her now. But still,

Diego, even in all his arrogance, even as he was, caused her pulse to race. And not only from anger.

"But that isn't what you're paying for," she reiterated. "You're paying for me to be your wife. That includes—" She swallowed hard. "That includes sex. It is part of being married. It's different than paying for sex."

"However you twist things so you don't feel like a whore, *querida*, it is not my concern. Twist them at will. The fact remains, that I am promising you this money."

"And I require a document."

His lips turned up into a wide grin and he reached toward the heavy oak desk that sat in the center of the room. He grabbed a piece of stationery and slid it to the center, taking hold of a gilded pen and making strong, bold lines across the paper. It made her wince, watching those thick, dark strokes of ink mar the page. As if she were watching something indelible take place before her that she now regretted bitterly, even though it was what she had asked for.

He slid the page toward her. And there it was, in black and white, the promised sum of money, her promised declaration to provide him with marital duties and an agreement to divorce when his inheritance was settled.

"This is not binding." She sniffed. "You wrote it on a piece of paper, and we have no witness."

"It will have to do, sadly. I can procure a last-minute priest, but the acquisition of a last-minute lawyer might be a bit ambitious."

"I'll keep this," she said, folding it up and holding it tightly in her hand.

"So little trust between us. Hardly a good start to a marriage."

"No, I think the kidnapping was perhaps the bad start."

"If you say so." He looked at her, his dark eyes assessing. "If you want something binding to seal that document, I do have a suggestion."

"What?"

That was when she found herself being hauled toward him, her hands pressed against that hard chest, his dark eyes cutting through her as if she were nothing. An insubstantial waif so easily flayed by all that raw power that he possessed.

And before she could protest, his lips were on hers.

And it was…

It was the explosion she always feared could occur inside of her. It wasn't a slow build, a gentle introduction into sexuality. No. It was like being hurled into space, cast into the darkness, so black, so intense that there was nothing else. No way to see through it. No way around it.

No way through it.

His kiss was hot, vast and slick and endless and everything she had ever hoped and feared a kiss could be.

Her heart was thundering hard, her entire body going weak and breathless from the onslaught of sensation that had tumbled over the top of her.

He forced her lips apart, his tongue sliding against hers savagely as he claimed her. And suddenly something bubbled up inside of her, something entirely foreign. Or perhaps, not so now.

It was the same thing that had struck her after the phone call with her father.

She had power here. She was not simply an object. He wanted her. *Diego* wanted *her*. And that made her a force of her own kind. Made her something powerful and strong. Something that he couldn't control or manipulate. Or at least, not without consequence.

She returned the kiss, some unknown intuition inside of her driving her movements. She traced his outer lip with the tip of her tongue and relished the feral growl that exited his lips as she did so. He wrapped his arms around her tightly, pressing his pelvis against hers, allowing her to feel just exactly what her kiss had done to him. He was hard, long and strong and so much bigger than she had imagined a man could be.

Classical paintings had not prepared her for the aggressive outline of Diego's masculinity. Had not prepared her for the overwhelming heat and hardness, for the leashed strength.

And nothing, no erotic turn of phrase or illicitly penned fantasy, had prepared her for the desire that welled up inside of her. For the need that overtook her, wrapped itself around her throat with a decisive click, like a collar, binding her to him.

She found herself clinging to his shirt, holding on to him tightly as he continued to savage her mouth with his own.

If she had not been a hostage before, she certainly was now. Hostage to him. To pleasure. Her own weakness.

She whimpered, and as if it was the magic turn of phrase to break a spell, he pushed her away from him, taking a step back, his dark eyes blazing with black fire.

"Dios mio," he rasped, pushing his hands through his dark hair. "You are a witch."

"I'm not," she said, her voice small, her mouth bruised, her entire body buzzing with rampant heat.

"You must be." He turned, as if to go, and then he paused. When he faced her again he reached his hand out, pressing his thumb against the center of her lower lip and staring at her intently as he held it there. Then without a word he released her, walking out of the room and leaving her there alone, feeling somehow trapped and untethered at the same time.

The fact that she was unchaperoned had hit her in a particularly strange way just before he had come to kidnap her. And oddly, though she found herself in his custody now, that sense was even stronger now.

Because there was no one here to stop her from going after him. To stop her from stripping off her nightgown and climbing on top of that hard, masculine body.

She shivered. She didn't know where these thoughts were coming from. These feelings. She shouldn't have them. No, not at all. She wasn't experienced enough, first of all. And second of all… She should despise him.

She didn't.

She was terrified of him. Of what he made her feel. She was fascinated by him. By this man who was essentially a marauding modern-day pirate.

"I'm alive," she whispered into the silence of the room.

She was. She was alive and she was free.

What a strange thing, because she was also a captive. But it occurred to her then that in many ways she had never not been a captive. Captive to her father's wishes. Captive to her own desire to do whatever it took to appease her father. Then she'd been given over to Matías. And now…

She might have made a bargain with the devil, but at least it was a bargain of her choosing.

"I'm free," she said again.

And tomorrow, she would be Diego Navarro's wife.

CHAPTER FIVE

THE DAY OF the wedding dawned bright and clear. Diego hadn't slept. He had been waiting. The priest was due to show up at six to finish last-minute paperwork. Concerns regarding the church. Diego was no traditionalist, but he was a Catholic. And though he might be a bad one, there were still certain things that were nonnegotiable down deep in his soul. That everything be recognized by the church was one of them.

The divorce... He would concern himself with that later.

He imagined it would be fairly easy for Liliana to make an argument for annulment, considering coercion had been involved.

His mouth twisted into a wry smile. She had not been coerced last night when they had kissed.

He had known that there was heat between them. Heat and flame and all manner of dark desire. He had not realized it was quite so strong.

He was a man who had sampled many flavors of hedonism. A man with vast experience in the sensual pleasures of the flesh. But he had never in all his life felt anything like that kiss. A kiss.

Of all things.

It had made him shake like a green virgin.

It had also made him…jealous.

Had his brother been accessing all that passion? It made him want to kill Matías.

The world already thought him a murderer, so, he might as well have the pleasure of actually being one.

It didn't matter. Though it galled him, it didn't matter. When he was through with Liliana, he would be the only lover that she remembered, regardless of who had been there before him.

She had seemed surprised by the explosive attraction between them too. And that, at least, had been gratifying.

He wanted to own her desire.

As he would own her in only an hour.

He adjusted his cuffs and went out onto the grounds, making sure that everything was in place. It would not be a wedding ceremony anything like his first. Which had been, granted, formal at the behest of his wife, and in the confines of a church, his bride in a grand, dramatic veil and train that had taken up the entire aisle she'd walked down. No. This would be different. He had chosen a place for them that overlooked the sea, where the sun would be rising just as they spoke their vows.

And he would see all that golden light over her skin, tangled in her hair…

He closed his eyes, not bothering to question why this mattered to him at all. It was about winning. Nothing more. Winning and sexual desire. Both things he understood well enough. Anything else… He would pay it no mind.

The sooner this marriage was finalized the better. And then, Liliana was going to have to have a talk with Matías.

In the meantime, he owed his *abuelo* a phone call.

The old man answered on the first ring. "You have taken your brother's fiancée!"

He sounded delighted. "I have," Diego said. "Though I think she prefers me. Women do love a bad boy."

Sadly for Liliana, he wasn't a bad boy. He was a bad man. And the two were worlds apart.

"And I admire a man willing to stoop to such levels to win."

Winning. Was that what he was doing?

Sometimes he didn't know what drove him to do this. Except...

It wasn't fair his brother should move on to some happy life at the *rancho*. With Liliana, most of all. The very idea was like acid in his stomach.

The *rancho* had been a torture chamber when they were growing up and Diego could hardly bear to set foot on it. He would have it destroyed. Leveled to make a housing development or just left to rot. Perhaps he'd salt the earth and let nothing grow.

As for the money...

He'd gamble it away.

Finishing destroying his father's legacy while the old man rolled in his grave.

If Matías was the hero, trying to redeem all that had been dark and terrible, Diego was the villain. He just wanted it all to burn.

It was what he did. It was who he was.

A destroyer.

"I do not play to lose," Diego said. That much was true. Whether it was in a casino or in the business world, Diego had never lost.

He had a sharp mind and no morals. The two went hand in hand to create some very nice fortune, he found.

"Indeed you don't. But watch out for Matías. He may yet surprise you."

"He won't find me. And when he does? Liliana and I will be married."

"He will still have the rest of the term to find a new bride. Then the inheritance will be split," the old man reminded him.

"I have not forgotten the details of your devil's bargain, *abuelo*. No need to remind me."

"Play to win, Diego. I am rooting for you, if I'm honest."

Diego hung up, feeling that same sour stomach he'd felt when his father had looked at him with recognition, rather than hatred.

The strange thing was…

He wanted to win. He wanted everything.

And yet, he had Liliana.

His brother might find a new bride but Liliana was his.

In the moment that seemed to matter most of all.

He waited. Standing down at the bottom of the stairs, keeping watch on the time. She was late.

He would think nothing of going upstairs and dragging her back down to him if need be.

But then, he heard footsteps, the swish of fabric. He looked up, and for a strange moment felt as if he was caught between that breath before the second hand on the clock moved. Because there she was, her pale blond hair spilling loosely over her shoulders, and that gown…

It was more than he had imagined it might be. There was a spray of glittering glass beads that seemed to cling to her skin, as the fabric they were sewn into was so sheer it was as if it wasn't there. They started as a pale glisten, then built into a startling shimmer as they cascaded down. The neckline was a deep V edged in those rhinestones, and the bodice fell loose and nearly sheer, the entire gown somehow managing to conceal her body just enough, while also giving the idea that at any moment it might give way and reveal her full glory.

He had seen it and known he wanted to tear it off of her body later. And that was why he had selected it.

But just then, that was not what he wanted.

He did not want to tear it from her body. Didn't want to lower her down to the floor.

He wanted to gaze at her in that piece of art forever. Wanted to place her upon a throne and call her his queen. He wanted to worship her.

For he had never seen anything so beautiful in his entire life. Not a woman, not a sunrise, not one single thing.

She was like a ray of light floating toward him, each step she took down the stairs making the fabric swish around her legs, making it appear as if she were floating.

She was an angel.

He had brought an angel into the underworld.

If she had makeup on, it was as translucent as the gown. She looked pale, but there was a shimmer about her skin, her lips a natural pink like the first blush of a rose against the snow. She looked so young. So innocent.

He had not felt young or innocent when he had been young. Now, in his thirties, he felt nearly ancient, and as for innocence...

He had been raised by a murderer.

He had never trusted anything in the world. He had been born jaded. At least, that was how it had felt.

As if from the first moment his mother had held him

he had sensed that once she put him down his father would raise his fists to her.

And yet part of him had always craved the softness.

Because it had been there. In his life, for a moment. Just a glimmer of light in his youth that had otherwise been a horrendous log of pain.

His mother. The light shining out in all of it.

He wondered if that was why he had been so drawn to Liliana. Not because she reminded him of his mother. Not even a little. But because he sensed she had that kind of light that might cut through the kind of darkness he lived in.

But he knew how that ended.

He knew it well.

Karina had not been an innocent, and so he had imagined he might be able to hold her, at least for a while.

But there had been an innocence caught between them. Caught in the darkness of their marriage. A chance at light that had been extinguished before it had ever truly burned.

Their unborn child. Another sliver of hope, of promise, held before him and then cruelly extinguished.

He gritted his teeth, and he did his best not to think of any of it.

Not now. Not now when the most beautiful creature in all of God's creation was floating on a cloud toward him. If there was happiness to be had for a man like him, it was fleeting. And this moment might well be it.

"Happy wedding day," he said.

Her eyes met his. "Yes."

She sounded detached. Slightly dazed. But she had put on the gown, and she was here. He did not require her to be enthusiastic about it.

"Shall we?"

"Where are we…?"

"I'll show you."

He reached his hand out to hers, and this time, he had no gloves on. This time, when she took it, the soft, delicate skin of her hand met with the callused skin on his. It was like lightning, and he knew that she felt it.

She was silk. He wanted to touch her everywhere.

He voiced none of this.

He simply led her out the front door and walked her across the silent grounds. Mist clung to the grass, to the tops of the trees, and she didn't speak as they walked.

They cut through the trees and made their way to the edge of the cliff side, the ocean raging down below. The priest was already there, his expression one of utter neutrality. He had been paid to perform the ceremony. Not to have an opinion on the ceremony itself.

If he sensed that it was a strange arrangement, he did not say.

Diego looked down at Liliana's left hand then and noticed that she was still wearing his brother's ring.

He gritted his teeth but said nothing as the two of them took their positions in front of the priest.

He began to speak, delivering the standard words for the marriage ceremony. Standard vows, which Liliana spoke without meeting his gaze.

For his part, he spoke his without ever looking away.

He had done this before. Had promised this very thing to someone else.

He had kept his vows too. It was just that death had come much sooner than he had anticipated.

But the fact he'd done this before only made it more essential he keep his eyes fixed on Liliana. That he not look away. That these words be for her, and her alone.

"Do you have rings?" the priest asked.

"Yes." Another purchase he'd made before he'd actually taken his bride. He had been confident they would end up here.

He reached out and took hold of her hand, and she looked down at the ring that was there. Diego slipped it from her finger. He held it up to the light, letting both her and the priest take a long look at the glittering diamond ring that was no doubt worth a small fortune for men who did not possess the wealth he and his brother did.

Then he hurled the gem into the sea.

"I have my own rings."

He reached into his jacket pocket and produced a long velvet box. He opened it, and inside was a set of rings. Both made from a dark metal that had been twisted into ornate knots around the band. His was plain beyond that, while hers had a simple band and a second ring that was set with large, square-cut diamonds. He slipped both rings onto her finger.

Like turning the key in a lock. She was his now.

His wife.

Liliana was his wife.

Then he held the box toward her, offering her his ring.

She took it out delicately, and then with trembling fingers slipped it onto his.

He cast the box to the ground and, without waiting for instruction, pulled her into his arms and sealed their vows with a kiss that burned him all the way down.

"Your services are no longer required," Diego said to the priest, then added, "Bless you, Father."

The older man nodded, and Diego seized his bride's hand and began to lead her back toward the house.

"What was that?" she asked as he rushed her back toward the house.

"What?"

"Why? Why the rings? Why all…this? Why did we get married there? Why do I have the dress?"

"It was a wedding," he bit out. "What would you have had us do? Wear sweatpants and sit in a recliner?"

"There was no one there," she continued. "No one there but a priest. And now it's over. I don't understand what the point of all the ceremony was."

Because he'd wanted it. And he didn't know how to say that. He didn't even know how to justify it to himself. He was not in the habit of justifying things to himself. If he wanted them, he took them. He had wanted to see her dressed as a bride. He had wanted to see her in this gown. He wanted to have a ring that matched hers, so he would know even when they were apart that she belonged to him. He had wanted to say vows, real vows, not simply sign a piece of paper. He had wanted to be married in the eyes of the church, because he was Catholic enough to feel it wasn't real if that were not the case.

He did not want to think about why those things were. And he did not want to have to give reasons for them. Not to her, not to himself and not to anyone.

Particularly not now that he had agreed to a temporary term on the marriage. He just wanted. With a blinding, endless desire, and had done so since the first moment he had met her. He had thought that this might make it stop. Had thought that this might make it feel the way that he needed to.

But the need was the same. Maybe once he had her…

He stopped walking, stood with her there in the middle of the mist-covered ground. "You're mine," he said.

"For as long as it takes, you're mine." For as long as it took for his grandfather to give him his portion of the inheritance. For as long as it took for this need in him to go away. "I wanted there to be no doubt about that. I wanted you to feel like my bride. Do you?"

"If I had married Matías there would have been a party. My father would have been there. My friends. I would have chosen my dress. And then…"

"And then you would have gone back to his room, spent your wedding night with him. Is that your regret?"

She said nothing.

"You did not marry *him*," Diego continued. "You have married *me*. And this is the wedding that I wanted."

"I don't understand why you care about the wedding at all."

"Because you're mine." It was all the reason he was going to give. And he'd give it as many times as she needed to hear it.

"You're a bit crazy—do you know that?"

"Creepy. Crazy. Again, I'm not sure why you imagine I would be bothered by such things." He took her hand and began to walk again. "What I know about life, *tesoro*, is that things slip through your fingers easily. As do people. Whatever chains I can put around you to keep you with me, I will do. Never doubt that."

"Until the end," she said softly. "We agreed."

"So we did. You cannot back out now," he said. She was his. She was his. She was his. He owned her now, until the end when he sold her back to herself.

He could do exactly what he wanted with her. She had agreed. He could take her straight back into the house and rip that dress from her body as had been his original fantasy. He could. There would be no one to stop him. Least of all her. She wanted him. He knew that she did. The way that she responded to his touch, to his kiss told him everything he needed to know. Forget a wedding night, he could have a wedding morning if he so chose.

But he found he did not want it.

He had bound her to him in the deepest way possible. He had procured a priest, of all things. They were bound not just by the laws of men but by the laws of God. It did not feel like enough. No. It would not be enough until his bride begged him. Until she came to him. And then... Then he would brand her in a way that she would never forget. But he would not allow her to spin tales of how Matías would have given her a gentle and respectful wedding night. Of how she would have had a more civilized groom and a grander wedding. No. There would be no regrets. There would be no comparisons.

She would beg. He would have her beg.

"I just require one thing from you," he said.

She went stiff, and he knew exactly what she imagined he might ask for next. "You must call Matías and tell him that you've married me. That you do not wish to leave me."

He took out his cell phone and held it toward her. "That's all?"

"That's all."

"And if I tell him to come rescue me?"

"To what end?"

She looked defeated by that and took the phone. He had dialed his brother, and she put it to her ear. "Matías? I'm so glad I reached you."

He could hear the intonation of his brother's voice on the other end. Angry. "I can't say." He didn't know what she couldn't say, but her blue eyes went to his for a moment, then away again just as quickly.

"I'm not injured. I'm perfectly safe. In fact, I need for you to stop looking for me." She squared her shoulders, her posture determined. "I didn't mean to deceive you, and I never meant to hurt you in any way. But I cannot marry you because Diego is the man I really want. I left with him of my own free will. The only reason that I screamed is because he startled me. But it was always my intention to waste your time and make it difficult for you to complete your task, and then marry him. I was not kidnapped. You don't need to look for me."

His heart was pounding heavily. She didn't need to say that to his brother, and he wondered why she did. Why she was changing the story like this.

"It's okay, Matías. Truly. I regret my behavior, but there is nothing to be done. Diego and I have already married. And that means… You know what that means. All of it will be his. If you fail to marry, then all of it will be his. It's too late. We have paperwork. Everything is legally binding. We're married. It's too late."

He watched her face closely, looking for any hint of regret. But there was one thing he came to be certain about as he stood there watching as she broke the news to her former fiancé. She did not love him.

And why he should care about that he didn't know. But he did.

When she was finished, he took the phone from her.

"That was terrible," she said.

"Is he heartbroken?"

"No. Of course not. Matías is a good man but I doubt him any more capable of love than you are, to be quite honest."

"Why do you suppose that?"

"I don't know. It's a feeling I have. He treated me like a baby duckling. Like he wanted to place me in a nest safely somewhere. He did not want to love me."

"I don't see you as a baby duckling," he said. "And I do not want to place you in a nest."

No, he wanted to place her on his bed, lay her on the soft mattress and lick her from her delicate ankles all the way to her sensitive neck. He did not want to protect her. He wanted to defile her.

But he kept that to himself.

"Happy days for me," she said dryly.

"Why did you lie to him?" he asked.

She looked bleak. "I want control of what little I can get. I don't want to be a victim. I don't want to be a woman who was sold into marriage or fought over by two brothers. If it makes the news, and it will, given who my father is and who the both of you are... I'd rather be seen as a vixen." Her mouth curved upward slightly. "I'd rather be a player in the story, rather than a pawn. I am so very sick of being a pawn."

Nothing much burned his conscience. But that did.

"You have free rein of the house," he said. "You may do whatever you wish. There's a library, as we discussed last night. The grounds are yours to wander. There is no method of escape, so you can forget that."

He didn't want her falling to her death from one of the rocky cliffs in a desperate bid for too much freedom. It was difficult to gauge just how sick of being a pawn she was.

"We have a deal," she said. "Whatever I think of it. Whatever I think of you... I gave you my word."

"Yes. And I have offered you a lot of money."

"I'm not going to try to leave."

"I have some business to attend to," he said abruptly,

not releasing her hand, leading her back into the house. "I am very sorry that you do not have a grand reception. However, you will find there are some freshly made pastries in the kitchen. I shall meet you tonight for dinner."

And with that, he led them both into the house, and left her standing in the entry. He could feel those ice-blue eyes on his back as he walked away.

He knew that she had expected him to play the part of the villain. That she had expected him to be the marauder who demanded his husbandly rights.

He smiled. All the better for delaying gratification. If she wanted him to make things easier for her by taking the choice away... She would be sadly disappointed.

She would come to him of her own free will. More than that, she would be trembling with desire by the time she did.

There were few things he understood about himself right now. But this... This made sense to him.

And more than that, the very idea of her begging him...

It was a delicious temptation he had not imagined he could feel. Until Liliana, life had been distinctly boring. He felt like he'd had nothing to look forward to. And then he'd met her.

Suddenly he'd *wanted*.

Prolonging that want—this pain, this need in his gut—it was such a novelty that he found it almost enjoyable.

Of course, the truly enjoyable part would be when she was on her knees in front of him.

He was happy to wait for that moment.

CHAPTER SIX

LILIANA FELT A sense of disquiet that lingered for the entire day. She had expected him to... Well, after the wedding, she had expected him to take his *rights*. She had told him that she would sleep with him. She had expected he would see to that sooner rather than later. She certainly hadn't expected to be left to her own devices for the entire day.

Her wedding outfit had been... It had been nearly obscene. The way that the jewels and the flesh-colored netting at the top had only just covered her breasts, and the tiny pair of white panties that had been provided for her... It all seemed like she was being made into the perfect virgin sacrifice for him. Surely, he had been intending to see that underwear, or he would not have chosen it.

Her cheeks heated just thinking about it.

She had been so certain. So very certain.

But no. He hadn't demanded anything. Not at all. And why she still had those panties on, and a matching white lace bra, now beneath a rather slinky emerald green dress, she didn't know.

But perhaps he would want to *consummate* after dinner.

She shifted restlessly just thinking about it.

She had had a great many hours to wonder what that would be like. To go from trying very hard not to think about sex with Matías to thinking a bit *too* hard about sex with Diego.

The fact of the matter was she'd wondered about it from the first moment she'd met him. Before she had found out her father had planned on marrying her off to Diego's brother.

The connection she felt with him had been instant. Electric and unlike anything she'd ever felt before. So yes, she had thought about his hands. Rough and large, and she had pondered what it would feel like to have them skim over her skin. Yes, she had more than pondered it. Even now, even now that he had proved to be—whatever he was—her body responded to him. It couldn't be helped.

It also scared her.

She felt like she was waiting for a lion to come eat her.

Now she was meeting him for dinner, and she thought she might crawl out of her skin. She was going to have to sit there at the table with him and wonder... Wonder if they would be together like that in only forty-five minutes.

She licked her lips and shifted again, making her way down the stairs and heading toward the dining area.

The house was beautifully appointed, and the food was delicious. Liliana had led a privileged life. Had never wanted for beautiful things or delicious foods. But there was something different about being here with Diego. About being in this house where there was no one else, and yet somehow there seemed to be limitless freedom. She had eaten delicious, flaky pastries for breakfast and lunch, had read an extremely sensual book she'd found in the library, and had thought about doing each and every one of the things on those pages with her captor.

He was the one that made it feel like she was on the verge of something reckless. She might be under his lock and key, but the fact of the matter was as rebellions went…

Diego was going to teach her things about life, about her body, about being a woman, that no one else ever had. And that was where the sense of freedom lay. She would no longer be innocent. No longer be cosseted.

She would… She would *know*.

When she walked into the dining room, he wasn't there.

But there was a spread on the table that was like something out of a fantasy. And, as there was still no staff anywhere that she had seen, it appeared that it had been brought by magic.

There was an array of breads, thin slices of meat and cheese, crackers and fruits. Two terrines filled with soup, a large bowl full of paella and two glasses that were already full of wine. It all looked too beautiful to touch. She wandered down to the end of the table, looking over the spread. Her stomach growled, and she found that the breads from earlier were no longer substantial enough. Not as she stared down at this.

But then, there was the insistent, uncomfortable gnawing in her stomach over what might take place after the meal.

She sat quickly, taking the seat to the right of the one at the head of the table. It was natural for her to do. Her father always sat at the head of the table, and she knew well enough to know that was not her place.

A kick of rebellion hit her stomach. Why? There

was no one here. It was just herself and Diego. Why did he get the head of the table? Because he was the man? Because it was his home? If she was his wife, for no matter how long a period of time, it was her home too. Philosophically if not legally.

She stood abruptly, and then sat in the other chair, feeling bold and empowered. And not altogether the pawn she'd been feeling like earlier. Not just earlier. For weeks now.

It was just as she'd told Diego after the phone call with Matías. She was tired of feeling like she was the last person in the world that had control over her own life.

Was it so wrong to want to be the heroine of your own story? To want to have some say in what went on?

To sit at the head of the table. To control the headline.

She might be in a situation that wasn't entirely of her own making, or her own choosing, but she was going to make of it what she could.

About two minutes later, Diego walked in. He saw where she was, his dark brow corking upward. But he said nothing. He sat down to her right, easily, lifting his wineglass and taking a sip.

"Is all of this to your liking?" he asked.

Liliana lifted her own wineglass to her lips. "Yes."

"Have you started without me?"

"No," she said. "I didn't want to be rude."

The corner of his mouth curved up into a grin, one that was becoming quite familiar to her. It was wicked, slightly dark, and it appealed to something inside of her that she could scarcely understand, let alone identify. She had never thought that a smile could be indecent, but his was. At least, it licked along her skin in an indecent fashion, made her feel heat down in her stomach that was in no way rational or reasonable.

Again, she became unbearably conscious of the underwear she had on beneath her gown. Underwear that he had selected for her. In fact, she had the feeling that every article of clothing in her closet, in the drawers of her dresser had been selected by Diego himself. And she had to wonder if he had touched them. If those rough, masculine fingers had run along the delicate lace fabric.

Which made her wonder what it might feel like if those rough, callused fingers ran along the delicate lace fabric while it was still on her skin.

Her cheeks heated, and she lifted her glass to her lips again, counting on the heady flavor of the wine to distract her. Of course, alcohol might be a bad idea. As it would simply lower her inhibitions.

Fortunately, her inhibitions were very high, so it would take a great deal of lowering before it got her into any trouble.

"Did you have a good day?"

"An uneventful one," she said.

"Well, that can be good."

"Indeed. How was your business?"

"Businesslike," he responded, taking a healthy portion of meat and cheese from the platter and putting it on his small plate. He ate the food with his hands, the action sensual, sending a strange sensation skating down her spine. She opted to start on the soup. Soup was a safe food.

"Well, I suppose that can be good as well."

"Indeed." He echoed her, and much to her irritation she felt a bit of amusement at the exchange. Anger was one thing. Illicit sexual feelings another. Amusement… She did not want to feel amused with him.

"Tell me, Liliana," he said. "What was your favorite thing to do at your father's house?"

"You already know," she said. "Read."

"Did you read today?"

That made her face get warm again, due to what she had read earlier. "Yes."

"That's good. I'm gratified to know you're not needlessly punishing yourself by lying around doing nothing but wearing a hair shirt."

"Martyrdom has never suited me."

"Really? Because you seem like a fantastic candidate for martyrdom."

"Why do you think that?"

"Well. You were willing to marry a man of your father's choosing in spite of the fact you didn't love him."

She frowned, reaching out and taking a piece of bread off the platter at the center of the table, peering into it fiercely. "Is that what you think?"

"Yes."

"I have a sense of obligation to those I love," she returned. "If that's martyrdom…"

"It is. Essentially."

"I don't see it that way. It's just that I'm not selfish. You don't…" She took another bite of bread. "You don't understand."

"Make me understand. Here we are, at our first meal together as man and wife. Make me understand you, Liliana."

"Will you make me understand you?"

"I'm creepy and crazy," he returned dryly. "Can you truly understand either of those things?"

"My mother died giving birth to me," she said, seeing no point in stringing him along. In giving him the satisfaction of toying with her as a cat did a mouse. "My father lost my mother right as I came into the world. He lost her because I exist. Tell me, how can I do anything to try and please him?" She blinked. "I… I wanted to please him, that is. For that reason. Not because I'm a martyr. But all of this has led me to the conclusion that my life really has never been mine. It's a frightening thing, Diego, to realize that you have never truly been free until the moment you were kidnapped from your intended path."

He picked up a piece of bread and dunked it in olive oil, taking a bite and making a musing sound. "Never truly free until you were in my arms? Is that what you're saying?"

"No," she said. "And yes, I'm in a cage after a fashion here, but it's a different one. And… I don't know. I don't know the right answer. That's the problem. I've wanted to please my father all this time, but… Part of me knows that it isn't fair for him to hold my mother's death over my head. Not that he blames me directly, but he definitely uses it. Has used it to keep me in line. To make me into the daughter that he wanted me to be."

"And he's a bastard for doing it," Diego said. "Though, in my experience fathers tend to be bastards."

"Your father…"

"We are not talking about my father." His words were hard, definitive. "Continue to talk about yours. About you."

"Obviously, I never knew my mother," she said. "My father's all I had. I don't think of myself as a martyr, primarily for that reason. It's just… He's all I have."

"You have me now," he said.

The air between them thickened. She… He meant it. Whatever it meant to him, she didn't know, but the words he'd spoken had been spoken with absolute conviction. She had him. And there was no tart response for that. Not when he had spoken with such sincerity. With such gravity.

She had him.

He had her—that much was true. He had kidnapped her out of a window.

But those simple words he had just spoken gave her power as well.

"And very good bread," she said, not sure what else to say. "Who is… Who is making our food?"

"I've hired some people on the mainland to supply us with meals. It's being brought over in a helicopter by one of my men that I trust implicitly. No one else knows where we are."

"I don't know where we are," she said.

"That isn't going to change. While I understand our agreement does benefit you, you must understand that our trust is somewhat limited."

"Well. I understand why my trust toward you would be."

As soon as she spoke those words she felt guilty. He had been…

She thought of the way he had taken her hand today. Of him throwing that ring into the ocean. Giving her his rings. The way he had looked at her the first time he had seen her in the wedding gown. None of it was normal. But it was…

Somehow, she had the feeling that Diego had stronger feelings for her than anyone else ever had.

"Thank you," she said. "For dinner. For… Oddly, for rescuing me from your brother."

He lifted a brow. "I thought Matías was a good man?"

"He is. But a future with him is not actually what I wanted. Having options… Which our deal has provided for me… I don't even know what I'll do with that kind of freedom. I've never had money of my own. I've never done anything but exactly what my father asked me to do. And I felt obligated to do it. But this… It's like you gave me permission to find another way. Somehow, taking away my choice gave me a world of choices I didn't know I had."

"Are you thanking me for kidnapping you?"

"Not in so many words."

"Well, I'll take whatever I can get. Even if it's not in so many words."

"What business do you do?" she asked. "That isn't gambling."

They spent the rest of the meal talking about his various investments and endeavors. He grew animated when he talked about the different restaurants and clubs he had been involved in. His mind was fascinating, filled with creative solutions to all manner of problems. Ways to get attention that she doubted anyone else would think of, methods of erasing formerly bad reputations, the process by which he managed to take an unknown location and turn it into the hottest destination for anyone with money and cachet.

She imagined that it was that darker side of his nature, the one that saw kidnapping her as a viable solution to his present problem, that made him such a brilliant businessman. He wasn't bound by societal restrictions. Wasn't bound by law, or really anything.

He didn't have to work hard to think outside of the box, because he had never been in one.

She, in contrast, had spent her entire life in a little box. One that she had stepped in and stayed in of her own free will. Being around a man like Diego was electric. She wondered then if that was part of their instant connection. Or at least, the connection she felt on her end. That fascination.

After they were through with dinner, there was hot chocolate and churros, and by the end of that, Liliana felt almost content. Warm and sleepy. Something in her wanted to move closer to Diego. Curl up against him like a cat. She couldn't figure that out.

She didn't feel entirely motivated to figure it out.

He would ask now. For their wedding night. They just had their wedding feast, after all. And they had talked. Gotten to know each other better. She hadn't anticipated that being part of any of this. But she wasn't sad about it. Not at all.

She felt happy.

Like this moment between them had nourished a deficit in her soul she hadn't even known was there.

"Are you finished, *tesoro*?"

Treasure. He called her his treasure, and sometimes she felt like he meant it.

The entire scene from their wedding played itself back in her mind again.

Yes. Sometimes, she felt like he meant it.

"Yes," she said, nerves quivering in her belly.

"Good. I imagine it's time to retire. We've both had a very long day."

"Yes," she agreed.

He stood from his chair, then reached down to help her up as well. She took his offered hand, electricity zipping from her fingertips down the rest of her body.

He lifted her hand to his lips, brushed them over her knuckles. "Good night," he said softly. Then he lifted his head, straightened and walked out of the room, leaving her standing there. Alone.

He didn't possibly mean to… He wasn't…

And she certainly couldn't be disappointed if he were. She was a prisoner. She had agreed to the physical aspect of a marriage under sufferance.

Immediate heat rolled over her. Not just because she was lying—to herself, in a bald and blatant fashion—but because just thinking of being with him made her feel hot with longing.

She went to her room, stripped her dress off and left it on the floor. Then she crawled beneath the blankets, restless and edgy. Sure he would come to her. Any moment. Any moment.

She lay there in the dark, nothing between her bare skin and the sumptuous comforter she was resting beneath, and that insubstantial underwear selected by Diego himself.

Every time she shifted beneath it, it stimulated her. Made her nipples feel sensitive. Made her breasts feel heavy. And that place between her thighs felt hollow.

She would be ashamed of her own weakness except…

He had said this would be part of the relationship. He had gotten her thinking about it. And now he wasn't here. It wasn't fair.

He was supposed to take the mystery out of all of this. He was finally supposed to be the one who…

It was just about sex. Not him.

She was twenty-one years old. It was past time she knew what all the fuss was about.

She flopped around like a discontented fish beneath the blankets for at least an hour. And then, it became abundantly clear he had no intention of coming to her room.

What game was he playing? And what was she supposed to do about it?

Suddenly, she felt hot. She pushed the blankets off her body and curled into a ball when the cold air hit her.

She felt goose bumps break out over her skin, and still, inside she was burning up.

She shoved the blankets down toward the bottom of the bed, pushing her feet beneath them, and finding that uncomfortable as well. She tried the reverse, shoving the covers up, and placing them over the upper half of her body while leaving the lower half exposed. Still, she was restless. Another hour had passed with her shunting the bedding down from one end of her mattress to the other, and sleep still eluded her.

She was well past the point of being jet-lagged. She'd been in Spain for nearly three weeks. It was him. Him.

He was the one who had gotten her to agree to this wretched devil's bargain. And now he wasn't even calling in his end of it.

He was keeping her in suspense on purpose. Torturing her.

It was two years of torture. That's what it was.

She growled and rocketed up out of bed, pacing the length of her bedroom. She could go into the library and read. And that was what she decided on. But after an hour of that and two sentences read, she gave up.

And she found herself walking down the hall, barely conscious of the fact that she was still only wearing that white underwear.

She hadn't been to his room before, she realized, but somehow, she was walking as if she would find it easily in this maze of rooms. But she sensed somehow that he wouldn't have placed her too far from him, and she was gratified to find she was correct when she pushed open the door just on the other side of her library door, and found it looked inhabited.

There was a large bed back in the darkness, and she could only just make out the shape of him.

"What exactly are you playing at?" she asked, the veil of darkness provided by the room covering her near nudity and making her feel bold.

"Liliana?"

She felt like a virgin sacrifice standing on the edge of the Dragon's cave. She could hear him beckoning from the darkness. And she was just stupid enough that she was going right toward it.

"No. It's your other wife."

"I wasn't expecting you. You went to bed hours ago."

"So did you. And you're still awake."

"True."

"What game are you playing?"

"I'm not playing any game. I'm sleeping. Or rather, I was attempting to."

"You know what I mean," she said.

"No," he said. "I find that I don't. Perhaps you would care to elaborate?"

"We agreed. We agreed that physically this would be a real marriage. And this is our wedding night… And you…" She huffed out a breath. "Stop torturing me. You have me on edge. Waiting for the moment that you're going to… Just take it."

"I told you," he said, his voice like dark silk, "I have no intention of taking anything from you. I intend for you to give it to me. Enthusiastically. I intend for us to give to each other."

"I don't… I don't understand. You said you wanted sex. And I agreed to give it to you."

"What sorts of sex have you had, Liliana? Because the fact that you seem to view this as a commodity that you hold, for you to take or give, mystifies me. Sex is meant to be shared between two people."

Her blood was pounding so hard in her face, her cheeks throbbed. "I don't... I... If we're going to do it, I don't see why we can't just do it now."

She heard the sound of his bedclothes rustling, heard footsteps as he began to walk toward her. "I asked you a question. Is my brother such a selfish lover that your view on sex is that it's a chore?"

"I'm a virgin," she said, ignoring the thick shame that wrapped itself around her throat and made it nearly impossible to breathe. She hadn't meant to announce it like that. She hadn't meant to announce it at all. It wasn't his business. It wasn't anyone's. She hadn't wanted to make herself so vulnerable.

But she felt vulnerable. The very fact that she had gone in here to confront him about leaving her alone on their wedding night proved that.

Because it wasn't the anticipation that had driven her. It was the fact that it had...hurt her feelings.

Good heavens. She was wounded over the fact that her kidnapper seemed to be able to resist her.

He might be crazy, but she wasn't much better. Clearly.

She heard his footsteps and saw the dark outline of his form as he moved nearer to her. "A virgin?"

He was big. So much bigger than she held him in her memory. It made her feel very, very small. He could break her with one hand. Destroy her.

She sensed he could also make her feel things she'd only ever dreamed of.

It made her tremble. There had been spare few unknown things in her life. She'd been protected by her father, her husband selected for her. And this...

This was very, very unknown.

"That's what I said." She sniffed, keeping her posture rigid, trying not to shrink back from embarrassment or anything else.

"That's very interesting. And especially interesting you didn't see fit to let me know until now."

"I didn't see that it mattered."

"And yet, you think it does now?"

"I wanted you to understand why it feels…unfair. It's not like I have a lot of experience. It's the unknown. I don't know what to expect. As far as sex goes. I'm just… I was just lying in bed, waiting for you to come. And I don't even know what exactly I'm waiting for. Can't you understand how that frays one's nerves?"

"First of all," he said, his tone almost gentle, "you're not waiting for an execution. If all goes well, you're waiting for an orgasm. Perhaps several of them. And that shouldn't terrify you."

"Orgasms don't terrify me," she said, grateful that the light wasn't on. Grateful he couldn't see how furiously she was no doubt blushing. "But the idea of…"

"Penetration?"

Her mouth flew open, then snapped back shut. She couldn't speak.

"Yes," he said. "That, I think, is what worries you."

Yes. It did. But, it was more than that. And she didn't want to have this conversation with him. Didn't want to talk about it at all. Because she couldn't put into words exactly what scared her. Beyond the element of the unknown and the physical pain. It was the fact that they were going to be so… So close. Skin to skin.

And of course, now she was standing there in his room wearing nothing but her underwear. At least it was dark. But still. What had she been thinking? She should have put on a robe. Or that green dress. Her wedding gown. Something.

"I'm turning on a light," he said.

"No," she protested, her voice an impotent squeak as he flicked a lamp on.

He was standing there wearing nothing but a pair of tight black briefs and she forgot for a moment to be embarrassed, because she was too busy taking in the sight of him. His chest was broad, covered with dark hair that tapered down to a thin line as it bisected his well-defined abs. His hips were narrow, his thighs muscular, and it made her curious what exactly he did to acquire such a physique. But she imagined that wasn't polite conversation. Of course, they were both in their underwear. So polite conversation might very well be out the window.

She was embarrassed, for a moment, when she realized she had been standing there staring. But only for a moment. Because then she realized that he had been staring right back. That he was looking over her body. And she forgot to be embarrassed at all, because he looked…hungry. For her.

And yet again, she tried to remember if she had ever felt like anyone particularly cared about her. Matías certainly hadn't cared whether or not *she* was his wife, or some equally suitable woman. Sometimes she wondered if it mattered much to her father who she was as a daughter. Or if any child willing to do his bidding would have done. He didn't know her, after all. Not really. He only knew who she tried to be for his benefit.

Diego seemed to care.

That heat and black fire in his eyes told her it was something more than caring too. Something dangerous and illicit that she had never imagined she would ever inspire in a man. She hardly knew anything. Had barely been kissed. Why would a man want her that way? She didn't have bombshell curves, or dramatic beauty. Whenever she made the style section of the papers they praised her slim figure, it was true, but the kind of figure that clothes hung off had little to do with the kind of figure men found sexually desirable.

Except, Diego seemed to desire her.

But he hadn't come to her. It didn't make sense. Particularly not with how he looked at her now.

"Beautiful," he said.

"Then why didn't you come for me?"

"I meant what I said to you before. I was not going to force myself on you."

"We had an agreement," she said weakly.

"That is not why a man wants a woman to come to his bed, *tesoro*. Not because there is an agreement. Not even because we spoke about it. I want you in my bed because you desire me. You're here now because you are…curious, I think. But curiosity is not enough either."

"What do you want from me?"

"I want you to need it," he said.

She blinked. "I don't even know what that means."

"Then you don't need it yet."

He turned away from her, and she was stunned for a moment by the sight of his sculpted back, her throat going dry. And then, indignation took over. "Are you rejecting me?"

"Does it bother you?"

"Yes," she said.

He turned again. "Why?" His tone was savage, intense.

"Because I… Because I…"

"What?"

"I want you." The words spilled out of her mouth, and she was too upset to be embarrassed by them.

"Do you?"

"Yes," she said.

"Does your body ache for me?"

"Yes," she said, her voice low and steady. "Does it make you happy to hear that?"

"Yes," he said, his voice transforming into a purr. "It is what I want to hear. But I must know more. When you were lying in that bed were your nipples tight?"

She flushed. "Yes."

"And between your legs… Did you ache for me, my darling?"

Shamefully, even as he spoke the words, she felt it happening to her. As if it were by magic. As if he were magic. A dark, dangerous kind of magic that she should want to run from.

Except, she had already made the choice to run to him. And fleeing now seemed silly. Especially when he had tried to turn away and she had stopped him.

She tilted her head up, did her best to stand there before him, proud and unashamed, even while her knees shook and her stomach pitched. "Yes."

"We can start with that," he said, closing the distance between them, grabbing her chin between his thumb and forefinger. "You want me. From there, I can teach you need."

Before she could speak, he claimed her mouth with his, and her entire world bloomed into color, and she found herself being dragged against his hard body, found herself surrendering to his touch, his kiss. To every slick pass of his tongue against hers.

This wasn't about what she should want. Wasn't

about what she should do. It wasn't about being good. It wasn't about anyone but her.

And she realized then, that it was about taking. Because she felt claimed already. But he was also doing something to her, giving her something that she had never imagined she needed.

Need.

He angled his head, parting her lips, taking the kiss impossibly deep. And the shaft of near pain that seated itself between her thighs made her understand that word in a way she never had before. *Need.*

This was need.

She expected fear to come and overtake that need, but it didn't. There was nothing. Nothing beyond the slick glide of his tongue against hers, those large, warm hands skating over her curves. His body was hard, crisp chest hair rough, where she was smooth. Where she was soft.

She had known that reading about things like this with a layer of fantasy between herself and the words couldn't compare. But she hadn't fully appreciated just how overwhelmingly tactile making love to a man would be. It was everything. Overwhelming all of her senses, his musky, male scent intoxicating her, making her feel dizzy and bold and like a stranger inside her overly sensitized skin.

But she liked it.

"I had such fantasies," he said, his voice rough. He slid his hands down to her rear, cupping her and lifting her, urging her legs around his back as he carried them to the bed, lifting her and setting her so that she was standing on the mattress and he was still rooted to the floor. "Fantasies of tearing that wedding gown off of you earlier, throwing you down on the floor and making love to you there. Did you know?"

"No," she said. "I didn't. Because you didn't do any of that. You didn't do anything at all."

"No. Because something changed."

"What?" She nearly whispered the question. She was desperate to know what had changed since the moment he had stolen her out of her bedroom window. What had changed between them. What had changed in his heart, in his soul.

"I don't know," he said, looking up at her, his dark eyes filled with a wildness that she couldn't quite guess at. "All I know is suddenly I wanted to lift you up. To put you up above me. I wish to gaze at you, just like this. To worship you." He reached up, grabbing hold of the clasp on her bra and making quick work of it, dragging the insubstantial lace down and away from her body. Before she fully took on board the fact that she was topless in front of him, he was already dragging her panties down her thighs. He was eye level with… With her.

And then, he was moving, his large hands holding her steady as he pressed his mouth to the heart of her, tasting her deeply, his tongue sliding through her folds, the blunt tips of his fingers digging deep into her hips. She began to tremble, began to shake. She forgot to be shocked. Forgot to protest. Her entire world was focused on this moment. This man. So powerful, so ruthless. Ruthless enough to pull her out of her bedroom window at midnight, to steal his brother's fiancée. To force her into a hasty marriage.

And yet, he was down below her, that dark head bent as he lavished her with pleasure. As he licked and sucked and kissed that most intimate part of her. Her thighs trembled, her knees turning to water, her entire body beginning to unravel beneath that expert mouth. And still, he kept on. Still, he ravished her.

She clung to his shoulders, her fingernails digging into his skin as pleasure crested over her like a wave, her orgasm out of her control and she was like a wholly new creation because of it.

Giving control of her body, her pleasure, to another person was…

Then, he looked up at her, and their eyes collided, and she felt something twist in her chest, shifting, turning on its side. She had the strangest suspicion that it might never right itself. That she might never be the same again.

He looked… Like a fallen angel. That wicked mouth was curved into a grin, that wicked mouth that she now knew could do indecent, obscene and delicious things. It had been so intimate, and yet, she wasn't ashamed.

She found herself kneeling, her knees pressing into the mattress. And she leaned forward, kissing his lips, tasting her own desire there, the evidence of what had just happened between them. He growled, wrapping his arms around her and holding her, not so tightly as he typically did when their mouths met, but like she was a fragile thing that he was afraid he might break.

Then, she found herself being pushed backward, that large, muscular body looming over her as he gazed down. He kissed her neck, on down to her breast, sucking her nipple deep into his mouth, then tracing a circle around it with his tongue before turning his attention to the other. She became lost in a world of sensation. An erotic dance of Diego's making. She could make no more comparisons between reality and fiction, because she could make no more comparisons at all. She could hardly form a thought. She could only feel.

By necessity she had been a cerebral creature for most of her life. Someone who observed life with a healthy dose of distance between the ivory tower her father had placed her in and the world around her.

But there was no distance here. It was raw and intense. Skin against skin, mingled breath and pounding heartbeats that tangled together. His tongue against hers, his fingers in her hair. His sweat-slicked chest rasping against her breasts as he held her close, as they kissed.

And somehow, by her own hands or his, she didn't know, his underwear was gone, and she could feel the blazing hot length of him against her hip as they continued to kiss, as he pressed his hand between her thighs and tested her readiness with his fingers. First one, then another. She gasped slightly at the unfamiliar intrusion, but that gasp gave way to a moan as he slipped his thumb over that sensitized nub between her legs, as he drew a response from deep inside her body, echoes of the climax she'd had only moments before.

He removed his hand then, settling between her legs, murmuring something in Spanish against her lips. "I don't…"

She had been about to tell him that she didn't speak Spanish, but her breath caught in her throat when he pressed against the entrance to her body. He murmured something else, but she couldn't understand. And then he was filling her, the pain blinding. She gritted her teeth, battling the urge to push him away. She wished, badly, that she could recapture the pleasure she'd found in him only a few moments before.

But then he was inside of her. He was breathing hard, his breath hot against her neck, and she became dimly aware of the fact that she was hanging on to his shoul-

ders like a cat trying to claw its way far from danger.
She forced herself to relax, to grow accustomed to the
sensation of him being inside of her.

"I'm sorry," he said. "I told you it might hurt."

She was about to tell him that he had not told her
that, except she realized it had been buried in that broken Spanish she hadn't understood. She would tell him
later that she didn't speak Spanish. An absurd thought
to have when a man was inside of you, probably.

Then he was kissing her again, and things began to
feel a bit more pleasant. He shifted, sliding his hand
down beneath her lower back, skimming over her bottom, down to her thigh as he lifted her leg, urging it
around him as he withdrew slightly, then thrust back
home.

It didn't hurt that time. It felt…

By the time he did it again it almost felt good.

And then, he began to make magic inside of her yet
again. That same, sensual veil that had been wrapped
around them before was suddenly there again as she
got lost in his kiss, the way his hands moved over her
body, and that slick, deep glide of him inside of her. She
felt full, but it was good now. Felt invaded, but she welcomed it. This was what it meant to be possessed. To be
desired. If she could have taken him deeper, she would
have. She would have taken more. Taken everything.

She clung to him, lifting her hips in time with each
thrust, chasing the building release inside of her. In the
end, it wasn't even that delicious friction inside of her
that did it. In the end, it was him. He began to shake,
lowering his head, his movements becoming wild, his
face buried in her neck. The sound that rumbled in his
chest was feral, came from deep inside of him. He froze
above her, looking as though he were in the most in-

tense, wretched pain. And he looked at her. Those dark eyes unveiled for a moment. And in them she saw…

She didn't even know what it was. A depth. A need. All she knew was that it called to her. That it reached inside of her and seemed to find a matching piece she hadn't known was there. She clung to him as he shuddered out his release, and her own caught hold, dragging her right down with him.

They clung to each other in the aftermath, like shipwreck victims in the middle of the sea, storm tossed and broken. But together.

He tried to move away from her, but she held on to him. She didn't know why. Didn't know why she wasn't showing a little bit more self-preservation. Why she wanted to hold on to him when really, it was the last thing she should want. But she didn't know who he was. Not anymore. Any more than she knew who she was. Something had changed inside of her and she didn't know if it would ever be right again. She didn't know if she wanted it to be.

The outside world… Well, out there they made no sense. He was her kidnapper. More than ten years older. She was an overprotected heiress who shouldn't exist outside of books or the nineteenth century. Individually, they were difficult enough, and together they were impossible. But somehow, on this island, secluded in this bedroom away from the rest of the world, it all seemed right.

She couldn't explain why. Not if pressed. Not at all.

She only knew that it was.

And she wanted to prolong this moment, this one of peace and rightness, for as long as she possibly could.

Finally, he rolled away, dragging her with him, bringing her half on top of his body. She laid her head against his chest, against his raging heartbeat.

"I will get condoms," he said.

She felt a slight pang at the realization they hadn't used protection. But it wasn't followed by any sense of panic. Which she couldn't quite understand.

Her mother had died giving birth. And while she'd always expected to have children of her own, she had always felt connected to the danger of it. Even in the modern era.

But she'd made her peace with her desire to have children versus any potential danger years ago. And that wasn't what she expected to scare her now.

It was the fact she would be linked to Diego forever.

She waited for the fear.

It didn't come.

She suspected she might be linked to him forever already.

"Okay," she said.

"It won't take long."

"I'm surprised you didn't have them here already. Considering you took care of every other detail."

"I intended to bring you here to make you my wife in a permanent sense," he said, his voice betraying no hint that such a thing might be strange. "But, now things have changed. I suppose precaution should be taken."

"Of course," she said softly.

She didn't want to think through what he'd said too deeply. So instead, she pushed it aside. And she clung to him. Marveling at how she felt. Altered. Changed. Closer to this man than she had ever felt to another human being.

"Diego," she said. "Why did you want a wife?"

"My inheritance."

"No. That's why you needed to get married. Why did you want a wife…?"

"I'm Catholic," he responded simply.

"Still. I would imagine you could make whatever deal you needed to make... From a religious standpoint... That it would be legal and not recognized by the church."

"I imagine. But, I have never much seen the point in marriage if it wasn't forever."

"Do you...? Do you believe in love, Diego?"

She was afraid of his answer. Very much. Because she feared that she might believe in love, and she feared even more deeply that she might be falling into it with the last man on earth she should.

"Yes," he said. "I believe in love."

For a moment, relief washed over her. Then he continued.

"I believe there are soft, brilliant people in the world with a capacity for love that the rest of us don't deserve. I believe in the power of love to heal, to change. But I also know that love can be twisted and turned, used as a weapon. That there are people who can never be reached with it. People who are beyond it. Love is a powerful force, but there are enemies it cannot defeat."

"So you believe in love, but don't believe that everyone can...feel it?"

"Yes."

"Why?"

"I've seen it," he said. "It's not a secret..." He cleared his throat. "It is not a secret that my father murdered my mother, *tesoro*."

"What?"

"My father is a murderer."

CHAPTER SEVEN

DIEGO HAD NO idea why he was telling her this. Especially after what they had just shared. He should make it about pleasure. About spending the night exploring her beautiful body. He could be more careful the next time they made love. Could withdraw before he climaxed. Though, part of him rebelled at the idea. Still, when the subject of birth control had come up Liliana did not seem as horrified as he had imagined she might.

But they were not making love again. They were talking about his father instead.

"Tell me," she said.

"My mother was a wonderful woman. I think we should start there. She was my introduction into the idea that there was good in the world. Believe me when I tell you there was little evidence of that elsewhere in my house. My brother and I were terrified of our father. He was a tyrant. If he had one emotion in his body beyond selfishness and rage, I would be surprised. He was like a black hole. Consuming and destroying everything in his path. And so, we did our very best to stay out of his path. Matías, he tried to be a good son. And for a while I did too. But then our mother had an accident. She was out riding and she… She fell from her horse. That was the story."

He paused, looking away from Liliana. From her impossibly beautiful, innocent face that was so shocked to hear such a story. It was his reality. His childhood. He had never been shocked by it. He had been broken the day he'd found out his mother was dead. Had cried the last tears he had in him. Even as a man, when he had endured hideous loss, he hadn't been able to weep. He had expended every last tear back then. But he had not been surprised.

What must it be like to not immediately assume the worst of people? She would. After this. After him. He had kidnapped her, for heaven's sake. Had brought her here. Was holding her... Well, it wasn't exactly against her will, not now. But... She would learn. She would learn at his hand. And this story would be part of it.

"She didn't fall from her horse?"

"She did. But my father was in pursuit of her. He shot her. I do not believe that it killed her. But the horse was spooked and threw her. Her official cause of death was a broken neck."

"Diego..."

"My father told me all of this in a drunken rage only two days later. I was eleven years old. And after that... After that I didn't care, Liliana. I did not care if he killed me. I tempted it. I welcomed it. I found my matching darkness and I let it bleed free. He had a shop with classic cars inside. I lit it on fire."

She was staring at him still, her blue eyes round.

"And I laughed as everything he cared about burned."

You must learn to let go of things when they're broken, Father.

He remembered saying those words back to the older man, defiant and filled with his own murderous rage.

"I really did think he would kill me that day," Diego

continued. "He beat me within an inch of it. But then, he laughed. He laughed, because he said he knew my anger. He said if I would only feed it, I would become just like him. Matías… He did not understand him. But me… I'm a chip off the block."

"You aren't," she said ferociously.

"No. It's true." He would not go into Karina. He would not speak of her at all. It didn't matter. Not now. Not now that this marriage was temporary. "And I did not tell you this story in order for you to talk me out of my vision of myself. But you asked what I think of love. Love is why my mother married my father. A misguided sense of love is why she stayed with him. And love is what killed her. It did not change him. It did not shine a light on his dark places. Instead, his darkness consumed her. They say that love redeems people, but there are those who are past redemption."

"Didn't you say you were Catholic? Shouldn't you believe that too?"

"I'm into Catholicism mainly for the guilt."

"Don't you think you deserve something other than guilt?"

"No," he said. "In fact, I cling to the guilt. That might be the one thing that separates me from my father. The fact that I have the capacity to feel it. Even if it is difficult."

"Do you feel guilty for kidnapping me?"

A strange bleakness flooded him. "No," he said honestly. "And that is a concern."

"But, here we are."

"Yes. Because whatever I feel, it's not strong enough to make me want to give you back. You're mine, *tesoro*."

"Yes. You continually remind me of that."

"Does it bother you? Do I scare you?"

She shook her head. "No. But you have to realize… If I'm yours… I believe that makes you mine." She kissed him then. He should stop her. He should yell at her and ask her if she had heard the story at all. Tell her not to speak to him again of love. To not kiss him so tenderly when he was trying to make sure she understood that he was a monster.

But he didn't.

He simply let her kiss him.

Let her drag them both to the edge of that place where nothing existed beyond pleasure and need. Where there was no him and no her. No light or dark. Just a brilliant blending of the two.

She had just asked him if he would let himself have something other than guilt.

Well, he would let himself have her.

So he did. All night.

CHAPTER EIGHT

TWO WEEKS IN Diego's house. Two weeks in his arms. Two weeks in his bed. Liliana hardly knew who she was, and she was all right with it. In fact, she liked this new version of herself better than the old her anyway. She laughed easier, for one. She felt bold.

The night before, at dinner, she had sat on his lap during the meal and fed him meat and cheese with her hands. Then, he had licked her fingers, put her up on the table and licked her everywhere else.

He was strange, her man. Complicated and, yes, filled with darkness. But there was something else too. He needed. He needed her to touch him. Periodically, during the day, she could sense restlessness falling over him, and when she placed her hand on him, she could almost instantly feel that unsettled energy leaving his body.

It always made her think of the boy he had been. The boy who had lit his father's shop filled with cars on fire. The boy who hadn't known another way to let his anger escape. The boy who had lost his mother. His softness. His reference point for love.

Diego believed in love because to not believe in it would be a dishonor to his mother's memory. She understood that.

Just as she understood he thought that he was like his father.

Thought that there was something inside of him that meant love was not for him.

She wanted—more than anything—to change that.

She only wished she knew how.

So she touched him whenever she could. Held him at night while he slept. She was his, and she made sure that he knew he was hers.

Today he had been particularly moody, and she wasn't sure why.

She was sitting in the library reading a book when he stormed in. He had that look on his face like he might throw her down and ravish her, and she was more than ready. But then he stopped, his posture rigid. "Pack a bag."

"Why?"

"We are going back to Spain."

"Why are we going back to Spain?" He wasn't getting rid of her, was he? Was their time together already at an end? That was impossible. Two weeks would not be enough time for his grandfather to be convinced of the legitimacy of their relationship. It couldn't be over. Not now.

Suddenly, the idea of having money, having a life that was full of things and freedom, but lacking in Diego, seemed desperately sad. And not like something she wanted at all.

"We have a wedding to attend," he said.

"We do?"

"Matías is getting married." He looked blank when he said it. "It was in the paper. She's the daughter of some famous...horseman, I guess."

"Oh."

"Does that bother you?" The question was asked with an almost-savage intensity.

"Why would it bother me? I'm married to you."

"Temporarily."

The word was like an ice pick straight through the center of her chest. "Yes. I suppose that's true."

"I thought perhaps it might bother you to see your ex-fiancé married to another."

"You know for a fact that he was never my lover," she said. "That I did not have any sort of real relationship with him."

"Does it bother you to attend his wedding?"

"No. Unless you're planning on leaving me there in Spain without you."

He looked completely taken aback by that. "Why would I do that?"

"You're acting very strange."

"Because I…"

It occurred to her then, the implications of the marriage. Of course if Matías was able to marry it meant that Diego would not get the total sum of the inheritance. They'd be sharing it. Considering Diego had stolen her from Matías in part to prevent that, he couldn't be very happy.

"Are you upset about the money?"

He looked genuinely confused. "What?"

"The money. Now you'll have to share it with Matías."

"Right. I suppose so. But I will get what's coming to me as well. I don't need any of it."

"Do you hate your brother?" She had to wonder if he did, with the way he was going after him like this, the way he'd tried to sabotage his chance at his inheritance.

"No. I don't understand him, not any more than he understands me."

"Then why does this matter?"

He made a sound that would have been a laugh if there were any humor in it. "My father tortured us. He took our mother from us. Now my *abuelo* is playing games with the only compensation we have for being sired by a madman. I don't like my life to be under the control of anyone else. I don't like being manipulated."

"But you allowed it," she said. "You married me."

"I won," he bit out.

"Then what's bothering you?" He said nothing. "You're still afraid that I'm going to run away from you, Diego. Is that it?"

"What has happened here has not felt real," he ground out.

Those words echoed that deep feeling inside of her. That somehow, secluded on this island, the two of them were a fortress. A fortress that could never be destroyed, but once exposed to the outside world, to the elements...

She had no confidence in it there.

In the ability of a sheltered, recently deflowered heiress to hold on to the attention of a man as complicated and interesting as Diego. That was the problem. She imagined that, mostly, to him she was a novelty. And novelty didn't last.

"What happened here has been as real as anything else in my life," she said softly. "At least... At least it was of my choosing."

"Was it?" he asked. "I kidnapped you. I brought you here. I certainly didn't ask for your permission."

"No. You didn't. But I gave myself to you of my own free will, and I have most certainly given myself to you of my own free will since. Can you doubt that the last couple of weeks were anything other than my choice?"

"That," he said, his voice hard, "is sex."

"Fine. So it's sex. Very good sex, I might add. That doesn't mean it isn't real. It doesn't mean I didn't choose it."

"It doesn't mean it was wise of you."

She put her hand on his face. "Was it wise of you to kidnap me?"

His dark eyes stayed trained on hers, and he turned his head, kissing her palm. "Of all the things I've done, kidnapping you was perhaps the wisest."

"Let's go to the wedding," she said. "I'm more than happy to attend as your wife."

The moment he set foot on the dry, cracked ground of the *rancho*, Diego's stomach twisted. He had not felt this way when he had returned to procure Liliana. Possibly because he had been distracted by the idea of claiming her as his own—which he had done repeatedly in the days since—but now... Now he felt consumed by the memories. This place. Which contained so many wonderful, terrible things.

The hacienda had not changed, not the red roof and wrought iron details. Nor had the grounds, arid and wild with the only real green the lawn stretching out before the house. The rest was all tangled vines and olive trees, washed pale in the midday heat.

He'd have thought that if he were to gain half ownership of the *rancho* he might burn the place to the ground. As he had already started to do years ago.

But for some reason, now that thought forced him to imagine what Liliana would think of such a thing. Needless destruction.

"Do you like this place?" he asked as the two of them walked to where the grounds had been set up for the wedding. Chairs positioned toward a flowered archway. He vastly preferred the ceremony he and Liliana had shared.

"Yes," she returned.

"You think it's beautiful?"

"Why?"

She stopped walking and looked at him, her blue eyes far too keen.

"Because if you like it then I should not allow anything to happen to it."

"Why would anything…?"

"If I have ownership of the place it would be my inclination to not let it stand."

"Because of your father?"

"Yes."

"To continue to destroy his dream."

She knew him so well. Understood him. She had that gentle way about her, soft and searching, and far more than he deserved. "Yes," he confirmed, his voice rough. "I might as well burn it all to ash, no?"

"Is this where…?" She cleared her throat. "Is it where your mother was killed."

"On these very grounds, yes. You can see the appeal of destroying it."

"Matías loves this place," she said. "I didn't spend a lot of time getting to know him. I often felt like he was more a guardian than anything else. We didn't have deep conversations. But he told me a great deal about the *rancho*. And he… He is consumed with it. It's everything to him. I'm not sure that he has much passion in his entire soul, but what is there… It's for this place. If you destroyed it, you would be destroying his dreams. Not your father's."

Something inside him twisted. "You forget, I kidnapped his bride. You think that the fact he cares about this place might deter me from doing something to it?"

"You wanted me," she said, her hand on his arm. "That's different. If you want the *rancho*...you should have your part of it. But if you want to ruin it... You didn't take me to destroy me."

There was something about her touch. It always made him feel calm. Made him feel something that was otherwise often beyond his reach. And it made him want more. Futilely.

"That doesn't mean it won't be the end result."

"You said you didn't hate him," she said, quietly.

He didn't think he did. But sometimes...sometimes it felt a lot like envy.

That Matías seemed whole.

When he'd seen the headlines of the upcoming wedding and the story of it being a love match, he'd nearly choked on that envy. Why should his brother be able to love? After everything they'd been through, Diego could not. That Matías seemed to find it wasn't just. But then he'd realized who the fiancée was.

Camilla Alvarez. The daughter of the recently deceased Caesar Alvarez. Matías had purchased the entirety of the older man's estate, and to Diego's mind, it all seemed a bit convenient for the two of them to suddenly find love.

He intended to look into that at some point over the course of the day.

Neither of them spoke as they continued to walk into the venue. They were ushered to their seats, and Diego stood again, driven by something. He didn't know what. Some need to get his footing back. Because God knew Liliana had made him feel like he was slipping.

He was so possessive of her he could hardly think straight most of the time. Work held no appeal. Truly, nothing did. He wanted to hold her close. Keep her forever. He had gotten condoms, as he had promised he would, and he had used them. But he would be lying if he said part of him didn't wish that the first time they were together had resulted in a pregnancy. Because he did not want to give her up. He wanted to keep her forever, as impossible as that was.

For so many reasons.

Even if they had not made the deal, by now he would have come to the conclusion that at the end of all this, once his half of the inheritance was his, he would have to let her go.

He already knew what became of things he cared for.

Already knew that he left nothing but destruction in his wake.

He would not tempt those feelings again. Not with Liliana.

He was the dark one. The bad one. Diego Navarro, beyond redemption. Everyone knew it. The people here certainly did. He had felt the judgmental eyes of everyone in the place from the moment they had come in, and Liliana was oblivious to it. Because Liliana had no idea.

His father was a murderer. And everyone here thought he was one as well.

He was the villain.

It was high time he reminded himself of that.

"I'll return in a moment. Do not disappear, Liliana. Remember, I can destroy your father with a phone call."

She said nothing to that, the brightness of shock in her blue eyes making his gut twist. The threat had been unnecessary and he knew it. But he'd still felt compelled to issue it. To remind her, not of what he held over her head.

But of who he was.

He left Liliana sitting in her chair, and walked toward the hacienda, his mouth set into a grim line. When he opened the door, it was not his brother he saw standing in the antechamber, as he had expected. It was a woman, standing with her back to him. The woman he had seen in a picture with Matías only a week or so ago. She had very short hair, and she was beautiful, much like a little dark-haired pixie.

"Well," he said, drawing on all his experience playing the bad guy to make sure he sounded just like one. "Don't you make a radiant bride."

She whirled around, her dark eyes wide, her expression full of all the fear that hadn't been in Liliana's eyes when he'd taken her from her room that night. This woman knew what he was.

"Diego, I presume," she said.

"You make this sound very like an overdramatic soap opera," he drawled, moving closer to her. "I must say, I am impressed with my brother's resourcefulness. Often, his scruples prevent him from claiming certain victories. I myself have never understood why he'd limit himself the way he does."

"I'm not entirely sure what you're talking about," she said. "Matías is my lover. He has been. Liliana's defection was only a good thing for us."

She was a good liar, was the little pixie. And Diego had to wonder if the part about the two of them being lovers was true enough. Though, Diego doubted they had been before. Matías was far too good to plan to marry Liliana while keeping a woman on the side.

"It is a very nice story," he said. "But I already read

it in the paper. You know, my brother fancies himself a good man, but he is not so different from me. He simply draws lines around moral dilemmas as he sees fit. And I have never seen the point of doing so. He decides that certain actions are *right*, and certain actions are *wrong*. He has decided that his motivation for inheriting the *rancho* is higher than mine, and therefore, he must win at this game. I require no motivation myself beyond my need to win. To be satisfied. I don't need to pretend I am being *good*."

"Is that why you took Liliana?"

She was spirited, this woman. He admired it.

"She was simply a means to an end." As he spoke the words, he thought of their weeks together. And again of her coming down the stairs in that dress. The tightness in his chest. His heart. The darkness in his soul that cried out for her light. "Like everything else."

"Did she go with you of her own free will? Or did you kidnap her?"

"Oh, I kidnapped her." Images of her in his bed, in his arms, flashed through his mind. And that drove him on. A reminder of who he was. A reminder of what this was. "But, she was convinced quickly enough to marry me. I just had to have her throw out that lie to Matías so he wouldn't come searching for her. He's not very trusting. He believed so quickly that she would betray him. It's a character flaw, for sure. If I were you, I would watch out for that later on. If he were to walk in now, I imagine he would have a lot of follow-up questions for you. Particularly if he were to walk in when you were in my embrace."

Diego took another step toward her, and the woman took a step away. "Don't come anywhere near me," she said. "You're a villain."

She had no idea. Truly, no idea. "To you. But a villain is his own hero. I read that somewhere once. I quite like it. Although, I am not overly concerned with being either. I'm simply concerned with winning."

"Well, Matías and I are getting married today. So you're not going to win."

"Am I not? Because I will get my share of the family fortune, if I choose to press the issue with my lawyer, I will probably end up with a stake in my brother's company." He didn't care. He wondered if he ever had. Or if he was still a small boy lighting things on fire because he didn't know what else to do with his rage. "And he has had to settle for second best when it comes to wives. Yes, I think my victory, while not total, was handily done enough."

The door to the house opened again, and a small woman in a black dress walked in, casting him a severe look. "It is time," she said.

"I had better go take my place in the audience, then," he said. "But rest assured and remember this. My brother might talk about being good, he might talk about doing the right thing, and in the end he might do the right thing by you, whatever that means. If it looks like a permanent marriage, or an attempt at commitment. But he will not love you. That is something the men in our family are incapable of."

He walked back out into the brilliant sunlight, repeating his own words back to himself as he took his seat next to Liliana, who looked at him and smiled as if he were the stars, and not simply the dark night sky.

He was not capable of love. And neither was Matías.

He couldn't be.

If after all they'd been through, Matías could find love, while Diego lived in the darkness...

He would be alone in it.

Sitting out there in the midday sun, surrounded by people, with Liliana's hand on his arm, he felt more alone than he ever had.

And the truly startling thing was, he found it unbearable.

CHAPTER NINE

THE WEDDING HAD been beautiful, and Liliana was not at all surprised to discover that she wasn't envious in the least. Not of the spectacle. Not of the groom. And not of the gorgeous reception that followed. The bride and groom were scarce during the event, but there were a lot of people eating and reveling, and she was ready to do the same.

The venue was made into something so beautiful. It was hard to believe such a place could have such a dark past. But Matías had worked very hard to turn it into something else. Something new. White lights strung over a clearing surrounded by olive trees, a stage with a band playing off to the side. There was an elaborate canopy with cakes and other sweets set beneath it that looked incredibly tempting after a long day in the sun.

It was so wonderful to be here, and she couldn't quite explain why. Except she felt free and happy.

Except… Diego was like a storm cloud at her side.

Diego, who could not see a way to redeem this place. Diego, who only saw the darkness.

"I'm going to go get cake," she said, touching his face, trying to see if she could conjure up some of that magic between them now. It didn't seem to be working. She shifted, dragging her fingertips along the line of his jaw, down to his chin, rubbing his lower lip with her thumb. A spark ignited in those dark eyes, and he looked at her.

"Would you like cake?" she pressed.

She doubted even sweets could improve his mood, as dark as it was, but she would do her best.

"What I would like is us to return to our hotel room in Barcelona," he said, his words filled with meaning.

She knew exactly what he wanted to do in that hotel room. It was the way he felt most comfortable connecting with her, and it was most definitely the best way for him to break one of his moods.

Not that she didn't like it. She did. But just for a while she wanted to be here with him. Out in public and on his arm. Wasn't that reasonable enough?

"Yes," she said. "And we will." Her body felt warm just thinking about it. "But, I would also like cake."

"Far be it from me to stand in the way of you and your sweets. By all means, *tesoro*, go and get yourself some cake."

She didn't want to leave him, not now. Not when he was in such a strange space. He hadn't said anything but she could feel it. Being here was hurting him. She wanted desperately to fix that.

"Will you dance with me first?" she asked.

He looked at her, his expression unreadable. "You want to dance with me?"

"Yes. I don't know how to dance, though," she said. "You'll have to teach me. Like you've taught me to do… other things."

Her words seemed to propel him forward, and he took her into his arms, holding her close as he led her to the dance floor.

His hold was firm and sure as he wrapped his arms

around her and led her in time to the music coming from the band on the stage. He spun her in a circle beneath the lights, a blur of glitter above her head. She felt like she was flying. And when she landed, she was safe in his arms.

· When he drew her back to his chest, she pressed her hand over his heart. It was racing, like it always did when they made love.

Like just touching was an echo of that intimacy. She carried it with her—there was no denying it. It made her feel linked to him in a way she'd never felt linked to another person. Ever. Not by friendship, not by blood.

It was the same for him. She knew it was.

The song ended and she could sense that people were staring at them. He released his hold on her, and she slowly let go of him, looking around with a growing sense of disquiet.

Several of the older villagers were giving Diego exceedingly hard glares, and then moving to her with looks of pity. She couldn't fathom why anyone would pity her. She was with the most beautiful man here. She stared right back, hoping her expression said exactly that as she allowed Diego to lead her back to a table.

"Get your cake, *querida*," he said, his eyes focused somewhere past her.

She nodded and moved away from him, feeling strange to be so far from his side after weeks of isolation with him.

She had felt that way when he had gone off to wherever he'd gone before the wedding ceremony. She wondered what he'd been up to. If he had gone to see his brother. And if so… What words had the two men exchanged? Diego was in such a strange headspace, she had no idea exactly what his goal was for being here.

To show his grandfather that he was married, perhaps. To prove that she was real.

Maybe he had gone out searching for his grandfather. But she hadn't seen a man she thought could be Matías and Diego's grandfather anywhere in attendance anyway.

She chewed her lip as she wandered over to the cake table.

"Señora Navarro."

Liliana looked toward the sound of her name and saw a small woman dressed in black, a severe expression on her face. Maria. The housekeeper. She had gotten to know her over the course of her stay with Matías.

"Hello, Maria," she said.

Maria shook her head. "I cannot believe you married *him*."

"I… I'm sorry for any pain I might have caused Matías," she said. "I am. But Diego…"

"He's a murderer," Maria said. "I doubt your darling new husband has confessed that to you."

The air rushed from Liliana's lungs, leaving her dizzy. "He is not," she said, feeling rage sparking her blood. How dare she say such a thing about Diego? He had been a victim of his father's horrific darkness when he had been a boy. And to tar him with the same brush…

"He is," the older woman insisted.

"How dare you say such a thing about my husband," Liliana said, her voice trembling. "This is his home as much as Matías's and he should not be insulted here."

"He killed his first wife," Maria continued, ignoring Liliana's tirade. "Everyone here knows it. I hope that you are entertaining him in his bed, or you will likely meet the same fate."

A *wife*? Diego had never mentioned having a wife before.

They say worse things about me.

Feel free to peruse the internet.

Those words came back, echoing in her mind. It didn't matter what this woman thought. She knew Diego. She knew that wasn't true.

"Do you know where he was before the wedding? He was menacing the bride just before she prepared to walk down the aisle. He mentioned you, of course. He says you're a means to an end. If his end is money, then perhaps you are safe. But if there is something else that he has his mind set on, then if I were you I should be concerned. He is a very bad man. A *diablito* from the beginning. The staff who have been here from the beginning have all said this. Matías is good. He has defied all expectation, everything his father taught him, and he is a good man. He is like his mother. Diego is his father. He is the devil. He was then—he is now. And everyone in this village knows it. They all remember. They know that he is responsible for the death of Karina Navarro as certain as his father is responsible for the death of Elizabeth Navarro. Ask him. *Ask him* and see what your husband tells you. But perhaps make sure there are witnesses when you do."

Liliana's head was spinning. She felt dizzy. She felt ill. She couldn't imagine Diego harming anyone, least of all a woman. Which seemed insane considering that he had kidnapped her, but she knew him. She knew him intimately. Had felt his body move inside hers more times now than she could count. She cared for him. She cared so very much. And she could not imagine that she might have come to care for a murderer. Or a man who saw her simply as a means to an end.

But why had he gone to talk to Camilla, Matías's wife? What had he been thinking doing that? What was the point?

She didn't want cake. She wanted answers. And she had a feeling she wasn't going to get them easily.

Her husband wasn't a devil. At least, she didn't think he was. But he was a brick wall.

She walked across the dark garden area, beneath the string of lights that hung like a glittering web overhead. And she went to find her husband. "I want to go," she said.

His dark eyes flashed. "Why the sudden change of heart?"

"We need to talk."

One corner of his mouth tipped up into a rueful smile. "I see. Perhaps one of the villagers has come to set you straight about the manner of man you married?"

"Something like that."

"We can talk here." He spread his hands wide.

"No. We're not going to talk here. We're not going to make a scene."

"Why not? I live for a spectacle."

"I don't," she said. "I don't, Diego. And this is *our* marriage. *Our* business. I will not trot it out for all the world to gawk at." Their relationship was private and special. It wasn't about what other people saw or thought. At least, it hadn't been on the island. That had mattered to her. As a woman who had been raised to care more about appearances than anything else, that they'd built a relationship in the dark, with only each other as witnesses, meant more than just about anything.

"That is the entire point of us attending the wedding today, *tesoro*," he said. "To cause a spectacle."

Of course. He had wanted to come to his brother's

wedding with the woman who would have been the bride. And Liliana had been foolish enough to not realize that. She had let go of Matías completely and utterly. Simple for her, since she'd never truly cared about him.

Their marriage was about two people: Liliana and Diego.

It was so strong inside of her that she had imagined it had to be the same for him.

She was a fool.

"Yes. Perhaps for you it was about creating a spectacle," she choked out. "But not for me. I wanted to attend a wedding with my husband."

"We do not have a real marriage," he said softly. "And that is because of you."

"Nevertheless. Whatever our marriage, however long it lasts, is our business. It was just you and me on the island, Diego. Just you and me." No past. No Matías. No Camilla. No angry housemaids intent on spoiling the fantasy that Liliana had built up of her husband.

She had *known*. While she had been there, something in her had known. The moment the rest of the world was invited into their union, it would introduce ugly, hard reality. Reality she did not want to cope with. Oh, as silly as it seemed, she preferred the fantasy.

"Then we will go," he said, his voice hard. She didn't know why he had decided to agree. Maybe what Maria had said was true. Maybe he was, after all, a stone-cold murderer intent on destroying her the moment they were in private. But she didn't believe that. Not really. Her sense of self-preservation was strong enough that if she felt that were true on any level she would not go off with him. But she didn't believe it. Not really.

He took her arm, and the two of them walked away from the revelry, waiting until Diego's impossibly ostentatious sports car was delivered to them. He got into the driver's seat, and the engine roared as he sped toward the roadway. And she had to wonder if he intended to kill them both with the way he was driving.

"Don't worry," he said. "I've done a bit of racing in my day."

"Not on a public road, I should think." She sniffed.

"All kinds of places." He laughed. "You are truly so sheltered, Liliana. You have no idea what kind of man I am. Or maybe you do, and you don't want to know."

Those words stung. Because they were true.

She wanted him to be all that she imagined him to be.

She wanted him to be the fantasy husband she'd created in her head.

Tonight was the first night she had been afraid— truly afraid—that he might not be. That she might be deluded by sex and a charming, dark voice that had made her fantasies a sweet and dirty reality all night long in his bed.

She had been so sure she was smarter than that. So sure that she wasn't enough of an idealist to buy into it.

She had trusted herself. Her feelings.

The low-slung car hugged each and every curve of the road as they made their way down into the city, all brightly lit as people began to emerge from their homes to take part in the celebrated nightlife of Barcelona.

They pulled up to the front of the hotel they were staying in, and Diego turned the keys over to the valet.

They walked up the vast front steps and into the ornate building, and Liliana barely had a chance to enjoy the gilded marble lobby with its rich, velvet furnishings, because Diego was whisking her to the elevator that took them to the penthouse. They hadn't stopped to look at the room earlier. Rather, Diego had simply brought their things and had the staff handle them. She didn't have time to enjoy it now. Because when the door shut firmly behind them, Diego rounded on her, his dark eyes blazing with black fire. "Go ahead. Make your accusations."

"What accusations do you expect me to make?" He knew. He knew because...

There were only two options. He either knew because he'd heard them as rumor... Or because it was true.

"I'm not playing a game with you, Liliana. Tell me what you think of me now, wife? Tell me what manner of man you were told you married."

"My first question is, why did you go off to play the villain with Camilla? What did that serve? Why harass Matías's bride?"

"I *am* the villain," he said, his tone dark. "It would be disappointing if I didn't make an appearance in the last act to menace, wouldn't it? It's just bad storytelling."

"Why? Why are you obsessed with the idea that everyone see you that way?"

"I wanted to see what this marriage was. If he'd found a woman to fall in love with him." His words were dripping with disdain. With hatred.

"And are you satisfied with your answers?"

He looked shocked by that line of questioning. "It would seem to me," he said, his voice dark, "that there is a certain amount of injustice in the fact that my brother could escape the life we lived being who he is. Finding love. Finding marriage. Living on the *rancho*, redeeming it."

"Why isn't that fair?"

"I can redeem nothing. I can only play in the darkness that my father instilled inside of me. Matías is our mother. He is…he is made of different materials. And I have never understood *why*. I've never understood how that was fair."

"Life isn't fair, Diego, or did you miss the class they gave on that?"

He made a scoffing sound and turned away from her, pacing the length of the room like a caged tiger. "Such a rich thing to be lectured on from a cosseted rich girl."

"My mother died giving birth to me," she said. "I never knew her. I never had the chance. She never even got to hold her child. Tell me how that's fair, Diego? My father didn't take the opportunity to then become two parents in one. To love me enough to cover my loss. No, he saw it as an opportunity to manipulate me into doing his bidding. Tell me again about fairness."

"I tried. I tried to overcome my past. I tried to love. It ends in nothing. It ends in darkness."

Disquiet filled her. She remembered the words Maria had spit at her.

He's a murderer.

Like his father.

"What happened, Diego? Tell me." She would rather know. She would rather know and face whatever demon came with the truth.

"You are not my first wife."

Those words felt like a punch to the stomach. She didn't want them to be true. She didn't want what Maria had told her to be true. But now, looking at him, at the horrible bleakness etched into his handsome features, she worried that it was.

"You never mentioned you'd been married before," she said.

"I don't like to talk about Karina. But the people in the village where I'm from have little else they like to talk about. The beautiful, vivacious woman that I married when we were both far too young." He shook his head. "They think they *know*. They think that it was the same as my father, and sometimes I wonder… I *wanted* to be in love, Liliana. I wanted to believe that I could escape what I was. I'd spent years losing myself in debauchery, trying to forget. Thinking that if I divorced myself from any and all connection I could at least keep those around me safe. And hell, in the process I might kill myself. And then the world really would be safe."

He was rambling, a string of words that ran together in a dark endless river. And none of it was answering the most important question she had.

"Did you kill her?" she asked.

"Yes."

CHAPTER TEN

THE WORLD FELT like it was tilting and she had to grab the back of the couch in order to keep from falling down. "Diego... I don't... I can't..." It made no sense. He wasn't a good man, her husband, but she couldn't imagine him killing anyone apart from his father. She had no trouble imagining he would happily put an end to the man who had made his life so miserable and stolen his mother from him.

But a woman? His own wife?

She couldn't believe it. She wanted to run away from this. Wanted to hide. But she had to face this. And him.

She wasn't a little girl locked in her father's house anymore. She was a woman. Her own woman.

"Diego," she said, her voice so much stronger than she had expected it to be. "Did you kill your wife?"

"Not with my hands," he said, his voice rough. "But the fact of the matter is, she ran off with a man who was worse than a coward, and she found him preferable to me."

Relief washed through her, and perhaps it shouldn't have. But he hadn't killed her. Not really. And that was all that mattered to Liliana. "Start at the beginning."

"It is not a pleasant story, and you won't like the outcome. The most that I can say is that what I love, or what I strive to love, tends to meet tragic ends."

"Diego…"

"I married her. I cared for her. She is dead," he said, his voice flat. "Does the rest matter?"

"Yes," she said, "it matters to me. Because you matter to me. And I want to know…"

"We were married for two years," he said. "Only two. I was twenty-five. She was twenty-seven. We met at a club, and we were both intoxicated. Not with each other, mind you, but with a substance of some kind. It was instant lust. She was wild and possibly the only person I had ever met who was more untamed than I was. How could I be anything but fascinated by that? I thought… I thought that would be the way. My mother had been sweet. She had loved my father in spite of all that he was. And I imagine that if I found a woman who was my equal in debauchery that then perhaps it would all work. But our marriage was never anything but toxic. Fighting, and then…"

"Sex," Liliana said, jealousy prickling over her skin. She was angry with herself. Angry for being jealous of a dead woman. A woman who clearly hadn't had the happiest of relationships with Diego.

But still. She'd been with him. Touched his body. Been brought to ecstasy by him.

No other man had ever touched her. It didn't seem fair.

"A year and a half into the marriage she became pregnant."

That word truly was like a slug to the stomach. Another woman. Pregnant with his baby. It burned her up inside.

"I had never wanted children," he said, "but I was… happy. Though Karina and I had our differences I thought we would have incentive to make our marriage work because of the child. I was happy to have a child."

"But you don't…"

"No. I don't have one. Because when Karina was about six months pregnant she informed me that she was leaving me for another man. My wife. My pregnant wife had found someone else. Someone infinitely preferable to me and my moods."

"What happened?" she asked, keeping her tone gentle.

"This is why people imagine I killed her. But the truth of the matter is it was nothing so nefarious as a car accident. It was just that… She was the only one in the car. And she was in the passenger seat."

"How?"

"She was with *him*. And he is alive and well, though he will not tell his version of the story. The truth is he was high and he ran their car into a cliff. The side that Karina was on. And he left her there. He escaped the car, leaving his pregnant mistress to die slowly. Leaving *my child* to die slowly inside of her. Karina was not innocent—that much is true. But she didn't deserve that. My child was innocent, Liliana. The only innocent in that entire tangled web. It can't be escaped. This darkness in me. It doesn't matter what I do. If I touch it, it dies. I might as well be a murderer."

"How? How can you possibly come to that conclusion?"

"She preferred the sort of man who would leave her in a car to die over me."

"I hate to speak ill of the dead," Liliana said, "but your wife sounds like an idiot of the highest order. Her bad decisions have nothing to do with you."

"And yet she's gone. And my child…"

"I'm sorry," she said. "I'm sorry about your child. And I'm even more sorry that everyone blames you because of your father."

"They blame me because they know that I must have been a truly terrible husband, whether she died by my hand or leaving me, it doesn't matter. The evidence of what I am remains. I might as well be a murderer."

"No," she said. "You're not a murderer."

"A kidnapper. A villain. A blackmailer."

"You have been gentle with me. You knew that I liked books. You talked to me. You have shown me pleasure. You've given me pleasure before you've taken your own every time we've been together. You have asked me more questions about myself than any person I've ever known. Do villains do that, Diego?"

"You are different. You always have been. You… You are the thing that I fear most, Liliana. And yet, I still couldn't stay away from you. That tells you everything that you need to know about me."

She frowned. "You are afraid of me?"

"You are that rare piece of light. You remind me of my mother in that sense. Make of that what you will."

He was trying to make it sound sordid in some way. Trying to take what they had and reduce it. She wasn't going to let him. "Say what you mean, Diego. Stop making menacing, leading comments. You might as well tie me to the train tracks if you're going to be this much of a cliché."

"Why I was drawn to you," he said. "You remind me of what it's like to have a light shine in the darkness. But I also know what happens in the end. The light is consumed. And I know what I am."

"I know what I am," she said. "And what I am is much stronger than I thought it was. I'm not just a creature created to atone for someone else's death. I'm not a weak-willed socialite. I am not your kidnapped victim. I'm not Liliana Hart. I'm Liliana Navarro and I am not afraid of you."

"You should be," he said, his voice rough. "I consume all that I touch. I destroy beauty. I break delicate things."

"No. That's giving yourself way too much power. You're an angry boy who has never learned to let go of the pain in his past. But that doesn't make you damaged beyond repair. You think that you were born a certain way and there's nothing you can do about it. You think that Matías was magically gifted with something that you can never have. That isn't true. It's not. You have a choice, and you can make it."

"A choice to do what?" he asked, his tone dripping with disdain. "What choices do I have in my life? The choice to keep you prisoner for the rest of forever? The choice to date until I fall in love and settle down in a suburb somewhere and have children with my lovely wife? What choices? I learned what men are capable of when I was a boy. I have seen the very worst end to a relationship that exists. I hate my father. And I hate even more the fact that he looked at me and saw not only his blood, but a soul he seemed to understand. I have tried to overcome it. And I will not try again."

"But you wanted to stay married to me."

"I wanted to *own* you, Liliana. I never wanted to *love* you."

His words fell flat over the top of all the pain already roiling around inside of her. They didn't surprise her. Not at all. He was so very committed to this. To this idea that he could not overcome what he was. And again, she saw, with a startling clarity, exactly why. Exactly what he was doing.

He was protecting himself. He had always done that.

From the time he was a boy he'd had to. He had endured hideous loss, and the loss of his wife… Of his child… He talked about it now with a kind of defiance, a certainty that it was the darkness in him that had caused it, but she recognized it as the same kind of blame she had taken on herself for her mother's death all her life.

She had always known that she wasn't truly the cause of her mother's death. But there was a comfort in taking on the mantle of that blame. It gave her a purpose. And most of all, it gave her protection. It allowed her to hold herself separate from the world around her. In her case, it had allowed her to justify the fact that she let her father tell her what to do. And by giving her father that kind of power she took away all responsibility for herself. She didn't take risks. She didn't make choices. She read books. She observed life rather than participating in it.

And because of that, she never had to risk anything.

Diego was doing much the same, but he didn't have a father to tell him what to do. He simply had one who had given him a monster's blood. And he could blame that monster for anything. For everything. And it kept him from ever loving and losing someone again. Yes, she could see him.

That angry, scared little boy who wanted to burn everything down. It was what he still did.

He was afraid. Afraid of being hurt. Afraid of loss.

But he wanted her. And that was the thing. He hadn't been able to stop himself from taking her. And whatever justification he was using for that now, she could see the truth. He was caught between wanting to protect himself, protect her and keep her locked away on his island.

Whether it made sense or not, her touch did calm him. She made him… Maybe *happy* wasn't the word.

She didn't know if she had ever seen Diego truly happy. But he was settled within himself when they were naked, lying in bed together. More at peace with the demons in his soul than he was otherwise.

If she could make him happy, it would be the most amazing thing.

She was strong. And he was good. And those were the two things he did not seem to be able to believe. He was afraid he would break her. But she would not be broken. Moreover, while he might possess the strength to destroy her, he never would. She trusted that. She doubted her father had spent one moment worrying about the darkness in him. Doubted he had ever agonized over the ways in which he had harmed his wife. Yet Diego took on the guilt of every sin committed not only by that man, but by his wife's paramour. That was not the act of a bad man.

He had sparked something in her from the moment they had first met. It had been like finding another piece of herself. She couldn't explain why. How something could be so strong and instantaneous with no evidence behind it. But since then, it had proved only to be the truth. He was a man separated from the world by his own fear. A man who had experienced everything, while she had experienced very little. But that common bond of loss, of wrapping themselves in a shield so strong and tight the world could never touch them, remained. "You're *my* light," she said. "Don't you understand that?"

"No," he said.

"It's true. I was just drifting along in the gray. Maybe it wasn't the blackest night like you've experienced, but it was a haze. I didn't know who I was or what I wanted. And you gave me this… This chance at freedom that I had never once imagined for myself. You shone a light on all these hidden places inside me. You made me understand passion. You are not darkness, Diego. Not in my world."

"You understand nothing."

"I understand everything that I need to. Diego…"

"Don't talk," he said. "Not anymore. Do not forget who it is you're dealing with."

"A man who wants to watch the world burn so that it will all go away and he can be safe from it?"

"If you insist on keeping your mouth so busy, perhaps you could do it in a fashion that I might find more pleasurable."

She found herself being pushed to her knees in front of him, and she realized what he was doing. The exact same thing he had been doing earlier when he had gone to seek out Camilla before the wedding.

He was trying to put her in her place. And put himself in his. That preferred role of villain, rather than a man who seemed as if he no longer knew who he was or where he fit into the world.

Lost. He was lost. Beneath all that certainty, all of his hardness, he was a man so desperately lost and alone who needed someone to take his hand.

But if he couldn't accept that yet, then perhaps she could reach him by taking hold of another part of him.

She knew that he expected her to get angry. That he expected her to fight back.

She refused. She would show him just how strong she was.

She lowered her head, her hair falling into her face. Then she looked up, reaching her hands toward his belt and undoing it slowly, then moving to the rest, making quick work of the button and zipper, drawing them partway down his hips before reaching inside his underwear and curving her fingers around his hardened length, drawing him out toward her.

"How could you think this would be anything but my pleasure?" she asked just before she closed her lips around him. He was intoxicating. Masculine and beautiful, and essentially Diego. The man who had become her entire world so very quickly. He forked his fingers through her hair, and pulled at her for a moment, as if he was trying to get her to stop. But she knew the moment that he gave up, surrendered, guiding her head rather than trying to pull her away. A rough groan escaped his lips, and she took pleasure, pride, in the fact that she was reducing this man to nothing. He thought he was so very strong.

He thought that he could break her.

But she was going to break him. Utterly. Completely. He was hers.

She lifted her head, meeting his gaze, glorying in the tortured expression etched across his handsome face. "You're mine," she said, her tone hard, possessive. Every bit of her meaning it, as deeply and truly as he had all the times he'd said it to her. And he had. From the beginning. This was beyond both of them. That he thought he could turn away from it, that he thought he could scare her away was laughable.

The only thing that scared her was a life without him in it.

He was her opposite in so many ways. Dark and dangerous. Jaded. Experienced. And yet…they were the same.

In their souls, they were the same.

She angled her head, dragging her tongue along the

length of him, a feminine satisfaction rolling through her when she felt him shake, tremble.

She took him in deep, and she put every bit of her motion into it. There was so much. So much that she wanted him to understand. About himself. About her. About the two of them together.

She could stay on her knees like this in front of him forever, pleasuring him, making him feel good, and it wouldn't be a sacrifice. Because every ounce of his pleasure echoed inside of her. Didn't he know? Didn't he understand?

Everything that he felt she was, he was for her.

She wrapped her hand around the base, stroking him as she continued to pleasure him with her mouth, as he began to lose hold of his control, his grip tightening in her hair as his hold on the world went slack.

It was back to that feeling. That there was just the two of them and nothing else mattered. She wished she could hold on to it forever. Even though she knew it wasn't possible. The world would always be out there. The opinions on Diego's past. The temptations and distractions that came with everyday life.

But here, in the bedroom, with nothing between them, they could get back to this. Back to each other. Back to themselves.

She was never more her than when she was naked with Diego inside of her.

He growled, hauling her to her feet. "Enough. I need you. All of you."

"And you can have me. All of me." Slowly, ever so slowly, she began to remove the dress that she was wearing. It was red, a much-bolder color than she usually favored, as typically, something so rich and intense washed out her already-pale features even more. But there had been something about this gown that had set Diego's eyes alight, and she had wanted to hang on to that. Had wanted to pursue it. And now, she pushed the delicate straps down her arms, lowering the zip slowly. Grateful she had decided to forgo wearing a bra, only a pair of matching red lace panties remaining as she let the dress slide into a silken pool at her feet.

He looked hungry, and she wanted to be the thing that filled that need.

It was deeper than sex. She knew it. She wondered if he did. There was a hunger in his soul, the thing that responded when she placed her hands on him.

They had both been lonely for so long. So very, very lonely.

It was his turn now to drop to his knees, wrenching her panties down and parting her legs. She wobbled slightly on her high heels, and he gripped her tightly, clinging to her bottom as he pleasured her the way he had done that first night they'd been together. As he worshipped her, drawing her pleasure tight inside of her like a bowstring, making her feel as if he might snap her in half.

She didn't know how long it went on. She simply lost herself in it. Not just the physical pleasure, but the intense, spiritual connection that came with it. That sense of her soul being wound around another person's. They weren't alone. They were together. Every intimate act, so deep and personal, would have been shocking to her if it had been with anyone else. But with him it was communion. With him, it was a deep exploration that went beyond bodies. It was necessary. The fulfillment of this aching emptiness she hadn't fully realized had existed in her before her eyes met Diego's across a crowded room at her father's house.

He flicked his tongue cleverly, his fingers plunging deep inside of her, and that string broke. She gasped, clinging to him as she rode out her release, as he continued to eat into her while her pleasure pulsed on and on.

He was everything. *This* was everything.

And she knew without a shadow of a doubt what it was.

He believed in love. That some could give it, and some could never properly receive it. She knew that he thought it wasn't for him. But it was. Because the love inside of her heart had been created just for this man in front of her. She had never believed in soul mates. A woman who was convinced of the fact that her father was going to select her husband could not afford to be sentimental about such things. But she believed in him. And he had changed everything she had imagined to be possible. He was her soul mate. It didn't matter if it was a cliché. Not when it was true.

There was no other man she could love. And that meant there was no other man built to receive that love.

It occurred to her then that no matter what he called it, no matter what he felt in return, it would always feel like enough. Because giving him her love was what she was made for. Worshipping his body, being with him. Being the one whose touch calmed him… It fulfilled something in her.

Whatever he gave back would be enough. She would love if it could be everything. But the fact of the matter was, she knew that whatever it was, it would be everything he had to give. And because she had been made for him, it would be enough.

She bit her lip, trying to decide if her next move was the wisest one. Ultimately deciding she didn't care at all. "I love you," she said.

That fire in his dark eyes turned sharp, his expression going molten. "What?"

"I love you, Diego. I love you so much." She dropped to her knees, so she was on the same level as him, and she kissed his lips, tasting him deeply, tasting the intimacy they had just shared on his mouth. "I love you."

"No," he said fiercely. "No." He grabbed hold of her wrists and hauled them both to their feet. "Don't say that again."

"I love you," she said.

"Don't be like my mother," he said, the words tortured. "Don't love me."

"You're not afraid you're going to hurt me. You're afraid that I'm going to hurt you."

He laughed, cold and hard. "How could I possibly be afraid of you? You are nothing but a waif. I can snap you in half with my hands."

"But you don't. You won't."

"You don't know that." His voice went rough. "I don't know that."

"You do. You know it. You're not afraid you're going to hurt me."

"So confident in your feelings," he said.

"I am confident in that. Because I know you. I do. I know us. Deep down in my soul, Diego, I know who you are. My soul recognizes yours."

"My soul recognizes nothing but my own needs," he said. "And what I need from you right now is not love."

He wrapped his arms around her, lifting her up off the floor and carrying her back toward the bedroom. He undressed, his movements savage, filled with rage. But she knew it wasn't at her. It was at himself. He set her down on the bed, his movements rough, his hands unsteady. "Turn over," he bit out.

"What?"

"Do as I say, *tesoro*. If you want to please me, if you love me, then love me through this. Give me what I actually want. Not words. Your body. Can you love me then?"

It was a dare, and he expected her to fail here. Expected her to turn away.

But she saw him. Saw right through him.

And she would meet him, match him.

He wasn't actually demanding submission as proof of love. He was asking that she prove she could handle his darkness. And he was betting she would not.

But she could.

She obeyed him, turning over onto her stomach, allowing those large, unsteady hands to position her so that she was up on her knees, a pillow propped up beneath her chest. He cupped her, sliding his fingers between her legs, pressing both inside her, testing her readiness. She cried out at the intrusion, feeling almost shameful excitement over the intensity of the moment.

He was trying to make this impersonal. He was trying to kill those feelings that she claimed to have for him. But this... Even his darkness was beautiful to her. Even now he appealed to her body in ways that went beyond logic.

He curved his fingers inside her, stroking some deep pleasure center there she hadn't been aware of before, making her shake and shudder. He smoothed his thumb between the crease of her bottom in time with that motion, pleasuring her there, making her face hot, shock nearly overtaking her pleasure. But not quite.

All she could do was submit to it. Submit to him.

And by the time he positioned his arousal at the entrance to her body, tears were filling her eyes. Because even now, even in his anger, his denial over what was between them, he was working to pleasure her first.

He thrust into her, deep and hard, deeper than he had ever been before, his grip on her hips tight as he rode her roughly, desperately. Like a man trying to exorcise a demon.

She felt it. That desperate need and effort he was putting forward to rid himself of the feelings that he had for her, of the fear. But the harder he pushed, going deeper inside of her even as he tried to get away, the softer she let herself become. She rocked back into him, taking everything he gave, finding a deep, unimaginable power within that decision.

He thought he could use anger to frighten her. He had likely done it all his life. His safety. His protection. That rage that he had learned early on could be so terrifying. But only in the hands of a madman. A sociopath who didn't truly care about anyone or anything but himself. And that was not Diego. Whatever he wished to pretend. It wasn't.

He might have convinced himself, but he would never convince her of that. Fevered, desperate words escaped his lips. Some in Spanish. Some in English. All of them, she had no doubt, profane. But to her, they were a prayer. Because he was fighting a losing battle. One that she would win. One that love would win.

He pressed his hand between her legs, toying with the center of her pleasure as he thrust in deep. And she stopped thinking. Gave herself over completely to the moment. She could feel his anger, almost blinding with its power, could feel his need. In the dark, deep emotion that lived down in the bottom of his heart that he feared more than anything else. His need for love.

"I love you," she whispered, as her pleasure burst

inside of her, white light shining behind her eyelids as her orgasm rocked her.

He growled, a feral denial, even as his body surrendered, as he slammed inside of her one last time and gave himself over to their need.

Then it was done, and they were breathing harshly, both of them reduced by everything that had just happened.

"Liliana…"

"Don't say anything," she said. "Let's not speak."

"Let's go home," he said.

She nodded. "Yes. I want to go home."

CHAPTER ELEVEN

DIEGO DID HIS very best to forget the day of his brother's wedding. And most especially the night that had followed. The way he had taken Liliana back to the penthouse and tried to push her away from him. The way she had clung to him, even while he had played the part of villain in a way that far surpassed his behavior at the wedding.

He didn't understand. He didn't understand how she could know everything she did, about Karina, about the baby, and still say that she loved him. He didn't understand how she remained. It made no earthly sense to him, and yet, while he had been on the verge of sending her away when he had finished making love to her, she had said they should go home.

She had meant the island. The place where he had taken her by force the first time. Home.

As if it were hers too.

And he had been utterly powerless to turn her away. They had not stayed in the penthouse suite. Instead, he'd had his helicopter readied, and the two of them had flown back to the island that very night. They had spent the dusky hours of the morning in bed together, and then when they had arisen, he had found Liliana at the breakfast table eating pastries and looking cheerful, as if none of the previous night had happened.

He didn't know what to do with that. With this woman who stayed.

Who stayed even though she knew exactly what manner of man he was.

He had been an abominable monster to her the night before, and this morning she was just sitting there, unaffected and cheerful.

She looked up at him, her blue eyes shining, her smile brilliant. Did she really love him?

The thought made his stomach turn violently.

And even so, there was a dark, unsavory part of him that thought it was a good thing. If Liliana wanted to lock her own manacles, keep herself prisoner in his world, why shouldn't he let her? He wanted her. He could not foresee a future where he would tire of her or her body. So why shouldn't he have her?

Why shouldn't he allow her to bind herself to him?

"I have been thinking," he said, taking a seat at the table next to her. "I have been thinking that perhaps our agreement is…outdated."

"How do you mean?" she asked, giving him an impish look as she lifted her coffee mug to her lips.

"I am not certain either of us wants this to end."

The smile that earned him lit up her entire face. "No," she said. "I don't."

"Are you certain? Because you were quite enamored with the idea of your freedom…"

"I'm free here," she said. "With you."

"We will not stay here forever. I have houses in major cities all over the world. And that is typically where I conduct my business."

"I'm happy with that," she responded.

"Do you like Paris?" he asked.

"I love Paris."

"London?"

"Yes," she said happily. "I would love living in London for a while."

"We can do that. All of that and more."

She was happy. He was making her smile. He could not recall the last time he had made another person happy. It was so foreign, so unexpected and oddly…satisfying.

He had never much cared for the happiness of another person. Mostly, he had looked to the happiness of himself. Or perhaps *happiness* wasn't even the right word. His own satisfaction. The temporary satiation of his desires, however dark. He had never taken into account what another person might feel. It was just one of the many reasons he had been an awful husband the first time around. One of the many reasons Karina had left him for the sniveling coward she had gone off with. Because at least—by all accounts—he had been a pleasant man.

Even if, in the end, he had been selfish enough to leave his lover to bleed to death on a roadside.

Seeing Liliana's happiness rearranged something inside of him. And he found the corners of his own mouth lifting into a smile. One that lacked cynicism, one that lacked any sort of edge.

He felt her happiness.

That lightness… He felt it in him.

He had been affected by her from the moment he met her, and always, her touch had done something strange to him, something that went beyond the sexual. But this was… This was something else. It was something quite singular.

That moment when she'd come down the stairs in her

wedding gown he'd had that momentary desire to place her up above him and give her whatever she wished.

This, he realized, was the reason for that instinct.

That nothing would ever truly satisfy him except for Liliana's joy.

"Good," he said. "Then it is settled."

"We're married," she said, her smile turning soft and dreamy. "Forever."

The idea didn't terrify him. Not in the least. It was what he had wanted from the moment he had first taken her.

The strength of the obsession that had gripped him from the first moment he'd seen her had been beyond anything he'd ever known, and nothing had come close to dimming it. He doubted time ever would.

There were cursed objects all throughout literature that bewitched men and took hold of their better instincts.

He would call Liliana his own personal cursed object, except...

He was the one who was cursed. And she was simply...

She was everything good and beautiful.

Everything. And he ignored everything inside of him that said it was wrong to know that and claim her anyway. Everything that reminded him that he was the opposite to all that goodness.

He had made her smile. He had made her happy. He could continue to do that. He would.

The important thing was she was his now. She had agreed to it.

And now, he would never lose her.

Liliana was so happy with her new life on the island. With her husband. In the fragile bubble they'd created in this isolated manor, on an isolated island.

It felt so fragile, this little world. Like any intrusion at all might spoil it.

She knew that eventually they were going to have to see how their marriage worked and functioned in the real world, but for now, it was something quite like bliss. For now, she wanted to stay here.

No, he had not said he loved her. But she had known that would be difficult for him. She was prepared to wait. She was prepared to wait for as long as he needed.

She went to sleep with him every night, woke with him every morning, and they shared breakfast. Then, he went off to work, and she set about her day.

She was starting to realize that she wanted to do something with her life. She was no longer living it for the pleasure of someone else. It wasn't like that with Diego. She brought that up with him one night while they were sitting by the fire. She wanted to find her passion, and he had spent the next hour making increasingly ridiculous suggestions about what she might do for a career. And then he had kissed her, brought her down to the ground and told her that of course she didn't actually have to do anything if she didn't want to. She could make her passion his body.

She had told him that of course she was quite passionate about his body, but perhaps needed something to occupy her day.

The next morning at breakfast he had spoken to her about the possibility of her doing freelance editing.

"You love books," he said. "You love to read. Perhaps that would be a good place for you to start?"

"It's more than just reading. With my limited knowledge about how things work, even I know that."

"Certainly, but you're very bright, and I have no

doubt you could learn what you needed to learn to accomplish the job."

"Maybe."

That had started her enrollment in some online classes, in addition to a hefty amount of research.

It was exciting. To think that she was embarking on a whole new part of herself. Husband and a career... Doing something she loved. She had never imagined that she might have those things.

Still, as happy as she was, she found herself feeling weepy and shaky at strange moments. She wondered if it was that impending sense of disquiet that came whenever she thought of them leaving their bubble. Then she wondered if it was nothing more exciting than a little PMS.

Except that was the thing. She was actually quite overdue to have her period.

The realization hit her while she was standing in the middle of her library.

She might be pregnant. And she had no way of finding that out without letting Diego know, because they were the only two people in residence.

She swallowed hard. He would be happy. He had wanted a baby. She worried that it would unearth some bad memories for him, some old grief. But if it did, she would be there.

It was funny that she thought of him, because when she paused for a moment, her own eyes prickled with tears.

She had never known her mother. Her mother had died in childbirth.

She waited for fear that the same fate would befall her, but it didn't come.

She wasn't scared. She never had been, really. Childbirth was dangerous, but with modern medicine, everything should be okay. The odds of something happening to her were low, not higher than they were for any other woman, she was sure.

No, she wasn't afraid. But thinking about being a mother when she had never had one…

It was her chance. She could never be the daughter in a mother-daughter relationship. But she could be the mother.

The thought filled her with awe. She pressed her hand to her womb, hoping.

She had been thinking that she and Diego wouldn't have a baby yet, but they were frankly not overly careful with birth control. And with the frequency they made love, it wasn't terribly surprising.

She was happy. Genuinely and truly happy.

She just had to hope it was real.

She walked down the hall quickly, toward Diego's office.

She pushed the door open without knocking, and saw him leaning back in his chair, his feet propped up on the desk. She smiled. She could watch him like this all day. With him not knowing. She loved him. And now they were going to have a family.

"Diego," she said softly.

He turned, a smile on his face, the kind she had been seeing from him more and more. Not those cruel, dark smiles she had seen so often in the beginning. But happiness.

"I'll have to call you back," he said, hanging his phone up. "*Tesoro.* Come in."

"I… I have something to tell you. I think… We'll have to go get it confirmed. But, Diego, I think I'm pregnant."

She couldn't trace all the emotions that flashed through his eyes. "We have to leave," he said. "We need to get you to a doctor."

"I can just have a pregnancy test brought here," she said. "I'm fine."

"That isn't good enough," he responded. "We must get you to a doctor, and we must do it now."

"Diego."

"Your mother died giving birth," he said. "I think that means we should go to a doctor and get you seen."

"You clearly weren't worried about that enough before to use a condom every time you had sex with me."

"I… I didn't think of it."

"You didn't think of pregnancy?"

"I didn't think of your mother," he said.

"Don't worry," she said. "Most women have babies and they're fine."

But he didn't say anything. Instead, he picked up his phone and began to make calls in rapid-fire Spanish, and before she knew it, she found herself bundled up and back on his helicopter, headed toward Spain.

Only a few hours later, she had the results to the test.

And Diego's reaction told her that things between them weren't going to go back to how they were.

She worried they might be broken. Irrevocably. Forever.

CHAPTER TWELVE

HE SLEPT IN his own room that night. He could not possibly sort through all of the feelings in his chest. Liliana was having a baby. *His* baby.

It was not the first time a woman had carried his child.

But this… This was different.

Part of him had wanted this. Had wanted a way to bind her to him. He'd been lax with birth control and he knew it. But it had seemed like a good thing, a way to keep her. But now…

Now something had changed. Something in him, and nothing could have prepared him for the reality of it. He was having all manner of thoughts that hadn't occurred to him before, and they were running through his head on a loop he couldn't stop.

Liliana's mother had died giving birth, and he could not get that out of his head.

His mother had died because of his father.

Liliana's mother by extension had died because of hers. And he just knew. From the moment he had found out she was pregnant he had been gripped by this terrible, awful sense of knowing. He would not be able to keep her. There was no possible way. He had convinced himself that it might be. Had told himself that they could make an arrangement that worked for both of them. And so far, it had been so.

But then there was reality. It was the other shoe, and it had dropped hard.

A child. His child and Liliana's.

After enduring the terror of her being pregnant, the uncertainty of her giving birth, then there would be a child.

And all his past fears rose up around him. The loss of Karina. Of the baby she'd carried.

He couldn't think. His brain was screaming, but it wasn't words. It wasn't anything other than a dark terror that he felt utterly and completely strangled by.

Liliana was having his child. His baby. There was no power in the world he could call upon to protect her.

Because the men in his family lived. They lived and endured, and the women they cared for suffered endlessly.

He knew that she was upset about being sent to her room alone, but it was a kindness, given how he felt.

He couldn't touch her. Not now. Her body was so fragile at the best of times… And now…

He swore, and stomped over to the liquor cabinet, taking out a bottle of vodka and tossing back a solid amount without bothering to pour it into a glass.

That had been his life before Liliana. Drinking. Doing whatever he felt like to keep the demons at bay. To keep the darkness around him a little bit more bearable.

Liliana had given him hope. A hope that he had never deserved.

It was all far too much.

"You're still awake?"

He turned and saw Liliana standing in the doorway. He paused, the bottle poised at the edge of his lips. "Yes."

"Why don't you come to bed?"

"It would be best if I left you alone."

"Don't you think I should be the one to decide that?"

"No, *tesoro*, I don't. I think that my feelings on the matter should come into play."

"We're having a baby, Diego. It's not supposed to be an upsetting thing."

"You say that as if you don't understand why I have concerns."

"I do understand," she said. "I went through my own feelings when I first thought that I might be pregnant. Whether or not I was afraid about my safety. But I'm not."

"That's because you don't remember loss." He took another sip of vodka. "I remember it far too well. More than one."

"But you wanted a child. You wanted to be a father."

"I did," he said, his voice hard. "Because for a moment in time I thought that maybe it could change things. But it didn't."

"You had a tragedy. It wasn't your fault."

"Maybe. Maybe not."

"Come to bed, Diego."

"No," he said.

"You're going to just stay out here and get drunk? What a fine solution to what you apparently see as a terrible problem."

"Do not force the issue, Liliana," he said. "Do not try to talk to me about something you don't understand."

Liliana drew back as if she had been slapped, and he felt a rising tide of guilt. It all felt far too much like his first marriage. Mistakes. His inability to respond correctly at a given moment. He had never felt wrong with Liliana. Even when he had been, taking her from her window. All of it had felt justified. But this felt wrong, and he didn't know what he could possibly do about it.

"Good night," he said.

She nodded slowly, and then turned away from him. And he felt as if she had taken a part of him with her. Peace. A slow-growing peace he hadn't realized had begun to take root inside of him. Gone now that she had turned her back on him.

And so, in the absence of Liliana, in the absence of that peace, he would get drunk.

He didn't know what else to do.

If he was the dark brother, the debauched one, then that was where he would retreat to now.

He didn't know another alternative.

Liliana kept waiting for things to get better. For Diego's smile to return. But there didn't seem to be anything she could do to fix the mood he had fallen into since she'd given him the news of her pregnancy.

He acted as if he was afraid to touch her. Afraid to have any kind of connection with her whatsoever. She felt… She felt defeated.

She had been happy, happy making her life all about finding ways to inject his with hope. With happiness.

Why wasn't that enough? She just wanted to give to him. She didn't understand. Couldn't comprehend why he wouldn't take it. And here they were, back in that same penthouse that had been the source of that hideous fight where they had decided that they were going to make things work between them. Where she had told him that she loved him, and he had said nothing. But it had made him happy—she had been able to see that. She had known it.

Now… Nothing seemed to make him happy at all. His mood was black, and there was no way she could penetrate it.

He had left her alone in the penthouse for the entire day, off to see to some work, he had said. Meanwhile she had set about hatching a plan she'd come up with recently. It had involved no small amount of skulduggery. She had gotten into his things, and thankfully, he had gotten lax, because she was able to get hold of a contact who made deliveries to the island.

And she was able to procure her wedding gown, which she had left back at their house.

With that done, she had set about to collecting all of Diego's favorite foods. She knew what they were, as she had spent the past few weeks grilling him on everything he liked. From music to movies to food. She was determined that her fact-finding mission would pay off.

He hadn't touched her in the days since they'd found out about the baby, and she was suffering for it greatly. She knew he was too. He needed that closeness. That intimacy.

He needed her. She knew he did.

If they could just get back to where they were then things would be better. She could make him happy again.

She could be what he needed. If only he would let her.

Now she had everything arranged. A dinner table with ham, mashed potatoes and a pasta salad. She had fresh baked rolls and a date cake, all of which she had procured in the city. And she was wearing her gown.

He had said that he'd fantasized about tearing it off her, but he hadn't done it.

Perhaps tonight she could bait him into it. Perhaps tonight, they could find their way back to what they'd had.

When the doors to the hotel room opened, she held her breath and stood there, waiting. He walked inside, and his handsome expression froze as he took in the scene that was set before him.

She'd made use of her name as a Navarro and had gotten the hotel concierge to aid her in setting a banquet, a table and two chairs brought up, the table now laden with the food she had gotten.

There were candles, everywhere. It was an extremely romantic scene, if she did say so herself.

But Diego did not look charmed. Not in any way.

"What is this?"

"Dinner," she said, shifting, purposefully moving her hips so that the skirt on the wedding gown swayed.

"How did you get that?"

"Your security is not as tight as it once was," she said dryly.

"I have work to do," he said, breezing past her and heading toward the room he'd been using as an office.

"Don't walk away from me," she said, stamping her foot. "I made dinner for you. Well, I acquired dinner for you. And I expect you to sit with me."

"My apologies, *princesita*. I didn't realize that you were in the position to make demands now."

"You know that I am," she said, walking up to him slowly. She touched his face, sliding her fingertips down, gripping his chin between her thumb and forefinger. "I know you want me. No matter that you're avoiding me now. You can't pretend that you suddenly don't."

"Is that what's bothering you? That I haven't had sex with you?"

"That's just a symptom."

"Perhaps I'm not hungry," he said, his voice cold. "In any of the ways that word might apply."

"I don't believe you."

"That is fine," he said.

Desperation kicked through her chest as he began to pull away from her. "No," she said.

She flung herself at him, wrapping her arms around his neck and kissing him, his lips remaining firm and unresponsive.

She didn't know what she would do if she couldn't reach him. If he didn't need her. She didn't understand why she couldn't make him happy. The man had kidnapped her from her bedroom window so that he could have her and now he was acting like he didn't care at all. She had no idea how she could survive this. How she could endure it. She didn't know what to do to fix it. She had tried. Had tried being everything to him, and he wouldn't take it.

She traced the outline of his lips with her tongue, and he groaned. She felt the exact moment she had breached his control.

"Now's your chance," she whispered against his lips. "Tear this dress off me. Do it like you wanted to then. On the floor. I'm not so fragile, Diego. Do what you need to."

She knew then that she had done it. Because he growled, his hold on her suddenly strong. And then, he grabbed the bodice of her dress and ripped it down violently, the fabric wrenching apart, a glitter of beads spraying everywhere, scattering all over the floor. Leaving her bare, leaving her exposed. Exposing him too.

His movements were dark and rough, and he reduced the dress to nothing but delicate tatters that shimmered like diamonds on the floor.

It felt far too close to how she felt in her soul. Torn, but still hopeful.

His lips were rough on her breasts, his teeth, his whiskers abrading her delicate skin. He gripped her tightly, so tightly she was sure he would leave a bruise. But she didn't mind. She wanted him to. If this was what he needed, she wanted him to expend all of that darkness, in her.

He was hers. It was her job to make him happy. She would do whatever it took. Anything.

If she couldn't do that, then he wouldn't need her. And if Diego didn't need her...

She cried out as he sucked one nipple deep into his mouth, the sound an expression of the desire that was riding through her body, and of the desolation that was echoing in her soul. The very idea of him not needing her, period, of him sending her away.

She closed her eyes tightly, trying to keep the tears from escaping them. She hated this. This feeling of not being able to reach him. Of being separate. She needed him. Needed to connect.

Needed him to love her.

And that was never supposed to be it. It was supposed to be enough that she keep him happy. That should be enough to make her happy. It could be. It would be.

Why did it feel like it wasn't?

A tear rolled down her cheek, and he paused, catching it with the corner of his thumb and brushing it away. When he looked at her, his expression was concerned.

But she didn't want him to worry about her. She wanted to fix him.

So she kissed him, hard and deep. And with every ounce of desperation inside of her. To make him feel what she knew he should.

We are going to have a life together. We're going to have a baby. Please let that be enough for you, please. Please let that be what you want.

She smothered a choked sob as she deepened the kiss, as she let him lift her up off the ground, as she wrapped her legs around him, clinging to him while he lowered them both to the floor.

She jerked his tie loose, ripped open his shirt, moving her hands over as much of his bare chest as she could. While he made quick work of his belt. He opened the front of his pants, not bothering to take any of his clothes off all the way. And he thrust inside of her, deep and hard. His movements erratic and intense. She wanted to take all this, all his rage and his pain and take it down inside her, hold it, take it from him.

She wanted to fix him.

Please. Please. I want to be enough. I want this to be enough.

She didn't realize she'd whimpered that out loud until he caught her lips with his and swallowed the words. And then he was stroking that sensitive place between her thighs, his thumb sliding over her as he thrust home, and she could think of nothing but her own pleasure. She cried out as it crashed over her, as she shook with the power of her orgasm. And he still wasn't done. She felt like she had failed somehow. Like she had been meant to serve him, and had ended up taking her own pleasure so greedily she hadn't done enough. But then he was shouting out his orgasm, and she couldn't worry about it anymore. She just held him.

But when it was over, and he looked down at her, he didn't look better. He didn't look happier.

He looked tortured.

He moved away from her, looking at the casualty of their coming together. "You have to stop this," he said.

"Stop what?"

"You need to be more careful with your body."

"I'm not the one who ravished me on the floor."

"You tempted me," he said. "Don't bait the darkness in me, Liliana. You cannot fix it."

He turned and left her standing there, the table still beautifully appointed with dinner, her dress destroyed in pieces all around her.

"I just want to make you happy," she said.

"You can't," he responded. "I'm not your father for you to spend your life serving, Liliana. You will not find a magic formula to bend me to your will and make me into the man you want me to be. You must stop now. I will not endure it."

"Don't make it sound like that. Like I'm being selfish. I am…giving to you."

"Are you?" he asked, his words like the crack of a whip. "Or are you trying to make me into a tamed thing that you can control as you see fit?"

"I am not."

"Then what is it you're trying to do to me, Liliana?"

"I want to make you happy."

"Why?"

"Because I love you." Desperation clawed at her. "You already know it. Why are you acting surprised?"

"Because I thought you would understand by now, my darling wife, that it doesn't matter how you feel about me. It isn't going to change who I am or how I feel."

"You *need* me," she said.

"I *desire* you," he said. "For a man like me that is a very different thing."

"No," she returned. "It isn't. It isn't that. If it was only desire then you wouldn't still whenever I touched you like you're a spooked horse who needs a gentle hand."

"You vastly underestimate the male libido, *tesoro*. When you put your hand on my arm, I'm imagining it somewhere else on my body. And that is the beginning and end of that."

"Liar."

"You're not the first woman I've been fascinated by, Liliana," he said, his tone sharpening to a knife's edge. "I was married once before—do not forget it. I imagined myself in love with her, but I've since learned the realities of myself. I like soft things. I like beautiful things. And I have never especially cared whether or not they liked me. My wife, Karina, intoxicated me. She fascinated me. Our connection was sexual… It was dark. I wanted that thing she had. That deep, dirty debauchery. I wanted to get it all over me. And I did. But then I did what I do, and the end result was that she was broken."

"Diego…"

"No," he said sharply. "You need to listen to this. You need to listen to me. I saw you, and I wanted your light. All that sweetness. You must understand I don't care if I use it up. I wanted you, and so I captured you. And in the end I will break you too, Liliana. If you allow it. And then I will find the next thing. Because that is the man I am."

"I don't think it's true."

"No. Because you want to change me. You want to

love me so much that I will love you too, because I can't resist the force of it. But isn't that what you spent your entire life doing with your father? And didn't he simply use you as a pawn in the end? Men such as us are what we are. We cannot fight it. And you cannot change it."

"So you're telling me that the best I can hope for in life is to be a discarded husk that lives in your house as your wife and doesn't have your attention?"

"I will not betray our vows. I'm simply telling you what I know to be true about myself."

"Will you fantasize about other women? Wish that it was them because I'll never be enough for you."

"No one and nothing will ever be enough for me, Liliana. Some people are born black holes. And we swallow them. Everything. We take. We don't give. You will not change me, my dear. Love me all you want, but it will never matter." He looked around the room. "Did you think a nice dinner was going to change that?"

She had. She had imagined that if she were good enough, if she were strong enough, made him enough dinners and touched him, kissed him, made love with him when he needed it, that he would love her. That he would need her. She was staring down her very worst fear.

She had fallen for him desperately and she didn't know what she could do to make him—to make him feel the same way. To make him need her like she needed him.

Maybe he'd been right before. Maybe she was trying to turn him into the man she wanted him to be, and not the man he was, for her own ends. Her own comfort.

She loved Diego. But she wasn't sure she knew how to love someone in a way that wasn't this.

And she wasn't making him happy. So what was the

point of it? What was the point of any of this? They could have a baby and not be married. It wouldn't be the end of the world. It wasn't what she wanted, but plenty of people did it.

She blinked back tears as she looked at the table still set with dinner.

She was torturing him. He wasn't happy. And she didn't know what she could do to fix it.

She needed to leave, but she didn't have anywhere to go. Even the very idea filled her with a strange kind of desolation.

Her life had been so much about her father, and now Diego, and beyond the two of them, she had nothing. No connections.

No friends.

She was about to have a baby and she…

She was going to pour all her love into that baby the way that she had done for Diego and her father.

And she wasn't having a sudden crisis where she realized she wanted to live her best life or be more selfish but…

She felt like she needed to know some things about herself. About what she wanted, what she was made of.

What she wanted beyond making someone else happy, because she had no idea how to make Diego happy if she couldn't even figure herself out.

She needed to make herself happy.

She'd never even tried to do that. She'd always gone with what she was told. And even going with Diego…

She hadn't taken responsibility for it. It had been something she'd wanted, but protecting her father's reputation had played a part in it. As had a kidnapping, which she had not chosen.

She wanted Diego. But she needed…

She needed to go. She needed to make a choice.

"I need to go," she said, looking around at the remains of her dress.

"What?"

"I need to go," she said again, striding off toward her bedroom. She began to dress herself quickly, ignoring Diego standing there in the doorway.

Once she was decent, she took her purse and started to march toward the door. Diego caught her arm. "Where do you think you're going?"

"Away from you," she said, jerking her arm back and breezing out the door, shocked when he didn't follow.

She got in the elevator, stabbing at the buttons with numb fingers.

She spent the entire elevator ride down to the lobby blinking back tears. She stumbled across the marble floor, headed toward the double doors, only dimly aware that she had no idea where she was going. Or who would take her there.

But, she supposed that finding a driver to take her to a destination was not as important as finding the destination itself.

"Liliana!"

She turned around to see Diego push open the doors to the elevator that was next to the one she had taken down, his expression wild, his dark hair in his eyes. "Where do you think you're going?"

"I'm leaving," she responded.

"Come back up to our room," he said. "Let us discuss this like reasonable people."

She remembered what he had said at the wedding reception. How he had wanted to talk about the allegations that had been made against him in public. And she had told him no. That they would take their business back to their private space and deal with it between the two of them.

But that wasn't what she wanted. Not now. If he wanted to make a scene, then she would make one. She had been...so well behaved. All her life. She had tried so hard to be good, and it had gotten her nowhere. She had been the best daughter her father could have possibly wanted or asked for and it had never earned her a damn thing. All it had gotten her was an arranged marriage, and then he had...

He had left her with her kidnapper. Had told her to marry him to protect his reputation.

That wasn't the action of a man who loved her. Nothing that she had done had managed to accomplish that. And then there was Diego. She had done her best to make him happy. She had given and given. She had promised to stay with him. She had worn the wedding dress he had picked out, had given him all of herself.

And what had he given her in return? She was eternally hoping that if she threw herself over the top of the sacrificial altars that eventually someone would halt the execution and spare her out of a sense of great love. But no. They just sacrificed her. Again and again.

She had to want more. She had to be more.

"Do you love me?" she shouted.

They were drawing looks from both the hotel staff and the guests, but she didn't care.

"Liliana," he said, his tone warning.

"No," she said. "It's a simple question, and it shouldn't be difficult for you to answer. Do you love me?"

He looked around, and then seemed to decide that he didn't much care what anyone thought either. "Is that suddenly a requirement for you?"

"Yes. I want you to stop hiding. Stop hiding behind that 'broodier than thou' thing. I'm sorry that your wife died. I'm sorry that she left you. I'm sorry that your mother's dead. And that your father is an unrepentant asshole."

"He's a dead unrepentant asshole," Diego said dryly.

"Well. I'm sorry about that too, just because it means you can't torture him to death. But there's nothing you can do about any of it. There's nothing I can do about any of it. You are the one that's deciding to be unhappy."

"I never said happiness was a goal, Liliana," he said.

"Why isn't it?" she shouted. "Why isn't it a goal? We could be happy. We could be. Together. We're having a baby. I love you. Why isn't that enough for you?"

"What is it you want from me? You want me to make you my entire life? You want me to entrust my happiness to you? Look at you," he said. "You're such a fragile thing. So easily broken, and you want me to embrace a potential future with you and assume nothing will ever happen? You live in a fantasy world, Liliana. I knew that you were innocent, but I had no idea that you were this innocent."

"What are you saying exactly? That you can't love me? Or that you won't love me?"

"It doesn't make a difference," he said. "I'm not a man who wants love. Not anymore. Perhaps there was a time when I would have. But that time is past."

"So a dead woman who betrayed you gets to be your only attempt at being in love, and I get left out in the cold even though I'm carrying your child, and I'm practically down on my knees begging you to love me?"

"You're not on your knees, *tesoro*. But, if you wanted to go ahead and make that a literal truth, I'm not opposed to it."

"You wouldn't want me to beg," she said. "That isn't what you want or need. You need someone to stand up to you and tell you that you're not scary. The only person terrified of you is you. And that's because you're terrified of the fact that there might actually be hope living inside of that granite chest of yours. It's not your darkness that scares you—it's the light. The light that won't go out no matter how many times you tell yourself and other people it isn't there. In your heart, you want to love me. You want to love this baby. All of that stuff that you say about wanting to keep me, the way that you quiet when I put my hands on you... Diego, you love me."

"I don't," he said, his face horribly blank.

He was scared—she knew that he was. She knew better than to take his word as truth. At least, she was hoping it was a lie. If it wasn't, she didn't know what she would do. She was trying to be strong, trying to stand there and cling to the realizations she had had only moments before, but it was so hard. So hard when she just wanted to fold herself into his arms and tell him it didn't matter if he loved her. That she would give him whatever he wanted as long as they could be together.

But she needed more than that. She had to demand more than that for herself, no matter how difficult it was.

Because what she had just said to Diego was true in the end. He would not love a woman who got on her knees and begged. If he had wanted a captive, he would have kept her a captive. If he had wanted someone weak and wilting, he wouldn't have boosted her strength over the course of the past few weeks. He wouldn't have latched on to their banter, rewarded her sharp comments with witty banter of his own.

If she wanted him to love her, then she had to be herself. Not the creature her father wanted to shape her into. Not the woman she had been imagining she could be for Diego. That was the real test.

When they had made love the night of the wedding, she had imagined that because she had been created for him that meant taking on board his endless darkness if necessary and asking for nothing in return. But the fact of the matter was, he didn't want her to just give. Not only that. He would want her to push too. To pull. She had to trust that she was made for him not simply when she was being accommodating, but when she was demanding more from him. When she was standing up for herself, for him, for all that he could have. When she was telling him things he didn't want to hear and demanding what he wasn't ready to give.

"Coward," she said.

"What?"

"You heard me," she said, taking a reckless step forward, crashing into a potted plant and sending it falling sideways, the ceramic shattering, soil spreading everywhere on the white floor. It hadn't looked like an accident. It looked like she was having a tantrum. She didn't care. She just didn't care.

"You're a coward. You could love me, but you're scared to. And you can give any reason you want, but that doesn't make it true. You're trying to protect yourself. Maybe you should think about someone else. About what they want. About what they need."

She turned away from him. "Wait," he said. "You can't leave me."

"I have to leave you," she said. "Because if I don't, then I am going to be that wilting, sad girl that you met living at her father's house, willing to marry whatever man he handed her over to when she really wanted another one."

"If you really wanted me that whole time, then why won't you take me now?"

"Because I need more. I need more than you at your worst, Diego. I can love you through it, but I shouldn't have to live with it for my entire life. Not when you can be more. More for me. More for our child. I'm going to leave. And I'll probably love you that whole time, but I need to be somewhere else. To be better for our child. To be better for me."

"You can't go," he said. "I won't allow it. I will chase you down to the ends of the earth. I will ruin your father with all the evidence I have against him. I will... I will have our child taken from you."

She drew back, feeling as though he had struck her, and he continued to advance on her. "Do not test me, Liliana," he said. "You will not like the consequences."

"If you won't allow me to be happy with you, Diego, then I beg you allow me to be happy somewhere. You might choose to live in the darkness, but I'm not doing that. I'm sorry if that diminishes your bank account, Diego, but as you refuse to care for me, that's all that will be left diminished."

"So in the end you are just like Karina."

"No," she said. "I'm not leaving with another man. I'm not leaving to hurt you. I'm leaving on my own. I'm leaving to heal me. In the end, I hope it heals you too. But if not... I can't live solely for someone else for the rest of my life. And you wouldn't like the woman I became if I did. Let me go. If you have any humanity in you at all, let me go."

Then she turned and walked outside into the night. And she waited. Waited for him to follow after her.

Waited for him to wrench the doors open and call her name as he had done in the lobby. But he didn't.

She called a cab, and on her way to the airport used that same contact she had used to get the ill-fated wedding gown collected. She figured out a way to find a new place to stay. Then after boarding a private plane using her husband's name, she landed in London several hours later, and procured lodging using her father's name.

And she decided that whatever she did after that, she would use her own name. She couldn't figure out how to be enough for Diego. But maybe... Maybe she could figure out how to be enough for herself. And if she could do that... Then maybe she had a hope of being a good mother. Of being a whole, happy person.

The rest... Her broken heart, her need for Diego... She would worry about that later.

She laughed ruefully in the empty hotel room. Tonight, she had kidnapped herself, in a way. Taken herself out of that life that she had built with him, so that she could find something else.

Because if she didn't, the kind of despair that she felt after he abandoned her would be all she really had.

And she was beginning to discover that she needed to find more.

The revelations she'd had at the hotel, that continued to unfold on her flight to London, were the kinds of self-realization that settled in her stomach like rocks. She didn't feel lighter. Didn't feel magically healed. But still, she couldn't ignore them. That she didn't know how to be with someone without constantly trying to fill the gaps. Without constantly trying to make herself invaluable.

She needed to fix that. And when she did, maybe she would feel better.

But for now she was lost in the in-between. Where she knew what she needed to become, but felt miles and miles away from it, when all she wanted to do was lie on the ground, curl up into a ball and howl.

And since she was by herself, that was what she did.

CHAPTER THIRTEEN

DIEGO COULDN'T FATHOM what had possessed him to simply stand in that hotel lobby while Liliana walked out of his life. While the people around him practically cheered at her strength, clearly taking her side in the matter.

And why wouldn't they?

She'd asked if he loved her. He'd told her no.

And then she'd begged him to let her go. Her eyes had been full of tears, her voice heavy with pain, and he'd… He'd done it because what other choice had there been?

She was miserable. He could see it in her eyes. She was breaking apart right in front of him, and he… He cared. He had never cared about anyone else like this in his life. Not since his mother's death.

She was gone. She was gone, and he should continue to allow it. He should let her go. Because she wanted and needed more than he could give.

That thought stunned him. He had never cared before what someone else wanted or needed. Always, his whole life it had been about himself.

About surviving.

He gritted his teeth, thinking about that moment when he had set his father's shop on fire. Thinking that certainly he would have tempted the old man to murder.

And all he could think was that Matías had somehow sidestepped this. That his brother was married and his wife...

He didn't know how to have it. He didn't understand. He was far too broken to have this. To have her.

Here he was nearly prostrate on the ground in a penthouse in Spain, while his brother was likely off honeymooning.

He picked up his phone, weighing it in his hand for a moment before dialing his assistant. "Find out where my brother is," he said.

"Yes, Mr. Navarro."

A few moments later his phone rang. "He's at his office in London."

Diego hung up the phone. He wondered why his brother was at his office, rather than at the *rancho* enjoying his new wife's body. It's what Diego would be doing if he hadn't sabotaged his entire life.

He needed to talk to Matías. It was the one thing he hadn't done. Beyond their thinly veiled threats made to each other when he had taken Liliana.

Diego had let Liliana go. And for the first time in longer than he could remember, he felt hope. She had changed him. Only two months ago he would never have released her. Not ever. He had taken her not giving a damn whether she wanted to be with him or not. Had forced her into marriage the same way. But something in him had changed. She had changed and he needed to...

He needed to know. How Matías had done it. How he was a good man. He needed to be a better one, for Liliana.

Liliana.

He thought of her, so brave and bright, facing him down and calling him a coward. She wasn't wrong.

No. She wasn't.

His phone rang, and he answered it, his heart in his throat. It was his assistant.

"Your brother has a message for you, Mr. Navarro."

"Does he?" Diego asked.

"He says it's all yours."

What was all his? Diego couldn't think straight for a moment. Everything wasn't his, or Liliana would be here. But she wasn't. So it couldn't be.

The inheritance.

Which meant…

Which meant all was not bliss with Matías and Camilla. Did that mean that there wasn't hope after all? Or did it mean Matías wasn't magically good?

If that was the case, did it mean Diego wasn't beyond help?

"I need a plane to London," Diego said. "Immediately."

There were some things that needed to be handled in person, and this, Diego had a feeling, was one of them.

When Diego walked into his brother's high-rise office, Matías was standing in front of his desk, a panoramic view of London behind him, two drinks in his hand and a smile on his face.

"You would only smile when offering me a drink if it was poisoned," Diego said, reaching into his jacket and pulling out a flask for his brother to see. "I'm good."

Matías normally looked…

Diego and his brother had many features in common. Both over six feet tall with black hair, dark eyes and strong noses. But Matías always looked at ease with his surroundings, and as a result, people in his presence always seemed at ease. Diego had the opposite effect. Creating waves wherever he went.

But today… Today there was no easy way about his brother at all.

"To what do I owe the displeasure?" Matías asked.

"I heard that you had forfeited our little game," Diego said.

"Because it quit being a game to me."

"Oh, I see. So it was still a game when I stole Liliana right out of her bedroom, but it's not a game now. Fascinating."

The bastard. He hadn't called it off when Liliana had been taken. The very idea of his brother marrying Liliana when he cared so little for her made Diego's stomach turn.

"Liliana said that she wanted to be with you," Matías pointed out. "I was hardly going to rescue a woman who didn't wish to be rescued."

"Yes," Diego said. "She did tell you that. Because I'm blackmailing her. Her father is not the upstanding citizen that he appears to be, and Liliana was quite shocked to find out the Hart family name was not built on the pristine foundation she had once thought. A tragedy all around."

"Not for you, though."

"Indeed," Diego said, "I have met very few tragedies that I didn't want to exploit. And this was no different. However," he said, "I think it is time we finish this."

It was another thing he could do. The last easy thing, he realized. He needed to make sure there was no external benefit to him being with Liliana. If he were going to go after her…

There was some deep work he had to do. Inside his very soul, and that would be difficult. But this… This he could do.

"I agree," Matías said. "And you've won."

"No," Diego said. "Abuelo has won. At least if we allow him to." His brother rubbed his chin thoughtfully, then took a drink from his flask. "So, you wish to discontinue this, to call your marriage a sham and be done with it. I wish to do the same."

Matías could only stare at his brother. Shocked at the words he'd just spoken. "Why?"

"I suspect for the same reasons you do," Diego said, taking a drink from his flask. "It got away from you, didn't it?"

He was desperate for the answer. Desperate to know if he was alone in this or if Matías was similarly afflicted. And what the hell his brother, the better man by all accounts, was going to do about it.

"Has it gotten away from you?" Matías looked surprised.

"Liliana Hart," Diego said, "was supposed to be the simplest and softest of targets. I have watched her for years while doing business with her father. Sheltered. Meek, or so I thought. She is such an innocent, Matías, you have no idea. At least, she was."

Diego felt like his heart was being squeezed even as he spoke of her like that. But it was the truth. He'd imagined her a piece of light he could capture easily. A lightning bug he could keep in a jar and claim for his own without consideration.

But Liliana wasn't meek. She wasn't soft or breakable. She was a force.

She damn well might have broken him.

"So, neither of us play?" Matías asked. "That's what you're proposing?"

"Yes," Diego responded. "I already called Grandfather and told him that Liliana was divorcing me."

"Is she?"

"I have already put her on a plane back to America. Along with all of the evidence of her father's misdeeds so that she has no fear I will use it against her."

"We are in a similar place, then. As I have sent Camilla away. Back to her family *rancho*, and have just finished procuring documents for her to sign that will restore ownership."

Diego laughed darkly. Then he reached out and grabbed hold of the whiskey tumbler in Matías's hand. He took a drink, quick and decisive. It burned all the way down. He hoped it would blot out some of the pain that he felt. It didn't.

"I thought you were afraid that was poisoned," Matías pointed out.

"At this point, I feel it would be all the same either way."

Matías shrugged, and took a sip of his own whiskey. "You may not be wrong."

"I have always found it astoundingly simple to take what I want," Diego said. "Why was it not with her?"

Matías sighed heavily, his gaze on the wall behind Diego. "You're not going to like my conclusion."

"Oh, probably not." Diego didn't like anything about this. Why should he like his brother's conclusions?

"Love."

The word was like a dagger straight through his heart. It was all that he wanted. All that he feared.

"I've already tried love," Diego said. "Against my better judgment."

But he hadn't loved Karina. Not really. He'd seen the chance for oblivion in her and he'd taken it. But he hadn't loved her.

"It ended badly," Matías said.

"Yes," Diego answered slowly, "though not in the way that people think."

"I knew that already."

The two brothers stared at each other for a moment. They had never been close. The way they had grown up had simply made it impossible. Diego had acted out. He'd made himself into a man that Matías would never want to speak to, much less spend any time with.

His brother had always wanted to escape the kind of debauchery their father had reveled in, and Diego had played on the outskirts of it. Why would Matías want to be close with him?

Maybe that had been the whole point. To push him away. To not risk anything with his brother. To not ever be close with another living soul because loss hurt too badly.

Maybe it was time to try. To talk about something they never had. If they could do that, if they could deal with that hideous childhood they'd both managed to survive, maybe they could take a step toward a different life.

Diego hadn't imagined Matías needed that, but now he wondered. He'd lost his wife, the same as Diego had lost his.

"I know that our father killed our mother," Diego said, his tone grave.

"Dios," Matías said. "Why did you never say?"

"I don't know how to talk about such things," Diego said. "And he…threatened me. And as a boy I was too frightened to stand against him. I am a coward, Matías, and I have to live with that."

"You were a child, not a coward."

Diego went on as though Matías hadn't spoken. "And I know that… That I am broken. Just as he was."

"No," Matías said, the denial so swift and fierce it shocked Diego. "You're not. He was. Abuelo is. We can be something else."

"Can we?"

"Does Liliana love you?"

I love you. Don't you love me?

"I don't think so."

How could she? How? It didn't make any sense. He was the monster who'd kidnapped her, and then denied her love when she gave it freely. She'd asked to be let go, and he'd obliged. The only good thing he'd ever done for her.

But if she still could...

"Camilla says she loves me. And I feel that... I feel that if she can love me then perhaps I'm not broken."

"The concern," Diego said, his voice rough, "becomes breaking them."

"Yes," Matías agreed. "But I wonder... If love is the difference."

"That is the one thing I can confidently say our father and grandfather do not possess at all. Though, that highlights other failures of mine, sadly."

"No one ever taught us how to love, Diego," Matías said. "They taught us to be ruthless. They taught us to play these games. To be cold, unyielding men who cared for nothing beyond our own selfish desires."

"I would say they taught us everything we should have tried not to be. And you," Diego said, "have certainly come the closest."

"I still didn't have love. So I'm not sure if it made any difference in the end."

"Is it too late now? Do you think it's too late to have it now?"

He wished it weren't. He needed it not to be. He'd

lived half his life convinced his fate was set in stone, but maybe it wasn't. Maybe... Maybe he could change.

He'd let her go.

He wanted her to be happy.

He wanted her to know he chose her.

He didn't want money.

He didn't want to win.

If all those things could change, then maybe there was no limit to it. Maybe he could be whatever she needed. Maybe they could have any life they chose.

"It's never too late," he said. "I have to believe that. And then, even when it is too late, I feel that you have to keep trying. Beyond hope. Beyond pride or reason. Because love has no place in any of those things. Love is something entirely different."

"When did you become such an expert?" Diego asked.

"I'm not," Matías said. "But I know about pride. I know about failing. I know about loss. I know about selfishness. I know about anger. And nowhere, in any of that, did I find peace. Nowhere was there love. I can only assume it's this thing," he said, "this thing that feels foreign, this thing that I don't know at all. This thing that has taken me over, body and soul. And... I wanted. I would've given it all up for her. We were both acting fools for this, and we were willing to give it up for them. Would our father have ever done that?"

"No," Diego said, without hesitation.

"No," Matías agreed.

"Well then," Diego said. "Perhaps we are not broken after all."

Whether or not he could take the chance on breaking Liliana was another thing entirely.

CHAPTER FOURTEEN

SHE WAS DOING well in her online classes, so there was that. Liliana imagined that she should feel triumphant that she had managed to move forward with her plans, even with her heart nothing more than ground-up shards of glass in her chest. But it was difficult to feel pride around all the pain inside her.

She was becoming her own woman, and she was finding that it was not the easiest thing. It was going to take some doing before she was able to pay for her own lodging. Well, it would take less doing if she moved out of the city. London was obviously going to be impossible for a pregnant student earning freelance money. At least, it would be impossible for her to get herself into any neighborhood that didn't make her feel she was in danger at all times.

She supposed she could get roommates. And that was definitely a route she was considering taking.

But for now, she was just still hiding away in one of her father's properties.

He had no idea she was there. He owned far too many places to notice that one, pale blonde was holed up in any of them.

She wondered if Diego had been in touch with him. If he had threatened him.

Diego must be furious. It had all occurred to her later that of course she had destroyed his chance at getting his family inheritance.

She almost felt guilty.

But…

She couldn't worry about him, and she couldn't live for him.

Oh, her heart still beat for him, but her actions needed to be for more.

She needed to be more.

If there was one thing she had done a lot of over the past few days, it was think about the future. Her future as a mother. She didn't know what a mother was supposed to do, not beyond what she had seen in TV, movies and read in books. She'd never had a mother. And her father had been such a difficult parental figure.

She had made quite a few decisions about what she wanted to be.

She was not going to expect her child to live for her. She couldn't put that on another person. She knew what it was like. To have someone care for you only as long as you were a vehicle for their goals.

But she had to be strong for her child, otherwise they would inevitably feel a sense of obligation. That meant she had to find her happiness in more than just motherhood, though she knew she would find so much joy in it. It wasn't for herself. It was for that child. Because if she didn't make a concerted effort, with just her and the baby she would put far too much on that little one's shoulders.

She didn't want to do that.

Didn't want to hurt people in the ways that she had been hurt.

And while she had been musing on that she realized

that the way she had loved Diego had actually done that very same thing to him.

If he didn't react in the right ways, if he didn't look happy when she wanted him to be happy, she was putting her expectation of fulfillment on him. Which, for all he had done, he had never done that to her. It was she who had done that herself. Diego was not like her father. But while hers manifested themselves in a much more altruistic way, she did have some similar tendencies.

She wanted Diego to be happy with her love because she wanted to feel good about herself. And that made it a somewhat selfish love.

Her father had said to her so many times that she was all he had, and there had been any number of addendums to that. She was all he had, and so she had to stay with him. So she had to be a good daughter. So she had to help him, because he needed her.

Diego had to be happy because she loved him. Diego had to love her so that she would feel good.

Yes, it might be different, it might come from a less manipulative place, but it was the same.

She was trying to figure out how she could want those things for him without imposing herself on him. And the only thing she could think was by being away like this. He would want to see his child, that much she knew. They would have to contend with each other eventually. But perhaps… Being forced to contend with each other as people, as parents, would be better.

She wanted less self-realization and more bread. Bread was all she wanted to eat. The craving was as real as it was intense. And her body didn't mind overmuch what kind of bread it was. Buttered and toasted brioche in the morning, a baguette and some cheese in the afternoon, a pastry in lieu of dinner. Just carbohydrates and fats.

She couldn't have love, so perhaps she could have butter, and that seemed about the best substitute she could manage.

With no small amount of guilt, she was using her father's means to procure food as well. Living at his address meant she was able to charge whatever she liked as long as it was delivered to the penthouse. She was awaiting her afternoon baguette, coupled with the evening's cinnamon roll. She was suddenly starving, and she had a feeling she would be eating everything all at once.

When the buzzer sounded, she immediately granted access and sat down on the couch, waiting. She felt like she was in the strangest emotional space she'd ever been in. Ready to be more independent on the one hand. And yet, nearly useless on the other. Lying around and allowing food to be delivered to her while she lounged on a couch.

Maybe it was hormonal. Maybe it was heartbreak. Maybe it was a unique combination of the two.

She would muscle past it eventually. She just didn't want to yet.

She didn't have the heart to yet.

The door opened. "Just set it on the table," she said.

"So very imperious," came a dark voice from behind her. "I assume you mean the bread."

She jerked upright into a seated position. "Why do you have my bread?"

"The deliveryman downstairs was more than happy to allow me to bring it up to my wife."

"Well, that doesn't seem very professional. He has no way of verifying that you're my husband."

"Don't you have other questions? Like how I found you and why I'm here?"

"I'm hungry," she said, her heart beating rapidly, her hands beginning to shake. "My concerns are centered around my lunch."

"Then have your lunch, *tesoro*," he said, handing her the paper bag that contained the baguette. But in truth, she was no longer hungry at all.

She clutched the bag to her chest, using it as some sort of defense. Against what, she didn't know. Maybe just the sheer force of him. Of all that he was.

He was still the most beautiful man she had ever seen. He called to her. Made her ache. Made her need.

All the grand plans for independence she had made felt diminished.

No. They weren't diminished. That was the wrong way to think of it. She could stand on her own. She has been doing it for the past few days. She was confident she could do it for as long as she needed to. But she wanted to lean into his strength. There was the life she could endure, and there was the one that she wished for. What she knew about herself now was that she could make hard choices. She could do what needed to be done. But she would rather... Oh, how she would rather have a life with him.

"I have brought you something," he said.

She crinkled the bread bag. "I know. I'm holding it."

"There is something other than bread in the bag, Liliana."

She rustled into the brown paper, and found a folder containing a stack of documents.

"What is this?"

"Proof," he said, "of your father's misdeeds. All the proof that I have. Beyond exploiting the connections to the people that I know, this is the only written proof that there is. It is yours now. You're free. I'm not going to use it against you. I'm not going to use it against him."

"Why?"

"Because you don't have to be with me, Liliana."

"What about your inheritance?"

"I forfeited it. As did my brother."

"What…? What's going to happen with that? What will your grandfather do?"

"That is up to him. I informed him that you left me. He wanted to know why I didn't simply force you to return, as I had kidnapped you once. I told him that forcing you to be with me no longer appealed."

"It doesn't?"

"And I need you to understand that. I need you to understand that I… I have never cared what another person wanted or felt, Liliana. The decision to kidnap you was an easy one. I wanted you, and I saw no reason I should not have you. I just didn't care what you wanted. I didn't care if you loved Matías, if you were his lover. It didn't matter to me."

He advanced on her, his eyes full of fire. "But when you asked me to let you go at the hotel… I cared. What you wanted mattered to me. And it has, Liliana, for weeks. But that was the first moment that what you wanted mattered more than what I wanted. Because what I wanted to do was chase you down in the streets and haul you back upstairs. To remind you that you're mine. To remind you that you wanted to be with me, no matter what. But I knew I couldn't force you, because suddenly your happiness meant more than my satisfaction. It has never mattered to me. I am not one of those altruistic men who avoided connections in order to spare people their darkness. You know I didn't. I married once, and the fallout was horrific, and still, I took you. Still, I wanted to marry you. And then it changed."

"How?"

"I don't know," he said, his voice rough. "I only know that the moment I realized that, the moment I let you walk away, was both the darkest and brightest moment I've had in years. Losing you, letting you go, was hell on earth. But realizing that I could change…"

"Of course you can change," she said. "Anyone can. We've changed each other, Diego. That first moment I saw you something in me changed, and in all the time since, it has only been made stronger. The fact that I was able to walk away from you was a change in me. I've spent my life only understanding a strange kind of codependent love. And I… It's the strangest thing, Diego. But I realized two things. Not only that the way I loved you wasn't fair to me. But that it wasn't fair to you. I cannot subject you to a life where my happiness is dependent on you reacting the way I want you to. To every little thing. That isn't fair. And you're right. It is me trying to control you to make you safer. To make you easier to deal with. I imagined that it was a giving, selfless love, but it isn't. It's just martyrish, and it isn't fair. You never asked for a martyr. But there I was, more than willing to play the part. And now… I would be okay, if we couldn't be together. I could stand on my own feet. I would figure it out. I'm going to find a way to not need my father's money. To not need yours."

"Well, that is extremely good to hear, *tesoro*. It sounds as if you don't need me to survive. And I don't need you to fulfill my dark purposes. There is now no more blackmail. So it seems to me that there is only one thing left."

"What is that?"

"Choice. It is the one thing both you and I seem to have been afraid of all this time. If it's all the world, if it's fate, if it's duty, then the pain that results is not ours, is it?"

"I don't suppose it is."

"If I am simply destined to be my father, then as much guilt and blame as I take on for our failed marriage, it's still hollow. Because I'm blaming my blood. Not the choices that I made that brought me there."

"If I am the daughter my father wants me to be, then when I find myself unhappy with the choices that were made for me…"

"You blame him."

"And if my husband blackmailed me into marriage, kidnapped me out of the bedroom window… I suppose when times get hard I can blame him as well."

"Yes. And when I find myself resisting loving my wife because the very idea terrifies me, then I can blame the loss in my childhood. The manner of man my father was. All the failures that have come since. It is so much easier to cling to the past and use it as a scapegoat than it is to move on to the future and realize that everything that happens from here on out… It will be my choice."

"Yes," she said softly.

"I chose to let you go. The first choice that defied what I considered to be my nature."

"I chose to walk away."

"And so now here we are again," he said. "With choices to make."

"And what choice have you made, Diego?"

He shocked her then, dropping to his knees in front of the couch, taking hold of her hands. "I choose you, Liliana. You said that I was your light, when all I saw in myself was darkness, but that too is a matter of choice.

I want to be your light. I want to love you, even though it is hard for me."

She pulled back slightly, her heart twisting. Hard to love her? She didn't know quite what to do with that.

He reached up and cupped her cheek. "No, don't mistake me. It is not hard to love you. It is hard for me to accept that I do. Because what terrifies me most is all that I cannot control. All that love costs. All that loss can cause a man to endure."

"Well. It's scary," she said, pressing her hand over his, holding his palm to her face.

He looked down. "But the real failing in my first marriage was not that I am like my father. It was that I married someone I never intended to give myself to completely. I convinced myself that as long as I was faithful that was all there was to it. As long as I didn't murder my wife, then perhaps I was better than my father, but I had a conversation with my brother. And we both realized something."

He looked up, his dark eyes meeting hers. "Love is the difference. Love is what makes you choose someone else's happiness over your own. Love makes walking away from your family inheritance seem easy. Love makes letting go of fear seem worth it. Love is what makes you a better man. A better person. And love is what I have found with you. Fear held me back. It made me want to push you away. Running from love made me say things I deeply regret. Made me treat you in a way I should not have. But now I'm before you, kneeling. As I wanted to do that first moment I saw you in your wedding gown. You are my queen, Liliana. The queen of my heart. And I am begging you give me a chance. I no longer want to own you. I simply want to love you."

She touched his face, tilting his chin up so that his eyes met hers. "I love you," she said. She set the bag down, and slid off the couch, so that she was on her knees with him. So that neither of them were above or below the other. "You are my king," she said. "The ruler of my heart. And you do hold me captive, but as long as I hold you, it will all be right in the end."

"I think I loved you from the first moment I saw you," he said. "But it took a great effort on my part to attempt to deny it while also trying to bring you into my possession. I suppose I can only be grateful that Matías intended to take you as his bride, because it pushed me to act sooner than I might have."

"Are you so afraid now? About the baby?"

"I'm more terrified than I have ever been in my life," Diego said. "Because I love more in this moment than I ever have. I love my life. I love you. I love my vision of our future, and with that comes…fear. Of all that I cannot control. But know this, Liliana. That which is in my power to do, I will do."

"I don't need you to control the whole world, Diego. I just need you to love me."

"I do. I will."

"I knew it," she said, leaning in and kissing him on the mouth.

"What did you know?"

"That we were made for each other. That if I trusted in that we would find our way here. I think we could have stayed together as we were. But it wouldn't have been this. It wouldn't have been everything."

"Thank you," he said. "For trusting in that, even when I could not."

"I'll trust in it forever," she said. "In our love."

"I trust in our love too. And more than that, in that

the moment I met you, my soul recognized yours. Recognized his other half.

"You're the light to my darkness," he said.

She smiled. "And isn't it funny, how you're the light to mine."

"I think, *tesoro*, that that is exactly how it should be." His lips curved, still pressed against hers. "It was never the inheritance," he said.

"What?"

"The real reason I wanted you. It was never the inheritance, Liliana. It was always you. The rest was an excuse."

"Really?"

"Yes," he said. "You were always the true treasure, my love. Always."

EPILOGUE

WHEN HIS SON made his entrance into the world, Diego Navarro was overwhelmed by a sense of relief and joy. The birth was easy. Everyone said so, even Liliana, who seemed surprised by how smoothly it had all gone.

Diego, for his part, had left nothing to chance. He had hired the best team of doctors in the world, had installed her in the plushest delivery suite available from the moment her first contraction had hit two days before the actual birth.

But now he was here, his son.

And so was his wife. The love of his life. The center of his whole world.

His grandfather had already called with his gift for the child. The inheritance. Part of Diego wanted to reject it, and he himself might not take any of it. But for his son… He would allow it for his son. And as for Matías, it meant that his brother could keep the *rancho*, which he loved. And Diego was more than happy to let his brother have full ownership of all that was his.

He no longer felt compelled to chase after the darkness inside of him. Not when Liliana's light had done so much to drive it out.

"What should we name him?" Liliana asked, gazing down at their precious boy.

"I don't know," he said.

"Is there no family name you want to use?"

For them, family would never be the blood that had made them. Liliana had given all the evidence of her father's wrongdoings to the women who had been harassed by him, and they had set about dismantling the legacy he'd built on so much corruption.

There had been no reconciliation possible for them after that.

But they were family. A family that was growing, with love that would grow right along with it.

"No," he said decisively. "I want our family to start with us. We are new. Because of our love. We are not tied to any legacy."

"No," she said, smiling slowly. "We are not. I do have a suggestion, though."

In the end, they named him Matteo Navarro. In honor of Matías, who Diego had always seen as the best of their blood. And more than that, as a man who could change, a man who could love, even when it was hard. And in the end, it was his talk with Matías that had helped him win back Liliana.

"Matías and I are the beginning. You and Camilla are the beginning," Diego said.

"Yes. That is true," Liliana said. "Though, I think that love is the beginning."

Diego Navarro spent all his life making a very good habit of loving his children, loving his wife.

It started with the first moment he set eyes on Liliana. When the flames that had always been inside of him had seen her and leaped upward, toward destruction, he had thought.

He had thought that fire in him meant he was lost, but she'd taught him different. It could do terrible damage, there was no doubt about that. But love made the difference. It was love that made it burn bright enough to light the way. That made it burn hot enough to keep them warm, but not so hot it destroyed.

Love, he had learned, made all the difference in the world.

* * * * *

LET'S TALK
Romance

For exclusive extracts, competitions
and special offers, find us online:

f facebook.com/millsandboon

🐦 @MillsandBoon

📷 @MillsandBoonUK

Get in touch on 01413 063232

For all the latest titles coming soon, visit

millsandboon.co.uk/nextmonth